SCAR

Alan Campbell was born in ... ...
to Edinburgh University. He worked for a while as a coder/
designer on the phenomenally successful Grand Theft
Auto video games, but then decided to pursue a career in
photography and writing. He now lives in south Lanarkshire
and *Scar Night* is his first novel.

Praise for *Scar Night*

'Stunning debut fantasy . . . Campbell has Neil Gaiman's
gift for lushly dark stories and compelling antiheroes, and
effortlessly channels the Victorian atmospherics of writer
and illustrator Mervyn Peake as well. This imaginative first
novel will have plenty of readers anxiously awaiting his
follow-up' *Publishers Weekly* (starred review)

'This book is far too good to be anybody's first novel, so
expect a lot of established authors to get cross . . . As the
first in a sequence, it's a hard act to follow' *SFX*

'His decaying city is so well realized it could be a character
in its own right. As for the characters, what a wonderfully
original bunch of misfits and grotesques they are!' *Starburst*
(5-star review)

'Campbell's novel neatly sidesteps all traditional fantasy
stereotypes' *Dreamwatch*

'A brilliant and richly imagined creation . . . hugely powerful and remarkable . . . Highly recommended' *SF Revu*

'Thrilling, chilling, and downright unputdownable'
LiteraryMagic.com

'Vampires, angels, assassins, priests and more . . . A terrific start to what promises to become a thrilling saga . . . Excellent!' Spinetinglers.co.uk

'An impressive debut, a real page-turner' SFFWorld.com

'With undead armies, psychotic angels and exploding airships, *Scar Night* is a gripping, ripping yarn which rattles along at a great pace. Tether all that to the knock-out image at the heart of the novel – Deepgate, a Gothic city built on a network of chains over a great abyss – and you have urban fantasy at its best' Hal Duncan, author of *Vellum*

'A book really has to compel me – and right away – for me to finish it. *Scar Night* did that . . . I felt caught in Deepgate's chains immediately – the action and suspense were nail-biting' Greg Keyes, author of *The Briar King*

'A chain-wrapped industrial city so real you can feel the iron and smell the fumes – and a violent tale told in murderously beautiful prose' Sharon Shinn, author of *Archangel*

'Vividly imagined, visceral and intensely involving . . . a stunning debut. I can't wait to see what follows in the next volume' Sarah Ash, author of the *Tears of Artamon* series

'*Scar Night* is a strong, slyly written, and very assured debut from a fantasist to pay attention to. Campbell mingles action and atmosphere with the grace of a seasoned pro' Scott Lynch, author of *The Lies of Locke Lamora*

SCAR NIGHT

ALAN CAMPBELL

THE DEEPGATE CODEX
VOLUME I

TOR

First published 2006 by Tor

This edition published 2007 by Tor
an imprint of Pan Macmillan Ltd
Pan Macmillan, 20 New Wharf Road, London N1 9RR
Basingstoke and Oxford
Associated companies throughout the world
www.panmacmillan.com

ISBN 978-0-330-44476-7

7 9 8

A CIP catalogue record for this book is available from
the British Library.

Typeset by Intype Libra Ltd
Printed and bound in the UK by
CPI Mackays, Chatham ME5 8TD

For my Dad, who might occasionally have scratched his head at my dreams and ambitions, but has never failed to do everything he could to help me achieve them.

ACKNOWLEDGEMENTS

Sincere thanks and appreciation to Simon Kavanagh, Peter Lavery and Juliet Ulman, three people who possess such a formidable wealth of talent that I wonder how there can be any left in the gene pool for the rest of us.

To Susi Quinn for the exhaustive crits and the zillions of printer cartridges she used up (I'll get you some new ones, honest), and to Justin Chisholm, Barnaby Dellar and Jocelyn Ramsay, three more good friends who gave up oodles of their time and ink to offer advice.

A huge thanks to my writers' group: Gavin Inglis, who helped me nail the start of the story, and Martin Page for his knowledge of old weaponry and those quirky verbs which I nicked – also to Stefan Pearson, Andrew J. Wilson, Hannu Rajaniemi, Charlie Stross, Andrew C. Ferguson, Jack Deighton, Jane McKie and Guthrie Stewart, all of whom gave encouragement and feedback.

My gratitude to the kind folks at Macmillan for all their hard work – Rebecca Saunders, Liz Cowen and Jon Mitchell among many others. If I haven't mentioned you, it's only because I was feeling euphoric when we met.

Cheers to Oliver Cheetham and Dagmar Tatarczyk for

the cool video, and to Bret, owner of the Welsh Nun Pub in Koh Chang, for the chats and the dental work.

And love to Caragh. Without your support this page and the ones after it would probably be blank.

PROLOGUE

Chains snarled the courtyard behind the derelict cannon foundry in Applecross: spears of chain radiating at every angle, secured into walls with rusted hooks and pins, and knitted together like a madwoman's puzzle. In the centre, Barraby's watchtower stood ensnared. Smoke unfurled from its ruined summit and blew west across the city under a million winter stars.

Huffing and gasping, Presbyter Scrimlock climbed through the chains. His lantern swung, knocked against links and welds and God knows what, threw shadows like lattices of cracks across the gleaming cobbles. When he looked up, he saw squares and triangles full of stars. His sandals slipped as though on melted glass. The chains, where he touched them, were wet. And when he finally reached the Spine Adept waiting by the watchtower door he saw why.

'Blood,' the Presbyter whispered, horrified. He rubbed feverishly at his cassock, but the gore would not shift.

The Spine Adept, skin stretched so tight over his muscles he seemed cadaverous, turned lifeless eyes on the priest. 'From the dead,' he explained. 'She ejects them from the tower. Will not suffer them there inside with her.' He tilted his head to one side.

Below the chains numerous Spine bodies lay in a shapeless mound, their leather armour glistening like venom.

'Ulcis have mercy,' Scrimlock said. 'How many has she killed?'

'Eleven.'

Scrimlock drew a breath. The night tasted dank and rusty, like the air in a dungeon. 'You're making it worse,' he complained. 'Can't you see that? You're *feeding* her fury.'

'We have injured her,' the Adept said. His expression remained unreadable, but he pressed a pale hand against the watchtower door brace, as if to reinforce it.

'What?' The Presbyter's heart leapt. 'You've *injured* her? That's . . . How could you possibly . . .'

'She heals quickly.' The Adept looked up. 'Now we must hurry.'

Scrimlock followed the man's gaze, and for a moment wondered what he was looking at. Then he spotted them: silhouettes against the glittering night, lean figures scaling the chains, moving quickly and silently to the watchtower's single window. More Spine than Scrimlock had ever seen together. There had to be fifty, sixty. How was it possible he'd failed to notice them before?

'Every single Adept answered the summons.'

'All of them?' Scrimlock hissed, lowering his voice. 'Insanity! If she escapes . . .' He wrung his hands. The Church could not afford to lose so many of its assassins.

'She cannot escape. The window is too narrow for her wings; the roof is sealed, the door barricaded.'

Scrimlock glanced at the watchtower door. The iron brace looked solid enough to thwart an army. That still did not give him peace of mind. He looked for reassurance in the Adept's eyes, but of course there was nothing there: only a profound emptiness the priest felt in his marrow. *Could* they have injured her? And what would be the cost to the Church? What revenge would she seek? God help him, this was too much.

'I will not sanction this,' he protested. He waved a hand at the heap of dead bodies, at the blood still leaking onto the cobbles. 'Ulcis will not accept these opened corpses; every one of them is damned.'

'We have reinforcements.'

'And they will die too!' the Presbyter snapped. Yet he recognized a lack of conviction in his own voice. *They've managed to hurt her.* In a thousand years, no one had accomplished as much.

'Sacrifice is inevitable.'

'*Sacrifice?* Look at this blood! Look at it!' Scrimlock stepped back and lifted his cassock clear of the blood pooling around his ankles. 'Hell will come for this blood, for these spilled souls. This courtyard is cursed! Evil will linger here for centuries. A hundred priests could not lift Iril's shadow from these cobbles. Nothing can be saved here. *Nothing.*'

The Presbyter could not decide which horrified him more: the thought that their Lord Ulcis, the god of chains, would be denied the souls of so many of his Church's best assassins, or that hell might be lurking somewhere close by. The Maze was said to open doors into this world to take the souls from spilled blood. Scrimlock searched the gloom around him frantically. Perhaps hell was already here? Were these souls passing even now through some shadowy portal into Iril's endless corridors? If so, what might come through the *other* way? What might *escape*?

'End this hunt now,' he said. 'Let her escape. It's too dangerous.'

'You wish her to survive?' the Adept said.

'No, I . . .' The Presbyter's shoulders nudged against something, and he wheeled round in alarm. A chain. 'I only wish to preserve the Spine,' he said, clutching his chest. 'Pull your men back before it's too late.'

A howl of laughter came from above.

'Reinforcements have reached the window,' the Adept said.

Scrimlock looked up. Smoke leaked from the jagged watchtower roof and spread like grease over the stars. The stone falcons and battlements had crumbled inwards, exactly as the sappers had promised, blocking access to the roof and thus blocking escape. The sulphurous smell of blackcake lingered. Halfway up the tower, the assassin nearest to them squeezed through the window.

A sword clashed loudly.

Scrimlock moistened dry lips. 'She's armed,' he said. 'God help us, she's defending herself with steel.'

'No,' the Adept replied. 'Barraby's stairwells and passages are narrow. Combat in such confines is treacherous. You merely heard a Spine blade strike stone. She remains unarmed.'

'I don't understand.' The priest cast another glance over the corpses piled to one side. 'There must be abandoned weapons in there. You cannot have removed them. Why does she not arm herself?'

A scream – followed by terrible laughter. Scrimlock felt nauseous. Both scream and laughter had seemed to issue from the same throat.

'We believe,' the assassin said, 'she wishes to be defeated.'

'But that makes no sense. She—'

A noise from above distracted the Presbyter and he looked up in time to see a body being forced through the narrow watchtower window. Bones snapped, and then the body fell till it struck a chain. Arms and legs twisted around the massive links, and for a heartbeat it hung there, limp as a straw doll. Then it slipped free, bucked and snagged on the chains further below, until it crumpled to the ground. Spans of iron tensed and shivered. Four more Spine had clustered around the outside of the tower window. They clung to bolts and hooks in the walls whereby the chains gripped stone. Others were climbing closer, from below. The assassin nearest to the window, a lean man, eased himself inside, after his sword.

He called down: 'She's cut, she's—'

A wail, half torment, half rage, pierced Scrimlock's heart. There were sounds of sobbing, like those of a frightened child, followed by a hellish cry. The assassin's broken, bloodied body reappeared at the window and dropped a dozen feet before its neck snagged on one of the tower's protruding bolts.

A third Spine peered in through the window. 'She's coming down.'

'What?' Presbyter Scrimlock retreated from the watchtower door. 'We must get away from here. Now, quickly, we—'

'She cannot break through this door,' the Adept said. 'Nothing can break through this.'

Scrimlock's sandals slipped on blood-soaked cobbles. His lantern shook, dimmed, then brightened. Shadows clenched and flickered around him. Above them, Spine were climbing, one after another, through the window: three, six, eight of them.

'She will die now,' the Adept said flatly.

Boom.

Something struck the watchtower door from within, with the force of a battering ram. Dust shuddered free from its thick beams, and the Spine Adept pushed against the door brace.

'Get away,' Scrimlock said. 'Leave her now, I beg you. This is *her* night.'

'Her *last* night,' the Adept said.

Boom.

The brace jumped. Wood cracked, splintered. The Adept pitched backwards, then lunged forward again and threw all of his weight against the door. Scrimlock looked around, searching for the best way to escape. 'It won't hold,' he gasped. 'She'll—'

Steel rang inside the tower: sharp, furious strikes, like an expert butcher hacking meat. The assassins had descended to the other side of the door. Then another scream. More rapid concussions as blades struck stone. Scrimlock pressed his fists over his ears, sank to his knees. His limbs were trembling. He began to pray.

'Lord Ulcis, end this, I beg you. Let your servants prevail.' *Let this door hold.* 'Spare these souls from the Maze, spare us all, spare me, spare me.'

Silence.

'It's over.' The Adept shifted his weight from the door brace.

Boom.

The watchtower door exploded outwards, its timbers shattered like rotten boards. The brace crashed to one side. The Adept was thrown clear, colliding with a chain, but Scrimlock was astonished to see the man's sword was already out; he was already rising to his feet.

Then the Presbyter looked at the gaping hole where the watchtower door had been.

Something stood there, darker than the surrounding shadows.

'She's here,' he hissed.

The angel stepped out into the lane, small and lithe and dressed in ancient leathers mottled with mould. Her wings shimmered darkly, like smoke dragged behind her. Her face was a scrawl of scars: more scars than could have been caused by the current battle with the Spine, more scars than a thousand battles could have caused. Blood spattered her similarly scarred arms and hands, and her eyes were the colour of storm clouds. She wore flowers and ribbons in her lank, tangled hair. She had tried to make herself look pretty.

She was unarmed.

Scrimlock, still on his knees, said, 'Please.'

One corner of the angel's scarred lips twitched.

'Run,' she whispered.

The Presbyter scrambled to his feet and bolted. Fast as his leaden limbs could carry him, he stumbled and weaved though the chains. Spine were slipping soundlessly to the ground all around him, pale faces expressionless, swords white with starlight. They converged on the angel.

Scrimlock didn't stay to witness the slaughter. Clear of the tangles of iron, he ran and ran; away from the crash of battle, away from the howls of pain and anguish; away from the unholy laughter. And away from the Spine, who never made a sound as they died.

2,000 YEARS LATER

PART ONE

LIES

I

DİLL

Twilight found the city of Deepgate slouched heavily in its chains. Townhouses and tenements relaxed into the tangled web of ironwork, nodded roofs and chimneys across gently creaking lanes. Chains tightened or stretched around cobbled streets and hanging gardens. Crumbling towers listed over glooming courtyards, acknowledging their mutual decay. Labyrinths of alleys sagged under expanding pools of shadow; all stitched with countless bridges and walkways, all swaying, groaning, creaking.

Mourning.

As the day faded, the city seemed to exhale. A breeze from the abyss sighed upwards through the sunken mass of stone and chain, spilled over Deepgate's collar of rock, and whistled through rusted groynes half-buried in sand. Dust-devils rose in the Deadsands beyond, dancing wildly under the darkening sky, before dissolving to nothing.

Lamplighters were moving through the streets below, turning the city into a bowl of stars. Lanterns on long poles waved and dipped. Brands flared. Gas lamps brightened. From the district known as the League of Rope, right under the abyss rim, and down through the Workers' Warrens to Lilley and the lanes of Bridgeview, lights winked on among thickets of chain. Chains meshed the streets, wrapped around houses or punctured them, linking, connecting, weaving cradles to hold the homes where the faithful waited to die.

Now all across the city, sounds heralded the approach of night: shutters drawn, bolted with a clunk and snap; doors locked, buttressed; padlocks clicked shut. Grates slammed down over chimney tops, booming distantly in all quarters. Then silence. Soon only the echoes of the lamplighters' footsteps could be heard, hurried now, as they retreated into the shadowy lanes around the temple.

The Church of Ulcis rose unchallenged from the heart of Deepgate, black as a rip in the blood-red sky. Stained glass blazed in its walls. Rooks wheeled around its spires and pinnacles. Gargoyles crowded dizzy perches among flying buttresses, balconies, and crenellated crowns. Legions of the stone-winged beasts stared out beyond the city, facing towards the Deadsands: sneering, grinning, furious.

Lost amidst these heights, a smaller, stunted spire rose from the shadows. Ivy sheathed its walls, smothered one side of a balcony circling the very top. Only a peaked slate hat broke completely free of the vegetation, skewed but shining in the waning light. A rusted weathervane creaked round and round, as if not knowing quite where to point.

Clinging to this weathervane was a boy.

He hugged the iron with thin white arms. Tufts of hair shivered behind his ears. His nightshirt fluttered and flapped like a tattered flag. For a long time he held on, all elbows and knees, turning regularly with the weathervane, studying the surrounding spires with quick, nervous eyes. His toes were cold and he was filthy.

But Dill was happy.

Warily, he stood upright. The North–South crossbar tilted under his bare feet, moaned in protest. Rust crumbled, murmured down the slates below. A flock of rooks broke around him, screaming, then uncoiled skywards to scatter among the gargoyles and jewelled glass. Dill watched them go, and grinned from one pink ear to the other.

Alone.

He took a deep, hungry breath, and another, and then unfurled his wings and let the air gather under his feathers. Muscles in his back tightened. Blood rushed through his veins, reached into his outstretched wings. The wind buoyed him, tugged him playfully, daring him to let go. He leaned out and threw back his head, eyes bright. The weathervane spun him like a carousel. An updraught swelled under him. He flexed his wings, straightened them, and pulled down on them. His feet lifted and he laughed.

Someone hissed.

A hooded figure hunched at a window, yellow lantern raised.

Dill scrambled to clutch the weathervane to his heaving chest. He folded his wings tight and dropped to a crouch, heart thumping.

The figure hovered for a while, the shadow of its cowl reaching like a talon over the temple's steeply-canted roofs. Then the figure lowered the lantern and moved away.

Dill watched the priest's shadow flit over the glass before the same window went dark. A hundred heartbeats passed while he clung there shivering. How long had the priest been there? What had he seen? Had he just then happened to pass by, or had he been hiding there in the room, waiting, watching, *spying*?

And would he inform on Dill?

The tracery of scars on Dill's back suggested he certainly might.

I didn't fly. I wasn't going to fly. He'd only unfurled his wings to feel the wind. That was all. That wasn't forbidden.

Still shaking, Dill climbed down from the weathervane and squatted where the moss-covered cone capped the surrounding slates. At once there seemed to be watchers hovering at every window, hooded faces scrutinizing him from all around, unseen lips whispering lies that would find their way back to the Presbyter himself. Dill felt blood rise in his cheeks. He tore free a scrap of moss and feigned interest in it, scrunching it in his palm without feeling it, examining it without seeing it. As he let it go, the wind snatched it and carried it out over Deepgate.

It was said that once you could have stood on the lip of the abyss and peered into the darkness below the city with nothing but the foundation chains between you and the fathomless depths. A sightglass, perhaps, might have offered views of the ghosts far below – but not now. The great chains were still down there, somewhere, hidden beneath the city that a hundred generations of pilgrims had built. But time had seen cross-chains, cables, ropes, girders, struts and beams grow like roots through those ancient links. Buildings had been raised or hung, bridges and walkways suspended, until Deepgate had smothered its own foundations.

Dill lifted one calloused foot and thumped it down. A slate shattered under his heel. He picked up a fist-sized chunk of it and swung his arm to throw it at the window. But he stopped in time. The windows were old, maybe even as old as the temple and the foundation chains. As old as the roof tile he'd just broken, he thought miserably. Instead he hurled the slate into the sunset and listened hard to hear if it hit anything before falling into the abyss beneath the city.

Glass shattered in the distance.

He flopped back, not caring if he crushed his feathers, and gazed past the twinkling streets to where the Deadsands stretched like rumpled silk to the horizon. Purple thunderheads towered in the west, limned in gold. To the east, the Dawn Pipes snaked into the desert, and there a ripple of silver in the sky caught his attention. He sat up.

An airship was purging its ribs for descent, venting hot air from the fabric strips around the liftgas envelope. Turning as it descended, it lumbered toward the Deepgate shipyards, abandoning the caravan it had escorted in from the river towns. The caravan threaded its way between water and waste pipes, the camels trailing plumes of sand. Behind the merchants, a line of pilgrims shuffled in their shackles between two ranks of mounted missionary guards.

'See you tomorrow,' Dill murmured, but he didn't really imagine he would. It would be days before the pilgrims died.

Darkness was creeping into the sky now, pierced by the first evening stars, and so he slid the rest of the way down the roof, hitting the gutter with a thump and a tussle of feathers. A rotting trellis, overgrown with ivy, formed a rustling, snapping ladder back down to his own balcony. When his feet finally found solid stone, he was shaking more than ever.

Once inside, he closed all four of the bolts in the balcony door then checked the window, making sure both locks were also tight. The fire was uneasily low, and deep shadows lurked at the edges of his room. Dill piled on more coals then knelt before the hearth, prodding them with a poker. The fire snapped and popped and sparkled briefly, billowing heat. Orange embers spiralled up the flue; coals crumbled and settled. He tapped the poker against the iron-toothed fender, and hung it back on its hook. Then he took an armful of the big temple candles from their chest and circled his cell, lighting each with a taper from the fire before pressing it down on yesterday's melted stub, where it would best keep the night at bay.

When he was satisfied, he looked up to the wall above the mantel, to the sword.

His sword.

He raced over to the weapon and slid it free from its mount. His soot-smeared fingers barely managed to close around the leather-bound hilt, but that didn't worry him. Tomorrow he would wear it, all the same. Firelight washed over the curved hand guard and blade. He dipped the sword and raised it again, measuring the solid weight of it. It was still too big for him, too heavy, but he took a step back, thrust forward the blade, and raised his other hand the way all great swordsmen supposedly did. His nightshirt sleeve slipped down to his elbow. The sword tip wobbled.

It took a moment to muster his grimmest expression. He covered his uneven teeth with his lip, thrust out his chin, and spread his wings.

'Are you afraid?' he asked the wall.

His brow furrowed as he swished the sword through the air, once, twice.

'Do you fear this weapon? Or its wielder?' He arched an eyebrow. 'My name?' He snorted, rubbed a sooty hand on his nightshirt. 'That doesn't matter. I'm an archon of the Church of Ulcis, Warden to the Hoarder of Souls.' He hesitated, thinking. 'And mortal blood of his herald, Callis.'

That sounded right.

In his mind's eye, an army of heathens advanced, sword hilts drumming on their shields. They cried out in voices edged with fear:

One archon against a hundred warriors.

'A hundred?' Dill laughed. 'No wonder you tremble.' With a twist of his wrist, he spun the sword end over end like a propeller—

—and caught it by the wrong side of the guard, on the sharp side.

'Balls on a skillet!'

The weapon clattered to the floor. A chip flew from the tile where the hilt struck, but the mark was tiny, barely noticeable among all the others.

Dill sucked at his finger then examined it. The scratch, like all the previous ones, wasn't serious. For the priests had neglected to sharpen the blade in his lifetime – and Dill knew why. He picked up the sword, slammed it back into its wall mount, and dropped to his haunches before the hearth.

Mortal blood of his herald, Callis.

This time he resolved not to look up at the sword, not as much as a glance. He wrapped his arms around his knees and rocked backwards and forwards, gazing into the warm currents between the coals, brooding.

Darkness gathered outside his cell. The wind picked up, whispered behind the windows, and teased the flames in the hearth. Only once did Dill's eyes flick back to the sword. He grimaced, hugged his knees tighter.

Tomorrow he would wear it . . .

Dill cursed, then rose and yanked the sword free again. He'd owned the weapon for six years now, almost half his life. He ought to be able to use it by now. The priests had said he'd grow into it. It was a good sword, they'd said. He wheeled about, snapped his wings out, and addressed the wall once more. 'Are you afraid?'

This time there was no army of heathens: nothing but the cold temple stones between Dill and the night sky. He swung the sword backwards and forwards in fierce arcs. 'Are you afraid?' Slash. 'Are you afraid?' Cut. 'Are you afraid?'

He leapt, stabbed the sword into the wall. The tip of the blade sank an inch deep between the stones. Mortar crumbled. The hand guard jarred against his fist. Wincing, he dropped the weapon again.

Dill squeezed his stinging hand under his armpit, and folded to his knees beside the fallen sword. 'Why are you afraid?' he asked himself.

Why *was* he afraid? Temple service was a privilege, an honour, Soul Warden a position of respect. Hadn't his ancestors performed this duty? His father, Gaine? But they'd been Battle-archons, they'd trained with the Spine, flown far across the surrounding Deadsands on behalf of the temple. They'd warred against the Heshette and carved the will of Ulcis into heathen strongholds. While Dill himself . . .

Dill lifted the sword in both grubby hands.

Who am I? An angel who reads about the exploits of his ancestors in books, who stands on his balcony day after day watching the airships return from the river towns, the Coyle delta, the bandit settlements where Battle-archons once fought and died.

Places he would never see. Now churchships and warships ploughed the skies, and an angel's place was here in Deepgate among the chains. While his father's armour rusted in a locked storeroom deep in the heart of the temple, ivy had grown unchecked around Dill's spire. Dust had thickened the old stained windows. Now spiders lived among the jumble of rafters high above his cell, softened the wood with their cobwebs. Now damp crept up the stairwell and saturated the rooms below, all of them empty but for mould and snails.

Dill had been born *too late*.

But they'd still given him a sword. That meant something. Didn't it?

A hammering at the door startled him. Dill scrambled to his feet, replaced the sword in its mount, then brushed soot stains deeper into his crumpled nightshirt and padded over to open the door.

Presbyter Sypes stood wheezing on the landing. A black cassock engulfed the old priest, melted down the spiral stairwell behind him. Only his head and hands were visible: the head shaking like a bone loose in its socket; the hands grinding his walking stick into the stones. 'Nine hundred and eleven steps,' he said. 'I counted.'

For a moment Dill just stared at him. Then he stammered, 'Your Grace, I didn't expect . . . I mean, I thought . . .'

'No doubt,' the Presbyter growled. 'I seem to have been climbing up here since breakfast.' He hobbled into the cell, dragging his robes, scowling. 'So this is where all the temple candles get to. Place looks like the Sanctum itself. Your clothes,' – he handed Dill a rumpled bundle tied with string – 'but you'll need to fold them again. I dropped them, twice.'

'Please, sit down, your Grace.' Dill scraped a stool closer to the fire.

The Presbyter eyed the tiny stool. 'A terminal manoeuvre, I suspect. My bones are still climbing steps. No, I'll rest here by the window until they realize I've finally arrived.' He gathered the folds of his cassock and perched on the window ledge, folding his hands over the silver pommel of his walking stick.

'Well,' he said.

Dill fumbled with the bundle against his chest.

'I said, well?'

Dill hesitated. 'I'm looking forward to it,' he said, lowering his eyes.

'Are you really?'

Dill nodded.

'Not nervous?'

Dill shook his head.

'Really?' The old man's eyes narrowed. 'Good.'

A long moment of silence passed between them. Coals shifted in the fire. Dill glanced back up. His sword was still there, glinting in the candlelight.

'Callis's own sword,' the Presbyter observed.

Dill gave the weapon another brief look. His head dropped even lower as he turned back.

The Presbyter's gaze travelled round the cell, lingering on the cracked tiles, Dill's stool, the candle-chest, snail-bucket, and sleeping mat. There was little else to snag anyone's attention. His hands twisted on the top of the walking stick. 'Well—'

'Thank you,' Dill interrupted, 'for bringing my clothes.'

Presbyter Sypes coughed. 'I was coming up anyway, on

my way to the observatory. Thought I'd wish you luck for the big day.'

Dill's cell wasn't on the way to the observatory. It wasn't on the way to anywhere.

'Thank you, your Grace.'

'Not nervous?'

'No.'

The Presbyter chewed his lips, struggling with something. Finally he said, 'Been up on the roof again, have you?'

Dill flinched. 'I . . .'

'Certain priests have nothing better to do than spy and snipe.' The Presbyter's entire face wrinkled. 'I won't name names.' The wrinkles deepened. 'It was Borelock, that bloodless pickthank. Skulking in the shadows like a damn Shettie saboteur, watching everything, as if it were any of his business. At least he came to *me* this time . . .' His voice trailed off.

'Still,' the old man added eventually, 'can't say I approve. Parts of the temple roof are rotten through.' He rapped his stick against the window ledge. 'Dangerous. Don't want you falling off and breaking your neck.'

Dill stole a glance at the Presbyter but saw no trace of insincerity there. 'It won't happen again,' he said, and right then he meant it. The whip scars on his back tightened, reminding him that Borelock hadn't always taken his discoveries to the Presbyter.

Presbyter Sypes was examining the window ledge, as if he expected the stone to crumble at any moment. 'Just be careful,' he said. 'The temple is no place for foolish mistakes. Dangerous, you understand?'

A gust of wind shook the window glass in its lead surrounds, howled in the chimney. The fire crackled, wavered. Candles guttered. Dill felt the night outside crowding in on them, a pressure behind the windows, pushing, searching for a way in. He swallowed, nodded quickly.

The Presbyter sucked in his cheeks then let them slacken. 'I'd better be off,' he grumbled. 'Far too much paperwork for me to be wasting my time here.' He rose unsteadily, his eyes focused inwardly on whatever toils lay ahead of him. 'Power shifts among the nobles,' he muttered. 'Trade, sciences, censuses, accounts, everything from supplies to bills to taxes to wages to stories to recipes to . . . hah! . . . poetry.' His shoulders slumped. 'It never ends. The Codex grows fatter, the pillars in the temple library are full of books, stuffed to bursting, and I'm buried under the pages yet to be squeezed in. No place to put it all. How long does it take to build a new storage pillar, eh? Stonemason's been at it for months now, for months.' He glanced around. 'You haven't seen him, have you? The stonemason?'

'No, your Grace.'

'Thought not. I think the fellow's died. Or gone and thrown himself into the abyss.' He sighed. 'The fools still do that, you know? One whiff of hard work and they jump, disappear, slip down between the chains like heathens. As if Ulcis would accept unblessed corpses!' The Presbyter rubbed his eyes. 'I don't know, Dill. I don't know where it will end.'

It seemed to Dill that Presbyter Sypes was ageing ten years for every one that passed. His fingers were wasted, ink-stained, curled into claws, as though still clutching his quill. But the Presbyter would struggle on, year after year, collating, ordering, and binding the city records, filling the pillars in his library with books that no one would ever read.

Until it finally kills him.

Back hunched, the old priest shuffled across the cell. 'God help me,' he said, 'if I spot him down there, plotting with the dead, I'll wring his neck. I'll have no skulduggery in my temple, or *under* it. None. I won't stand for any of their nonsense.'

Dill rushed to get the door.

'Someone's got to keep an eye on them.' The Presbyter jabbed his walking stick at the floor. 'Got to make sure they aren't up to anything unsavoury. This blasted wind, I swear it's them. Listen to it: the dead moan more than the living. They're restless, always restless before the ceremony.' He paused on the landing, and his expression softened. 'Not nervous, Dill?'

'No, your Grace.'

'Good lad.' Presbyter Sypes squeezed Dill's shoulder, then released it. 'About tomorrow . . .' He looked uncomfortable. 'Your overseer will be here to collect you in time for the mourners' bell. Your instruction will begin after the ceremony.'

Dill had been expecting this. John Reed Burrsong had been overseer to his father and to his father's older brother, Dill's uncle Sewender. A highly respected soldier and scholar, Burrsong had been instructing temple archons for more than fifty years. Dill had been eight or nine when he'd last seen the old overseer. Burrsong had looked to be more than a hundred years old back then, but he was as tough as old armour – still able to wield his great iron sword to best men half his age.

'That's right,' the Presbyter said. 'Your sword. You

ought to know how to use it, yes? And there are other things: poisons, decorum, and diplomacy.' He waited for an acknowledgement.

'Yes, your Grace.'

'The overseer can explain it all better than I can. Be here in the morning. You'll get along – bound to get along. Pretty little thing, if you don't mind that haunted look. You don't mind *that* do you?'

Dill hid a look of surprise. Clearly, the Presbyter had become lost in one of his fuddles, slipped into another conversation. Not by any stretch of the imagination could John Reed Burrsong be described as pretty, little, or a thing.

'No, your Grace.'

At once the old man came alive. 'I *am* glad we had this chat.' He turned quickly away. 'Best of luck. For tomorrow.'

Stone steps spiralled down into darkness. Wind whistled through the broken windows and murderholes below. 'Shall I escort you down?' Dill said weakly, torn between his duty and the dread of descending into that terrible gloom. He edged closer to the top step. Presbyter Sypes might stumble, hurt himself in the dark. Had every one of the torch brands down there blown out?

The old priest studied him for a moment then rested a hand on the rough-surfaced wall and lowered himself down the first step. 'No need, no need,' he said. 'Get back to the fire, lad. Only nine hundred and ten steps to go.'

Dill wavered. A boot fell from the bundle he still clutched. He reached down to pick it up and dropped the rest of the garments, his hands were trembling so much.

'Nine hundred and nine.' The Presbyter gave him a strained smile as he waved the lad away with his stick. 'Nine hundred and eight!'

The young angel gathered up his bundle and returned to his cell. He gave the bolts and window a final check, found everything secure, and for a moment considered lighting yet more candles. Night was just beginning, and his cell full of draughts. If the dead beneath the city were restless, some of the candles might blow out.

2

MR NETTLE

He carried her with the confidence of a man used to finding his way in darkness. Wooden boards creaked underfoot; ropes groaned and stuttered. With every step, the walkway bucked and swayed closer to the shacks on either side. They called it Oak Alley, those who lived here, but there wasn't a splinter of oak in the whole damn place. Pulpboard more like, and tin. Mr Nettle dipped his shoulder to avoid snaring his daughter's shroud on a stray tin panel. As he ducked, the boards sank with him, bobbing the gangplanks that lay between the walkway and the doorsteps like tongues. The shacks hung motionless over the dark, quietly crumpled in their cradles of hemp.

Up ahead, a brand guttered over its blackened drum, spitting tar. Giant shadows swept around him as he passed. Mr Nettle raised his bottle and took another slug, wiping his mouth on the back of his hand, and settled back into the beat of his own footsteps.

The hood itched against his skin. The whole bloody robe itched. The rough sacking rubbed his wrists like stocks, drawing sweat despite the chill.

Gossip spread faster than disease in the League of Rope, and his muttered lies about Abigail's murder had done nothing but feed those rumours. Unable to disguise his dead child's wounds or pallor, he'd shooed away the shroud widows who'd come knocking at his door, cleaning and wrapping the body by himself. There'd been no viewing, no death ale. Curious voices soon turned angry and fearful. To avoid the gauntlet of his neighbours' stares, he'd figured to deliver her at midnight, when the streets were as quiet as the yawning abyss beneath them.

Oak Alley dipped below the Tummel cross-chain – named after the Glueman who'd fought and died at Sourwater – and rose again steeply. Mr Nettle stuffed his bottle under one arm, then strained on the rope to pull himself up the slippery boards beyond. When he reached the top, he saw that his secrecy had been in vain.

Barterblunder's Penny Tavern depended from one of the foundation chains, some eight feet out from the walkway itself. Dented, pot-bellied, rivet-stitched, and belching smoke, it had lost none of its charm from a former life as a tar boiler. Rowdy laughter came from the open hatch in the tavern roof. Four men were outside. A heavyset fellow with the look of a cutpurse stood on the main walkway, shaking the guide-ropes as a second, scrawnier man wobbled across the tavern gangplank to join him. The other two crouched among the curtains of chains around the hatch, sharing smoke from an old tin hookah. Blaggards, the lot of them, they turned at Mr Nettle's approach. Drunken grins collapsed. The cutpurse let go of the guide-ropes.

One of the smokers exhaled. 'Where does he think he's going with that?'

'It's the big scrounger from up Dens way,' the man on the gangplank said, 'with the cut-up girl.'

The cutpurse lowered his head and the shadows under

his eyes darkened. He took a step toward Mr Nettle, all brazen like he owned the road.

'Leave him to the temple guard,' the smoker said. 'Man doesn't know better. He's drunk or stupid with grief.'

'Got no right to take that thing to the temple,' the cutpurse said.

Mr Nettle tightened his grip on Abigail and shoved past him. The walkway lurched. The other man spun and gripped the street-rope to steady himself. 'You think they'll let that in?' he called. 'Think they won't know?'

'Might be someone tells them first,' the man on the gangplank said. 'Best bury her in the Deadsands, save yourself the walk.'

Mr Nettle kicked the plank from under him.

The man threw an elbow over one of the guide-ropes. The hemp stretched dangerously, groaned, but held, leaving him swinging over darkness. The smokers laughed.

Mr Nettle grunted. Damn right he was drunk.

When the men were out of sight, he shifted Abigail's corpse to a more comfortable place on his shoulder. His heart was beating painfully. For a long while he searched the ground, seeing nothing.

What would Abigail have made of his present mood? How many times had she brooded and sulked, fretted and cried and shaken him to break his silence over one of her worries? He'd never gotten angry; never raised a hand to her like some fathers might have done. He'd just sat there and watched her through his whisky, quiet like. The bottle felt cold in his hand. He took another slug.

After a while, the path brought him to the edge of the Workers' Warrens. Here the sprawl of timber huts and walkways lapped the walls of stone-built tenements. Frost clung to the cobbles and flint in Coal Street, a wending fissure which led the scrounger into the district of Chapel-funnel. Fog smothered the ground and writhed amid the swish of his mourning robe. Wisps of it coiled around his knees.

Maybe four hours until dawn. He was running out of time. He drank deeply, savouring the burn in his throat. Mutilation was not the answer. Not for *his* child. Those that took knives to their dead were worse than blaggards, or thieves, or cutthroats. They were worse than the heathens. Yet what choice did he have? If he was to see her safe?

Under his robe, the cleaver hung heavy from his belt.

Coal Street narrowed as he went deeper into the Warrens, pressing the fog into a dank vein. He passed Boiler's Inn, silent and shuttered, and followed the long curve round Fishmarket. Smoke drifted through the locked grates. He narrowed his eyes and pushed on through it, hoping the shroud would not retain the smell. Past Fishmarket the tenements grew taller and slouched inwards. In some places the upper storeys buttressed those opposite, like exhausted brawlers, and then Mr Nettle's footsteps echoed in utter darkness. Unseen tunnels burrowed into the walls here, gaping maws that leaked chill draughts, odours of damp straw and horses, hookah smoke and weed. Once, he sniffed the spice of the censers at Sinners' Well: his stomach clenched at that.

Beyond the tunnels there was scarcely more light. With the brands here long out, moonlight fell in grey slabs that made the shadows all the darker. He trudged past bolted door after bolted door. Rusted bridges linked the districts of the Warrens, spanning narrow canals of empty space. He left Chapelfunnel and crossed into Merrygate, iron ringing under the hobnails of his boots.

He was deep in the Warrens, where Merrygate merged
into Applecross and the road skirted the broken watchtower to follow Dolmen's Chain, when he noticed a heap
of blankets on the ground ahead stir. A voice chimed out:
'Coin for a pilgrim, sir, a penny or a double? Look at the
moon grin – one night before she's dark. A double for a
room to keep me safe.'

Blankets hid the boy's face, but Mr Nettle saw the cup
out-stretched.

'Hungry,' the beggar said, reaching for his own mouth.
'No mother, no father.'

Mr Nettle spat at him without breaking stride.

Fifty years a scrounger had taught him plenty. Expect
nothing, ask for nothing. If you need a thing, you find it
or you pay for it. If you can't find it or you can't afford it,
you never needed it. A double would make no difference
anyway. Didn't matter what night it was any more. Full
moon or dark moon, the lad wasn't safe. No one was safe
these days.

'Ragman!' the beggar cried. 'Keep your League-filth
coin, you're no better than me.' He banged his cup against
the wall and began to sing. 'Come out tomorrow. Come
see the moon. Out tomorrow. See the moon.'

Mr Nettle's pace faltered for an instant. Thrashing the
beggar would only delay him. He held Abigail more firmly,
straightened his back, and pressed on. The city soon
swallowed the boy's lunatic song.

Dawn was close, but the districts of Deepgate still slept
in frost: air held like a breath for morning. Stars glittered
like spear points in a ragged strip between the eaves.

The bottle was nearly empty. He raised it to his lips,
then lowered it again without taking a drink. What was he
to do? He had to think. A headache was creeping into the

base of his skull and his thoughts ran like tar. Had he sleepwalked into this godforsaken maze? Where was he now? On Tapper Road, where once he'd broken an oil-seller's jaw for weighting his barrel with stones. He was almost out of the Warrens. How much time left? Not much. He'd wasted it. He'd listened to his own footsteps and watched his breath curl up before him, and drunk his whisky. The cleaver blade felt like ice against his thigh, the bottle neck like a knot in his fist. He threw the bottle away and heard it smash.

Around the next bend, the Tapper Road plunged into deeper fog. Gas lamps bloomed in the distance: the temple districts. He was almost there.

Mr Nettle paused by a luckhole, a gap where the street-stones had fallen through, lost to the abyss below. Some-one had put down planks, but those would come up easy enough. There would still be iron down there, lots of it. Often you could remove three or more girders without weakening the street and making more holes. But some-times you lifted too much iron and the whole lot would cave in when a loaded cart went over. It was hard to judge.

He pulled Abigail down from his shoulder so that she lay in his arms. Her face sparkled with a patina of ice, as white as the linen in which he had wrapped her. This was good linen, better than any you'd get in the League. He'd found a bolt beneath the Coalgas Bridge fourteen years ago, unsullied, for all the stink of that place, and kept it for himself. Even so, merchants sold silk out in Ivygarths, and he'd walked the miles there yesterday to price it. And walked the miles back empty-handed. It was fine enough linen.

There was nothing delicate about Abigail's appearance.

She had not been pretty: the strong jaw, wide forehead, features as blunt as his own but softer. Her too-wide shoulders and hips were now far from those of the young girl he still saw in her. Despite this, even after all this time, she weighed nothing. He could have carried her for ever.

Mr Nettle closed his own eyes and imagined Abigail opening hers. She would lift her arms around his shoulders. *You don't have to carry me*, she'd say. *I can walk.* Then he'd lower her to the ground and they could turn round and go home. He pressed his forehead against hers. She was still cold as stone. He opened his eyes again, blinked at the gas lamps in the distance, and pushed on – crossing the Flint Bridge into Lilley.

Abigail had often come here to paint. She'd liked the crooked old townhouses with their slatted shutters and delicate iron balconies, and she'd liked to sit under a shady tree in the cobbled rounds and listen to birds chirrup while she worked. But she'd liked the gardens best.

They'd been down here together once, trying to sell a rake he'd scrounged in Ivygarths, and Abigail, being little, had done the door-knocking. An old fellow had let them in to one of the gardens and stood haggling with Mr Nettle like a Roper, while Abigail had run in circles gawping at all the different flowers. After that, she'd wanted to go in all the gardens, but Lilley folk kept them locked tight. Still, he'd gotten eight doubles for the rake and was put in a fine mood, so he'd lifted her up on his shoulders so she could peek over the walls.

Southeast of Lilley the road veered away from Dolmen's Chain and rose to Market Bridge, and here were the pedlars out stamping their feet, rubbing their hands, and hollering through the morning mist.

'Coal oil coal oil.'

'Hot bread, fruit bread.'

'Birders, ratters, guarders.'

Some Lilley servants were already out, milling round the carts, buying, arguing, and laughing like it was their money they were spending.

There was no other way but on through the market. Mr Nettle kept his head down and quickened his pace, and no one bothered him until he reached the flower sellers at the far end.

'You, mister?' The man got right up off his stool and stood in front of him, blocking his way. 'Got daisies and poppies and Shale Forest milkflowers, all fresh and nothing over a double a bunch.'

He had a thin, dirt-coloured beard and a loop of gold in his ear, big enough to slip a finger through.

'Nothing over a double, and halfpenny sprigs of sickle-berry from Highwine – and look here.' He picked up a bunch of the white roses and cradled them like he was holding a baby. 'Lilley roses, home grown, six a penny.'

Mr Nettle was staring at the earring.

The pedlar was looking at Abigail's shroud. 'Nobles been buying them up for twice that. Soil comes all the way from Goosehawk's Plantation in Clune. Listen, give you another couple on top, same price.' He pushed the flowers into Mr Nettle's hand.

They were a tired-looking bunch: curling petals and brown stems.

'That's eight for a penny,' the pedlar urged.

Mr Nettle gripped the stems and shook hard. Petals scattered.

'Hey.'

'Withered,' Mr Nettle said. He snatched a fist of petals from the ground and threw them at the pedlar. 'Dead.'

The sky was flat white when he carried Abigail into Bridgeview, where the road unravelled into dozens of deep lanes. He wove through one after another, checking the signs to keep from losing his way. Victoria Lane, Plum Lane, Silvermarket. On Rose Lane he heard the shuffle of feet and looked up. High above, the soft silhouettes of the nobles' bridges jagged between the townhouses. Muted conversation drifted down: they were going to see the angel; they were tired and cold, and if this dreadful fog didn't lift they'd see nothing. Mr Nettle reached the end of the lane, clumped down four steps, and came at last to a misty courtyard abutting the open abyss. Here he stopped.

The Gatebridge shattered the dawn. Arcs and struts of iron rose in a skeletal fan. Along the deck, low bolted gasoliers burned feverishly, lighting wedges of the thick oak beams which ran all the way to the temple steps at the opposite end. The dead lay there: six or seven that he could see. So few? His stomach tightened like twisted rope. He brought his hand to his mouth before he remembered he'd thrown the bottle away. His gaze lingered a while on those pale shrouds. Why could there not have been more today?

The Church of Ulcis rose up behind, its walls like black cliffs. Fierce convolutions of stone, sharp in the glare of the gasoliers, spread outwards from the doors, softened, and faded into the fog, so the building itself looked like it stretched to the ends of the world. Mr Nettle knew how vast it was. On clear days you could see its fist of spires clear from the League, so big you felt you could reach over and grab it. But this was as close as he'd been in twenty-three years. There had been thirteen dead that previous day, fourteen including his wife. He'd left Abigail asleep in her tiny cot and carried Margaret here. A week before Scar Night and the guards had been lax: they'd opened none of the shrouds. But that day he'd had nothing to hide.

The courtyard nurtured a silence like a pause in the clangour of bells. He felt it in his bones and it set his skin crawling. The cleaver was a cold weight under his belt, the steel pressing against his thigh. It had to be now or never.

He held his daughter firmly. For a long moment, he almost felt inclined to turn away.

And then he yanked the hood lower over his face and advanced. He stepped onto the bridge, his boots loud on its deck.

Other mourners crowded the bridge. Some stood in silence; others huddled in whispering groups. Black robes seethed around him as they parted to let him through: robes of silk and velvet, some finely cut and sewn in folds that rippled as they moved, some cut plain, but all were as black as his own. Most of the mourners turned away at the sight of him, but a few hoods bowed as he passed them, white fingers steepled underneath in greeting – Warreners, he figured. Mr Nettle ignored them, pushing through towards the temple doors, with his jaws clenched and his heart bruising his ribs.

At the far end of the bridge, he laid her with the others, taking a moment to smooth back her hair and brush away some of the frost crusting her shroud.

She looked now just as he remembered seeing her asleep only a few nights before, her hair like coils of copper round her cheeks, her mouth slightly open, as if even now she might draw a breath and wake. He remembered thinking at the time how peaceful she looked, as pretty as one of her own paintings. She would have made some lad a fine wife.

He opened his hand and took the three white rose petals resting there and tucked them in her shroud, and then gently he covered her face with the linen. In a moment she was as anonymous as the rest. Mr Nettle stayed on his knees, tugging creases from the stiff fabric of the shroud long after it was smooth.

Dark figures stood around him and waited. The gasoliers hissed. Mr Nettle counted thirty heartbeats before a hand gripped his shoulder, another thirty before he turned round.

The temple guard wore oiled armour, as black as the abyss. Threads of gaslight slipped over its surface, never settling. On the breastplate, the talisman of Ulcis, the Hoarder of Souls, shone dully. The guard's face was clean-shaven, wrinkled and red from the cold; the eyes beneath his helm were heavy with sleep. In one hand he held a pike like an iron mast. 'Open the shroud,' he sniffed, rubbing a leather gauntlet under his nose.

Mr Nettle looked up, his face still hidden by the hood, his hand still clutching his daughter's shroud.

'I'm to check them all,' the guard said.

Still Mr Nettle didn't answer.

The guard regarded him impassively for a while, his breath misting in the cold air. Then he moved to one side, laid his pike on the deck and knelt by Abigail's corpse. Plates of steel on his shoulders slid against each other as he loosened the folds of cloth and pulled her arm free.

Both men stared at the torn flesh on her wrist.

The guard dropped the arm like it was a plague rat. 'This one's been bled,' he announced, louder than he had to.

There were murmurs from the mourners behind. Mr Nettle heard them push closer to look.

The guard traced a circle around his talisman and touched his brow. 'A husk,' he said. 'Been on ice for a while.' Slowly, he reclaimed the pike and rose to his feet. 'Why do you bring this thing to the temple doors? Gods below, man, don't you realize the danger?' He threw his arms wide. 'She cannot enter.'

Mr Nettle continued to stare at his daughter's exposed arm.

'You understand? There's no soul.'

The guard's words rang out like bells in the still morning. Deep inside, the scrounger felt some part of himself crumble. And with it, the gem of hope he'd guarded all night slipped away. Had he been wrong not to try to disguise her wounds? Suddenly he was weary, his head slumped to his chest. For the first time, he seemed to feel Abigail's cold weight pressing down on his shoulders. He sank to the ground.

And then his teeth locked together and his lips peeled back. Beneath his robe, the muscles in his neck grew taut, his shoulders bunched, his hands tightened to fists, and he was on his feet with a snarl, grabbing the guard's throat with all of his strength, and forcing him back.

The man stumbled, flailing an arm. He tripped over one of the corpses and hit the ground in a clatter of armour, his neck still tight in the scrounger's grip. The pike toppled and landed with an unholy crack.

Mr Nettle's hood fell back; his face twisted into a blur of teeth and stubble and murder.

The guard wrenched at Mr Nettle's arm, and struck it, pulled at the fabric of his robe. The sacking ripped but the arm beneath remained hard as iron.

Mr Nettle tightened his grip.

Air burst from the guard's throat; his eyes rolled back; his face darkened to crimson. He scrabbled again at Mr Nettle's arm, then at his face, fingers gouging. His gauntlets, stiff with frost, raked Mr Nettle's skin.

Then something hit Mr Nettle hard above his ear, pitching him sideways. His head struck the deck of the bridge and he rolled awkwardly, twisting the muscles of his shoulder. Darkness flickered through his vision. He ended up on his back, gasping. His ear burned, and his skull felt like it was shrinking. He shook his head, looked up. Spans of iron spun against the still lightening sky.

A second guard stood there, livid in the dawn, armour gleaming, pike levelled.

Mr Nettle staggered to his feet. Blood streamed from a gash on his forehead, filling his eyes. The crowd of mourners backed away.

He charged at the guard – or tried to. Pain hit him like a nail driven into the top of his spine. Everything suddenly lurched to one side; the bridge slid out from under him. His legs folded and he stumbled, brandishing his fists like a drunk, and dropped to his knees.

The second guard stove the base of his pike into the scrounger's stomach.

Mr Nettle curled and clawed at the wooden deck beneath him. Splinters pierced him under his nails. He bit down hard, tried to rise, and was struck again. And again. And again.

The mourners looked on in silence. One of them crouched to inspect the injured guard. Pinned by his armour, the man coughed and spluttered and drew in great rasping breaths.

Mr Nettle had no idea how long he suffered this

beating. After a time, he stopped feeling the blows as they rained on him. They came as quick as licks of flame in an inferno. He was only distantly aware of the sting of metal on flesh, the deck of the bridge rough against his cheek, the blood bubbling in his nose as he sucked in air. It might have lasted minutes, or for hours.

Finally, the guard held back. 'Get lost,' he said, panting. His arms trembled as he levelled the sharp end of his pike at Mr Nettle's throat. 'Go! Out of here. Get lost.'

Mr Nettle tried to move, his muscles screaming protest. Torrents of fresh pain rushed through his arms and legs. He bit down on the urge to retch, and pushed back against the bridge, hefting himself onto his hands and knees. His left eye had swollen shut. At least one rib was cracked or broken. He spat a bloody tooth on to the deck.

But he moved away. Without turning to face his attacker, he crawled back to his daughter's body. Slowly, carefully, he replaced her arm in the shroud. Blood dripped from his face onto the linen.

Then he gathered her up and forced himself to his feet. For a moment he wavered: she was suddenly so heavy. His legs shook, but he wrenched himself upright again with a loud gasp that echoed back from the temple walls.

Unhooded now, with teeth bared and his face swollen and bloody, he started back across the bridge. His robe was torn and hung in strips about his arm. He swung a savage glare over the other mourners, who parted like a dark river before the bow of a ship, crowding as far from him as they could, only to follow his retreat with shrouded eyes. Nervous voices hushed as he passed.

Mr Nettle continued across the bridge with blood pounding in his ears and only silence in his wake.

In the shadow of the girders at the Gatebridge entrance,

he held his daughter over the edge, over the darkness, and looked down at the rumpled fabric covering her face, at the strands of hair that hung out from the cloth. Tears mixed with the blood on his cheeks as he dropped her into the abyss. The white shroud flamed for an instant in the gaslight and then she was gone.

The cleaver handle dug into his ribs and, for all its cost, he felt like throwing the damn thing far into the abyss too. What use would it be to him now? How could he ever get close enough to his daughter's murderer to use it?

To kill an angel, he'd need to find a far more dangerous weapon.

3

DILL AND RACHEL

Dill woke with a jolt, gasping for breath, still in the grip of his nightmare. He'd been alone somewhere in cold, crushing darkness. No, not completely alone: there had been a girl. *Black eyes, red lips, white teeth.* Even as he tried to remember, her face faded, leaving him with nothing but the feeling that, somehow, she'd been both beautiful and hideous.

Had she been crying – or laughing?

It was morning, and he was lying face-down on his mat in a pool of his own spittle. The candles had burned down to stubs of tallow. Ash smouldered in the hearth. Sunlight streamed through the stained glass in the eastern wall. Dill's gluey eyes focused on the image portrayed in the window. His ancestor Callis, Herald and commander of Ulcis's archons, held his wings outstretched and his sword aloft before a group of cowering heathens. Motes of dust drifted before the glass angel, changing from pink to blue to gold.

Dill sniffed, wiped his lips on the sleeve of his nightshirt, and rose stiffly from his mat. He stretched arms, legs and wings before he realized his eyes were itching terribly.

He groaned. *Please . . . not today, not for the ceremony.*

But no amount of pleading would make a difference. Dill's eyes were the wrong colour: completely inappropriate.

Nerves. He was bound to be nervous. The darkness in his dream had unnerved him.

And today I wear a sword for the first time.

He would have to attend to his eyes later, first he had to wash. The water in his bucket was freezing, but he drenched himself until he gasped, then stood naked, soaked and shivering, with his bony arms wrapped around his ribs, his feathers damp.

The uniform lay there on the stool, precisely folded where he'd left it last night, a stack of heavy velvet, fine brocade with glints of silver. The boots standing beside the stool were new and smelled of polished leather. But the sword above the mantel outshone all else.

The blade beckoned him, but he couldn't touch it, not yet. Everything must be perfect first, and he had to take care of the snails. There were only seven this morning: one by the hearth, one under the window, the others clinging to the walls at various heights. The largest was the size of a walnut, the smallest the size of his little fingernail. Gently, he removed them and put them in the snail-bucket along with the others. About forty in it now, he noted. The promise of rain must be bringing them out in such numbers.

Wherever did they come from?

Dill had spent years trying to figure it out. There was a narrow space under the balcony door, and also under the door to the stairwell, through both of which they might have entered his cell, and there were also a few dark holes where mortar had crumbled from the damp walls. But he'd watched those same openings for hours at a time without ever seeing a single snail slither through. The empty rooms beneath his cell were thick with them, but those rooms were permanently dark and there wasn't a brand or taper bright enough to make him want to venture far inside them. Not that those snails down there ever seemed to move either. Snails, being snails, only moved when no one was watching them.

A sudden roar rattled the windowpanes. An explosion? Dill wheeled, confused, expecting to see the walls topple, and he almost knocked over the snail-bucket. But everything remained solid. The noise outside died away.

The door to his balcony had jammed shut, as though its arched frame had shifted during the night, but he finally got it open with a kick and squeezed his wings through.

Crisp morning air: the flagstones chilled his bare feet; the parapet felt cool when he leaned against it. Deepgate spread below, bright in the sunshine. Had a chain snapped somewhere, some part of the city collapsed into the abyss? He leaned out further to get a better view.

Heavy with balconies, the townhouses of Bridgeview slumped at odd angles around their dappled courtyards, walled gardens, and fountains that glittered like smashed glass. Beyond that, neatly pitched roofs crowded the chains in Lilley and Ivygarths. Further out, smoke rose from a thousand chimneys in the Warrens. And, out on the fringes, the League of Rope clumped around the chain anchors, under the Deadsands, like driftwood on the shores of a lake. There was no sign of disaster.

Another deep roar. Rooks burst past his tower with cries of alarm. Dill raced around his balcony to investigate.

Fat black lettering on the tail-fin proclaimed the warship to be the *Adraki*. She was turning slowly, edging closer to the temple. Propellers twice the size of a man thrummed on either side of the brass-etched gondola suspended beneath the envelope. Four aeronauts in white uniforms stood on the aft deck, peering over the stern-castle rail between the aether-lights and docking harpoons. The signalman spotted him and waved his flag in a clipped semaphore message that Dill doubted was civil.

Dill gave a hesitant wave back. He'd never seen one of these ships so close. Its silver envelope filled half the sky; and it was getting closer, descending past him to where a dock jutted out from the temple's sheer walls. In his lifetime, no airship had used that mooring. Not even churchships were allowed this close, and this, the *Adraki*, was a warship, her deck-cages packed with drums of lime-gas and incendiaries. Clearly someone important was arriving. Abruptly Dill's nerves were on edge and his eyes itching all the more.

White as a coward's flag, as the captain of the temple guard would have said. At least the aeronauts were too distant to see his fright. He closed his eyes and thought about Callis's sword, *his* sword, but felt the white in his irises now edge towards purple. He shook his head and gripped the parapet tightly until their colour faded to a comfortable, respectable grey.

'Leaders,' cried an aeronaut, tossing down a first coil of rope. Evidently, they were not prepared to use the harpoons this close to so much ancient stonework and glass. A dockhand snatched up the rope, fed it through a pulley on the docking gantries and ran with it over to a winch. More ropes followed, and men scrambled after them.

A call came up from the dock, 'Leaders fixed. Ready to winch.'

'Bring her in.'

Ropes stretched and twanged as dockhands began to wind cables down from spools mounted on the airship deck. The warship's engines roared again. It trembled, eased closer to the dock.

'Hey, archon,' the signalman shouted, 'want a race?'

The other aeronauts laughed. 'Leave the poor bugger alone,' one of them said. 'Not his fault.'

'I was only asking.'

Dill lowered his head so that they couldn't see his eyes become pink, then he followed his own wet footprints back the way he had come. The aeronauts could stuff their warship. Dill had his uniform now. And his sword, of course. He brightened a little; there was still time for some sword practice. He ran the rest of the way around the balcony, folded his wings, and ducked inside the doorway to his cell.

But halfway through he halted, and blinked. A young woman stood waiting for him by the fireplace: small, gaunt, her fair hair drawn back severely from her face and woven into a tight plait in the style popular among nobles' daughters. But this was her only concession to fashion, for she was bereft of jewellery, and wore beaten leathers bristling with weapons. A worn hilt jutted from the scabbard on her back, blue throwing knives and silver needles ran the length of her leather-sheathed forearms, while her belt held poison pouches, a blowpipe, and three stubby bamboo tubes tarnished with age. She had taken Dill's sword from its mount, examining it. The sword was too big for him, but in her tiny hands it looked absurd.

'Put that back,' Dill snapped.

Dark green eyes turned to confront him. Her face was

so white she looked ill. 'Your sword?' she asked. Her gaze dropped to it briefly, then bounced back up to meet his.

Dill remembered he was naked. He snatched up his nightshirt, wrapped it round his midriff, and glowered at her. 'It is Callis's sword.'

'So they say.' She studied the weapon more closely. 'It's old enough. The steel is single-layered, brittle, heavy. Blunt. The balance . . .' She drew the back of the blade over her sleeve and then held it between both hands. 'Does not exist. The pommel was sheared off at some point, not that it makes much difference. The guard . . .' She snorted. 'Someone replaced this. It's gold-leafed lead. You could dent it with a spoon.' She slid the weapon back into its mount. 'Shiny though.'

Dill waited stiffly.

'Rachel Hael,' she said.

There was something familiar about her surname, but he couldn't place it. 'What do you want?'

'Nothing,' she replied quickly, flatly, as though it were a reflexive answer to that question. Then she hesitated, seemed to realize she ought to say more. 'I'm your over-seer.'

'What?'

'Overseer. Tutor. Personal guard.'

Rachel Hael was a foot shorter than himself, half his weight, and she couldn't be more than three or four years older than him. She exuded all the scholarly air of some-one who ate beetles.

'You're not my overseer,' he said.

She was looking around his cell. 'How many candles do you *need* here?'

'John Reed Burrsong is my overseer.'

'He's been dead for seven years.'

Burrsong was dead? That explained why Dill hadn't seen the old man around for a while. But surely there were other soldiers, or scholars? The temple teemed with them: dusty old men with spectacles and beards. Men who remembered wars, and times when the water tasted better and everyone was polite, and would tell you about them with flinching eyes and great weary sighs. There had to be someone more appropriate. Someone older. Less *fragile*-looking.

'Sypes told me to watch you,' Rachel said. 'And to train you, I suppose. Swordplay, poisons, diplomacy, that sort of thing.' She reached inside a pouch attached to her armour, produced a tiny book, and flipped it towards him.

Dill glanced at the title. *Desert Trade Etiquette for Merchant Noblemen by P. E. Wallaway.* 'What's this?'

'Something to do with diplomacy, isn't it?' She glanced at the cover. 'That's what they told me. You ought to read it, if you get a chance. I'm sure it's fascinating.'

'I don't—'

'I don't blame you,' she conceded.

Dill bit his lower lip. This seemed all wrong. Had Presbyter Sypes finally succumbed to his encroaching dotage? A young woman armed with a book she hadn't read and a sword she probably couldn't pull out of its scabbard without hurting herself did not amount to a proper overseer.

'I'm hardly thrilled myself,' she said. 'Let me guess, orange means annoyed?'

Dill looked away, tried to focus his eyes back to grey. Dust motes danced and sparkled before Callis's window. His snail-bucket sat underneath it. He felt like kicking it.

'Why do you have a bucket of snails in your room?' she asked eventually.

'What?'

'Snails?'

'Because.'

She waited.

'Because they climb up here,' he said. 'I put them in the bucket and take them away.'

'Where?'

He scowled. 'What training have you had, anyway?'

'*Where* do you take the snails?'

Why was she talking about snails? He batted the book at her impatiently. 'Down below, into the temple.'

'Why?'

'To let them go.'

'Why?'

'I don't know!' It was just something he did. He didn't want them here, so he took them away, released them in the corridors behind the priests' cells. She was trying to distract him, and he wasn't having any more of it. 'Why you?'

Rachel Hael let out a long sigh. 'A husk arrived at the temple doors this morning. There's talk of another soul-thief loose in the city, as if *one* wasn't bad enough. Maybe it's becoming fashionable.' She shrugged. 'I suppose they'd rather *your* blood stayed in your veins.'

This morning? 'But Scar Night is tonight. The moon's not yet gone dark.'

'Really?' She yawned theatrically.

So here was his pocket-sized overseer: a finch of a girl who thought she knew something about soul-thieves. Perhaps she'd read a book on the subject. The crackling in his eyes intensified. 'What does that have to do with you?'

'God knows.'

But Dill suddenly knew. He recognized her uniform. He looked again at her sword hilt, and this time he noticed just how well worn it was. A feeling of unease crept over him. *That's why she's so pale.* 'You're Spine,' he said.

'*Spine,*' she spat the word. 'I hate that title. Temple backbone, very noble. I prefer *Nightcrawler.* Isn't that what the commoners call us? Right up to the point where they get dragged off for questioning.'

What was she doing here? Spine weren't usually assigned other duties. They *couldn't* be assigned other duties, not after *their* training. What was the Presbyter thinking of?

Rachel interrupted his thoughts. 'A message for you.' She threw him a package wrapped in thick paper. Dill fumbled in catching it and the package dropped to the floor and burst open.

It contained an iron key on a chain, and a note from the Presbyter.

Make sure you lock the soulcage outside the temple. Until the dead are blessed, hell will be looking for them and I don't want the Maze opening any doors in here. God knows what might escape. And don't lose the key – it's three thousand years old and it's the only one we have.

Dill scrunched up the note and threw it into the hearth. *Don't lose the key!* Did they think he was an idiot? Callis looked down with disdain from his glass battlefield, while even his painted enemies seemed to cower less and leer more.

'Good news?' Rachel asked.

He frowned.

'It's that kind of morning,' she sighed. 'Which probably means it's only going to get worse.'

She was behaving very strangely for a Spine. Normally they just did what they were told without a blink or a wasted word. They were never angry or frustrated – and certainly not sarcastic or rude. Something to do with their training, he supposed. But this Rachel was unusually emotive, and he began to suspect something other than her recent appointment as his overseer was troubling her. He could not, however, have cared less.

'I'll see you after the ceremony,' she said.

'That won't be necessary.'

'You don't have a choice. Neither do I.'

Outside, the warship's engines rumbled again. The distant shouts of dockhands filtered up, followed by the clanging of bells. Dill felt the ruckus reverberate in his teeth.

Rachel Hael's expression soured. 'The *Adraki*,' she said. 'Looks like Mark managed to dock the flagship without knocking the whole temple over,' then, seeing his confusion, 'Mark Hael, my brother.'

Now Dill recalled where he'd heard her surname before. Mark Hael had been appointed commander of Deepgate's aeronauts after his own father, General Edward Hael, had lost his warship to Heshette arrow fire in the northern Deadsands. Hampered by sand storms, aeronauts had been searching the wreckage for the general's body for days. The significance of the *Adraki*'s arrival at the temple dock became apparent. They had now located Edward Hael – Rachel's father was to be among the dead given to the abyss at this morning's ceremony.

'They must have found him, your father.'

She folded her arms.

'Then you will be at the Sending ceremony,' he said.

'Not if I can help it,' she said, turning away.

'But—'

But she was already striding towards the door.

'Hold on,' he called after her, waving the book. 'Wait, you mentioned swordplay, poisons.' He didn't care a whit about either, but he wasn't about to let her walk out that easily; not with his cauldron of questions still bubbling. 'If you're supposed to . . .'

She halted midway across his cell, slipped a tiny black phial out from a pouch on her belt and tossed it over to him. 'You want to know about poisons?' she said. 'Drink that.'

Then she left.

Dill stood there for a while, juggling the phial, book and key, and tried to untangle his thoughts. He felt cheated. Why a Spine overseer? His first day of service, and he was to be shadowed by a temple assassin. Worse, he was to be *instructed* by a temple assassin. They weren't scholars. They weren't even proper soldiers. *Nightcrawlers!* What would people think? He gripped the soulcage key so hard it stung his hand.

Don't lose the key.

Gods below, he was a temple archon, not a child. He coiled up the chain and slammed it on the mantel, then placed the phial and book beside it. A tiny snail he'd missed clung there. Dill pinged it away with a flick of his finger and heard it ricochet off the far wall.

'Bastard.'

He shoved on his boots, then cursed and yanked them off again before pulling his trousers on instead. The trousers were too large, but the sword belt kept them in place. The shirt pinched his back around his wings, and the straps were all too fiddly and complicated to tie up properly. He left half of them undone: it didn't matter. No one would see them under his jacket. The jacket itself was stiff and equally difficult to get into – another garment adapted to fit around his wings by incompetent temple cassock-stitchers who never had to wear the stupid thing.

Finally fully dressed, he took a deep breath and forced his eyes from their throbbing orange back to the appropriate grey. Then, at last, he looked himself over.

Snails had left their greasy trails down one side of his jacket. One silver button was missing. His boots were loose, and somehow already scuffed, his trousers creased and covered with wisps of cobweb.

He looked like a fool.

'I'm a temple archon,' he said to his ancestor's image in the window, but that didn't make him feel any better.

Then he grabbed his sword and thrust it into the scabbard at his belt. So what if the pommel had been sheared off? Maybe it wasn't a Spine sword, or even a good sword, but it had once belonged to Callis, and that was enough for him. He patted the replacement guard. The Spine assassin was probably just jealous. Dill plucked a loose feather from his sleeve, brushed away imaginary dust, and then, proudly gripping the hilt of his sword, set off for his first proper day at work.

He returned a moment later to collect the key.

4

THE WEAPON SMITH

The whole city got out of Mr Nettle's way. Crowds parted at the Applecross fleshmarket, merchants hushed their hollering, pedlars and servants and jugglers and fools stepped aside, and even the beggars shut their whining mouths and stilled their rattling cups. It might have been the size of him, or his battered, bloody face, or the way he trudged past with his jaw set and fists swinging at his sides like he wanted to punch someone. He might have, too, had they not been quick to avoid him.

He had meant to go straight back to the League, meant to go home and lose himself in a bottle, but somehow his boots led him on east of Merrygate, to the warrens of the weapon smiths.

To support all the forges and the heavy stone, there were more chains here than elsewhere in the Warrens, yet there seemed no sense to them, no way to see how they all connected. The smiths themselves had gone to work on these chains, adding to them, linking them, strengthening old iron with new, so Mr Nettle found he had to duck and weave to get through. Huge staples, as big your arm, bound one chain to another, or were bolted to links where the welds had split. Great pins drove up through the cobbles or through walls, and in places there was nothing but iron underfoot. This resulted in a tangle of metal that the smallest breath of wind set quivering and singing – a song that might be heard for miles in the deep darkness below the streets.

Blacklung Lane was rightly named. Soot covered the brick in a foul fur. When you breathed you tasted coal and felt you could scrape it from your mouth, and when you spat you looked to check if it was black. Smithies packed the lane on both sides. Smoke from the forges boiled through pipes in the walls and then hung in a seething canopy between the buildings. Rusty wrought-iron signs hung over the doors, all swinging and creaking though there was no breeze. The sun had barely burned away the dawn mists, but already the place was bustling. A constant stream of porters shuffled past, carrying coal, wood, and heavy crates of raw or worked metal. The whole lane shook with their footsteps. With Scar Night looming, folks had woken early to make the best of the day, eager to get their work done before the coming sunset.

Iron rang. Steel clattered. Fires roared. Shovels scraped and men sweated. Hammers beat anvils, *clang, clang, clang*, and Mr Nettle pushed on past the porters, through the chains, and ducked inside a low door on one side of the lane.

Two men with flame-reddened skin were stoking the furnace. A third leaned over an anvil, working the steel of a red-hot sword.

'What?' this man said without looking up.

'I've come to trade,' Mr Nettle said.

The man gave him a quick glance without pausing in his work.

'What for what?'

Mr Nettle told him.

The man snorted. 'Next door,' he said.

Laughter followed Mr Nettle out.

And so he went from door to door, from furnace to furnace, from scowl to scowl. The smiths' laughter spread down the lane like a plague, and the calls, earnest as some were, were all the same: *Next door, Next door.* Of the many smiths on Blacklung Lane, none would offer more than fourpence for the cleaver and none would accept it as trade for what he needed. By the time he reached the end of the lane, the laughs, the calls and the pounding of metal threatened to split his skull.

Blacklung Lane ended in a slump where it had come loose from the chains. It might slide into the abyss next week, or in a year, but then sometimes slipped lanes stayed this way for good, and people nearby just made do. Rubbish had gathered in festering piles where the rain had washed it down the slope. The last smithy of all hung in an impossible cradle of chain and girders, all meshed together like a great iron bonfire tied up with cable and rope. The door was skewed, half obscured by crates, so Mr Nettle had to climb through with difficulty.

The smith had his anvil propped to one side on a stone slab to make it level, and worked away at it with a mighty hammer, pounding a spike of hot iron so hard it seemed like every strike would bring the whole lane toppling down. He was old for a smith, his muscles thin and knotted, his face creased with years of grime. By the light of the forge his skin looked flayed and roasted. When Mr Nettle's shadow fell over him, he looked up and said, 'So it's a hard bargain, then? No one comes here who will pay what the others ask of him. Folk must expect my mind to be as crooked as these walls.'

'Those others are thieves,' Mr Nettle said.

'Aye, well.' The smith didn't pause in his work. He continued to hammer the iron while it cooled, flattened both ends, and then bent it in the middle to form a bracket. 'But men have to eat, and must bargain to eat, and me more than most. Sixty years I've been at this forge and trade is thinner than ever. Folks who can afford any better don't come down here. They're afraid the lane will crumble under their weight.'

'I want to trade.'

The smith took up the bracket in a pair of long tongs and dropped it into a trough of water. Steam hissed furiously. He mopped his brow with a rag. 'Let's see what you've got.'

Mr Nettle handed him the cleaver.

'Well, I can use the steel, but what you after for it?'

Mr Nettle hesitated. 'A crossbow.'

The smith gave a look that might have been a wince, or maybe just weariness. 'Do you see weapons in here?' he said. 'I make pins and brackets for walls. Pins and brackets, and I'm lucky if I earn a penny for any of them. Nobody pays up front for iron worked over a slump unless it's cheap as sand.'

'Will you bend the iron if I get it? I'll cut the wood myself.'

'Not for this.' He gave the cleaver back to Mr Nettle.

'I'll pay, trade more for the work.'

'Aye well, come back again. If you can get more steel we'll talk.'

'I need it tonight.'

The smith shook his head. 'A hard bargain right enough. Fittings for a crossbow in a day, and so little up front.'

'I can work off the debt,' Mr Nettle said. 'Stoke your furnace, carry coal. I'll make these brackets for you if you show me how.'

'What you want the crossbow for?'

Mr Nettle said nothing.

The smith looked at Mr Nettle's torn mourning robe, at the bruises and blood on his face. After a moment he said, 'Moondark tonight, eh? If you're thinking to go out hunting, I'll not see the debt paid.'

Mr Nettle bristled. He hadn't thought past Scar Night, didn't think it important. But the man had a right to be wary: a debt was a debt, and you paid your debts. Each man had as much right to eat as any other, and if Mr Nettle didn't come back he'd be leaving the smith down on this deal. That was as good as stealing food from his table. Right then Mr Nettle had a queasy, empty feeling in his gut, and wanted more than ever to go back to his bottle.

'Listen,' the smith said, 'you talked about cutting the wood for a crossbow. Are you a carpenter? Do you know how to make such a thing? Have you ever shot one? Ever seen one?'

'No,' Mr Nettle admitted. He felt as he had on the Gatebridge: imprisoned by circumstance and, for all his anger and strength, the walls containing him were stronger.

'Aye, I thought not. Maybe it's best you give up. Let it go.'

'I can't.' The scrounger's teeth clamped shut.

'I'm sorry.' The smith turned away.

Sudden desperation took hold of Mr Nettle. He grabbed the man's shoulder, harder than he meant to, to halt him. Then he eased his grip. He'd almost said *help me* but the words lodged in his throat. Quickly, he said, 'I'll pay, I'll work for you,' and was surprised at the tremor he heard in his voice. It sounded odd, as though another man had spoken.

The smith turned back to look up at him, his face seeming hard as bronze in the firelight. What was it Mr Nettle saw in those eyes? He'd never seen such a look before. And then he realized it was pity. He let go of the other man, turned to leave, at once ashamed and afraid the smith had heard his unspoken plea. He was a fool to have come here. A bloody fool. He didn't need anyone's help, not now, not ever.

'Hold on,' the smith said.

Mr Nettle hesitated, his ears burning with more than the blows the temple guard had given him.

'Come through the back. I've some stuff maybe you can borrow – if you work for it.'

The floor sloped away so steeply that Mr Nettle had trouble crossing it. He had to walk sideways, his arms held out for balance, his feet sliding. The smith didn't seem bothered by the slope. He loped across the room in an odd, shambling way that made him look like a cripple.

They climbed through a lopsided door into a dim stone cell barely high enough for Mr Nettle to stand upright. His head brushed stone that might have been either a wall or the ceiling. Straw covered a pallet over to one side, which lay at a steep angle against the far wall, or floor.

Noticing his gaze, the smith said, 'Righted my pallet at first so it was level. But one day I found I couldn't sleep in it. Can't sleep on a flat bed no more. You get used to such a thing, eh?'

The tilt of the room made Mr Nettle feel faintly sick. Long nails in the walls held dozens of iron brackets and pins that hung skewed, like clock hands pointing at seven or eight. The smith knelt before a huge poppywood chest, solidly built with stout iron bands around its deep red grain. He unlocked it and rummaged through, then brought out tools, mostly hammers and tongs of various sizes and states of repair, and laid them to one side. 'Here it is,' he said. 'Give us a hand.'

Together they heaved out a big sack-wrapped bundle and set it down on the floor.

It was full of weapons: four knives, without handles, but with good, sharp blades; a plain shortsword of the size Deepgate reservists sometimes used; a morning star with oiled, fluted blades; and a large crossbow. The last possessed a wide yew bow bound in iron and backed with steel, and a clunky device, like a winch, at the butt of the stock.

'Used to be better paid before the lane slipped,' the smith said. 'Made more than wall pins in my time, eh?'

Mr Nettle picked up the crossbow. With all the iron and layered wood, it weighed as much as a sack of coal.

'It's not meant to be carried about,' the smith said. 'Great crossbow this – made it for a merchant who wanted to mount it on his cart for travelling out to the Plantations. It's not the finest-looking thing, but it'll put a bolt clean through a man. This at the back's the windlass, see, for winding back the bowstring. Got the bowstring here too somewhere, wrapped in oilcloth.' He reached back into the chest, spoke over his shoulder. 'Only have three bolts for it mind; just the samples I got from the bolt-maker. Was going to have more made, but the merchant never came back. I figure the Shetties got him on his last trip. Still, they're a fine three. Here they are, and here's the bowstring.' As he turned round his eyes were glittering.

The first bolt had a glass bulb full of sluggish liquid attached to one end. 'Incendiary,' the smith explained. 'You'll want be careful with that one.' He laid the bolt down carefully. 'There's plenty of reservists with glass eyes and leather skin from lighting up their pipes near these.'

The next had a crescent-shaped steel end. 'Hunting tip,' the smith said. 'Merchant must have fancied going after hawks or vultures when he wasn't defending his carrots from the heathens. Kind of figure you might find a use for this, eh? Not poisoned, but just dip the end in birdshit and the smallest graze will do nasty work.'

The last bolt had a thick leather hood over its tip. The smith took up a pair of tongs and, very carefully, removed the hood to reveal a plain, sharp steel point. 'Now this,' he said, 'is a rare one. Maybe it's not still potent now, but maybe it is. I'm not touching it to find out.' The smith turned the bolt over like it was made of fine glass. 'Craw plague – Devon's finest. Milked from spiders that grow inside men's flesh, no lies. Know what that'll do?'

Mr Nettle shook his head.

The smith grinned. 'Wound will never heal. Never. Won't stop bleeding till there's no blood left and the Maze comes looking for its share.' Gingerly, he replaced the hood over the tip. 'Soultakers, they call these.' Again, he glanced at Mr Nettle's tattered mourning robe. 'Maybe you like the sound of that, eh?'

'You'll lend me this?' Mr Nettle asked.

'Aye, *lend*. And I want work in payment. I've two ton of pig iron needs brought from the yards and a hundred-weight of brackets to go out to Rins before dark. Mind you pay this debt *before* sunset.' He shifted uncomfortably. 'No offence meant, but I recall what night it is tonight.'

Mr Nettle lowered the crossbow. 'Can't take it.'

'Eh?'

'Too much. Can't repay this.'

A day's work wouldn't pay the debt. And chances were, the smith would never see the weapon again. They both knew it. The man's kindness felt like a punch, and Mr Nettle turned away to hide his discomfort. He'd have to find another way.

'Listen, son,' the smith said, 'you'd be doing me a favour. With the bastards paying twenty doubles for a crate of iron, I can hardly afford the porters to bring it in. And what good is this bow to me, sitting here, gathering dust?'

Mr Nettle couldn't look at him. 'You could sell it,' he suggested.

The smith grunted. 'Who to? Ever seen any reservist with coins in his pocket? Those sods can't afford to eat these days. The regulars have money, aye, but the temple buys their arms for them, and they don't buy old junk like this.'

'A merchant?'

'They got their airships now. Gods below, they have to pay enough taxes for it, too. Aye, find me a merchant without the temple's hand in his purse, and maybe I'd have a sale, but those without pockets deep enough to stave off the Spine and the Avulsior are gone now, branded as heathens. Do the work for me, but take this damn thing out of my sight before the priests find it and claim it as tax.'

Mr Nettle hesitated.

'Buggers like us got to help each other. No bugger else will.'

At last the scrounger nodded.

'All right.' The smith then showed Mr Nettle how to fasten the bowstring and load a bolt by winching back the windlass. 'But know there are just these three bolts, no more. If, say, you want to shoot at something way up high, you'll need to be a damn fine shot or have a fair bit of luck, eh?'

Mr Nettle had never even picked up a crossbow before this moment, let alone shot one. And as for luck, he'd never had much of that either. But now at least he had a small chance to put things right, and he began to feel more like his old self. He'd pay his debt before nightfall, be square with this man as much as he could, and then, come tonight, he'd be square with the angel. He hefted the crossbow to his eye and squinted along the sight, imagining wings in the shadows. 'What's your name?' he asked the smith.

'Smith,' the man said, grinning like a conspirator.

5

GHOSTS, POISONS, AND PASTRIES

Presbyter Willard Sypes was observing and recording the movements of ghosts. To facilitate viewing of the abyss beneath, he had extinguished the observatory lamps, leaving only a few scattered candles sparkling in their crystal lanterns. In the gloom, the Presbyter's black cassock had no discernible shape. His head floated phantom-like over his desk, as cracked and yellow as the parchment beneath, while his quill sprouted from the arthritic grip of what appeared to be a disembodied hand.

To Adjunct Fogwill Crumb, the Presbyter's face seemed to have halted momentarily, as it melted towards the book. From the mottled expanse of his cranium, skin hung in folds like an accumulation of tallow. Tiny, chitinous eyes shifted somewhere within as the old priest reached to dip his quill in ink, focused once more on the page, and then resumed scratching his words into the journal.

Sypes set down his feather and creaked himself forward to peer into the eyepiece of the aurolethiscope, and for a sinful moment Fogwill wondered if the sound had come from the chair or from his master's aged bones.

The aurolethiscope occupied most of the space in the

observatory. Sypes cranked a handle and the brass machine began to turn like the innards of an enormous clock. Wheels and cogs clicked and whirred at various speeds. The lens column rotated smoothly, raising itself a fraction above the hole in the floor as the Presbyter adjusted focus. Reflections from the lantern winked on the spinning, polished surfaces and gave the machine the look of burnished gold.

Fogwill stood before his master: short, round, and splendid in his ceremonial robe. His pate was smooth and hard as a nut, his face softly plump and dusted with his favourite poppy talcum from Clune. Jewelled rings glinted on his fingers: fat rubies mounted in gold, subtle seastones in silver, and amber sandglass to match his smiling eyes. 'Are the soul-lights bright this morning?' he asked.

The Presbyter squinted into the eyepiece. 'Nothing for days now. I suspect my eyesight is failing.'

'Perhaps the dead grow less restless.'

Sypes sank back into his chair. He looked like he'd been hunched at the aurolethiscope all night. 'Or more wary,' he said. He scribbled another sentence into the journal then banged it shut.

Dust settled in time.

'You asked to see me,' Fogwill said.

Sypes turned with a succession of creaks. 'I don't think so.'

Fogwill steepled his fingers under his chin, trying to decide if the old man was baiting him. He produced a scroll from his sleeve. 'I received a message.'

'Yes, yes.' Sypes looked irritated. 'Is everything in order for the Sending?'

Fogwill rolled up the scroll and replaced it in his sleeve.

'Preparations are almost complete. The Sanctum has been scrubbed and blessed, I've arranged for fresh candles—'

'Not perfumed?'

The Adjunct's face slipped a little, before he caught it.

'I see,' Sypes said. 'Must we always suffer these brothel odours?'

'Perfume masks the smell of rot.'

Sypes hunched forward and sniffed. 'Clearly.'

Fogwill shuffled back a step, but kept his expression patient. There *was* an odd odour in here, now that he thought about it. He glanced at the hearth. A thick ream of parchment smouldered on the coals, blue smoke curling around its singed edges.

'Poetry,' the Presbyter said, catching Fogwill's glance. 'An Applecross butcher's contribution to the Codex: one hundred ways to skin a cat.'

'A humorous piece?' Fogwill asked. *Certainly a long one, for poetry.*

'Not for the cat,' Sypes grumbled. 'God forbid any more of the commoners learn how to write.' With a dramatically despondent shake of his head, he leaned back. The chair, or bones, protested softly. 'How is Dill?'

'On his way to meet the soulcage.'

'Do you think he's ready?'

Fogwill shrugged.

'Humph.' Sypes's lips quivered. 'The lad's what – now ten?'

'Sixteen,' Fogwill said. *As you well know.* Dill was already a full year older than the age Codex law dictated he become Soul Warden, and the populace knew it. In the years following Gaine's death, Borelock had been required to perform the angel's duties and, although competent enough, his presence did little to inspire the faithful. Dill was more than just a servant of the Church, more than a symbol. He was a link to the past, to the founding of the same Church. As the living descendant of Ulcis's own Herald, his line had become the thread which linked man to god. But outside the temple, gossip was rife. Had Callis's line died with Dill's father? If the bloodline had been severed, would Ulcis still honour his promise to those who worshipped him? Or would he abandon them to Iril, the Maze of Blood? Life in Deepgate was often bleak, sometimes turbulent. The Church had long known that to pull the faithful through, it was necessary to give them something to hold on to.

Fogwill had been surprised at Sypes's repudiation of the Codex in this matter, but at the time had put it down to the apparent decline of the old man's mental faculties. Only later had he begun to suspect otherwise. The Presbyter was only senile when it suited him.

Sypes rubbed an ink-stained finger across his chin, leaving a dark blue smudge. Fogwill couldn't help but wonder if this action too was deliberate.

'You can't keep him hidden in that tower for ever,' Fogwill said.

The Presbyter gave him a weary nod. 'Of course, you're right. But I can't help worrying about the lad. One arrow, one knife, one poisoned cup: that's all it would take.'

'It's not too late to have him combat-trained,' Fogwill said. 'The temple guard could do it . . . or even the Spine, I mean . . .' He had meant any of the Spine except Rachel Hael. The absurdity of her assignment had not escaped Fogwill. Sypes had chosen the worst assassin in Deepgate to oversee Dill's training.

'I'm sure she can teach him the basics at least,' Sypes said.

'Well, quite,' Fogwill said. Whatever the angel learned from *her* was sure to be basic. She hadn't even been tempered, for god's sake. 'With your permission,' he said. 'I think it's time we found him a wife.'

Sypes looked up, his eyes colder.

'The families have always been well compensated,' Fogwill continued. 'Before, and afterwards.'

Sypes grunted. 'The sort of woman *he* needs is the sort who'd marry him without any of this . . .' He waved his hands at everything and nothing.

'The girls have other motives I'm—'

'Rot! I remember Gaine's wife on her wedding day, her frozen smile.' Sypes let out a long sigh and his gaze shifted to the hole in the observatory floor. 'And now she's down there, watching us.' He rested his chin in his hand and stared into the abyss. 'The dead, Fogwill, what are they up to, hmmm? Hiding, sulking, plotting, scheming in their pit.' His voice dropped to a whisper. 'And up here I'm fading all the time. Like old ink on parchment. I'll join them soon.' He punctuated this last word with a tap of his finger. 'And I think they know it.'

Looking at him sitting there, with his stained skin and trembling fingers, Fogwill thought the old man was probably right.

'Nonsense,' he said instead. 'You're as strong as a courser.'

'The marriage,' Sypes said, 'I'll leave it in your hands. I've no stomach for such matters.' He picked up his blue-inked quill and plunked it in a bottle of red ink.

'A message, your Grace.' A boy had appeared in the doorway, fidgeting with his scuffed cuffs.

'Gods,' Sypes said, 'does no one knock?'

The boy grinned, handed the Presbyter a scroll, bowed briefly, and bolted, fast as a rat.

Sypes unrolled the message, held it out at arm's length, squinting. 'Good, good,' he said. 'The *Adraki* has docked. Edward Hael's body is here.'

'Wonderful news,' Fogwill said. Sypes had been worried about the general for days. 'His son and daughter will be relieved.'

The Presbyter was still reading, frowning.

'The body?' Fogwill ventured.

Sypes ignored him. Finally, he set down the message and rose from his chair. He grabbed his walking stick and said, 'Come with me.'

They left the observatory and plodded up the stairs that wound around the inside of the Acolyte's Spiral. A gaggle of priests on their way to the missionary halls stood aside to let them pass. As they climbed, the floor disappeared far below. Sypes grumbled constantly, complaining about his heart, about dust, about everything. Halfway up, Fogwill unlocked a grate and they set off through the dim, aether-lit corridors in the direction of the dock.

Mark Hael was waiting for them in the dock anteroom. The aeronaut commander's face was pinched but lean, with desert skin, mud-brown against the white of his uniform. Three stripes of gold braid looped each cuff. 'We left the body outside,' he explained. 'The smell.'

A faint, meaty odour hung in the air. Fogwill held his breath, then opened the doors leading out to the dock.

Weathered and overgrown with weeds, the basalt wharf extended some fifty paces out from the temple wall. It was wide enough not to require handrails, but high up enough to make Fogwill miss their presence. Moored to gantries at the far end was the *Adraki*. Trapped by a web of cables, its silver envelope towered over them, flashing violently in the sun. Portholes and brass fittings gleamed in the gondola. Deepgate sprawled dizzily far below, slumped in its chains under the blue sky.

'Good lord,' Fogwill gasped, pinching his nose. His perfume stood no chance against this.

'We came in from Sandport overnight,' Mark Hael said. 'Ran our tanks dry to get here in time.'

But Fogwill wasn't listening; he was looking at the corpse.

The thing that had once been General Edward Hael lay on its back, with blackened fingers curled at its chest. Dry blood and ash-caked scraps of uniform matted the cracked skin, and there were charred, empty sockets where eyes should have been. The naked soles of the feet reminded Fogwill of burnt hams.

Sypes coughed. 'Are you certain it's him?' he asked.

Mark Hael nodded. He reached in his pocket and handed something to the Presbyter. 'Heshette savages brought the *Skylark* down near Dalamoor. She must have landed heavily, ruptured a gas tank. Took us a while to clear the area and get down to the wreckage. No survivors – the crew were all . . . like this.'

Sypes was looking at what he held in his hand. 'Nasty business,' he said.

'He's dry as leather,' Fogwill said.

'We'll send the soul down today,' Sypes said.

'But—'

Sypes raised a hand, and Fogwill saw that he was clutching a fistful of medals. 'Clearly some blood was lost, Adjunct. Some. Little enough for Edward, he's full of it, brimming.' He gave the body an uneasy glance. 'He was devout, a good soldier, a good man. I think it fair to say his soul survives intact.'

Mark Hael had his head bowed. 'Presbyter . . .' he said.

'You may leave us, Commander,' Sypes said. 'The Adjunct and I will attend to this.'

'Very good, your Grace.' Hael turned to go.

'Commander.'

'Your Grace?'

'I haven't informed your sister yet.'

Mark Hael nodded and went back into the temple.

As soon as he was gone, Fogwill threw up his hands. 'Look at this body, it's a husk! There's not a drop of blood left in its veins. The soul is already in Iril.'

'Mark Hael's a fine lad,' Sypes murmured, almost to himself. 'He'll make a fine general one day. Good blood, eh? Won't do to have friction between the Church and the military.' He squinted into the sun, gazing out over the desert. 'Not *now*.'

'You can't bless this *thing*! Ulcis would be furious.'

Sypes made a dismissive gesture. 'Pious soldiers like General Hael are rare. The god of chains needs good men.'

'But his soul is in the Maze!'

'Nonsense.'

Fogwill shook his head. 'I'll fetch some bearers,' he grumbled, eager to be away from the stench.

'No, Fogwill. There's not much time before the Sending. Try to round up Devon, will you? He ought to be there, too.'

Fogwill frowned. He opened his mouth to argue then changed his mind. Why bother? Sypes seemed determined to obstruct him. Finally he said, 'I'll send a boy.'

'I'd rather you took care of this personally.' Sypes

pinched the bridge of his nose with two ink-stained fingers, leaving more blue smudges. 'If you send a messenger, Devon will just have the lad off scrubbing vats in that infernal factory and we'll never see him again.'

'Scrubbing vats?' Fogwill couldn't hide the scorn in his voice. He had his own ideas about what happened to the temple staff who ended up in Deepgate's Department of Military Science.

Sypes's tufted eyebrows lowered till his eyes all but disappeared in the crenellations of his face. 'Will you go find Devon?'

'I won't have time to get out there. The ceremony . . .'

'Then I suggest you try the kitchen.'

'The kitchen?' The Adjunct's eyes narrowed. '*Our* kitchen? The temple kitchen?'

'I understand he's up to his old tricks again.'

Fogwill's gaze dropped past his freshly laundered robe to his favourite blue plush slippers – a gift from mother, each silver stitch lovingly wrestled by the old dear herself into vaguely floral splats. His powdered face sagged. 'The kitchen,' he said, 'of course. Where else would the Poisoner be today?'

Rachel Hael was hanging upside down in darkness. She concentrated on her breathing, her muscles, her heartbeat, constructing states of mind to control blood flow and respiration. She envisioned a bitter coldness to draw blood away from her skin, a threat to quicken her heart and brace her weary muscles.

Spine called this process *focusing*. Fatigue, hunger, even thirst could be controlled for a time by any skilled Adept. She ought to be able to hang by her feet on this rope for hours, perhaps even days, without ill effects. But she'd been here for ten minutes and already had a blinding headache. Her Spine master, a thin man whose name she did not know, would have been scornful of her inability to focus, had he been capable of scorn.

Of all the Spine Adepts, only Rachel herself was able to feel scorn, or resentment, or anger, or happiness. All of them weaknesses in an assassin, for emotion was anathema to the Spine. It marred purity of thought and purpose, precluded focusing, and hindered Adepts in the field. Emotion was not tolerated for long. In the Church's eyes she was the weakest Adept of them all. She'd already proved that to them more than once.

Someone tugged on the rope.

She twisted herself up, slipped her ankles out of the cuffs and climbed back towards her room.

Her brother stood by the hatch in the floor. 'Getting closer to god?' he asked.

Rachel sat on the edge of the hatchway and pulled up the rope, winding it into coils around her elbow. 'Helps me relax,' she said.

He gave her a blank look.

'The silence,' she said. There was a sea of silence down there in the abyss, miles of it all around, and for untold miles below her, but it didn't calm her as much as it once had. These days it just took the edge off.

'What if the rope snaps?' Mark asked.

She shrugged.

'Or someone cuts it?'

She shrugged.

'Gods below!' Mark cried. 'The monks told me you'd be down there, but I didn't believe them. Thought it had to be some kind of Spine joke – before I remembered the Spine don't have a sense of humour.'

'What do you want?'

'Nice to see you too.'

Rachel picked up her sword from the weapon rack and slid it into the scabbard on her back. She tied the poison pouches to her belt, plugged three short bamboo tubes into the harnesses beside them, and then sat down on the bed, feeding knives and needles into the appropriate slots in her leather armour.

'We found him,' Mark said.

She paused for a moment, then continued loading her armour.

'Sypes expects us both present at the Sending.'

'I've stuff to do.'

'You don't have a choice.'

A bitter smile stretched her lips.

Mark opened the window and leaned out, peering up at the foundation chains and the underbelly of the Gate-bridge. 'This has to be the lowest room in the temple. Is that some kind of symbolic statement? Keeping you lot down here in the foundations like this, in the darkness?'

'Access.'

'What?'

'Never mind.'

Mark looked round her room, but apparently spotted nothing of interest. 'They don't give you much, do they?'

Rachel slipped a blowpipe into her belt then hefted her crossbow from the dresser and began to oil the bowstring. 'I have everything I need,' she said.

'You any good with that thing?'

'I'm still alive.'

Mark sighed. He searched the room again, before his gaze returned to the crossbow in his sister's lap. 'I heard about the new soul-thief. The aeronauts are looking this way. Apparently most of the husks have been temple staff.'

She ignored him.

'Have *you* seen anything?'

'Like what? Someone carrying a bloodless corpse?'

Mark Hael was silent for a while, then said, 'If you're hiding something . . .'

She snorted. 'You know me better than that.'

He threw up his hands. 'No, Rachel, I don't know you. I've hardly seen you in a dozen years. They've moved you from one backwater hole to the next. If you aren't rotting down here in this monk-infested dungeon they like to call a school, then you're traipsing through stinking, Heshette-fouled caves under some unholy mountain.' By now he'd found the wine on the dresser. She heard the stopper slide from the carafe, heard him sniff. 'Low Coyle Valley,' he said. 'Hardly worth the effort of pouring it.'

'Then don't.'

Mark replaced the stopper. 'Listen, I'm sorry. It's been a difficult week for me.'

Rachel's teeth clenched. She set down her crossbow and went over to the window, her back to him. She leaned out and let the breeze caress her face. The foundation chains were silhouetted against the morning sky. She knew these chains well; they provided routes into every part of Deepgate – hidden routes. But she knew the city rooftops better. For four years now, she'd hunted them on Scar Night. Four years, totalling about fifty Scar Nights, and in that time she'd loosed nine bolts. The thing she hunted knew the rooftops better than anyone.

A rook hopped across the ledge below, black as the iron

around it. She watched it watching her. Was her quarry watching her too? Unlikely, she supposed, for Carnival shunned the daylight.

Mark said, 'Decent of Sypes to let Father go through. I don't think there was a drop of blood left in him. Crumb saw the truth of that. Dry as leather, he said. Felt like slapping the fat little princess for talking about our father that way.'

The benefits of being a Hael. Mark's rank in the aeronauts, her own acceptance for Spine testing, all won for them by the family name – a name dragged inch by inch from the League to Ivygarths by generations of iron smugglers, plantation slavers and temple bootlickers.

'You don't even care,' Mark said. 'After everything he's done for you?'

'Get out,' she snapped.

'There was a time I would have slapped you for speaking to me like that.'

Rachel remembered, but she didn't turn round. Twelve years with the Spine was armour enough against Mark. It was armour enough against everyone. She sighed. *Almost* everyone.

Mark's voice dropped to a whisper. 'I have the consent documents, the authorization for your tempering. The Spine masters are pressing me to sign.'

Rachel stiffened.

'I don't know,' Mark said. 'I've been thinking . . . Rachel, I don't want you like them.'

She closed her eyes.

'They're soulless.' He waited. 'Nothing more than walking corpses. I can't imagine you like that, my own sister. I don't want to—'

Rachel could no longer restrain herself. 'You liar!' she

cried, wheeling to face him. 'You're doing it to hurt me. You're bitter because *you* failed their tests and I passed. You blame *me* for Father's disappointment in you—'

'You're still an Adept.'

'Do you know what I had to *do* to earn that rank? Do you know how hard it was?'

Mark gave her a cold smile. 'I heard about your little display.'

'*Display?*' She'd beaten every Adept, one after another, in single combat, and that hadn't been enough. So, bruised and exhausted, she'd then challenged her master. An insult – had he been even capable of perceiving insults. In the end he'd been capable of nothing but focusing to keep his lungs clear of blood.

'Well . . .' Mark was looking around for something to distract him, but failed. 'All the more reason that you don't need to come under the Spine needles. If you can fight like that, untempered—'

'I had no choice! They don't trust me, won't accept me. I had to give them grounds to wait for your consent. If you don't sign those papers, they'll get rid of me, kick me out – or worse.' She paused, looked hard at her brother, and a sudden realization came to her. 'That's what you want, isn't it? You want them to boot me out. You want me to fail.'

'I want to protect you,' he muttered.

'You callous bastard.'

'Callous?' Mark's face reddened. 'That's marvellous, coming from you. How many Shetties did you clear from Hollowhill?'

Trust Mark to use a word like *clear*. His killing was done from an airship, from a distance. Whole tribes of Heshette were *cleared* by poison deployment. Men, women, and children were *cleared* by judicious, precise, carefully managed, cost-effective use of incendiaries. Mark was never close enough to hear them cry or beg. He never saw them bleed or foul themselves. They were simply *cleared* – never killed, never *murdered*. Her hand tightened on one of the bamboo tubes at her belt, then she relaxed it. She took a deep breath. 'Please,' she said quietly, 'sign the papers. Let them temper me. I can't live like this any more. I can't do the things they want me to do.'

'No, Rachel.'

'Then get out. I want to be alone.'

'You're always *alone*. Do you hate company so much?'

Did she? The monks didn't exactly *forbid* relationships. It was never that simple. They just kept her down here, training, focusing, or had her moving from one dark part of the world to the next. She remembered the very first time she'd held a sword, how she'd laughed, spinning with it like a dancer while her father looked on, grinning. That had been one of the last times she'd laughed. But she'd danced with it again: in Hollowhill and the Shale Forest, in Heshette caves and gin dens and Sandport brothels, until the sword had become as much a part of her as faith was to the tempered. She'd danced a hundred times before they'd assigned her to the rooftops, to Carnival. *You aren't ready*, they'd warned. *But it won't make any difference.*

She squinted up at the painfully blue sky beyond the foundation chains. Her eyes were not accustomed to the daylight, for to hunt at night, she'd had to live at night and train in darkness. For four years, she'd woken after dusk, and gone to sleep before the dawn.

'Sypes wants you to stay here,' Mark said. 'To look after that sparrow of his.'

'Dill.'

On the window ledge below, the rook pattered along, ripped up a scrap of moss, then took off. Rachel watched it soar toward the sunlit city. The Church had hobbled Dill as surely as Mark had hobbled herself. After Gaine, the temple had forbidden its archons to fly. With the Heshette war quashed and the introduction of airships, Battle-archons were no longer required. Or so the Presbyter claimed. Rachel suspected there was more to it than that. Gaine's older brother Sewender had died young, without heirs, and Gaine, who under the circumstances should have taken several wives, had married only once. Sypes, to the horror of the clergy, had not pressed him to marry again. Now that an unknown bowman had killed Gaine, the bloodline had again been reduced to a solitary angel. And what an angel. As Gaine, for all his notoriety, had been but a shade of his ancestors, so Dill, poor awkward Dill, was a mere shade of his father. Callis's blood had evidently thinned. No wonder Sypes kept him locked out of sight in that tower.

The Church had enemies everywhere. With Deepgate said to be full of Heshette spies, the Presbyter strived to hold on to his community's last tangible link to god. This interdict, this cruel, immutable law, had been impressed on Dill since he'd been old enough to fly.

Or to fly away?

Sypes had been foolish. Chaining a person would only make him more determined to break free.

'You'll enjoy that, though,' Mark said. 'You like animals, don't you?'

'Are you trying to annoy me? Is that what you're doing here?'

'Fine!' He slammed his hands together. 'I'm going. I'll leave you to your knives and bolts and your dark little cell. Just make sure you get yourself to the Sanctum for the ceremony.'

He hesitated at the door. 'You're not going to wear that stuff, are you?'

Rachel didn't reply. She was thinking about Dill. By hobbling him, had the temple spared his life or wasted it? And, as the rook disappeared between the foundation chains, she wondered if she cared.

From a round chamber at the bottom of his spire, Dill descended further into the main body of the temple, by way of a wheezing elevator. Little more than an iron cage ankle-deep in musty rugs, the machine creaked and shuddered down through a hole in the floor, past two fathoms of stone, till it emerged in a vast, seemingly bottomless space: the Hall of Angels. Sunlight glittered through huge orange-, lemon-, and cherry-glass mullioned windows lining the far walls, making tiny silhouettes of the multitude of priests who were busy preparing the temple for Scar Night. Figures swarmed over catwalks and ladders, closing enormous grates over the windows, checking and rechecking the locks, setting up the crossbows on their stanchions positioned before cross-shaped murderholes.

Dill pulled one of several tasselled cords which would, in theory, tell the hidden operators he wished to be taken to the Sanctum corridor. A bell tinkled far, far below, and somewhere beneath him, half a dozen men would be switching winches. The elevator paused, swaying, and then began to descend again, now easing closer to the southern wall. A pigeon settled on the bars immediately above, and began preening, before it noticed the angel and took off with a squawk.

Dill hated this elevator. The Presbyter had had it specially installed after the Church interdict on any of its archons resorting to flight. The contraption was slow, uncomfortable, and rarely arrived at the requested floor. And when it did arrive there, it often stopped so far out from the appropriate ledge as to necessitate a treacherous leap. Whether this was due to some failure in the elevator mechanism or to disgruntled winch staff, Dill didn't know.

Abruptly, the elevator halted. It hung, creaking, in empty space two hundred feet above the floor, and still eighty feet from the nearest wall.

'Hello?' Dill called out.

None of the priests heard him. They were much too far away, too busy securing the windows, or aligning and loading the Spine crossbows.

Hand on his sword, Dill stood in the elevator and waited.

And waited.

'*Hello?*'

Nobody answered. High above, the same pigeon fluttered by.

The kitchen was a battlefield. Strikes of countless knives rang out above the roar of roasting fires and the shouts of busy men. Battalions of cooks in tall white hats sweated over chopping tables, slicing, dicing, gutting, pounding. Cauldrons bubbled over open hearths. Potboys toiled before steaming sinks and scrubbed away at endless crockery, while stewards jostled by with platters of seared goat and sweet mutton, lark pies, rook pies and hot buttered potatoes.

Fogwill's face was already flushed, while trickles of sweat carved trails through the talcum on his cheeks. He decided that the faster he proceeded, the cleaner he might stay, so he wove quickly through stoves and sinks, ducked under rows of hanging copper pots, and hopped over streams of milky water. He held his sleeve over his nose, and almost collided with a grizzled porter carrying a pig. The animal squealed and wriggled in the man's grip and the aged porter spat a curse. A sneering kitchen-hand turned from the limes he was chopping and said something derogatory, but Fogwill couldn't make out his comment over the din.

'Beastly,' the Adjunct muttered. 'Utterly beastly.' The place was a menagerie. Just think of the germs, the dirt brought in by all the animals. After this, he'd have to steep himself in lemon-oil from top to toe.

His robes were sodden around the ankles, and his slippers – well, he didn't want to study them too closely.

Finally he found the head cook lying asleep on a makeshift bed of sacks heaped beneath a rack of eels, and he almost gagged at the stench. Even the smell of General Hael's corpse had seemed more wholesome. The eels above him sweated oil in greasy drips that spattered the sleeping man's fleshy jowls, making him mutter and twitch.

Fogwill prodded the dozing figure with his toe. 'Wake up, Fondelgrue. Wake up.' Oil pattered on his own scalp.

Fondelgrue twisted himself awake with a groan, and scratched his swollen belly beneath a tunic that had once been white. Seeing Fogwill, he squeezed an eye shut, farted, and exhaled. 'Crumb? What do you want?'

Fogwill noticed the dark spots now dappling his ceremonial robe and leapt back from underneath the eels,
praying with all of his heart that the foul odour emanated
from the man before him rather than the creatures above.
'I'm looking for Devon,' he said. 'Have you seen him anywhere?'

Behind them, plates clattered and something smashed.
Fondelgrue ignored the accident. 'What would that poxy
Poisoner be doing in here?'

'Maybe trying to tamper with the food again.' Fogwill
shot a contemptuous glance at the gurgling, frothing pots,
the smoking ovens encrusted with old food. 'But I see
you've got everything completely under control.'

The head cook slid a hand through his slick hair, then
paused to examine something caught beneath his fingernail. He gave Fogwill a sideways look. 'I think he tests his
poisons and diseases on us.'

'I've heard him claim he comes here for inspiration.'

Fondelgrue smiled thinly.

'Well, if you do see him,' the Adjunct said, 'please let
him know he's expected presently in the Sanctum – for a
very important service.'

The head cook stifled a yawn. 'It's always bloody
important with you lot.'

Behind them, a steward was yelling at a potboy. Something else smashed, but Fondelgrue didn't flinch. Finally
he grunted, and closed his eyes. 'Well, you can see Devon
isn't here.'

Fogwill surveyed his surroundings again. Two potboys
were wrestling in an aisle between banks of sinks and
chopping boards. As they skidded and rolled around on
the wet floor, one of them knocked against a table and a
basket of cutlery scattered to the floor in a metallic hail.

'You have new staff, I see,' Fogwill commented. 'Have they all been screened?'

Presbyter Sypes had a right to be nervous. With the Heshette enemy now decimated, there was always the risk they might turn to more subtle methods of revenge. *One cup of poison?*

Fogwill took a deep breath, and regretted it immediately. A dog whined nearby, then ceased abruptly. *A dog?* He didn't want to know. He glanced once more at the wrestling potboys, then set off in the opposite direction. The odour, he noticed with horror, pursued him.

Threading his way back through the great kitchen, he had to dodge countless cooks, dish-washers, and beaters, carvers, vegetable choppers, stewards, maids and porters. The kitchen was bursting with them – who would notice one less body here? Or even a dozen? How many had the Poisoner whisked away to his own foul kitchens over the years? Fondelgrue's words came back to him. *I think he tests his poisons and diseases on us.*

By the time Fogwill found the door, he was beginning to imagine that every one of these cauldrons might contain unknown terrors. That meat – suspiciously tinged with green? This pallid fowl – what ailment distressed it so? The Adjunct then and there resolved never to eat viands prepared by this kitchen again. At least for a week or so. He would meanwhile press Sypes on the matter of security, oversee the changes himself.

A steward glided past balancing a silver platter full of pastries.

Fogwill grabbed one, inspected it closely. Did the cream it contained have a faintly sulphurous odour? He dabbed his tongue to the soft pastry: was there a hint of bitterness masked by its succulent, buttery sweetness?

He stuffed the entire pastry into his mouth, and left the kitchen, munching.

Some risks were just worth taking.

Arch Chemist and Poisoner Alexander Devon lay awake, bleeding. Blood trickled from cracks furrowing his face and neck, across his chest, from the broken skin under his arms and knees, and soaked into his old stained sheet. Blisters burst on his back when he moved. His lungs felt furred: every breath bubbled and stung, every cough expelled strings of fluid which he spat into a bucket beside the bed. Raw eyelids rested like broken glass on his swollen eyeballs. When he turned to check the standing clock by the window, his bones grated and his muscles scraped against the inside of his skin. He was late for work, yet moving meant agony. But Devon rose from his bed anyway, and tried to force his grimace of pain into a grin.

Life, after all, was full of little challenges.

Elizabeth's side of the bed remained smooth and dry. He pressed fingers to his lips and touched the place where her head had once rested. Years of washing the sheets had thinned the outline of her wounded body until there was nothing left but a faint line of old blood. One day, he supposed, all trace of her would fade completely.

He removed the sheet and dumped it in a basket, then he set to work tending his own wounds. First his arms: he dabbed the weeping skin with a soft cotton pad steeped in alcohol, smeared away the blood, and then gently bound himself with clean bandages. Next his chest: once the skin was clean, he tucked the end of a bandage under one armpit and wrapped it around and around himself down to his waist. A jolt of pain shot through his knees as he bent to attend to his legs and feet, but he took his time. It was important to cover every wound, lest more infection set in. The Poison Kitchens harboured every type of infection.

When he was done, he dressed himself carefully in his old tweed suit and tried to regain his composure for the day ahead. Every inch of him felt raw and brittle. He placed his spectacles on his nose. Though his sight was fading, his eyes still looked clear and warm. Once handsome in a roguish sort of way, his was a good-humoured face, still etched with smile-lines – a face that people would instinctively warm to, were it not for the cracks and blisters and weeping skin.

Devon's flesh knew the touch of poison.

Morning filtered through the gauzy drapes of his bedroom window while, outside, the bricks and tarred roofs of the Depression basked in sunlight. Birds chattered incessantly, nesting here in thousands, away from the egg-thieves and from the scroungers who had stripped this derelict district bare so long ago. Devon closed his eyes, letting their melodies wash over him. Far away, the mourners' bell chimed solemnly in the temple.

Elizabeth would have loved it here. He had looked forward to showing her this place once its conversion was finished; it was to have been a surprise. Clay pots and trenchers still littered the warehouse roof, while pebbles marked meandering paths through heaped mounds of imported Plantation soil. He'd planted orangegrass, blue-wisps and roses, put up trellises, and built a slender whitewood gazebo. But the flowers he had planted were all withered now, the soil dry and dead. He'd taken too long to prepare his surprise. Now only traces of her

survived: the faded stains in the sheets he'd brought from
their Bridgeview townhouse, a few of her perfume bottles,
all empty now, and the painting of her that had cost him
half a year's salary to commission. Devon shared his new
home with memories.

He picked up one of Elizabeth's perfume bottles, and
inhaled deeply. Even the scent was faint – like the ghost
of some long-dead flower – but it bolstered his resolve as
it always did. Gently he replaced the stopper and set the
bottle down, his hand lingering on the smooth glass.

The sound of sobbing could be heard from his laboratory next door. Good, the girl was awake. He ought
perhaps to make her some coffee and try to calm her
down. But the coffee might interfere with the sedative he
planned to use on her. He sighed. Maybe he would speak
to her softly, and try to ease her pain. It wasn't going to
be easy, though: there would be a lot of pain. The poor
thing would struggle desperately.

But life, after all, was full of little challenges.

6

✝HE SENDING

The odour of limewax pervaded the corridor, but its sickly-sweet veneer did little to mask the smell of decay. Iron chandeliers hung from chains fixed in the vaulted ceiling, and tiny candle-flame reflections glowed deep in the marble floor, but the light they provided seemed thin: stretched by the vastness of the space.

At the innermost end of the corridor, Dill stood by the Sanctum doors, and wished there were windows. Shadows crawled all around him, like things moving at the edges of his vision. But whenever he turned to look, there was nothing.

Something creaked above him. A chain moving in a stray draught, probably.

Dill avoided looking up; the things up there were worse than anything in the shadows to either side. Instead he fixed his eyes on the stable doors, anxious for them to open, yet hoping they'd stay firmly shut. Borelock tended the stables.

Another creak above, and Dill looked up.

On tall columns hung the remains of the Ninety-Nine, displayed like ghoulish puppets in chains which held their skeletal arms in place and their tattered wings outstretched. Some wore scraps of armour or peered over dented shields, but all of them brandished weapons: swords, spears, halberds or pikes, all pitted, scarred and rusted.

Dill shifted his weight from one foot to the other. His uniform felt stiff and uncomfortable; the sword hilt dug into his ribs. He clasped and unclasped his hands, studied the floor, loosened some buttons and tugged at his collar, but he couldn't keep his eyes from returning to the heights.

Gaine had told him stories of this gloomy place: winter storms when the whole temple swayed and the relics rattled their chains in howling draughts. Dill peered along their ranks, half expecting to find his dead father among them, but there were only the bones of the Ninety-Nine, staring out at nothing, collecting dust.

With a clank the stable doors on one side of the corridor swung open. Torchlight fanned out over the floor, bringing with it the odour of straw and animals. Borelock led two huge mares out into the corridor. Behind them, the soulcage rumbled into view on its wooden wheels.

A heavy structure of iron and tarred wood, the soulcage had been specially blessed by the priests to ensure that souls given over to the temple's care were protected until the time they were released into the abyss. It was empty now, but when full, was big enough and sturdy enough to keep fifty souls safe. In the dead, unblessed blood was dangerous. Hell opened its doors to receive unblessed blood, and when Iril's doors were open there was no telling what might get loose.

With awkward precision, Borelock walked the horses across the polished marble floor. A sour line of a mouth jutted from his cowl; his chin protruded like a spike of bone. The rest of the priest's body hobbled and shifted beneath his cassock as if there were more than one set of arms and legs under there. Once he reached Dill he stopped, clutching the reins with yellow-stained fingers.

Dill wondered if the priest's eyes were yellow too. He swallowed, and said, 'Fine animals.'

The nearest horse bared its teeth and snorted. Its coat gleamed black as a temple guard's armour.

'Five years,' Borelock grumbled, 'I've been driving this cage in your stead. Five years until the Presbyter saw fit to pluck you from your tower and put you to honest work. Don't you think I've had better things to do with my time than face the scorns of those miserable bastards outside?'

'I'm grateful,' Dill replied weakly.

'Don't mess it up,' Borelock said. 'Mark Hael and his sister are in there.' He jabbed a thumb at the Sanctum doors behind them. 'The late general's son and daughter.'

Dill clambered into his seat at the front of the cage, and leather creaked. The seat was even higher than it had looked from the ground and Borelock had to throw the reins up to him. The horses bobbed their heads and whisked their tails, eager to be off.

'Wings,' Borelock said.

Dill spread his wings.

As the horses lurched into motion, Dill almost toppled back onto the cage bars. He pulled hard on the reins, but the animals ignored him. The soulcage lumbered forward, picking up speed.

'I'll be watching you,' Borelock called after him.

They clopped along, uncomfortably fast, under the scrutiny of the decaying angels. Rust had eaten the name plaques beneath the skeletons' feet, but Dill still recognized a few from his one previous visit down here.

He'd been eleven years old when his father had brought
him to this dismal corridor, ordered the temple doors to
be opened to let some light in, and left him with a slab of
parchment on which to sketch the relics. In daylight, the
skeletons had seemed less threatening, so Dill had relished
his task at first, writing each name in his best hand beneath
his sketches, determined to draw them all. That morning
passed quickly, and occasionally Gaine returned, bringing
him cups of sweet tea, to admire his handiwork. When
they paused for lunch at a rough table outside the kitchen,
Dill proudly displayed his drawings to everyone and anyone who passed by. Everyone had seemed impressed.

By mid-afternoon he'd drawn eight and was bored.
They all looked the same. So he squeezed the remaining
ninety-one of them into a giant battle played out on a
single sheet of parchment – with a dozen stick-like Heshette enemies fleeing into the bottom corner. At Dill's
insistence, Gaine counted the pencilled archons and
admitted that there were, indeed, ninety-nine in total.
There hadn't been space to fill their names in, but his
father had liked his composition all the same. It was one
of the last times they had spent together. Gaine had died
only weeks later at the hands of a Heshette bowman.
Presbyter Sypes had brought Dill extra candles that night,
helped him set them up around his tower room.

The soulcage now passed beneath the archon with the
lopsided wing, repaired at some point with brass staples,
and there over on the left was the one who leaned out too
far, ever threatening to drop its spear. Dill had originally
sketched that one from the side.

Looking up at them now, Dill tried to fit the names he
remembered to the skeletons' bones. This one standing
fierce and proud over his great sword, Simon perhaps – or

Barraby? This one, more melancholy, resting on his spear, could he be Dolmen? And here, the toothy grin of a shield-carrier made him think of Praxis, the last archon before Callis to die. He imagined these angels as they must have looked in life: Ulcis's elite sweeping into battle with their wings like shards of sunshine and their weapons glittering like ice crystals. Three thousand years had passed since the angels had risen from the abyss, and now their bones watched over the dead, and over the Soul Wardens who brought them into the temple.

He was twisting round, trying to identify the design on a shield that might have belonged to either Mesa or Perpaul, when the soulcage jerked to a halt with an irreverent thud. Dill spun round. One of the vehicle's front wheels had collided with the column to his left.

The next few moments stretched into a long, sluggish dream. Both mares lowered their heads, chopped their hoofs against the floor, and bulled forward. Dill yelled. The soulcage groaned.

The column shifted . . . and teetered.

High above, the archon's spine flexed and its legs seemed to move, as though the skeleton was keeping its balance. Slowly, the column rocked in the opposite direction. Chains creaked . . . Dill held his breath . . . the column tilted back.

And settled.

Dill breathed again.

There was a snap and the angel collapsed in a shower of bones. A helmet plummeted and hit the floor with a bang; a spear clattered on the marble and skittered off into the shadows. Bones rained down, hands and limbs and ribs smashed to fragments around him. The horses whinnied and stamped their hoofs in protest. The angel's skull struck the seat beside Dill and ricocheted away. It flew up almost as high as the top of the column before descending again to hit the stone floor with a sickening crack. Its jaw snapped off, teeth exploded everywhere. The skull bounced again, and again, shattering more teeth each time, until at last it rolled along the passage and came to rest a dozen yards away, facing him.

Bone dust drifted down.

Borelock screamed. He flew along the corridor like a wraith, his thin arms flailing about his head. Dill sank lower into the driver's seat and shuddered.

'Three thousand years,' Borelock was howling. 'Three thousand years – preserved, protected, safe from decay and intruders. But not from you! Not from the wretched, clumsy, gangling paws of fools and children. Three—' He choked on the word.

Dill's eyes flashed pink. A deeper, hotter pink than he had ever experienced before. He felt the blood leave his face, as though his eyes drew it into themselves like a searing beacon to proclaim his shame.

'A disaster,' Borelock wailed. He whirled round, finding yet more blasphemous evidence of destruction everywhere he looked. 'Dust! One of the Ninety-Nine in ruin.' He rushed over to peer at the plaque affixed to the column, then threw up his arms. 'Samuel. The Dawn Star, bane of Heshette, reduced to this. Destroyed!'

The Dawn Star's jawless, toothless skull gazed back up at them from a carpet of broken bones.

'What will Presbyter Sypes say? Eh? What will he do? A whipping for you no doubt. Yes, a whipping for you. Sorry and raw red you'll be. But me? What of me?' He faced Dill, his chin jutting knife-like from under the cowl. 'Go now. The Sending won't wait. Punishment will come later, but now, go, go, and cage the dead. I must attend to this disaster myself. Go!'

Dill flicked the reins with shaking hands. As the two mares snickered and moved off, bones crunched and popped beneath the soulcage wheels. Dill left Borelock on his knees, sobbing and muttering as he picked up fragments of the fallen archon.

The journey along the rest of the corridor lasted a thousand quick, sharp breaths. At the far end, the horses stopped before the huge banded doors which opened on to the Gatebridge, and Dill found himself looking up at the last skeleton of all. There stood the bones of Callis, the greatest of the first angels. Ulcis's Herald seemed to have deteriorated more than the archons he'd once commanded: countless staples held his old yellow joints in place. One bony fist clutched a mouldering book, the other a key enveloped by a hissing blue flame. The flame was supposed to burn eternally, but Dill had heard whispers that the priests often forgot to change the gas tank that fuelled it, leaving the light extinguished for days at a time. He bowed his head in reverence all the same.

Two guardsmen in black-enamelled armour pushed the temple doors inwards and bright sunshine leapt in.

Dill blinked. Six corpses lay wrapped in shrouds on the temple steps. Mourners crowded behind them, spanning the Gatebridge from side to side, and beyond them dozens of onlookers had climbed up to perch on or cling to the girders for a better view. A cheer from the younger elements of the crowd was followed by stern hushing from wives and mothers. Pillars of smoke rose from the Bridgeview townhouses. Somewhere distant, a blacksmith's hammer pounded out dull iron notes.

Dill edged the soulcage forward, out onto the wide

esplanade above the temple steps. Then he slid down from his seat and, fumbling with the key, finally managed to unlock the soulcage.

While the guards hefted corpses into the cage, Dill studied the mourners. Hoods hid their faces, but every head was turned his way. They were watching him. Someone pointed and whispered, provoking nervous laughs, and Dill suddenly remembered his eyes: they would be seashell pink in the sunlight. To his dismay, the colour only deepened.

When they had finished loading the corpses, one of the temple guards guided the horses round in a tight circle. Dill climbed back into his seat and flicked the reins. The beasts did not move.

The guard coughed, nodded at the soulcage.

Dill's eyes reddened further. Once more, he slipped to the ground, and locked the soulcage. At the familiar sound, the horses began to move, so Dill had to scramble after them. A mourner stepped forward and threw up a shower of petals that drifted over both the angel and the dead.

The temple doors were heaved shut behind him and he was confined once more in gloomy silence. A single guard remained inside to escort the soulcage back along the corridor, but even with this limited company the vaulted space felt emptier than before.

Dill urged the horses forward. They were no keener to obey the reins than they had been a moment earlier, moving off only after a while, when they were ready. The axle creaked and the horses snickered. Ten paces behind them, the guard marched along in his armour, his footsteps resounding like a slow, metallic heartbeat. Any guard with a relative among the corpses could claim the right to escort the soulcage, and Dill wondered if this was true today. Did this man have a loved one among the dead? He glanced back, but detected no sign of grief in the man's face, just weariness, and possibly boredom.

Borelock had meanwhile gathered the shattered bones into a pile beside their empty column and stood hunched over them, his rage still seething about him like an invisible cloud.

At last the small procession reached the Sanctum doors, where Dill checked his appearance. Flecks of dust and bone covered his jacket. He brushed them away as best he could then finger-smoothed his tufted hair. Rushes of pink still shifted through his irises: he screwed his eyes closed and tried to shed the colour, but it proved hopeless. Something jabbed him in the back: a small bone, perhaps part of a finger, snagged in his feathers.

A key clunked in a lock. Dill stuffed the bone in his pocket, sat up straight, and pulled his wings tighter against his back.

Wrought ironwork as sharp as thorns hedged the Sanctum walls. Spikes of tallow hung from brackets set deep inside, where candles burned and threw clawlike shadows around a wide aperture in the floor. Blessings had been carved in spirals fashioned around the hole, to keep the dead from rising from the abyss below until Ulcis should release them. A chain ran up from a winch fixed to one side, through a system of pulleys set high above, and back down to where it coiled in loops on the floor. This was the very heart of the temple, the heart of Deepgate itself.

Dill shook the reins again and, thankfully, the horses moved into the Sanctum without hesitation, the sound of their hoofs like whiplashes in the silence. The scent of flowers overwhelmed him, so thick he could almost taste it, and he forced himself to take shallow breaths.

Presbyter Sypes leaned on a hardwood lectern. Next to him, three others sat on high-backed chairs facing the aperture of the pit. There was Adjunct Crumb, sitting closest to the Presbyter, Rachel Hael beside him, and a young man who must be her brother.

Deepgate's new aeronaut commander?

The fourth chair was empty.

They expected someone else. But who would ignore a summons from the temple?

In front of the group lay a body wrapped in silk printed with a hundred blessings. Dill's gaze lingered on the shroud for a moment before he remembered his duty and climbed up beside the soulcage to help the guard hook it up.

Iron rattled and scraped as the guard dragged the loose chain over the floor. He passed the hook up to Dill, who attached it to the top of the cage, then clambered down to unhitch the horses. The mares trotted back into the corridor on their own, and he hurried to close the doors behind them.

Click.

The temple guard had by now unlocked the winch. He cranked the handle, drawing in the slack. The Presbyter, Adjunct and guests looked on silently as, slowly, the chain grew taut and, inch by inch, the soulcage began to rise, wheels and all.

'Frailer specimen than Gaine.' Mark's whisper was strikingly loud in the still of the Sanctum. The commander had leant closer to his sister, looking at Dill out of the corner of his eye. Rachel Hael did not reply, just sat there, staring ahead. The brother slumped back in his chair, nonplussed.

Mark Hael was just as lean as his sister, but there the similarity ended. Deepgate's aeronaut commander lounged in his chair, arms dangling, an expression of boredom on his deeply-tanned face. Rachel looked corpse-pale by comparison. She sat primly upright, dressed in the same grubby leathers she had worn earlier.

Presbyter Sypes was propped against the lectern as though it was all that kept him standing, his sunken eyes fixed on the aperture below. Adjunct Crumb sparkled beside him like a heap of treasure, hands folded neatly in his lap, his whole head scrubbed and pink as a perfume pot. He caught Dill's eye and gave him an oily wink.

The soulcage swung out over the open abyss and the guard paused to rest, flushed and panting.

Everyone waited.

For a long time, Presbyter Sypes stared down into the void below the soulcage, while Rachel, her brother and Adjunct Crumb all appeared to be deep in their own thoughts. A breeze stirred the air. Candles flickered. Shadows swayed like windblown branches over the floor. Minutes passed. Sypes's eyelids drooped.

Adjunct Crumb suddenly cleared his throat. The Presbyter's eyes flicked open. He sniffed the air, frowned, then muttered something Dill didn't catch.

The Adjunct grimaced.

Presbyter Sypes seemed to remember where he was, and nodded to the guard, who began to lower the cage through the aperture into the waiting abyss. Once it was out of sight, the guard locked the winch, and Dill heard a murmur like cogs whirring in a clock.

'Death,' the Presbyter announced, 'is always close.

Death is the pause between each breath, the space between each heartbeat.' He lowered his head. 'When Ayen sealed the doors to Heaven, she damned us all to Hell. Ghosts of good men abandoned, for ever destined to walk Iril's corridors among the wicked . . .'

Dill wiped bone-dust from his sword hilt. A fine weapon; solid and heavy – a sword worthy of a temple archon. And he would grow accustomed, he supposed, to its weight.

'. . . endless corridors, waist-deep in blood where purulent demons and wraiths, lunatics, murderers, foulest bastards, blasphemers and whores are damned to wander lost for all eternity . . .'

Flecks of gold leaf had come away from the curved hand guard. Dill ran a finger over its polished surface. Gold-leafed lead or not, old swords were definitely superior to new swords.

'. . . but Ayen's spite strengthened the Maze. Nourished with souls over which it had no claim, Iril grew sentient, cunning . . .'

Ancient weapons had a presence, a personality, and steel could be sharpened.

'. . . even now trying to find ways into this world. Had her eldest son, Ulcis, not sought to depose her . . .'

Dill would ask the priests to sharpen the blade for him. Now that he was actively in temple service, they would have to listen to him.

'. . . a hundred years of war in heaven. Only to be cast out, his shattered legion of angels fallen . . . and imprisoned in the abyss beneath our temple . . .'

The weapon's guard could be replaced too, restored to battle-readiness. Deepgate's smiths would probably want to emblazon it with a suitable design: something in the spirit of the Ninety-Nine—

'. . . Ulcis offered salvation in the abyss . . . For three thousand years we have entrusted him with our souls . . . An army waiting in the city of Deep . . . One day to reclaim Heaven and . . . Dill?'

—But not too similar. Using Dill's own design: an eagle, perhaps, or a sandhawk. He would begin sketching ideas right after the ceremony.

'Dill, am I boring you?'

Dill started. He had been idly fingering lines on the sword's wide, gold-coloured guard. Now he snapped to attention and feigned sombre interest.

The Presbyter's eyes twinkled. 'Had Ulcis's coup succeeded, our world would be a very different place today.' The smile left his eyes and he seemed to drift away for a moment before regaining his voice. 'Now, before the Gate to the city of Deep, we offer this blessed blood as a libation to Ulcis, Ayen's eldest, God of Chains, Hoarder of Souls.'

A gust of wind emerged from the pit. Candle flames leapt and brightened. Shadows reached closer towards the aperture, then withdrew. Dill stared down into the void, but saw nothing, only a stark, unsettling blackness.

Presbyter Sypes gripped the lectern, leaned over it, his voice booming. 'Deny Iril this blood. Free the souls bound within. Let them join your army, and rise again to smash open the doors of Heaven.'

Iron writhed around the walls. The scent of flowers thickened and Dill found himself struggling to breathe, as though something was squeezing the air from his lungs. The soulcage chain trembled. Metal clicked, clattered, whirred. And then suddenly it stopped.

Dill breathed at last. The soulcage was raised again, now empty. An open trapdoor in its base swung back and forward, knocking against the rear axle.

Presbyter Sypes stepped down from the lectern and approached the shroud of General Hael. He laid a hand on the corpse and said, 'Edward Hael died protecting everything I hold dear.' He glanced between Rachel, her brother and Dill. 'In his stead Mark will protect the city. And Rachel . . .'

Mark Hael was watching the Presbyter solemnly, but Rachel buried her face in her hands. When she looked up again, there were tears in her eyes. Adjunct Crumb saw this and failed to hide a look of surprise, but the Presbyter did not appear to notice; he was now busy straightening his cassock.

All at once she seemed even smaller, more out of place here than she had before. Dill offered her a weak smile. Perhaps she didn't understand: Death was a joyous occasion. Her father was to be reborn in the abyss, his soul released into the service of Ulcis. Tears were selfish, a display of faithlessness. Dill knew this, but he remembered his own father's Sending, and the tears he'd shed himself. Presbyter Sypes hadn't noticed those tears either. He'd been busy straightening his cassock on that occasion too.

The temple guard cast the general's body down into the abyss.

Dill didn't stay to ponder further. He had a whipping to receive.

7
MR NETTLE'S LUCK

With Smith's bill of sale clutched in his fist, and Smith's trolley creaking before him, Mr Nettle sought the gaffer on Berth Seventeen. Tradeships rumbled over a forest of docking spines and tarred chains where armies of men worked with hammers and hooks and aether flames to keep the whole thing hale. More men unloaded goods from docked ships: metal ores and coal from Hollowhill, wood from Shale, food, livestock and soil from the Coyle Plantations and wine from the High Valleys; salt, textiles, worked gold, silver and bronze from the desert settlements. Tremors ran through the girders and stones underfoot. The air smelled of fuel and iron.

The incoming ships were from the depots at Sandport and Clune, heavy with the collected wealth of the river towns, but the outgoing ships were swift and light. They carried little but tax demands and the occasional crate of armour or bolts for the outpost garrisons.

Mr Nettle remembered the days before the great ships ploughed the skies. Everything had come to Deepgate by caravan, and many of those caravans had never reached the city. At the height of the Heshette war there had been difficult years when the heathens choked the supply lines.

He was just a boy back then, but he remembered the food queues, the hunger and the bloodshed. In those times, Iril had taken many souls.

Great ragged holes pocked the shipyards, some of them big enough to let the airships manoeuvre down to moorings where stitchers and Gluemen could clamber over them and work their repairs. All of the holes he passed by were empty now, full of nothing but darkness and chains, and a queer metal wind sighed up from the abyss. But he knew there were men down there, in harnesses on ropes, strengthening the old iron with new. Mr Nettle could hear their faraway shouts and laughs, the pounding of their hammers. He wondered how men managed to face those chains each day, and if their wives could bear to look at them when they left home in the morning.

He found the gaffer bawling out a group of dockhands gathered beside an overloaded cart. The weight of coal sacks it carried had tipped the cart back on its wheels, leaving the harnessed donkey suspended a few feet above the ground. The donkey chewed its teeth and merely looked bored.

'Laggards, you think this is a joke?' The gaffer smacked his billet against his palm. 'You want my stick on the back of your heads?'

'Not our fault,' one of the dockhands protested. 'Donkey's lost weight since yesterday.'

'Aye, and you will too, when I cut your wage for this folly.'

Smiles faded from the dockhands' faces. They set to work unloading the cart.

'Pig iron,' Mr Nettle said, 'for Smith.' He thrust the bill at the gaffer, who ignored it.

'Tomorrow,' the gaffer growled, then, to his men, 'Take them from the top first, you dolts, you want to spill the lot?'

'No,' Mr Nettle said. '*Now.*'

The gaffer gave him a square look. He seemed about to say something, then to change his mind. Maybe he noticed the way Mr Nettle's shoulders had tensed. He sighed and grabbed the bill. 'Over there. Warehouse eleven, like it says here. Pallet three hundred and two.'

After Mr Nettle had got the bill checked by the warehouse boss, he found the crates where he'd been told, and heaved the first onto his trolley. Wooden axle squeaking, he set off back to Blacklung Lane.

He worked hard for Smith all afternoon. His ribs protested with every step, and at times the pain was worse than from the beating, but he just kept moving, planting one foot in front of the other and trying to clear his mind of everything but the cobbles ahead and the grumble of the trolley wheels. Each box seemed to weigh more than the last and there appeared to be no end to them. He could have sworn someone was loading up the pallet even as he emptied it. At this rate, he'd be lucky to finish the job by the time it got dark. *Lucky?* He scowled. What was luck? Bad luck was just what happened day to day. Bad luck was an icy morning, or finding nothing in the nets for a week, or getting ill when you had to work. Bad luck was just life. And good luck? It was nothing but a pause in the bad. That was when you didn't get ill, and therefore could keep dragging the nets every day. That was when you found something you could sell, and you could eat. But maybe his luck was changing. Smith was a good man. He didn't want to think about it, though. The more he thought about it, the more he felt he was tempting fate. Good luck, real good luck, didn't come to people like Smith and Nettle.

By the fourth afternoon bell he had delivered half the iron. His ribs were aching, and his muscles beginning to fold. The sun beat down mercilessly and sapped his strength. Sweat soaked into his mourning robes. He slumped to the ground by a common pipe under the Merrygate watchtower, there slaked his thirst and sloshed water over his face. Some folks looked at him strangely, and some even stared outright, but most ignored him like he was a beggar.

Only three bolts. What were the chances? If he missed with the first, the angel was sure to finish him before he could load the second, poisoned or no. One bolt would have to do it. But which one would he use? The *soultaker* was the most fitting – a soul for a soul. Though it would cost the most to replace, since diseased bolts were rare. Smith had never said anything about him paying for the bolts, but he figured he owed the man that at least – assuming he made it through the night. Mr Nettle rubbed his eyes with the heels of his palms. What if the angel killed him? The crossbow would be left on the streets for anyone to find, and Smith would never see it again. That was a poor trade for a day's work. He shunned the thought.

Mr Nettle rose stiffly and tilted back the trolley, resting it on his stomach. Pain shot through his ribs but he did his best to ignore it. He had a full afternoon's work ahead.

Even before he got back to Blacklung Lane, he knew something was wrong. As Mr Nettle wove through the narrow, winding lanes towards the weapon smiths' warrens, a sense of dread began to fill him. At first he shrugged it aside, thinking it a shadow of his grief, but when he drew nearer the feeling grew until, not knowing why, he found himself hurrying. He was still a street away when he realized what was wrong. The ringing and hammering of metal had stopped. Blacklung Lane was silent. Mr Nettle ran the last few yards, the crate rattling on his trolley.

Crowds blocked the entrance to the lane itself. The smiths were all outdoors, away from their forges, their coal-streaked, muscled torsos jostling as they tried to push past one another to see what was happening. Smoke billowed from somewhere at the end of the lane and someone cried, 'Get back, get back, it's going to go.'

Mr Nettle abandoned the trolley and tried to push his way through. The crowd threw him angry looks, shoved him this way and that, but he squeezed among them and managed to force his way forward. Big as these smiths were, Mr Nettle was bigger. The smell of burning rope hung thick in the air.

'Get back I say! Back, you fools.'

Up ahead, people were coughing; others were shouting. There was a *whoomph*, then the groan of stressed metal. Embers twisted upwards through the smoke, and suddenly the crowd surged backwards, carrying Mr Nettle with it. Men fought to get past him. Someone punched him, another kneed him hard in the stomach and he almost dropped. He grabbed the man's hair and dragged him down, sending him sprawling beneath the feet of others. And all at once there was space in front of him. And flames.

Blacklung Lane terminated abruptly: where once there had been a slump of cobbles, chains and soot-blackened walls, there was now a gaping hole rimmed with burning rubble. The far end of the lane had fallen through into the abyss, taking half the adjoining smithies and much of the surrounding neighbourhood with it. A circle of cross-chains hung down into the rift like a basket with the bottom fallen out. The collapse had ripped open a dozen houses. Walls had crumbled away, leaving girders jutting from the stonework and private rooms open to Mr Nettle's gaze, their furniture undisturbed but now inches from the open abyss.

Smith and his workshop were gone.

Mr Nettle took a step back as more cobbles dropped away before him. He pressed himself into the crowd. Coals from the furnaces had set fire to the torn nets below and, even as he watched, those flames grew higher and a cloud of smoke rolled over him.

'Back!' he roared, and pushed hard into the throng. Men stumbled and fell, but those behind him were still struggling, trying to free themselves from others, while at the back still more onlookers were pushing forward.

The crowd swelled alarmingly, and for a dreadful moment Mr Nettle felt himself being shoved towards the abyss. He tripped, grabbed something – a man's ear – and pulled himself upright. The man yelled, fell back – if he went over the edge, Mr Nettle didn't see. Others were now tugging at his robes from all sides, pulling him, pushing him. He kicked them away. He elbowed someone else in the face, knocked him to the ground.

Another *whoomph*, and a loud cracking noise. Behind him, more loose stone rumbled into the abyss.

There was no way out through the crowd. He had to go up, over them. Mr Nettle wrestled with the men nearest to him, forcing them down. Shouts and screams came from everywhere. He climbed over backs and faces and arms and legs, pushing, punching. He kicked out, grabbed hair or skin, and clawed his way forward. For a heartbeat he was carried above the crowd, and then he sank among them, among their legs and boots. Something hit him in the face; he tried to rise, but there were men on top of him, flattening him, suffocating him.

He heard the snap and hiss of parting cables. Suddenly he was covered in blood; his hands and arms were red, wet. He didn't know if it was his own blood or not. A boot kicked him in the teeth, then it stood on his head. Crushing weight bore down on his aching back.

The scrounger yelled, strained against the man's weight, and wrenched himself up on to his elbows. Another push and he got his feet under him. He heaved upwards: men fell on either side and Mr Nettle stood. Thicker smoke now engulfed him. He closed his eyes, struck out with his hands and pushed and pushed and punched and punched his way into the mass of people. His fists connected dozens of times.

A deep rumble erupted from somewhere behind. More men began to scream.

Eyes shut, lungs full of smoke, Mr Nettle battered his way further through the crowd.

And suddenly he burst free.

All around, the smiths were dragging fallen comrades from the panicking throng. Others were rushing to the scene with buckets of water, but hampered by the tangled mass of people, they could do nothing but drop these nearby and run to fetch more.

Mr Nettle paused there gasping for breath. His robe was now torn to tatters and covered in blood, too much blood to have come from the blows he'd delivered. The snapping cables, he realized, had torn right through the crowd. He checked his own limbs, counted his fingers. He felt dazed, bruised, but still in one piece.

He'd been lucky, he thought miserably.

8

THE BATTLE OF THE TOOTH

Dill couldn't decide whether Presbyter Sypes was still reading or asleep. The old priest's head hovered inches from the tome on the desk before him, while his face appeared to have subsided and set like Fondelgrue's porridge. Dry breaths rasped in his throat, but he wasn't snoring, so therefore he was probably still reading. Yet the old man hadn't turned a page since Dill had entered the schoolroom.

Dill's gaze drifted across the bookshelves behind the desk. From floor to ceiling the spines of the ancient volumes formed a mosaic of sombre hues with the occasional speckled gold of lettering. Apart from this assemblage of books and a couple of tired wooden desks and chairs, the schoolroom was bare. Late afternoon sunlight slid in through windows high in the western wall and lay in honey-coloured slabs on the floorboards. A single fly wove its languid way between the beams of light and seemed to labour through an air too thick with silence. All at once Dill realized the harsh breathing had stopped, and he turned to find the Presbyter staring at him.

'How long have you been standing there?' the old man said.

'I didn't want to interrupt you, your Grace.'

'No, I suppose not.' He looked Dill up and down. 'You're not scheduled for a lesson today, are you?'

'No, your Grace.'

'Then what do you want?'

Dill hesitated. 'I was told to come here,' he said. 'Borelock told me to come here.'

'Ah yes.' Presbyter Sypes straightened in his chair. 'The incident this morning. It seems the Ninety-Nine are now ninety-eight.' He paused. 'Well, what do you have to say for yourself?'

Dill hung his head. 'I'm truly sorry.'

Presbyter Sypes studied him carefully. 'I see.'

The fly buzzed angrily past Dill's ear, traced a wide curve, then settled on the Presbyter's desk. The priest slammed his hand down, missing the insect.

Dill flinched.

The Presbyter was examining his palm in apparent confusion. 'I understand that before you began temple service, Borelock usually dealt with this sort of matter.'

'Yes, your Grace.'

'What do you expect me to do, then?'

'I was told . . .' Dill's chin still rested on his chest, his eyes rooted to a point on the floor. 'Your Grace, I was told a whipping.'

'Hmmm, that would be the standard punishment, would it not? For tardiness perhaps, smudging a parchment or spilling ink . . . or other such crimes.'

'Yes, your Grace.'

'But do you think your actions this morning merit the standard punishment? As I understand it, we now have a barrowload of dust and teeth covering the Sanctum corridor. Samuel no less, the Dawn Star. Would a mere whipping suffice, do you think?'

'No, your Grace.'

'No indeed.' Presbyter Sypes shook his head. 'You know how old that relic was?'

'Yes, your Grace.'

'Son,' he closed the book gently, 'it was just a pile of bones before your accident. And now it is still a pile of bones. Very important bones, yes – sacred bones.' He let the words sink in. 'We will repair it, with some effort and at some considerable cost no doubt, but it will still be a pile of bones at the end of it all. However,' he hesitated, 'tradition demands a whipping, and a whipping you shall have.' Now he spoke softly, hardly above a whisper. 'But, Dill, there is a problem. I am a weak old man. I doubt I could lift a lash, let alone apply it with the force necessary to inflict pain.'

Dill cringed at the mere mention of the whip, nevertheless he replied, 'I understand. I will speak to Borelock.'

'No, lad, no. I will not have them think me a weakling, a crippled old priest who cannot perform his duties. In this case I think we will dispense with the whip.'

There were poisons a hundred times worse than the lash, poisons that could sculpt ingenious landscapes of suffering without permanent damage to the body. Dill's eyes flared white, his knees trembled, and it was all he could do to remain standing.

'When you leave here,' the Presbyter said, 'I suggest you walk with a stoop, wear a grimace on your face. Avoid looking directly at the priests – and say nothing.' He shrugged. 'Let them fill their heads with imagined beatings and poisons and God knows what else. Let them wonder at their old master's fury. Why should we not contrive the required effect without straining ourselves unduly? Would that not save us both a little pain? If any should grin, or mock you, let me know quietly. Do you understand?'

Dill was trembling so much, his nod became an extension of his shaking.

'Don't be so afraid, lad. Help me, cover for my weakness, and I will endeavour to have any future punishments administered in this manner too. Not that I expect to see you before me again like this. You are an adult now. Do we have an agreement?'

'Yes, your Grace.'

'Good.' Presbyter Sypes smiled. 'Mustn't let any of them think I'm a doddering old fool.'

'No, your Grace.'

'Well, now, my nap has been disturbed, and I am currently enduring one of those rare moments of lucidity, so we may as well make the best of it. I'd say we have thirty lashes worth of time together, and they expect me to administer them at leisure. This is a schoolroom, so why not read something. Where are you in the curriculum?'

'Your Grace, you threw the curriculum away, during our last lesson.'

'I did?'

'Through the window.' Dill pointed out a fresh pane of glass, still smudged with the glazier's fingerprints.

'Oh my. What book was it?'

'I don't know. A heavy one.'

'Good for me, I loathe the dense stuff. Did we then study something else?'

'You said that, as I'd turned sixteen, it was time to learn the most important lessons of life.'

'Did I?' The Presbyter frowned. 'Yes, yes, of course. I remember,' he said unconvincingly.

'Well, I was wondering . . .'

'Yes?'

'A topic we broached last time . . .?'

'Ah.' Presbyter Sypes stiffened. 'Oh, my memory.' He rattled his fingers against his teeth. 'Well, let's not be bashful. If I've started on this subject, I ought to finish it . . . I suppose it was only a matter of time. Sixteen years, so of course . . .' He opened the journal again and scanned a page, but Dill suspected he wasn't really reading it. The Presbyter had now turned an odd shade of pink. His lips thinned. He made a clucking sound. Finally, he fixed his eyes on Dill. 'Women,' he said.

'No, your Grace, it's not that.'

'No?'

'We were talking about the war.'

'The war?' Presbyter Sypes let out a long sigh. 'Ulcis's grace, yes, the war. I'll tell you about the war.'

For a moment he appeared to gather his thoughts, gazing past Dill. 'Mostly the Heshette,' he muttered. 'The others were too busy garrotting each other over goats or stealing each other's wives. But the Heshette . . .' He kept nodding. 'Three thousand years ago, Callis came to raise the temple over Ulcis's realm, but the Heshette vowed to tear it down. The first battle, the Battle of the Tooth, came when Deepgate was still a community of tents and mud huts raised around the abyss. With no city walls to keep the heathens out, one hundred archons and barely two thousand pilgrims managed to defeat a horde twenty-five times their size.'

The Presbyter smiled. 'But you already know this part of the tale?'

'Yes, your Grace.' Dill knew the story of that battle well. Many accounts had been written by scholars or past presbyters, and Presbyter Sypes himself had told him more than one.

'Then I'll skip it.'

'No, your Grace, please.'

The old priest's smile broadened. 'Scrimlock's account began with two questions.'

Dill remembered: this was his favourite anecdote of the battle.

'How many?' Callis had asked. 'And where?'

Balthus Brine hunched on his knees on the carpet of the Herald's sun-baked tent, his broad shoulders casting a wide shadow across the map spread before him. 'Herald, our best estimates put them at forty to fifty thousand. Eight thousand pure Heshette, with their trade cousins from Dalamoor at twice that number, and a score of Heshban tribes gathered from the northern Deadsands. Then there are camel herders from the steppes, branded nomads caught up in the war, and a small unit of salt mercenaries brought in from the Lowlands, some fifteen hundred men. There haven't been this many heathens in one place since the Poleman York boasted there was still a virgin in Sanpah. At present, the army is camped four leagues southwest of Blackthrone, *here*.' He pointed to a spot on the map. 'Ten to twelve days away.'

'Salt mercenaries?' the angel asked.

'Herald, the Heshette have paid them with salt from the Pocked Delta.'

Callis boomed a laugh. 'Then let's hope they bring

their wages with them to battle. We're out of salt, are we not?'

'We're out of a lot of things, luck being one of them.' Balthus squeezed the nape of his neck. 'Herald, the army marches quickly. All but these mercenaries are desert men. If we are to have any chance of reaching the Coyle and the shelter of the river towns, we must leave now.'

'Flee, Balthus?' Callis's eyes glittered. 'I will not flee.'

'Herald, we cannot defend Deepgate against such a force. We could construct defensive walls, but . . .' He left the rest unsaid. Would such fortifications delay their inevitable end by as much as an hour?

'Agreed. It would not be to our advantage to remain in the settlement.'

'Then we retreat to the temple? We might defend the chains, but we don't have the supplies to outlast a siege. The water pipe to Jakka is incomplete, and less than half our caravans will return before the horde is upon us. We would perish of thirst in a month.'

'That's true,' Callis said casually.

Balthus waited, but the angel said no more. At last he asked, 'Herald, what are your orders?'

'We march against them.'

Balthus almost choked. 'Against fifty thousand men?'

'You said yourself, it might be only forty.'

'Still . . .' But he found Callis's gaze too difficult to meet. The intensity of those dark grey eyes unnerved Balthus, so he stared down at the map as though a solution to their dilemma might somehow appear there. 'We have swords for seventy men,' he said. 'Four barrels of black-cake brought from . . . overseas. And the Ninety-Nine, of course.' He drew a circle around the talisman at his chest and touched his brow. 'If, by the will of Ulcis, they will answer your summons.'

'Do you doubt me, Balthus?'

'No, Herald, but one hundred archons, barely two thousand pilgrims . . .?'

'And a Tooth,' Callis said.

Balthus stared at the Herald for a slow moment, then a grin spread across his face. All this time the solution was – and the pun widened his grin further – right in their faces.

'Herald, I will begin preparations at once.' He left the angel still pondering the map and stepped outside, into the shadow of the Tooth.

The Tooth was a wonder: it towered over the settlement like a citadel carved from bone. Callis had brought the machine into Markeh forty years ago, and it had shaken the earth in more ways than one. The Herald had preached from the Tooth's high walls: how Ayen, goddess of Light and Life, furious at the wickedness of men, had sealed Heaven. How she had abandoned earthbound souls to the Maze.

At this there was much consternation among the men in Markeh, for they had no desire to wander Iril's bloody corridors among the souls of the wicked.

Callis had calmed the crowd. Seven of Ayen's sons had stood against her; they had raised an army of angels with which to displace the goddess. Their coup had almost succeeded, but at the final hour Ayen's own forces had proved too strong. The goddess had prevailed and expelled her sons from Heaven for their treachery, casting them down with the last of their defeated armies to join mortal man in his realm below.

Balthus had listened in awe and fear, with the others,

and had known it to be true. Last winter had they not seen the night sky blaze with Ayen's fury? Had they not witnessed seven stars fall?

All was not lost, Callis had then explained. Hope for man now rested with Ayen's eldest son, Ulcis. The god of chains had fallen to these lands, had been driven deep within the earth. Weakened but not destroyed, the god had sent his herald forth to build a temple: to proclaim that Ulcis offered salvation in his abyss. Souls sent down to him would be spared Iril after death. The god of chains was building a new army with which to storm Heaven.

Balthus had been so shaken by this revelation, he'd shed his old life, as easily as a cloak, to join the pilgrims constructing the temple.

Now outside the Herald's tent, he lifted his gaze past the Tooth's river-wide tracks, up its pale hull to the scorched funnels rearing hundreds of feet above, where smoke from its lungs poured into the desert sky. This thing was a fortress, Balthus realized, and more than that: it was a weapon. For the last four decades, the relic's massive cutters had bitten deeply into the slopes of Black-throne, gouged that strange ore from the flesh of the mountain, and brought it to Deepgate to forge the temple's chains.

Fifty thousand men?

They might as well be fifty.

Yet Balthus had failed to consider what this machine could mean to them in battle. The Tooth had become as much a part of the landscape as the abyss itself. How often does one really notice the ground beneath one's feet or the roof above one's head? Had he changed so much that he could take such a manifestation of the god's power for granted? Balthus walked over to the edge of the abyss and knelt in the sand to beg forgiveness from his lord down below.

All work had halted since news of the advancing horde had reached them. The walkways zigzagging from the perimeter in to the hub were deserted. A deep silence hung over the abyss itself. All ninety-nine foundation chains were now in place and the main skeleton of the temple was beginning to take shape. Balthus let his gaze roam over the vast scope of the construction: Mesa's chain, Perpaul's, Simon's; each as mighty as the legend of its namesake. They were Ulcis's greatest warriors, survivors from the war in Heaven. Forty years ago Balthus would not have believed mortal man capable of building such a thing.

Truly, he was grateful.

Preparations for the battle were made in earnest. The pilgrims loaded what supplies they had into the Tooth's holds. Men, women and children were housed in temporary quarters within. And Callis summoned the Ninety-Nine.

Ulcis's angels rose from the abyss to join their commander, their armour wreathed in death-light, their swords glittering under Ayen's furious sun.

Balthus shivered at the sight of them. 'Are they dead?' he asked Callis.

'They have given up eternity for us,' the angel replied. 'In this world they cannot survive. Ayen's light will destroy them, just as it destroys men.' His eyes narrowed. 'But while alive they will burn brightly.'

At the Herald's command, a bottle of black liquid was brought forth.

Balthus gave Callis an inquiring look.

'Angelwine,' Callis replied. 'A gift from our Lord.'

'A potion?'

Callis laughed. 'Of sorts. It will bestow great power, strength and longevity upon those archons who drink it. A magnanimous god, Ulcis, to share his divinity for a time, don't you think?'

Balthus eyed the angelwine. Could this elixir really contain the power of a god? The liquid boiled like smoke and it seemed to him he heard whispers within the glass.

'It is alive,' he gasped.

Callis held up the bottle. 'This wine,' he said, 'contains the souls of many men.'

'*Human* souls?'

'Enemies of Ulcis.' His tone warned against further questions.

Balthus watched as each of the Ninety-Nine supped the angelwine. He watched their eyes turn black and the death-light darken around their armour. And when the Herald himself had taken his share, Balthus could no longer contain his desire. 'Might a loyal servant be permitted to drink too?' he asked.

Callis seemed in the grip of a murderous fever. He wheeled savagely, face contorted, and for a heartbeat Balthus feared for his own life. But then the violence left the angel's eyes and he looked upon his servant with pity. 'Balthus,' he said, 'this elixir is too potent for man. It would drive you insane.'

On the dawn of the day of battle a great sand storm rose, as if the god of chains was beating his wings beneath the earth. Balthus Brine watched from the Tooth's bridge, with Callis at his side. Throughout the battle, the Herald did not speak. His rage had faded and he gazed down at the slaughter with an expression on his ageless face that might even have been regret.

'Do you mourn them?' Balthus asked.

'They are savages,' Callis said.

Balthus nodded, and his white teeth split his brown lips.

'Like us,' the Herald said, and he shared his servant's grin.

The storm raged and the Tooth ploughed through enemy flesh and the archons' swords blazed until earth was as red as the sand-choked sun. And when at last the winds died and the killing was done, the corpses of twenty thousand men lay strewn across the Deadsands. The remainder of the horde fled from the Tooth, and from the angels, and Callis stood triumphant upon a mountain of the dead.

'All who are still whole will be blessed and cast into the abyss,' he commanded. 'They will be redeemed.'

Balthus said, 'But they sought to destroy us. They do not deserve a place in our Lord's army.'

The angel smiled. 'A magnanimous god, Ulcis.'

'Did Callis really live for a thousand years?' Dill asked.

The Presbyter took a moment to focus on him, and then looked away. 'Records conflict,' he muttered, 'although most would agree with that estimate. Alas, his sons did not inherit their father's longevity.'

Dill considered this. A thousand years of life from one sip of angelwine. Had there been more of the elixir, would the angel still be alive today? 'But the Heshette returned,' he said.

'Returned, yes, but never again in those numbers. The Battle of the Tooth taught them a harsh lesson. It wasn't until two hundred years ago that the balance began to shift again. Our spies discovered a caste of shamans among the Heshette who were urging the desert peoples toward a second war. We struck out, hoping to halt their momentum, to slay the shamans, but our efforts only strengthened their cause.'

The old priest sniffed, rubbed at his nose, and went on, 'They rose again, and for many years our armies held them back with nothing but faith and steel. And with the aid of Callis's sons of course. The Herald's line held strong.'

Dill grimaced inwardly. The scratch on his finger seemed at once to sting. But the Presbyter continued, as though speaking to himself. His eyes had dulled a little, but he spoke with passion.

'Each time the heathens recovered, they returned, though rarely any stronger than before. Scattered tribes mostly – roused as always by the Heshette core and their snake-tongued witchdoctors. They remain loyal to Ayen, and have vowed to destroy her outcast sons.' Sypes seemed to drift within himself for a moment. 'Tattooed and bearded savages . . . cannibals too, it's said. They eat their own wounded and drink some foul brew fermented from blood and milk.' The Presbyter's brow furrowed. 'But, then, they say a lot of such things in this city.'

Dill tried to imagine the Heshette, their sun rituals and the human sacrifices the missionaries sometimes spoke of. In his mind they scrapped like dogs, fork-tongued shamans flitting among them like whispering ghosts. He imagined himself standing before them, on the abyss rim, the last archon standing guard before the panicked streets of Deepgate, his sword high, his eyes dark and deep as Ulcis's lair.

The Presbyter went on, 'Faith and steel, and god's will,

kept us safe for so long, but that summer thirty years ago galvanized the tribes and raised their hopes. A drought, the worst in history, withered most of our crops. Dust storms ruined the rest. The Coyle, never known to fail before, dried to a trickle. Everyone suffered equally; those of us in Deepgate as much as the desert folk. But the tribes saw omens in that drought. They believed the goddess Ayen was punishing *them* for our actions. For the first time since the Battle of the Tooth, they stopped warring among themselves and united. Once more they marched against us as one army, the shamans among them urging them on. Our troops were stretched too thin in the desert, so we retreated and fought them on the perimeter of the chasm.

'Even then we were outnumbered. Our soldiers had training, discipline, keener swords, but they struggled against the sheer weight of numbers. Gaine himself slew more than forty of the foe. The tribes always were afraid of your line, and understandably so. You should have seen him.'

Dill saw in his mind the tribes advance: all tattooed and wild-eyed, an army of rags and muscle. He saw his father alone, defiant, before them. Gaine's sword flashed, cleaved through flesh and bone. Heads flew from shoulders and blood rained. Men sank before him. Gaine took to the air and the heathens fled screaming back into the Deadsands.

'And Devon saved us,' Rachel Hael said. She had entered without knocking and, judging by Sypes's expression, it was a habit he felt she should shake off.

Dill spun round. 'What do *you* want?' he snapped, then glanced back at the Presbyter. Dill's eyes reddened.

Rachel's relief at finding the angel had been spared the whip was diminishing quickly.

The Presbyter eyed her warily. 'Adept Hael here is quite correct. Back then, Devon was apprentice to the Arch Chemist Elizabeth Lade, his future wife, in the Poison Kitchens.'

'Devon is married?' Dill looked surprised.

'Was,' Sypes said, turning back to him. 'The poor woman. Few survive to old age in that particular field of work – the fumes in there.'

Rachel bristled at Sypes's dismissive manner. She bit back a retort.

'Elizabeth was more concerned with the development of narcotics,' Sypes went on. 'We were looking for alternative ways to counter the threat posed by the Heshette without resorting to out-and-out genocide. Addiction to soporific chemicals was being considered.' He shrugged. 'But the possibilities were never fully explored. After his wife's death, Devon returned the focus of his research to straightforward poisons and the like, for military application. He had a certain . . . zeal for such work.'

'Gases to blister the skin and cause blindness,' Rachel said.

Sypes nodded hesitantly.

'Powders to spoil Heshette water and cripple their children,' she added.

Now the old man seemed flustered. 'They . . .'

'Frightening weapons.'

'Certainly . . .'

'Unholy weapons.'

Dill scowled at her.

The Presbyter shifted uncomfortably. He remained silent for a long moment, and then met her gaze, and spoke sharply. '*Necessary* weapons.'

'Efficient,' she said coldly.

Sypes growled, 'I believe pain interests Devon more than efficacy of slaughter.'

Rachel's eyes narrowed on him. Unlike her brother and his officers, the Presbyter did not hide behind euphemisms. She realized that Sypes's animosity was not directed at her. Evidently the old man felt some responsibility for setting Devon loose on the Heshette.

Sypes returned his attention to Dill. 'Towards the end, he helped design our warships as a way to aid the deployment of poisons. The tribes were—'

'Debased?' Rachel ventured.

'Decimated,' Sypes snapped. He pulled a handkerchief from his sleeve and mopped his brow. 'We had no choice: we lived in wicked times.'

Rachel folded her arms. Were these times any less wicked? Was the guilt easier to live with than the threat from Deepgate's foes? 'So we prevailed,' she said.

Dill kept his back firmly towards Rachel. 'Did the archons always protect the temple?' he asked.

'Up until that battle they did,' Sypes said, still eyeing the assassin warily. 'Things are different now. Swords and symbols have less importance in the world today. Instead of swordsmanship, you are taught ceremony, codex law . . .'

And too little of that. What did the old man expect her to teach the angel? His duties as Soul Warden? Sanctum etiquette? The way he should lace up his boots? There were other things, Rachel decided, that Dill might find more interesting, or at least more enlightening.

Presbyter Sypes smiled weakly. '. . . and history, when you can bear it.'

'But if the tribes attacked us again . . .'

Rachel snorted. 'The battlefield is no place for you.' She realized too late how harsh her words sounded. *He wants to fight. God help him, he actually wants to go out there.* She bit her lip.

Sypes shot her a warning look. 'There is no danger of another attack. Our forces are too strong for the heathens. The tribes are scattered once more, the Heshette and their confounded shamans all but destroyed.' The old man looked weary now.

Dill lowered his eyes. 'Thank you, your Grace,' he murmured.

'You should go with Adept Hael now,' Sypes said. 'I'm sure she can show you how to use that sword of yours.'

Rachel nodded. *And more.*

In the corridor outside the schoolroom, Dill turned on her. 'Are you always so *rude*?'

For once, she didn't have a reply. If she had an apology for him, it was now firmly stuck in her throat.

He stormed off, the point of his blunt sword scuffing the floor.

'Wait.' Rachel followed.

He ignored her.

She grabbed his arm, suddenly angry again. 'How old are you?'

He glowered at her.

'You're sixteen, aren't you – a man now?'

'So?'

'So I'm going to teach you a lesson.'

'I don't need a lesson from you.' He tried to pull away, but she held him firmly. His wings shuddered. Cool air rushed over her face.

'I don't care what you think,' she said. 'I'm going to teach you anyway. Forget swordplay. Now you're a man, there's something far more important you need to learn.'

'What?' He was turning red again: eyes and face.

She stifled a grin. 'Just come with me.'

'Where?'

'Somewhere private.'

He was now so red she could almost feel heat radiating from him. He shook his head.

But Rachel led him away anyway, feeling deliciously cruel.

9

CROWDS AT SINNERS' WELL

Hundreds had gathered to watch the execution. They waited silent and motionless beneath the rusted mass of chains around the watchtower, but Mr Nettle sensed an urgency in the air that made the hairs rise on the back of his neck.

Low in the west, spears of sunlight punched through growing thunderheads. Scar Night was close.

Barraby's watchtower reached up through the chains – a fist of crumpled, fire-blackened battlements. They had bricked up the door and window two thousand years ago, but it was said that footsteps could still be heard within, or even the braying and cackling of demons.

Mr Nettle shoved his trolley forward under spans of chain, clipping shins and ankles as he went. Flies buzzed around him. He made his way around the killing stage to where the temple carts waited, piled high with offerings for Ulcis: worked iron, copper and wood, flowers and swords, each gift the finest sample of the giver's trade. After the execution, the carts would be brought back to the temple, and the gifts cast into the abyss.

A bloody waste.

Two temple regulars in half-plate stood guard over the

carts. At the sound of Mr Nettle's trolley, the nearest looked up. 'What you got there?' he rumbled. 'Iron?'

Mr Nettle grunted. 'Nothing for you.'

'These shows aren't free.'

'Didn't come here to watch no pilgrims bleed.'

'On your way then.'

Shoulders hunched, Mr Nettle bruised past. Nothing worse than soldiers with nothing to do. The man ought to be grateful he had a job, as there were fewer than nine hundred regulars still in Church employ, the bulk of those garrisoned in the river towns. Thousands more had been demoted to the rank of reservist. They received no pay: nothing to show from their days spent in the army except their weapons and armour, and they had to keep those clean and sharp for regular inspection, on pain of the Avulsior's displeasure. Deepgate's cavalry had been similarly reduced, the warhorses sold to merchants for cartwork, or to the Fleshmarket butchers and the Gluemen.

A murmur swept through the crowd, and Mr Nettle turned to see Ichin Samuel Tell, the Avulsior himself, climb the stairs to the killing stage. A hollow-faced man in black robes, his thin beard oiled and sharp as a spike, Ichin Samuel Tell was head of the Spine. He spoke quietly to one of the two temple guards present, who straightened, then nodded, and began to drag the first pilgrim forward.

The bark-skinned Heshette warrior did not struggle or even raise his head from his chest. His eyes were closed: evidently he was praying. The rest stood in a line behind him, wrists and ankles raw from their manacles. Half a dozen men, two women, one young boy sobbing, they all wore rags the colour of sand.

Mr Nettle quickened his pace, shoving his trolley on past a flock of perfumed nobles and matching the glare of their bodyguards with his own. Maybe this cull was right, and maybe it wasn't: he didn't much like to think about such things. But, darkness take him, he was not about to stay and watch it.

The Avulsior consulted a scroll before he turned to face the crowd and spoke out in a dead voice. 'This man is a heathen and a blasphemer.'

The crowd roared. 'Redemption!'

'So be it.' Ichin Tell then muttered blessings while the first temple guard opened the Sinners' Well – a shaft through the killing stage into the abyss below – ready to receive the body after the soul had been redeemed. The second guard tightened a noose around the pilgrim's neck, before he stooped to unwrap the hatchets and wire saws from their burlap covering. Redemption by rope alone, the Spine had long ago discovered, lacked enough flavour to satisfy the mob. Blood must be shed over Sinners' Well.

Blessed blood, but . . . Mr Nettle saw the same look in every face in the crowd: avid repulsion mixed with a hunger for the horrific and the grotesque. And more than that: the *need* to witness something dangerous, to feel that space between each heartbeat. Baiting hell to validate the abyss.

Two faces of the Church of Ulcis: Sypes with his angel, the Spine with their Sinners' Well. An uneasy balance of power between them, but for how long? Most folks thought Sypes had grown indolent, or even senile.

Only one angel in the temple now, and the old man's to blame for that. Should have made Gaine take another wife. No shortage of girls who would become martyrs. Mr Nettle glanced again at the eager faces around him, and grunted. *Or families who'd force their daughters into it for temple coin.*

Maybe Sypes wasn't senile after all.

The manacled Heshette lad was wailing now. Ichin Tell had put him at the end of the line, so the boy would have to watch the others before his own turn came.

The scrounger clenched his jaw and shouldered his way through the rest of the crowd, his fists painfully tight on the trolley handles. Behind him rope creaked, the onlookers cheered.

Back in the League Mr Nettle beat his boots along the walkway planks, shoved past passers-by, not caring how much the bridges swung or the gangplanks wobbled or who had to hold on for dear life. Boards threatened to snap under the weight of the trolley he pushed. His mourning robe flapped about him, torn and filthy and thick with blood. The League folk frowned at him, shunned him, but none said a word of protest until the Nine Ropes Bridge, where a bow-legged spinster screeched after him, 'Rude! You big pig!'

Mr Nettle swung round, ready to slap her, but seeing her all hunched over and clutching the street-rope made him feel like a lout. He scowled instead, and spat on the boards at his feet, but he eased up his progress a bit so the bridge shook less.

He would have slammed the front door if the doorframe hadn't been held together with catgut and about to fall apart. Once inside, he unloaded the iron, one bar at a time, and spread it out over the strongest joists in his hall floor. When this work was done he stormed down the hall, kicking empty bottles and oil barrels aside. The whole house shuddered and swayed, ropes creaking dangerously. He didn't care: the ropes would hold or they wouldn't. To hell with his luck. In the living room he lit a lamp, tore off his robe, and threw his cleaver hard at the wall, where it stuck. Juddering.

Mr Nettle unplugged a fresh bottle of whisky and slumped in his chair, grinding his teeth.

Angel. He pounded a fist on his knee. *Angel, angel, angel.* Why did folks call her that? This one wasn't god-fearing like the temple angel. She was a leech, an abomination, a wound in the city that, like the wounds she gave her own victims, never healed. Like the wounds she'd given Abigail.

He drank, spilling whisky over his chin.

Scar Night or not, the murdering, soul-thieving bitch was going to suffer. She had it coming. He would be out tonight watching for her. Out under the dark moon, him and her – alone but for the beggars, the madmen and the Spine. *Those Nightcrawlers,* who did they think they were, with their sanctified swords, crossbows and poisons? The beggars had no choice, the lunatics no mind to make one, but the Spine – if they were so damn good, then why was this demon still loose? Why was his Abigail dead? He looked at the cleaver buried in the wall. He didn't need Smith's crossbow. Foolish idea. Eight inches of steel and a strong arm to swing it, that's all it would take. He'd find a way to get close to her. He took another slug.

And just *one* spot of real luck; he'd need that. Just one little bit of luck. Just one. The bitch would spot him all right, if the stories about her were true. She'd see him from a league away. He'd make sure of it – and she'd hear his shouts. The whole damn city would. This would be a Scar Night when no one got any sleep. But he'd need to see her too, and that would be harder. His enemy hated the light.

He sat there for a long time, brooding. If he could get

her down from the roofs somehow, lay a trap for her. Maybe he could lie down somewhere, pretend to be drunk. No, she didn't relish whisky-blood or Glue-blood, so they said. Instead he would make like he was hurt or, better, a madman wandering the city singing fool's songs like they sometimes did. Mr Nettle pushed the thought away. His wife used to say he'd a singing voice like a sick boar.

Probably just frighten the bitch off.

Abigail's paintings still hung from the walls, dozens of them. Bright little squares of pulpboard: all her imagined gardens – the flowers and trees painted in red and yellow. He'd never managed to find green paint for her, just those two colours. She'd never minded. Red and yellow were her favourite colours, she'd said, and then she'd hugged him. He'd grumbled and shaken her off. Told her to go paint something.

A shuddering breath. Mr Nettle rubbed his eyes: red and yellow trees everywhere blurring.

Two more fingers of whisky. Somehow, the bottle was almost finished. His eyelids were heavy, his head nodding. Limbs feeling like pounded meat. He'd work out his trap for her after some sleep. He needed to be fresh and clear-headed to make his plans. Exhaustion drained the last of the blood from his muscles, and he sank further into the chair. He closed his eyes. He'd need to be clever, cunning. And sober. Wouldn't do to let Carnival come at him while he was drunk.

He was standing on a high tower, looking out across a pale city of delicate spires and slender bridges. A black moon rose swiftly into a sky the colour of bone. Streams of dark cloud boiled across the horizon, as though dragged along by ferocious gales. Black stars pierced the heavens.

The streets below were empty, and at first he was sure he was alone, the only person in the whole city, but then someone touched his hand.

Abigail stood next to him, her shroud fluttering in the wind. She looked up at him with sad eyes and clutched his hand in her cold grip.

Deep, she said.

Aye.

Then he saw the lights. Warmth seeped through shuttered windows. The houses were suddenly full of people. Distant sounds of song and laughter drifted up. But up here on the tower it was bitterly cold.

Ulcis's army, Abigail said, *they're waiting for heaven.*

He shrugged.

You still have a choice, she said. *Do you really think you can defeat her? If she doesn't take your soul for herself, she'll send it to hell.*

What's one hell compared to another? he said. *Lived in Deepgate all my life, haven't I, and never complained. The Maze can't be any worse.*

Iril is endless, she said.

His heart cramped at the thought of her there. He wanted to say at least they'd then be together, but he knew it was a lie. Everyone who wandered the Maze was alone, damned to walk for ever through corridors of blood, searching for their soul. He couldn't bear to look at her any more, so he fixed his gaze back on the sky. A dark shape moved across the heavens. Wings? He reached for his cleaver.

Don't, Abigail said.

Don't what? he asked, like he didn't know.

She squeezed his hand tighter. *Please, Da, don't do it.*

He shook her hand away. *Don't bother me*, he said. *Go away.* He'd almost said, *Go paint something* – and the pain in his heart tightened.

I'm scared, she said.

He wanted to hold her then, wrap her in his arms, but he couldn't. *It's not up to you*, was all he could think to reply.

Go home, Da.

To what?

A SECRET PLACE

Hidden among the temple spires, an ivy-strewn tower broke free from a nest of rooftops. Its once arched crown had crumbled, but gargoyles still squatted between the remaining fingers of stone; beasts with lion feet, wings and tusks. Lichen scarred their soft scowls, moss furred their wings, and tiny white flowers sprouted from cracks between their toes, but the gargoyles kept their endless watch undaunted.

Dill sat on a fallen keystone with his wings out-stretched, the sunset warm on his feathers, and watched finches lace the air around him.

'Is this it?' he said.

Rachel Hael was leaning against a gargoyle. 'You cast the same shadow as these.' She patted the head of the stone creature.

Dill glanced round at his own shadow and his eyes began to nip.

'Pink is embarrassed, right?'

He felt the colour deepen.

She exhaled deeply and looked past him, out beyond the stones and the temple spires. 'I haven't been up here since I was little. They used to let me wander all over the temple whenever father was here. This was always my favourite place.' She circled him slowly, brushing stone dust from the gargoyles' wings. 'It didn't seem so neglected then.' She tentatively reached out and touched his feathers. 'Can you fly with these?'

Dill drew in his wings. 'I'm not allowed to.'

'But you must have tried. I would have.'

'Codex law forbids it. We have airships to defend us now, poisons, assassins.' He stressed this last word.

If she noticed his emphasis, she didn't show it. 'Are they afraid you'll fly away?'

He shrugged. 'Rules are rules.'

'What a stupid thing to say.'

Dill bristled. Her fingers brushed his wings again, and he drew them in tighter. He had felt tempted to fly in the past, but the priests would have known. They *always* knew whenever he did something wrong. 'My eyes . . .' he began.

'Are pink,' she said.

'Green when I feel guilty or ashamed.'

'Like mine.'

Despite himself, he smiled at that. 'Do you always feel guilty about something?' His smile dissolved when he saw the expression on her face.

I don't want to know.

'I'm sorry,' she sighed. 'People say the Spine have no sense of humour, and they're right. I should try to act more human.' She crouched down beside him, seemingly unsure of what to say next.

Dill didn't know what to say either.

Deepgate murmured beyond the surrounding spires, its chains and houses disappearing under the shadows lengthening from the western rim. Distant shouts and faint scents came to them on the evening breeze: whiffs of coal fires and green gardens, the dry spice of the Deadsands beyond. A pall of smoke hung over the shipyards and the Scythe, where the warship Dill had seen earlier was edging closer to a docking spine, glittering gold. From this height, the airship seemed no bigger than Dill's thumb.

'She's come in for refuelling,' Rachel explained. 'Mark's leaving for Sandport with a trunk of orders for the outpost garrisons.' She grunted. 'He'll be long gone before the darkmoon rises.' Her gaze lifted to a thunderstorm building in the west. Suddenly she looked away, breathed a curse. 'Do me a favour,' she said.

'What?'

'Fly.'

'I can't.'

'You can.' She grabbed his jacket collar and yanked him to his feet. Suddenly she was pulling him to the edge of the tower, towards the drop.

Dill tried to resist, but she was surprisingly strong. 'No, I . . .' Open sky loomed closer. 'Wait.' He dug his heels in. 'Please, don't.' Desperately, he tried to pull away from her.

Rachel released him, eyeing him strangely. 'Did you think I was going to throw you over?'

'Weren't you?' Dill's face was flushed, his eyes now white.

She seemed genuinely shocked. 'My job is to oversee you, not kill you. I was going to get you to fly from this side of the circle to the other.' She peered over the parapet, then back at him. 'That's an idea though. If I pitched you over . . . they couldn't punish you for trying to save your own life.'

Dill recoiled.

She grabbed his hand, stopped him from backing away. 'Spine humour,' she said.

He stared at her.

'Forget it.' She hesitated, then pointed to a gargoyle opposite. 'Just fly from here to there.'

'Why?' he said.

She thought for a moment. 'Because they won't let you.'

'So you can report me?'

Her expression darkened. 'You think I'd do that? That I'm trying to trap you? It's only a short flight, for god's sake. I'm not asking you to build a shrine to Iril.'

'I'll be punished.'

'Only if you get caught. You can survive a whipping, can't you? You've had enough of those before, don't get all sanctimonious on me now. The Spine aren't going to be coming for your bones.'

Dill started. 'What?'

She sighed. 'I'm sorry, that wasn't fair. This latest husk . . . everyone's talking about the Soft Men again.'

'The Soft Men?'

A puzzled frown. 'You don't know about the Soft Men?'

He stared at his feet.

'Does nothing reach that tower of yours?'

When he didn't answer, she continued, 'According to the story, the Soft Men were three scientists who once made angelwine in secret. They preyed on drunks and beggars, bled them for their souls. But when they eventually took the elixir, it drove them insane. The Church found out and sent Spine out to kill them. But the assassins couldn't kill the three scientists. The angelwine had changed them. In the end the Spine cut out their bones and buried the men in the Deadsands. People say they're still there, still alive after hundreds of years, but unable to dig themselves free. Camel merchants still talk about hearing moans and cries from beneath the sands.' She paused. 'It's a myth, of course. Like the Chain Creeper, the Hag, or the Roped Widow. It's not meant to be taken seriously. At least—'

'The Roped Widow?'

'A woman from Chapelfunnel who . . .' She broke off. 'Forget it. I'm not telling you that one. It's too gruesome.'

Dill didn't think it important to mention that he'd never heard of the Chain Creeper or the Hag either. But he was now in even less of a mood to be bullied into an illicit flight. He avoided her eyes, glanced at the trapdoor leading back into the temple.

'The priests never come up here,' she said.

But they always know. Didn't she understand that?

Rachel said, 'They told me there's an elevator in the Hall of Angels.'

Dill glowered at her. 'I don't *need*—'

'Honestly, I didn't believe them. I had to see it for myself, so I spoke to one of the winch operators after the Sending, a temple guard named Snat. You know they throw dice to decide which floor to take you to?'

Dill felt his eyes darken, white to grey.

'Sometimes they leave you hanging there for a while, don't they?'

A darker grey.

'It's a game,' she said. 'How many times will you pull the bell cord? They bet on that.'

Darker still.

'Snat was up three doubles, he claimed, when I spoke to him.'

Even darker.

'Big man, he couldn't stop laughing. Says he's only five wins away from buying a new sword.'

Dill unfurled his wings.

'From here to there,' Rachel said. She took a step back, still clasping his hand.

The angel gave his wings a flap, and then another. And then, slowly, he began to beat them. He felt the substance of the air, felt the muscles in his shoulders and back clench when his wings descended. He quickened the beats, snapped his wings back, dragged them down, harder, and harder.

His ankles lifted.

Wisps of Rachel's hair blew back from her face. She let go of his hand.

And he flew.

He rose breathlessly, heart pounding, his whole body tingling. Cool air caressed the back of his neck, rushed over his face. His cheeks prickled and flushed. His wings swept up–down, again and again, like hands plunging through cold spring water. He sucked in a shivering breath and it tasted crystal. Open, endless sky turned from pink to red-gold where mountains of dark cloud mounded in the west. The Deadsands simmered under the horizon, crumpled with orange shadows.

Rachel shouted something below him.

He turned to see her. This shifting of weight unbalanced him and he panicked, groped for something to hold on to, found nothing. Suddenly he was falling, flailing. His shin struck a gargoyle's head and he rebounded, tumbled backwards, and hit the flagstones with a jolt that stole his breath.

She was by his side at once, a look of furious concern on her face. 'Are you hurt? Is anything broken?'

Dill fought for air. Iron bands seemed to tighten around his chest and his breathing came in shallow gasps. Shakily, he got up and patted dirt from his trousers. Loose feathers tumbled around him. A twist of pain in his shin. He winced, staggered, then sat down on the tower's battlements. 'I'm fine. I just . . .'

'Just what? What's wrong?'

His legs were trembling. 'My fault. I panicked, lost control.'

'How do you feel now?'

He rubbed his shin. The pain in his chest eased and he could breathe more easily. 'I feel . . . I don't know . . . stupid.' Blood trickled down his chin.

'You cut yourself.' Rachel pulled out a handkerchief and dabbed his lip.

Dill looked at his hands. Grazes covered his palms. As soon as he noticed them, they began to sting. 'I think I landed on my sword,' he said.

'Lucky you had some good hard steel to break your fall.'

He smiled weakly.

There was a softness in her expression he hadn't seen before. 'You flew,' she said. 'Sort of.'

Dill cringed, and moved to stand up. 'It's getting dark,' he said. 'I have to go now. They'll be locking down the spires soon. The windows, the trapdoors.'

Rachel nodded.

'Will I see you tomorrow?' He'd asked the question lightly, even selfishly; still hoping, deep down, that this flawed day had not been real, that Rachel would understand his need for a *real* overseer and relinquish her job to someone more appropriate. But he saw from the tensed muscles in her face, the faintest narrowing of her eyes, that the assassin had heard a different question.

'I hope so,' she said.

Fogwill shuffled along beside his master while the old priest limped closer to his desk. He had seen Sypes move more quickly, usually when the old man wasn't aware he was being observed or when some pressing issue forced him to forget his infirmity for a while, but Fogwill remained patient. The Codex pillars towered over them, the shelves in each crammed with books from floor to distant vaulted ceiling – their grubby leather spines locked safely behind filigree-gilt gratings. Construction of the thirty-first pillar was currently under way. Segments of cut sandstone and slabs of facing marble lay propped on beams around the base of the half-completed column, but there were no stonemasons at work on the wooden scaffolding.

Where are they? Two months of this, and I've yet to see a stone raised. Are we paying these masons by the hour?

They weaved through great stacks of parchment, freshly inked and ready for the Presbyter's perusal. Reports from the garrisons and the traders' guild, theses by Poison Kitchen chemists, accounts, literature, history, lists, lists . . . and more lists. How did Sypes cope with all this? No wonder he burned the poetry.

When they finally reached the desk, Sypes eased himself into his chair, turned to Fogwill and said, 'Tell me.'

'Your Grace?'

'You've been hovering, Fogwill. Not in itself unusual,

but you've been hovering silently, which is rare. Out with it.'

'This husk – this girl – apparently she was a Roper's daughter.'

'Yes, yes.' Sypes opened a drawer and pulled out a heavy ledger embossed with the words *Unaccounted Souls*. 'The theft must be recorded nevertheless. Her name?'

'We don't know. There was a scuffle, and the guards sent the father away. I'll have to make enquiries. He ought to be easy enough to trace. A death like this will be on the lips of everyone in the League.'

The Presbyter inked his quill and started writing. 'I wouldn't bother too much. Most of these records are incomplete.'

'Carnival wasn't responsible.'

The Presbyter didn't look up from his writing. 'There's only one soul-thief in this city, Adjunct.'

'With respect, your Grace, the corpse was fresh on the morning *before* Scar Night.'

'Obviously it has been kept on ice.'

'For a whole month? Where would a Roper get that much ice?'

'These people can be ingenious, Fogwill. It proves nothing.'

Then why are you avoiding my eye? Fogwill took a deep breath. 'The guard reported seeing bruises on her arm, above the elbow . . .'

Sypes did not look up.

'Implying that whoever bled her tied her down first. Carnival's husks are bruised only around the ankles, from the manacles.'

Sypes was now blotting the ink in his ledger.

'This murderer is far more capricious than the Leech,'

Fogwill continued. 'Carnival is at least consistent in her method of slaughter. One soul for herself on Scar Night, the others . . .' He left the remainder of his sentence unvoiced. 'But these other husks, they're turning up at all cycles of the moon, their blood removed cleanly. Someone *wants* them to be found. Someone is sending us a message.'

'What message would that be?'

Fogwill wrung his hands. 'Angelwine,' he said. 'Someone is trying to make angelwine – and they want us to know.'

'Angelwine?' Sypes snorted. 'Listen to yourself, Fogwill. Angelwine cannot be made.'

'But—'

Sypes raised a hand. 'Myths, legends . . . old wives' tales.'

Fogwill frowned. He cast a glance back at the books locked within the Codex pillars. Ten thousand old wives' tales. 'The commoners still believe in the Soft Men,' he said. 'If Devon—'

'That's enough.' Sypes's tone was stern. 'I won't have you barging in here making accusations, undermining the trust we've built up with the military over this –' he batted a hand – 'ludicrous warren gossip. Do you really dislike the man so much?'

There it was. In the seven months Fogwill had endured Sypes's dismissals of his suspicions, four additional husks to those normally expected had turned up. Four extra souls claimed, their blood leached out, yet Carnival, for all her voracity, took only one for herself on Scar Night. But how could he convince Sypes of Devon's guilt without telling him the precise truth?

Do I hate Devon enough to suffer your scorn?

When Fogwill had last complained about the fumes

from the Poison Kitchens wilting his dear mother's geraniums, everyone in the temple had subsequently fallen ill. Suspecting foul play, Fogwill had kicked up a terrible fuss. The bout of sickness following *that* complaint had given him slurry for a month, and when he'd finally recovered, it was only to discover that Devon had since begun recruiting labourers from the temple kitchens. What became of them was never investigated. That swine Fondelgrue didn't know and didn't care, and nor, it seemed, did anyone else.

Except, of course, Fogwill. He hesitated. 'I had a friend.'

Sypes lowered his head into his hands. 'I don't want to hear this, Fogwill.'

'A kitchen porter,' Fogwill said, feeling bolstered now that the words were out. 'Devon said he had four ships coming in that night, and needed strong lads to load supplies. He claims an ongoing shortage of menial labourers, and refuses to use soldiers or scholars. Says he hasn't the time or resources to screen every cleaner and packhorse himself.'

'His words?'

'Not *mine*.'

'Unpalatable but necessary work I'm sure, and the war has hard-pressed us all.' Sypes closed his ledger. 'When was this?'

'Six weeks ago.'

'And what happened to your . . . friend?'

'Disappeared. The Poisoner pleaded ignorance, of course. Said he must have . . . well, I don't really want to go into that. It wasn't civil. His comments, quite frankly, were obscene. He hates me, so he always . . .' Fogwill couldn't find the words for his frustration. 'He always . . .'

'No *body*?'

A wounded look.

'Truly I am sorry you lost your friend, Fogwill, but that's no reason to suspect foul play. He may simply have wandered off. I understand that's common for those employed in the Poison Kitchens. Nobody in their right mind wants to work there. Despite Devon's official title, he is not a wicked man.'

'A moot point. Look at the weapons he devises. The level of suffering he strives for is quite unnecessary.'

'Your opinion of his work is hardly relevant.'

'Let me put the Spine on it – just to observe him.'

'Impossible.'

'We could use Rachel Hael. She's still untempered, has connections within the military, we—'

'No. I want her watching Dill.'

'Then let me speak to the Roper,' he said, 'find out where and when his daughter died, perhaps examine the body.' He surprised himself as he said it. The League of Rope was not the safest place in Deepgate.

The Presbyter shook his head. 'Fogwill, we denied this girl our blessing. Her father will be hurt and grieving. I don't want you salting his wounds. My answer is no.'

Why are you blocking me? Fogwill shook his head in frustration. Was Sypes *hiding* something?

A light rain began to patter against the window behind the Presbyter's desk. The sunset was now a rip of gold between the horizon and the towering clouds. A storm was coming. It would be dark earlier than usual this Scar Night, and Fogwill suspected there would be more than one murderer at large.

PART TWO

MURDER

II

SCAR NIGHT

Rain fell in sheets, rattled catch-pans or gurgled through gutters and into the throats of cisterns. Chains steamed and dripped endlessly, shifted, groaned under the weight of waterlogged buildings – like dull iron voices in every part of Deepgate. The evening light dwindled and died, but no lamplighters appeared to brighten the streets, and soon the Temple districts, the Warrens and the League of Rope filled with darkness.

Twelve Spine assassins had gathered in Pickle Lane: gaunt-faced ghosts, unmoving, rain hissing off leather armour, knives, swords and crossbows within easy reach of their pale hands. Of all the twelve, only Rachel shivered. She had seen the others many times before, yet knew none of their names.

A dead-eyed man with a hook-shaped scar that curled around his nose addressed her. 'You will be bait.'

'Why me?'

'You have the capacity to enrage her.'

'And you don't?' Rachel snorted. 'Don't flatter yourself. Open your mouth and say anything, she'll be pissed, I guarantee.'

'Provoke her, Adept. Carnival will respond to you – to

your insults. You have a talent for applying such emotional
. . . devices. You will be bait.'

Conversations with the Spine were typically wooden.
These were the times Rachel was almost glad she'd been
spared the needles, the torture, the brutal tempering which
would cleanse an Adept and allow one to function without
the burden of emotion.

Almost glad.

'And, of course, you are expendable.' This came from
a rakish woman with full, bloodless lips. She stood beside
a slender girl who might have been her sister, a young
thing with deep bruises under her vacant eyes.

God, do I look like this? Like these ghouls? These husks?

Rachel glanced from one hollow stare to the next,
found nothing there. 'Expendable,' she muttered. 'Yes, I
forgot. Stupid of me. Thanks for that.'

The rakish woman nodded stiffly.

Insults, sarcasm, irony – all wasted on her peers.
Rachel would have slapped the woman if she'd thought it
would anger her, but where was the satisfaction in striking a brick wall? And yet Rachel envied her, envied them
all. Tempering offered an inner silence for which she
would not mourn the loss of her sense of self. 'Just get
out of my sight,' she snapped. 'I'll meet you at the
planetarium.'

The dead-eyed man said, 'You will not engage Carnival
until the trap has been sprung.'

'And if she attacks me before then?'

'Do nothing.'

'Nothing?'

'That is correct.'

Rachel clenched her fists. 'Whatever you say.'

The dead-eyed man tilted his head. 'Darkmoon is

rising.' At this unvoiced command, the Spine slipped away into the night, leaving Rachel alone.

Do nothing? She turned one way, then cursed and turned back again. *No, I'm going to find a tavern, bang on the bloody door until they let me in, then sit and have a drink like a normal person. Maybe meet a man . . . Maybe . . .*

Maybe it wasn't too late for her.

She stormed off into the rain. The streets were deserted, but she sensed a *tightening* in the air all around her. A thousand noises came from the dark homes: shutters checked; nails driven into wooden boards; doorjambs and iron grates secured; chains and padlocks locked and tested. Deepgate was tensing for battle.

'Coin for a pilgrim?' A filthy figure huddled in a doorway, long, greasy strands of hair and a food-crusted beard poking from under his hood. 'Sir, the darkmoon is coming, the rain is fresh and clean, and here we are alive. You have blood in your heart, and I have glue in mine. What a glorious thing! Spare me a coin.'

A Glueman? The skin beneath those rags would be yellow and viscid; the tongue thick and weeping chemicals. His blood . . . unusual. 'Sir?' she replied.

'Ah, good lady, then. Young by the sound of your voice, pretty too, yes, yes, now I hear the breasts, oh my, the thighs, the strain of some tight fabric – is it leather? How wicked. Yet without a man to walk at your side on this foul night. Has he thrown you out, or died and left you wandering dazed and broken by grief? Severed? My condolences, poor puppet.'

Rachel realized he was blind. *That's why he heard me pass.* 'All this from one word?'

'Six words now, kitten, each weighted with enough pain to crack cobbles. And longing too. So conflicted, confused, poor thing. I hear an undercurrent of desire. I hear . . .' He paused, as if listening, then lowered his voice. 'Oh, my shame, that's it. You are quite wet, aren't you, quite wet?' He began to rock backwards and forwards. 'Speak two words for me. Two words to know your soul. For me, please, please.'

The assassin sighed. 'Which two words?'

The beggar shifted closer in his rags, whispered, 'Dirty boy.'

'You want me to say . . . those words?'

'Say them, I beg you.'

'I will not.'

'Please,' he said. '*Please.*'

'Not a chance, beggar.'

'Puppet, have pity. Look how broken and lonely I am, how desperate. My brothers lost in rendered shipyard nets. My wife disappeared with a penniless reservist of dubious gender. My old Glue-father snatched away for throwing pebbles at the Avulsior. My mother—'

'All right.' He was going to rouse the whole neighbourhood. Sheepishly, Rachel swung a look around her to make sure no one else was nearby, then quickly muttered, 'Dirty boy.'

'Lust! Delight!' the beggar cried. 'Now come here, sit in my lap.'

Rachel frowned.

'I heard that frown.'

'What are you doing here anyway?'

'Sitting on the ground, begging.'

Rachel's lips quirked. 'Very clever,' she said. 'Can't you find somewhere safer to sit than this doorway? Your Glue-blood might protect your soul, but not your flesh. Nothing is certain tonight. You're still in danger.'

'Ah, but Carnival and I have an understanding.'

'And what would that be?'

'I don't kill her, and she doesn't kill me.'

'A fair deal.' The Spine Adept found herself smiling. 'You've spoken to her then?'

'I heard her wings above me and called out to her. She swooped low and gave me a gift.'

'A gift?'

'A fine gift! A haunch of lamb, sweetly cured and smothered in redberry sauce. Look here . . .' The Glue-man reached inside his rags, drew something out.

A dead rat, the head chewed down to the bone.

Rachel's smile withered. 'She gave you . . . this lamb?'

'On my soul, I swear it. And so you see I have nothing to fear.'

'You are . . . fortunate.' She reached into one of the pouches at her belt, pulled out a copper double, and carefully pressed it into his hand.

'Vengeful Ulcis bless your nights,' the beggar said, then more quietly, 'and spiteful Ayen bless your days.' He winked a sightless eye. 'Not that I pray to either of them. I am bound for hell.' He said this with pride. 'So I embrace Iril: there are wonderful benefits in being damned. The Maze is growing. I hear its stone passages creeping through the derelict places in the city. Sometimes I hear the thump of blood.' He pocketed the coin. 'This will buy wine for our feast. You must share it with me, I insist. There's meat for two, and with you so recently widowed, so supple, we might—'

'Thank you, no. I must get back to work before . . .' The words were out before she realized.

'*Work?*' He scrambled away from her, and hissed, 'Spine. Get away from me, bitch.'

Rachel just stood there, unmoving.

'Ichin Tell's whore,' the beggar growled, clutching his rat. 'I've nothing for you.'

Rachel wheeled, her heart stuttering.

'How many knives have you cleaned in your life, Nightcrawler?' the beggar cried. He was eating his trophy now. 'Scar Night is her night . . . The dark of the moon . . . One soul for the angel . . . Spine blood for Iril . . .' He giggled. 'But no souls to nourish the Maze. You gave them away already!'

The assassin strode away, leaving the beggar to his feast. She walked on for miles, losing herself among the dripping chains, and passed four taverns, but did no more than glance at their solid, bolted doors.

The rain had ceased at last, leaving the night air scrubbed and cool. Fresh wind from the north gusted and dragged rags of cloud across the stars. Snake-scale tenement roofs glistened faintly, but the streets between were dark. Every shutter had been drawn against the night, every brand smothered, and every gas lamp left unlit. Very few were abroad in the city now. No one but herself and those who hunted her.

With ragged wings folded tight against her back, she squatted on the roof of the Ivygarths watchtower, bracing herself against the chill wind, savouring its force. Tall stone falcons perched at each of the eight corners of the octagonal watchtower, blindly observing the city with grim determination. Carnival's face was expressionless. Her long black hair whipped around countless scars: scars across her cheeks and forehead, scars across her nose, her neck; scars beneath her moondark eyes. All of them knife cuts, except one.

These watchtowers had been built an age ago: Carnival could not remember when, only that there had been a time when the skyline was different. From their weather-bitten stones she judged them to be more than a thousand years old. Perhaps the Spine had once used them? A vague memory stirred in her, like poison bubbling over the lip of a cauldron.

Another watchtower . . . Crumpled battlements . . . Smoke . . . Blood.

Scars tightened around her heart. She almost cried out, drove her nails into the heels of her palms until the emotion passed and she was left breathless and trembling. Something terrible had once happened in Barraby's watch-tower, the place they now called Sinners' Well. She did not want to know what.

Other parts of Deepgate pained her too: Canner's Nook and the Thousand Brick House and the nets below Cha-pelfunnel Market. Fragments of old, old memories sur-faced whenever she drew near to these places; memories that drove her away from them, snarling and gasping. She had been in those places once, she supposed, and people had died.

The abyss was the worst. She had tried more than once to fly down into that darkness, but each time the rope scar around her neck constricted until she clawed for breath and thrashed back up towards the city. The abyss terrified her.

Now she surveyed the city patiently. Her hunger was building – she could feel it behind her eyes and in her veins – but it had not yet grown beyond her control. So she waited, searching for some overlooked weakness: a forgotten attic window; loose tiles on a storm-damaged roof; a smokeless chimney or an unlatched shutter thumping against its frame in the wind.

Nothing. There were no obvious openings, no easy ways into the houses. Her prey had long since learned to be thorough.

Carnival was pleased.

A mile to the west, she spied a shadow move. One of the Spine, a heavy crossbow in his arms, ran crouching across the rooftop of the Goat and Crab Inn in Merrygate, and ducked out of sight behind a chimney. The ninth assassin she'd seen tonight.

His leathers so much darker than the slates. Does he know? Is this poor camouflage deliberate?

Carnival gripped the ledge tighter as the scars on the back of her hands began to itch. Her heartbeats quickened; she moistened her lips. Part of her wanted to go after this assassin, *yearned* to go after him. She clamped her jaws together, and squeezed the ledge until her fingers hurt, then gasped. The hunger subsided.

A trap. It has to be.

She closed her eyes and listened for quiet sounds beneath the buffeting wind. Fragments of hushed conversations drifted up from the nearest homes.

'. . . no, both of them, sleeping . . .' A mother's voice, concerned for her children.

'. . . it's locked, I checked . . .' Another woman, older, speaking to her husband.

She heard the crackling of coals on a hearth, footsteps on a wooden floor and the clink of cutlery. She heard someone crying and the shreds of an argument.

And then she heard the drunk.

'Goddamn bitching murdering bitch!'

Her eyes snapped open, and she darted to the other side of the watchtower, heart racing, blood pounding behind her scars, making them throb.

'Filthy scar-faced whore.' He was down in the street a few blocks away, shouting up at the rooftops. A big man, staggering all over the place, swinging a cleaver at the shadows with one hand and waving a bottle at the air with the other. He lurched suddenly to one side and crashed into a pile of crates. For a few moments he lay there, grumbling incoherently, then he picked himself up and continued zigzagging along the street. 'Come out, you murdering bitch!' Twenty paces later he fell to his knees, retched, then slumped to one side and lay unmoving.

Rushes of sharp, delicious pain prickled over Carnival's skin. 'Shhh,' she said, placing a finger to her lips, 'I can hear you.' Her finger traced the gossamer lines around her mouth, then down across the raised white scars on her chin, before it lingered at the deep rope-mark around her neck. A thin smile stretched her lips.

Then she sprang from the watchtower and dived into the night.

Oberhammer's planetarium perched on the clock tower of his pinched grey mansion like a huge glass egg ready to topple to the lane below. Vines and brickleweed clutched its western curve and reached inside the brass skeleton, where facets had been smashed by thrown stones or decades of winter frost. But most of the panes were intact, painted black and dotted with pin-holes. On sunny days these holes had once been stars to viewers within. A platform with twelve comfortable chairs remained inside, at one time kept perpetually level, through some mechanical wizardry, while the globe revolved on its wheels and simulated heavens rolled overhead.

Seated now in one of the observation chairs, Rachel gazed up at real stars shining through the broken glass and imagined illusions.

The planetarium had never been operational in her lifetime. Church intolerance had seen Oberhammer die poor, another crank who'd killed himself after his fortune dwindled. Like most developing sciences, astronomy had been frowned upon – decades of study brought to the temple, locked away and forgotten. The masses need not be educated. Where was the merit in that when Ulcis waited beneath their feet, when Ulcis was everything? In another generation few would remember the scientist's name.

Now Oberhammer's mansion mouldered: windows boarded, its walls wrapped in chains to keep them from bursting under the weight of his folly above. The clock tower forever displayed thirteen minutes past nine, the time for rats and bats and lunatics, for every ghoul and demon conceived by Deepgate's commoners. The scientist had stopped the clock at that moment, retired quietly to his drawing room and opened his wrists with a razor – his valediction to the Church. Now the place was said to be haunted. Iril's doors had opened here, and when the Maze opens its doors something is always left behind. Rachel recalled the stories from her childhood: the Grey Mummer, the Chain Creeper, the Nunny Lady – ageless sinners who had escaped an overflowing hell to walk in the house below her.

For an angel, there were so many ways into the planetarium, and so many escape routes. It was an impossible place to set a trap, and this, of course, made it perfect.

Rachel rose from damp cushions, feeling moisture seep into her trousers. Both planetarium and mansion hoarded old rain. Water dripped and trickled through the dank sealed rooms below and softened the fabric of the house. Corridors wept. Staircases slumped and ticked. Paintings blistered under bowed ceilings. She shivered, imagining the Creeper working his way up through the house to find her, the Nunny Lady stalking its corridors with her hatpins.

A flourish of controls reached towards her over the front of the viewing platform: a mechanical arm of tarnished levers and heavily corroded wheels. The chains linking this to the great clockwork engines below had been removed, presumably by the workmen who had originally closed down Oberhammer's house, but Rachel tried turning one of the wheels anyway. It was immovable, welded with rust.

A howl, somewhere close to the south, made her tense. Carnival was nearby. Rachel fought the urge to leave her post, to scale the planetarium and find a vantage point where she could watch the angel's approach. But her job was here in this cage. The Spine would steer Carnival towards the trap. All Rachel had to do was attract her attention. She slumped back into the seat, loosened the straps around her throwing knives, and waited. Oberhammer's mansion grumbled beneath her, the way old houses do.

A series of sharp concussions woke Mr Nettle. He lifted his head, winced at the pain in his skull. There was a stink of whisky and dung smoke, and he was lying in an alley he didn't recognize. Cobbles, wet with starlight, shifted and blurred before him, then bled together into a sloping channel that lurched sharply to the left, fifty yards ahead. Tenements brooded on either side, like flint muscles straining against chains. He heaved himself upright and tried to figure out where the hell he was and what he was doing here.

Then he remembered.

He turned round just in time.

Carnival flew at him like a demon, wings wide, hair wild, eyes black with fury.

Mr Nettle raised his cleaver.

She grinned.

Then veered to the left as a score of crossbow bolts smashed to fragments on the cobbles between them.

Mr Nettle wheeled.

Spine, dozens of them, on the rooftops. 'Civilian,' a voice called down, 'get indoors immediately. If you do not have a residence in this district, temporary sanctuary may be granted in one of the Church boltholes or beggars' nooks for a fee of six doubles or one and a half pennies—'

'Piss off,' Mr Nettle yelled. He turned back to the angel.

Carnival was thrashing skywards through a second barrage of crossbow bolts. Several ripped through her wings, while others punched deep into her ancient, mould-patched leathers. She howled and headed away from the Church's assassins.

Mr Nettle ran after her.

The alley emerged into a broader lane he recognized at once. Narrow and undulating, Cage Wynd sank gradually from the old planetarium in Applecross, running south over a series of humped bridges towards the shipyards. Its name came from the grates and spikes bolted over every window and door. The chainmen and yard workers who lived here had access, more often than not, to more iron than the smithies did. Everyone but the Church knew they were at it: for every two tons of iron that went missing in Deepgate, one of them ended up here, smuggled in and put to use securing local homes from attack. Whole façades of heavy bars and plate and needle-sharp points – it felt like you were standing in the open jaws of a monster. With its sheer weight of metal defences, it was a wonder Cage Wynd hadn't dragged the whole district into the abyss years ago. Even the old planetarium surmounting the mansion at the top of the lane had been stripped of its cogs and support joists – the brass and steel recycled into makeshift armour for the many tenements below. Little more than brickleweed held the heavy globe to the clock tower's summit.

Mr Nettle heard a sudden hiss and looked up to see dark shapes swarm over the rooftops opposite. The Spine were loosing dozens of bolts at a spot higher up on his side of the street, just a short distance to the north. The scrounger grunted and set off again, crossing the lane to give him a better view of the assassins' target.

They appeared to be driving Carnival north, towards the planetarium. Bolts glanced off flint, iron plate and roof slates, thudded into exposed beams.

'Bitch!' Mr Nettle threw his arms wide.

She twisted in mid-air, diving towards him.

Again, the Spine crossbows forced her back, further up Cage Wynd towards the planetarium. They would harry her thus till dawn, keep her moving away from the Temple districts and the Warrens. Out of his reach.

The scrounger roared, and surged after her.

Whenever the Spine hurt Carnival she took vicious revenge. The more she was hurt, the worse her retribution became. Even the strongest barricades couldn't keep the angel out when she was injured. Ropers and beggars hated the Spine for it, for they suffered most. Their pulpboard shacks in the League might as well have been made of paper. Those who could afford it had cages made inside their homes, and locked themselves and their children in. Sometimes it kept them safe, most often not. Carnival had been known to rip through a dozen such homes on Scar Night, tearing whole buildings free of the chains which supported them.

The Spine were hurrying now, their silhouettes converging on the planetarium under a vast expanse of stars. They had stopped shooting.

'Here, whore!'

But Carnival ignored him. Something else had caught her attention – something inside the planetarium itself. Cursing, Mr Nettle studied the mansion below the huge brass globe. The old house stank of Iril. The clock tower had been bound in chains to keep the crumbling stone together; the windows had been boarded up, but there were wide gaps visible between the planks. Mr Nettle thought he saw movement within: oddly shaped figures capering. Some said the corridors inside the house moved and shifted, constantly forming new mazes to keep the things trapped there entertained.

He hesitated for a heartbeat before setting off again. When he reached the chains around the clock tower, he began to climb.

*

A silhouette suddenly covered the stars that were visible through one of the missing windows. Rachel leaned back in her chair, just enough to make it creak. The silhouette changed shape. Carnival had seen her, but didn't move yet to engage.

No wonder you suspect a trap. Those idiots have stopped shooting, now they've got you in position. And I'm supposed to sit here and do nothing.

So Rachel threw a knife, aimed to kill.

Carnival flinched away from it, snarling. But still she didn't attack.

Come on, you bitch, come get me. The assassin threw another knife, and another, but the angel avoided them as easily as if they were windblown leaves. *How can she even see them coming?* Rachel pursed her lips. *Provoke her, they said.*

'Hey, freak,' Rachel yelled out.

That did it. Carnival dived.

Rachel leapt forward and sideways just as the chair she'd been sitting in smashed to pieces behind her. She rolled across the observation platform, pulling another knife from her sleeve, and at that same moment heard the heavy crossbow hidden on the mansion roof below fire its payload.

A steel-mesh net engulfed the entire planetarium. The whole structure shuddered as the heavy bolas wrapped around its base.

The angel growled.

Now the scary part. I'm trapped here too. Rachel threw the knife, but heard it clatter against a strut in a different direction to the one she'd thrown it in. *Shit shit shit. Carnival* knocked *that knife aside. I may as well be lobbing balloons at her.* She got to her feet, drawing her sword.

In the starlit gloom the angel's wings loomed huge and black.

'You are to be sacrificed,' Carnival hissed.

'Not if I can help it.'

Carnival charged her, a blur of darkness. Rachel lunged out with her sword, felt it deflected. The angel merely pushed the blade aside with the heel of her hand, moved inside Rachel's reach. *Oh god.* Suddenly Rachel felt over-stretched, vulnerable to attack, and Carnival was reaching for her throat. Rachel flexed at the knees, dodged beneath her assailant's hand and, thereby unbalanced, had no option but to throw herself backwards. Carnival's own momentum shot her clear.

Pain jarred through Rachel's neck, a chair collapsing under her shoulders. She didn't have the luxury of worrying about that, for Carnival was moving again, turning, coming for her. *So fast!* The assassin rolled over, scrambled away, lashing her sword blindly behind her. *I'm fighting like some frightened recruit.* By luck, the clumsy manoeuvre bought her just enough time to regain her feet.

Glass burst inwards overhead. *What?* Rachel whirled round. For a crazy moment, it appeared to be raining again, though the sky above was cloudless. Water streamed through missing panes, dripped from the planetarium's skeleton struts. Carnival recoiled from the downpour, widening the gap between them. A drip splashed over Rachel's hand, greasy on her skin. Then she recognized the dense, chemical odour, and she realized what was happening.

Not water. This wasn't part of their plan. Not part of the plan they told me.

Evidently the angel had noticed the smell too. 'Sacrifice,' she said with a mocking grin.

Rachel heard the flame arrows before she saw them. The first struck the brickleweed growing on the west curve of wall, fizzled for an instant, then erupted. The second smashed through one of the constellation-etched facets in the eastern side of the globe and lodged inside the viewing platform. Flames blossomed around it. Half a dozen more arrows followed.

Lamp oil – they've drenched the place in it. They're going to burn us both alive.

In as many heartbeats as there had been arrows, Oberhammer's planetarium was ablaze.

'Spine,' Rachel snarled. 'The utter bastards.'

Carnival's eyes narrowed to slits; her scars seemed to turn blood-red in the firelight. She lashed her wings and lifted herself six feet above the platform. Flames reached out and plucked at the air around her.

Expendable? Rachel lowered her sword. *They weren't joking.*

Carnival, however, did not appear to share her fellow captive's resignation. Wreathed in flames, the angel's wings thundered in the centre of the globe. She paused to gather her strength, then threw herself against the southern curve of the planetarium.

Rachel felt the jolt through the floor as all of the facets on that side shattered. Glass exploded outwards, showered into the lane below. Metal groaned under the impact.

Oh shit, she's not going to . . . She can't . . . This globe must weigh a hundred tons.

Carnival drew back, tensed, and then slammed herself again against the inside surface of the globe.

A deep grinding sound. The planetarium tilted.

Flames had taken good hold of the viewing platform and were rising, crawling over the rows of chairs. Smoke hissed from their padding, rose in billowing columns to spread across the roof. Twists of it spiralled behind Carnival's outstretched wings. The heat forced Rachel back, closer to the southern edge. Hand over her mouth, she hopped down from the platform itself and clung to a curve of metal protruding between two broken facets. She pulled at the steel net, uselessly. The planetarium's brass skeleton gleamed in the firelight, sweated streams of green and red and gold.

Carnival pulled back again, whipping the flames around her into a frenzy. She closed her eyes, gave a roar, and plunged forward again.

Grrrrrrnnd.

Rachel heard stone crack and crumble below her. Metal grated, moaned, buckled. The brickleweed trembled, crackled, and then tore apart.

Oberhammer's folly toppled.

Mr Nettle was two-thirds of the way up the external wall of the clock tower when the fire started. He paused, breathless and uncertain, his boots wedged between the supporting chains and the mouldering wall. He'd seen the metal net go flying over the planetarium and the bolas wrap themselves around the pinions at its base. He'd cursed the Spine for that, now he cursed them for the fire. Three thousand years of battle and they manage to best Carnival *tonight*? The notion sat in his belly like poisoned meat. Stinking luck: the angel didn't deserve to die at the hands of the Spine. She deserved his cleaver in her skull. Maybe he could still get to her before the fire took firm hold. Wouldn't matter if he burned too, as long as he got one good swipe at her, left one deep scar behind for Abigail.

He looked down. Spine had gathered on the roofs on either side of the lane below, twenty or thirty of them, armed with crossbows. Cage Wynd dropped away between them, sank down the hill towards the cranes and airship pits in the yards.

The scrounger sucked in a breath through his teeth. He wasn't going to let the angel burn until he'd gotten his revenge. He turned to face the wall again, began hauling himself up faster.

Above him, the planetarium tilted. Stone and mortar crumbled, showered past. And then the whole, huge brass globe came loose.

Mr Nettle pressed himself tight against the wall. Heat slammed into him as the planetarium roared by. It struck the tenements below, smashing into eaves on both sides of the lane with a thunderous boom. Clouds of dust and burning embers bloomed skywards. But the globe itself was wider than the lane. It had lodged there, pinned by iron façades, eighty feet from the ground. Spine scrambled away from it as chimneys toppled. Landslides of slates slipped from roofs into the lane below.

Mr Nettle grinned. He had her now.

Then his grin faded.

Still blazing and wrapped in the tight steel net, Oberhammer's planetarium let loose a mighty groan and pitched forward, smashing roofs on either side and crumpling eaves and dislodging gutters, and began to roll along the top of Cage Wynd down toward the dockyards.

*

The impact knocked Rachel from her feet. Every facet in the globe exploded, and painted shards of glass rained down on her. She fell through a square gap between adjacent brass struts, one leg dangling through the enveloping steel mesh. Far below, glass tinkled on cobbles. Rachel winced as Carnival howled with pleasure.

Shit.

The fall could have killed her.

Fortunately the planetarium was wide enough to get trapped above Cage Wynd, the lane's iron-plated façades proving strong enough to support its weight. They had fallen only thirty feet from the summit of the clock tower. Rachel eased her leg out from the mesh of net and lay back gasping. The globe was still on fire, and she was still trapped inside it with Carnival. She had to get out of here.

Then came a groan like the cry of a wounded god.

The whole structure began to roll.

Shit shit shit shit.

The viewing platform, chairs ablaze, tipped vertically, then rose higher till it loomed overhead like a burning ceiling about to collapse. Still clinging tightly to the net, Rachel followed it up and over. She looked down to see Carnival hovering six feet above the brass curves now shifting beneath her. Through the smoke, Deepgate seemed to be tilting towards Rachel, rising up to fill her field of vision: crowded alleys of iron-clad tenements, a labyrinth of rain-soaked roofs, the temple . . .

The shipyards.

Cranes loomed over spaces large enough to swallow airships.

Shit shit shit shit shit shit.

Rachel held on grimly. The globe revolved over and down again, crunching through slates and eaves on either side. When the metal structure beneath her levelled, she pushed herself upright and hopped from strut to strut like a rat in a wheel.

Carnival thumped her chest. 'Come on.'

Rachel closed on the angel, brought down her blade, and swung it hard to the right, anticipating deflection. But Carnival merely backed away, laughing, making no effort to push inside the assassin's reach. Now Carnival was behind her.

Unable to stop moving but vulnerable at the rear, Rachel ran even faster. She scrambled up the inside of the planetarium, gripping the steel net, and lashed back savagely with her blade. The blow hissed an inch in front of Carnival's chin, halting the angel's attack. Rachel kicked out and caught her opponent in the belly, sending her tumbling away.

The flames! She must be almost blind in this light.

Oberhammer's folly blazed. Burning brickleweed whined and popped and whirled through the turbulent air. Rachel picked herself up and ran. The viewing platform surged overhead again and back down towards her. She leapt onto it, sprinted along an aisle between burning chairs, and jumped down off the other side. She grabbed the net and pulled at its steel links, using all of her weight. Her muscles bunched, strained, but the net would not break. She held on. The globe rolled faster, bumping and pitching as it hurtled down Cage Wynd.

Carnival had by now recovered. The scarred angel took to the air again, pounding her wings to keep well in the centre of the globe, away from its spinning walls. Rachel slipped beneath her, rose up on the other side. Debris rained down: pieces of a broken chair, burning leaves and snarls of branches. Flames whipped and roared. Deepgate reeled across the heavens – cobbles, gas lamps, brickwork, chains – while stars raced underfoot.

Picking up speed now.

The force of spin pushed Rachel back against the net. She arced once more under Carnival, up one side, overhead, back down. She struggled to move but the impetus held her firm. Her bones felt brittle, ready to snap. Faster and faster – now she was directly above the angel. The planetarium struck something solid, jumped, and for a heartbeat Rachel was weightless.

She kicked away from the net with every shred of strength she had left.

Carnival twisted to one side, but she wasn't quick enough. Rachel's sword clipped the angel's knee, drew blood, and then the assassin collided with net below. The globe smashed back into the eaves above Cage Wynd, lurched forward faster.

Carnival launched herself at the spot Rachel had occupied moments ago.

But the assassin was already above the angel again. She ripped a knife from her sleeve, threw it. The blade sank into Carnival's shoulder.

Carnival shrieked, tore the knife free. 'Spine,' she snarled, her voice murderous, 'I'm going to come for you when it's dark. Do you hear me? When it's dark, when I can see, I'll find you and rip your fucking heart out.'

Rachel doubted the angel would get the chance to act on this threat. The globe was spinning so fast she herself could hardly move. And it was getting faster: each jolt punched her in the ribs and whiplashed her neck. Her leathers were singed from the flames, her hands blistered; she smelled her hair burning. Loose embers and burning feathers whirled and looped and spun. One instant Carnival was there in front of her, the next below her, the next upside down. Rachel felt sick. She pulled at the net behind her, tore at it desperately, kicked it. Though of steel, the mesh was thin. Any Spine Adept could have broken it apart.

Any Adept except her.

She focused, heaved herself at the net, muscles screaming.

Nothing happened.

Rachel Hael collapsed against the net, making no effort to quieten her breathing. Carnival was somewhere overhead, or behind, or below. It didn't matter now: she couldn't fight her, couldn't stop her. She had never been ready to confront the angel. Now she never would be. There was nothing more she could do. Her tenure with the Spine ended here.

And then she spotted the hole.

In a facet four feet away, the steel mesh had been shredded and hung in tatters. She hadn't noticed it before because of the flames.

Half the net must have been ripped away. Gods below, I'm lucky I haven't already fallen through.

Teeth clenched, the assassin dragged herself towards the gap. She could hardly breathe. She seemed to be climbing and falling all at once, didn't know which way was down or up. Flames spun and howled and tore at her exposed hands and neck.

'I hear you,' Carnival growled.

Rachel caught a glimpse of the angel: eyes screwed shut, wings smouldering, face livid with scars. Then everything around her was smoke and fire.

With a final push, she heaved herself through the gap, through the severed net, and out into fresh air. Cobbles and stars swam before her. The city wheeled drunkenly, rings of light and darkness. She felt Carnival grab her foot, kicked out at her, and then she was free and falling.

One moment she was sinking towards the heavens, the next towards grey slate roofs. Blissful silence but for the rush of wind, and so cool, the air silken. Exhaustion enfolded her, wrapped soft arms around her body. Rachel closed her eyes.

She hit something solid, felt her hip jar, but distantly . . . heard a crash, then she was falling again. Another collision, then more falling. Finally she landed with a thump in something soft. Grit pattered against her face.

'Mother!' The shriek sounded as though it came from another world. 'Mother, a woman fell through the roof!'

'Don't be ridiculous.' Another voice, this one from even further away.

'She's here in my bed!'

'Get to sleep. I won't tell you again.'

The Spine assassin smiled, but didn't open her eyes. The second voice was right: she desperately needed to sleep. And nothing was going to wake her until the morning.

'Why are you doing this to me?' the girl pleaded.

Devon stopped reading to glance at her. The poor thing was a mess: her eyes were red and choked with tears, her face much paler now, almost translucent, but slick with sweat and veined with inky hair. She still wore her blue and white striped scullery apron, now sprayed red up one side from his struggle to get the needle in. Purple bruises bloomed darkly on the white of her arms where he had manacled her to the chair, and again on one wrist where he had inserted the tube that leached the blood from her.

'I am looking for god,' he said.

When the girl started crying again, Devon wondered whether he ought to administer more sedative. The bottle sat to one side of the scattered pages on his desk, the syringe still protruding from its top. The flask at her feet was almost two-thirds full of blood, so he decided against it. There was too much at stake and sedation would only extend the purification process further. He could not afford to spend any more time on this. The previous flasks were set to one side against the wall, deep red, and safely out of reach. He'd moved them there once she'd started kicking.

Beyond the heavy shutters, Scar Night's dark moon would be rising over the city, and Carnival would be out hunting vermin in the cold streets. But here in Devon's study it was bright and warm. Rich with waxed wood and oil wicks smoking behind crystal, it had been transformed into an ad hoc laboratory. Firelight played across a clutter of glass receptacles, the steel distillers, and the brass clamps and stands that crowded every surface. Several gilt-framed oil paintings of long-dead scientists leaned neglected against the wall beneath the scrawled charts that had replaced them.

Only one portrait remained hanging on the wall. It depicted an elegant woman, austere in expression but for her soft amber eyes and the trace of a smile on her lips. His beloved Elizabeth. Devon looked deeply into her painted eyes, as though for reassurance.

Will the Spine come for me? Are they stealing up the steps to my apartment even now, blades oiled, crossbows coiled and ready?

No. Someone powerful was protecting him. Someone had already provided him with the means to save himself.

Someone high up in the Church.

It had happened seven months ago, when Devon had returned to his apartments to find an innocuous package: the ramblings of one of his chemists, he'd presumed. He'd left it for a while and almost forgotten about it, but when finally he'd opened it he'd been shaken to the point of terror. In his hands he held the journal of the Soft Men: three scientists named as Mr Partridge, Mr Hightower and Mr Bloom. It contained pages and pages of notes, hundreds if not thousands of years old. In archaic script the pages outlined the process for making angelwine.

There were no clues as to who had delivered this package but Devon had developed his suspicions. The journal could only have come from one place. The Codex.

Had Presbyter Sypes delivered it?

Why?

The question plagued him endlessly but he felt it would be imprudent to confront Sypes directly. His mystery benefactor clearly wished to remain anonymous. And what if Devon was wrong? One misplaced word could end his own life. The Spine would not look kindly upon the reappearance of such a work.

He let his gaze drop from his late wife's portrait to the mantelpiece below it. An ornate clock ticked the moments away, lost amid a clutter of chemical bottles with handwritten labels and sugar-crust corks. Poisons for making angelwine.

Devon sniffed. A faint odour of sulphur hung in the air, pleasantly unpleasant.

He went back to the journal, tapping a pencil against the gold rim of his spectacles. Fluids leaked from the bandages covering his back. A little fresh blood had gathered in the crook of his arm: not much, but enough to add yet another stain to his already ripe tweed jacket. Devon didn't care; his looks were of no concern. Elizabeth had still loved him.

Cracked lips pursed while he considered the pages before him.

Blood contained energy: a life-force – or *soul* as the Church named it. This journal presented him with a method of extraction, a way to remove the spirit from the blood. To bottle it. *Flesh withers. Everything material is poison, everything we consume. Even the air we breathe destroys us. But when we nourish the body with spirit, feed the flesh with something ethereal . . .* Somewhere outside was a creature who did just that, and had done so for thousands of years.

'Please,' the girl said, 'stop this.'

Devon glanced again at the flask of her blood before returning his attention to his notes. He had followed the letting and purification processes to the letter, but as yet there had been no sign of the expected results. Was his transcription at fault? Had he overlooked something? Impossible. There had been no error, he felt sure, in his preparations or implementation of the technique. What else could be missing? Some extra manipulation that had not been recorded? It seemed unlikely. The journal, for all it infused mysticism with science, appeared to be complete. Devon chewed the end of his pencil. A pollutant in his materials? Hardly. He could not make them any more sterile. He'd even had the containers blessed. *For all the good that will do.* And he'd used minimal sedative in the blood itself.

Then what? What was he missing?

The girl's pleas came in fainter gasps. 'You're . . . killing me. Please . . . stop.'

'Hush, girl,' Devon said.

'My name is Lisa,' she wailed. The effort left her breathless.

Devon rolled the pencil between his fingers. A blister opened, leaving the wood slightly damp. Perhaps the souls were tainted, in some way damaged by the process of removal? Or was he failing to extract the entire soul? The Soft Men had taken thirteen souls before the elixir reached saturation point, when spirit could no longer be absorbed by the physical solution. Only then had the recipient flesh been able to absorb the angelwine. Devon had already harvested ten souls. After this girl he required two more. But as yet there was no sign of the elixir nearing saturation point, and this troubled him. Was a soul quantitative?

'My father is Duncan Fry, a lieutenant of the temple guard,' the girl panted. 'We have money. He's saved some, I know he has. He'll give it to you.'

Devon slammed his palm flat against the desk. 'Can't you see I'm working?' Pain clenched his chest and he grimaced. 'For what, *what*, do you wish to be saved? What are you hungry for? A life toiling under Fondelgrue's sweaty palm? The grunt of some malodorous swine as he stuffs you? The skin-stretched years spent raising his litter? Iril take you, girl, have some self-respect.'

She flinched, her head twisting away as far as the bonds allowed. Her lips trembled as she spoke. 'I'll . . . do anything you want. I'll give you anything you want.'

He tried to review his notes again, but it was useless. The girl's pleas had broken his train of thought. Instead, he got up from his desk and approached her, then crouched on the carpet before her chair. He lifted her face to his, forcing her to look at him, at the sores and seeping cracks.

'But that is exactly what you are doing,' he said with a crooked smile.

A fresh bout of sobbing took hold of her. Mucus ran from her nose on to his arm. Devon wiped it on her apron and put his arm around her shoulders. 'Life's greatest mystery,' he said, 'is death. What happens to us? Where do we go? You believe in god, don't you? You believe in the soul?'

The girl sniffed and nodded, raised her eyes to meet his.

'Then you must believe Ulcis can release it from the blood.' He smoothed back some of the hair from her face. 'If the soul truly exists, take comfort in knowing that yours will not be wasted.' His expression softened. 'I intend to put it to great use. One more plump little grape in a rare bottle of wine, eh?'

She wailed and shook her head, sending more hair tumbling over her face.

'Hush girl, you shouldn't worry. It will all be over soon.' He gave her his warmest smile, wincing inwardly at the pain it caused him, and cupped his hand to her cheek. Tears spilled over his fingers. He leaned closer, speaking gently. 'Shhh . . . You must try to be brave. I know we shun death: we lock it away, forget about it, until one day it rattles the box and reminds us it's there. For me that day arrived when my wife fell ill. But Elizabeth had an implacable beauty that no force of man or nature could have soured. Even at the end, when her skin wept like mine, she remained beautiful – to me.'

The girl's breathing was softer now. The clock on the mantel ticked steadily and the logs crackled in the hearth.

Devon rested her head against his chest and held her gently until she died.

'For the love of God, woman, for the sake of all that's sacred and good, will you not shut up?' Doctor Salt's hands gripped an imaginary neck.

Rosemary Salt stood with arms folded, blocking his escape from the parlour. 'I will not let you talk your way around this one, Arthur. I don't give a damn what night it is.'

'She'll hear you,' Arthur Salt hissed. 'And then none of this is going to make a blind bit of difference. Do you want to get us both killed?'

His wife didn't budge. 'Twelve bottles, Arthur? How in God's name did you get through twelve bottles in a month? You must have been permanently ratted.'

Doctor Salt threw out his arms, his fingers splayed. 'I didn't drink them all myself. I've had all these functions to attend lately – you know that – and I can't very well turn up without bringing some token.'

'Oh, bring a token, yes, fine. Next time bring your own thick skull full of Warrengrog, but don't you dare dip into my bonus from the distillery. That case was supposed to do us for a year. What about the bottle I'd promised my father, and the one for your brother for that matter?' Rosemary Salt stabbed a podgy finger at her husband. 'You think I don't know what's been going on? It's Jocelyn Wilton isn't it? You're always round there.'

Doctor Salt eased his reply through clenched teeth. 'Visiting Patrick. I can hardly refuse an invitation from the faculty head, can I? He needs someone to talk to. He's worried about Jocelyn's health, that's all.'

'Her health!' Rosemary cried. 'Next to you, she's the biggest drunk in Deepgate. You could pickle eggs with her blood.'

'Will you keep your voice down? Surely we can talk about this another time. I'll buy you some more bloody whisky.'

'You're damn right you'll—'

There was a rap at the door.

Rosemary Salt froze. She stood with her mouth open, her tongue sticking out absurdly. Doctor Salt looked past her, wide-eyed, into the hallway. 'It can't be *her*,' he breathed. 'I can't imagine she'd bother to—'

Several more knocks, urgent.

Doctor Salt swallowed. 'We don't have to answer it.'

His wife had a hand pressed to her mouth. 'What if it's not her?' she murmured through her fingers. 'It might be one of your patients. We can't leave them outside tonight.'

'We damn well can.'

'What if it's an emergency?'

'Sod it.'

They stared at each other for a long moment.

Three more knocks.

'I'll go and ask who it is,' Rosemary said. She lifted the lantern from the dresser and crept into the hall, before stealing a backward glance at him. 'We don't have to actually open the door.'

He followed her, nerves tense as twisted wire. The front door was bolted; no sounds beyond but the wind gusting outside. The wooden panels shook with the force of it.

'Who's there?' Rosemary asked.

A cold voice answered: 'It's Jocelyn. Let me in.'

Doctor Salt's muscles unravelled. Breathing a heavy sigh of relief, he moved towards the door.

'Wait.' His wife grabbed his arm, and glared at him. She whispered, 'What's that smell?'

'What smell?'

'Like burning hair, or—'

More knocking. 'Will you let me in, please?'

Rosemary turned back to the door. 'Jocelyn, what's wrong? You sound different.'

'Of course I sound different. I'm terrified.'

The voice did not sound terrified at all, but what did Doctor Salt know? Women were entirely unfathomable at the best of times, scared women more so. He shrugged off his wife's arm and moved again towards the door.

Rosemary Salt grabbed his sleeve and yanked him round to face her. Her eyes, bulging with silent protest, held his own while she spoke. 'Why are you here, Jocelyn? You know what night it is.'

'It's Patrick, he's suffered a fit.'

Doctor Salt reached for the door but his wife stopped him again. She mouthed the words, *We can't be sure.*

'Sod you,' the doctor said. 'I'm not leaving her out there a second longer.' He shoved his wife aside, snapped back the bolt, and threw open the door.

This was going to hurt. Dying always hurt. She never got used to it. She had ratcheted the chain taut, then locked it. The excess swung through a dim beam of starlight, creaking under the hook in the rafters. She had bound the doctor's mouth and hands, manacled his feet, and hung him upside down so that his head brushed the floorboards. His breath hissed through the corners of his mouth. His eyes were wild, bare chest wax-white and heaving, face bruised and swollen with blood and streaked with his tears. He twisted his feet against the manacles, dragged his shoulders up from the floor, then collapsed once more, his body swinging in and out of shadow.

Carnival would abandon the attic after it was done. The smell would bring Spine, and the blood would bring demons. She'd take the hook, ratchet and manacles to another dark, derelict place, but she'd leave the blood-soaked chains. Deepgate had no shortage of chains.

She steadied him and scraped a pan across the floor-boards, edging it under his torso. Her stomach was a fist. She looked at him for as long as she could bear.

His eyes flicked to the knife in her hand and away, silently screaming. The air through his nose came in quick, insistent rushes. She could have removed the gag: now he would do nothing but fight for breath.

She grabbed his wrist and felt him spasm. His bladder relaxed and urine ran down his chest, over his chin, and pattered into the pan. Carnival ignored it, knelt, cut once. Blood welled. He trembled as she brought her lips close to his skin.

Delicious warmth filled the attic. The chains creaked gently back and forward as she drank. Back and forth, slower, slower.

Carnival gradually relaxed. The ache of hunger melted away.

Darkness slid in thickly and filled the attic. It soaked into wood, into flesh and blood. Above her, the chain settled to silence. The man was still now. Only Carnival's throat moved.

When she was sated, she stood up and looked down at the dead man's wrist. She had bitten it more than she'd meant to, torn the skin badly around the original cut. She let his arm fall loose, scattering stars of blood across the floor.

Carnival wiped her mouth, and lifted her knife again. Blood dripped from the tip.

She waited, trembling.

And then she died.

And was reborn.

Pain ripped through her, so intense it seemed to scour her soul. She fell forward, gasping, on to her hands and knees, her own blood screaming in her ears. Her stomach buckled and heaved. She clenched her jaw and forced herself upright.

Her head felt light. For a long moment Carnival didn't know where or who she was, and then she saw the blood and remembered.

What have I done?

A different kind of pain then consumed her, one that clawed her from the inside, like the talons of an animal trying to break free. She wheeled round, took a few steps forward, then turned back, not knowing where to go. Her fingers made vague shapes over her chest.

Blood everywhere. Blood on her hands, on her clothes.

What have I done?

She hesitated, turned away, turned back. A wave of sickness rose within her.

She looked down at her thigh and stabbed the knife in deep. She felt it glance off her femur. Blood spewed over her leg. The pain was frightening, exquisite. She savoured it, clung to it, twisted the knife and opened the wound further. Fresh pain blossomed; she closed her eyes and drew a long, shuddering breath. She wrenched out the knife, dropped it, agony building, hammering through her

heart and bones. Her hands contorted like claws. Saliva –
or blood – dribbled down her chin. She sucked in another
rasping breath . . . and wailed.

Gradually, the pain ebbed.

The wound on her thigh was already healing, leaving
its scar.

The pan was spattered and filthy. The man's arm still
swung back and forward over it, dripping. Carnival pulled
a filthy square of linen from her pocket and wiped her lips,
her face and throat. She bunched the linen and rubbed it
over her hands. She threw the scrap away, then picked
briefly, uselessly, at her cracked nails. She licked her teeth,
and spat, then spat again. She tried to drag her fingers
through her hair, but couldn't – her hair was too matted
and tangled. For the first time, she noticed the smell:
blood swelling over the floorboards, foul and sweet. By
morning, the attic would be seething with flies.

Carnival turned away, trembling, fighting the urge to
retch. She stumbled a few steps, her feet slipping on the
wet planks. She crouched, feeling the dull throb of the
new scar on her thigh and the heavy pounding of her
heart, until she couldn't bear the sensations any longer.
She cried out, spun round, and lashed a foot at the dead
man's head. His neck snapped like dry wood.

Carnival crumpled to the floor again, her arms wrapped
tight about herself. Chains and hooks creaked above her
as she wept. Her body convulsed with great racking sobs
from the pit of her stomach. She grabbed the knife again,
lifted the blade and drove it back into her thigh, splitting
open her newly inflicted scar – again, again, again.

The wound hurt savagely, but not nearly enough.

12

✝HE POISON
KI✝CHENS

While Dill waited for Rachel Hael in the schoolroom, he struggled with a question.

How do I dismiss her?

After all, she had been given no choice in the matter either. Presbyter Sypes had thrust her upon him. An overseer who wasn't a proper scholar, a teacher who couldn't be bothered to teach him, a Spine Adept who encouraged him to break Church law – nothing about her made any sense. She was supposed to be teaching him about poisons today, but was, of course, late.

She was probably still in bed.

The Presbyter had crumpled over his desk before the dusty wall of books, and lay there snoring. A fly traced lazy circles around his head. There always seemed to be flies around the old man, and Dill had been watching this one for an hour. Occasionally it settled on the Presbyter's ink-stained fingers or mottled scalp, until he twitched and it buzzed away for another circuit. Shafts of sunlight lanced down from the high windows, seething with dust. Full of the scent of ink and beeswax, the air hung like syrup on Dill's wings.

The hand of the clock on the wall clunked a minute

further from nine, but seemed no closer to eleven. It felt like he'd been waiting here for days already.

Dill stared at the book he was supposed to be reading, *A Hierarchy of Bell Keepers*, and he sighed. All the books in the schoolroom were like this: dry, dense, and reassuringly dull. Each possessed an authoritative weight he found oddly comforting, and yet he hadn't been able to finish a sentence today.

Yesterday's illicit flight still plagued him. Why had she encouraged him to fly? Not just encouraged, *bullied*. Rachel Hael was a bully. She was a bad influence. She was complicating his life.

Where was she?

Clunk. The clock hand took another tiny step into the wide gulf before eleven. The fly droned past his head. Dill swiped, and missed. For a while, he stared blankly up at the windows and imagined himself flying past them in golden armour, setting off to some distant battle.

The next Sending was tomorrow and he wasn't looking forward to it. Borelock would still be furious with him. Had they repaired the archon yet, or would the pillar stand empty? Empty, but full of accusation: a monument to his incompetence, his failure, standing tall before the remaining ninety-eight archons, and before the Herald himself.

Sparks of pink nipped through Dill's eyes.

Rachel's arrival at the temple seemed to have triggered his bad luck. First the fallen archon, then the flight. He steered the path of his thoughts away before his eyes took firm hold of it. The Presbyter would never discover what had happened if they both kept quiet. He could put the incident behind him. A life of temple service stretched like a winding river before him. To navigate it without foundering meant following the currents of temple law. Dill nodded slowly to himself. When Presbyter Sypes woke up he would tell the old man he didn't need an overseer. He would insist. All for the best.

Plates of blue sky shone high in the schoolroom windows, cool and distant.

Where *was* she?

For Dill's introduction to the art of poisons, the assassin had arranged for Alexander Devon himself, the head of Military Science, to be present. Dill had met Devon once, years ago: a charming fellow with lively eyes and a warm smile despite his wounded skin. The Poisoner had smuggled him some sweets when the Presbyter wasn't looking: Glassberry drops that stained Dill's tongue purple for four days, and a bag of Acidsnaps that he had hidden on his balcony. The rooks had stolen those, whereupon he'd spent hours throwing stones at them until the priests had shrieked at him to stop. They claimed he'd broken a dozen windows, but it was more like eight.

The clock hand clunked again. Now it seemed to be moving backwards. Presbyter Sypes snorted, and mumbled something under his breath before settling back to his snoring.

Dill forced his attention back to his book.

The schoolroom door creaked open and Rachel peeked in. 'Come on. Don't wake him.' She beckoned, and disappeared behind the door.

Dill looked over at the Presbyter, then at the clock. He rose and followed her.

Paintings of past presbyters, grim in their black cassocks, lined the wood-panelled corridor. Without exception, the old priests glared down at him with disdain, as if they knew exactly what Dill was up to and didn't approve. Gasoliers hissed yellow tongues of flame that smelled like burning cherries.

'Devon's waiting for us,' she said, hurrying ahead.

Dill ran to catch up. 'Listen . . .'

'He's in the kitchen. Again.'

'I've been thinking—'

'He can't come here without whisking someone off to his vats. Annoys the Hell out of Fogwill.' She smiled. 'Which is the whole point. Devon could requisition staff from anywhere in Deepgate but, no, he harvests Fogwill's own little patch. Bet you the Adjunct is on his way. Defending all those strapping young men from the Poisoner's clutches. Gods below, I don't know which one of them is worse. At least with Fogwill they have some choice in the matter.'

Dill noticed bandages on Rachel's left hand. Her leathers had been burned across one side, her hair singed. She looked exhausted. 'What happened to you?' he asked.

She waved her hand. 'Same old stuff. Listen, when you meet Devon, don't drink anything he offers you. He's got a very strange sense of humour.' She looked thoughtful for a moment. 'You didn't drink from that little black phial I gave you, did you?'

'Uh, no. Rachel, I want to—'

'Good, don't. Did you read the book?'

'Well—'

'Here we are, come on, hurry.'

A steep staircase led down to the lower banquet hall, the Blue Hall, where the temple guard took their meals. Breakfast had finished at nine and swarms of white-suited waiters were clearing cutlery and crockery from long tables, mopping up, and stacking chairs against the wall. Adjunct Crumb was already there. The fat priest glistened among his staff, a mirage of robes and jewels directing the cleaning-up operation, getting in everyone's way.

'Adjunct,' Rachel greeted him as they approached.

The Adjunct flinched. 'You? Why are you here?'

'Meeting Devon.'

'Well, he isn't here. Look at this mess, look at the carpet. Why can't our temple guards eat with their mouths closed?' A waiter collecting platters of pie rinds and pigskin from a nearby table grabbed his attention. 'You, what are you doing? Don't pile them up like that, you're spilling food everywhere . . .'

'Trouble with the grunts, Fogwill?'

Dill wheeled to see Devon approaching from the kitchen, and his breath caught. *How can he still be alive?* The Poisoner's wounds had worsened since their last meeting. Dry blood crusted the corners of his eyes and mouth. Skin peeled and blistered in a dozen places. Dark stains bruised his tweed jacket. Hairless and grinning, his head looked like a parboiled skull gleefully fleeing Fondelgrue's kitchen before it had been fully cooked. A skinny kitchen porter followed him, peered at them over Devon's shoulders.

'I would lend you some of mine,' Devon said, 'but they refuse to wear the uniforms. Too tight, hellish chafing, I'm told. Apparently, you never seem to order them the correct size.'

'I've been looking for you.' Adjunct Crumb's eyes kept flitting between Devon and the porter. 'They told me you were recruiting staff again.'

'The tenth time this year,' Devon replied. 'For some

reason, they never remain in my service for long. Perhaps the work is too much for them.'

'What work is that exactly?'

Devon's grin widened. 'I shall not bore you with the details.'

Adjunct Crumb flushed. All of his jewels rustled. 'Would you care to join me for tea?' he asked. 'There are some small matters I'd like to discuss with you.'

Devon removed his spectacles and cleaned blood from them with a handkerchief from his waistcoat pocket. 'I should love to, but sadly I must decline. I have been summoned to perform a service for the Church.' He returned the spectacles to his nose and arched his eyebrows. 'By the Spine no less. Our new archon is to be instructed in the use of poisons. I thought a tour of our facility might prove enlightening.'

'Of course.'

A tour? Dill shot a look at Rachel, but she ignored his glance. She hadn't mentioned a tour. How could he possibly visit the Poison Kitchens? That meant he'd have to leave the temple, walk through the city, and Presbyter Sypes would never permit that. There had to be some mistake. He looked to Adjunct Crumb for help, but the fat priest's attention remained fixed on Devon.

'If you will excuse me,' Devon said, 'the sooner I get this fellow back to the lab, the sooner he can be put to some use.'

The Adjunct's flush appeared to deepen. 'What *use* would that be?'

Devon leaned closer and gave him a conspiratorial wink, a trickle of tawny fluid curling around the eye. 'If I told them beforehand, I would never get anyone to take the job.' He bowed. 'Please, excuse us.' He turned to Rachel and Dill. 'Shall we?'

'Just a moment,' Rachel said. She lifted a strip of pigskin from a platter on the nearest table, tore it into three, and then slipped a piece into each of the tubes at her belt. She plugged the tubes again quickly, and said, 'Well, it was going to waste.'

Dill thought he saw the bamboo containers shiver.

'How wonderfully gruesome,' Devon said.

They left the Blue Hall by way of a vaulted passageway that curved around the eastern side of the temple towards the Gatebridge. Arched, stained-glass windows in the outer wall threw colourful fans across the flagstones.

'Thank you for agreeing to this,' Rachel said to Devon.

'My pleasure,' he replied. 'We can't have our angel ignorant of Deepgate's grandest export.' Taut skin stretched and cracked around the corners of his mouth.

A side door led them to the exterior end of the Sanctum corridor. The broken archon, Dill noted, had not yet been repaired. The porter opened the temple doors for them, and they stepped out into sunlight.

For every step forward Dill took, he glanced back twice at the temple. Armies of gargoyles crowded its black walls. Spires, pinnacles and battlements rose to impossible heights. Glass sparkled like shattered rainbows. And, all around, the city curved upwards in a great bowl of stone and iron towards the abyss rim. The chains shimmered behind a veil of watery air. Dill kept his head low, ashamed of his frost-coloured eyes.

At the end of the bridge they veered right and plunged into the tangled lanes of Bridgeview. Here the city lapped the moat of chains around the temple itself and, finding no more space to expand out, swelled upwards. The very rich bunched themselves here: their townhouses brawled for space, abandoning the passages between them to permanent shadow. To allow the privileged to walk in sunlight, walkways had been constructed high above the lanes: slender platforms of silkwood swung leisurely from one balcony to the next, like bunting. The tallest and oldest dwellings overhung the temple moat, while those behind, as though jealous of this prime position, leaned in as close as the width of the walkways in some places. Often it seemed that a resident could reach out his hand to knock on his opposite neighbour's window.

'Doesn't your family own a house here?' Devon asked Rachel.

'West of here,' Rachel said. 'If it's still standing. I haven't been there in years.'

'I was sorry to hear about your father – a fine general. I apologize for missing the Sending.'

'I'm sure you must have been very busy.'

'Work never stops.'

For once Dill was thankful for the gloom: it suited his mood. Of them all, only the porter seemed to share his dismay at being outside. The young man walked along all hunched, hands stuffed in his pockets, while Devon strode ahead with alacrity, his head high, and Rachel kept pace with him as lithely as a cat. Dill shuffled behind them and peered sideways at everything from the corners of his white eyes.

Tiny windows pitted the walls – only servants occupied the lower levels, and glass was expensive. Most of them were thick with grime or cobwebs, but occasionally Dill caught glimpses of the rooms beyond: gold-striped wallpaper, musty furniture, glazed figurines on a shelf. He heard a woman singing from an open window, where the smell of freshly baked bread wafted out.

The crabs he bought,
On Sandport dock,
He paid for more than once.

He glanced in there, but saw nothing more than a flash of an apron tied around a broad waist. Rachel, Devon and the porter ploughed ahead, oblivious to such sights and sounds. More than once, Dill found himself racing to catch up.

Although the cobbles ran seamlessly between opposing buildings, the foundations beneath were supported by vast webs of chain. Deepgate's engineers had constructed Bridgeview to some ancient, unfathomable design. Wrapped in ironwork, the narrow lanes spread out in a sinuous, organic fashion, weaving and curving, dipping and rising, like burrows tunnelled by mice.

They left one alley and followed the course of another for some time, before tacking back to continue their progress in the same general direction. So far they hadn't encountered another soul, but just as Dill was beginning to believe he might remain undetected, a door flew open and a little boy burst from one of the houses and almost collided with him.

The lad, plump and pug-nosed, gawped at Dill. Dill gawped back until Rachel called out for him to hurry up. The boy yelped, and bolted back inside his home.

'Don't let it bother you.' Devon grinned ghoulishly. 'Happens to me all the time.'

When Dill next glanced over his shoulder, there were

two children following them. The boy had returned, joined now by a little girl with red shoes and red ribbons in her hair. On being observed, they squealed and scampered behind some steps, peering over them with wide eyes. Rachel gave Dill a resigned look.

'We'd better take the road through Gardenhowe,' Devon said. 'They're still clearing up the mess in Lilley.' He arched his eyebrows at Rachel. 'Oberhammer's planetarium came loose last night. They tell me it rolled a mile through Applecross before it hit a foundation chain and leapt clear over the Scythe.'

'I heard,' Rachel said.

'Punched a hole clean through a factory owner's house on the other side. Poor fellow was at the temple this morning, cursing the Spine to Iril and looking for compensation.'

'I'm sure the Spine will find him some other accommodation.'

To Dill, the Poisoner's laugh seemed forced.

Pink blossoms dabbed the trees in Gardenhowe and lay in soft clumps beneath them. The two children had now become four. They kept a safe distance behind, giggling, flapping their arms, and kicking up showers of petals. When Rachel tried to shoo them away, they scattered behind the nearest trees.

It was early afternoon as they neared the Scythe. Gardenhowe grew denser, the buildings more substantial. Ash darkened flint walls. Heavily corroded chains and girders divided the sky into blue triangles. The lane narrowed, rose, and came to an end at a high wall between two towering roundhouses. A faded sign bearing the crest of Deepgate's Department of Military Science sagged over a small red door.

'Here we are,' Devon said. 'And not before time.' He gestured behind them.

Dill looked over his shoulder. Eight children now stood in a line at the end of the lane, flapping their arms.

'They appear to be multiplying exponentially,' Devon said. 'At this rate the neighbourhood will be overrun by dusk.'

The door opened to reveal a wooden platform hemmed by a rusty balustrade. A rope bridge dipped steeply away from it and rose again to approach the main gates of the Poison Kitchens, some three hundred yards distant. The bridge spanned a section of open abyss that curved away on either side like a black river running through the city. Monstrous foundation chains spanned the yawning gap. Obese and soot-blackened, Deepgate's Department of Military Science looked like a giant cauldron in which great chimneys and iron funnels boiled and steamed. Smoke poured from its roof and flares of burning gas erupted with distant roars. Gantries bristled underneath the structure, serving as airship docks. Dill spied the shadowy hulk of a warship tethered to one of them and edged closer to the balustrade to get a better look. The porter sank further into his pockets.

The rope bridge wobbled when they stepped onto it.

'Is it safe?' Dill asked.

'Certainly,' Devon replied, 'provided you do not fall off.'

They soon descended below the level of the buildings rising on either side of the gap. A confusion of lead pipes connected the factories and dwellings to the city's water and sewerage systems. Nets hung everywhere: billows of hemp, dappled by shafts of daylight from above, sagged beneath the adjacent streets. These nets kept discarded rubbish and the occasional drunk or attempted suicide from plunging into the abyss. Ulcis did not welcome the living into his realm, no matter how briefly they remained alive there.

'The domain of scroungers,' Devon said, noting Dill's interest. 'You would be amazed at the sort of things they dredge from those nets.'

Rachel was studying one of the foundation chains extending above the rope bridge. 'Callis forged those chains?' she asked.

'Among other things.' Devon glanced at Dill, a twinkle of amusement in his eyes. 'The machine he used to quarry the ores and then fuse these links still lies at the base of Blackthrone. Our warships rediscovered it some time ago. Priests call it *The Tooth of God*.' He snorted. 'You should hear their claims. The relic is waiting, watching over us, as though it possessed consciousness, sentience even.'

'You don't agree?' Rachel asked.

'More cogs than cognisance I think. Ancient, yes, and vast, as large as our facility here, but it is mechanical nevertheless. It once harvested metals from Blackthrone and brought them across the Deadsands to Deepgate. Now it sits derelict in the shadow of the mountain. The Heshette use it like a citadel. Can you imagine? A whole community of people, living and rutting inside like animals?'

'So you don't believe Blackthrone was once Ulcis's throne?'

'The mountain is unique, certainly. The ores it disgorged are singular, its very presence poisons the land around it for hundreds of leagues, but if it was ever a throne, then it was a damned uncomfortable one.' He paused. 'But I do believe part of the legend to be true: that Blackthrone fell from the sky.'

Rachel looked surprised.

'Why not? You have seen falling stars – I believe the mountain was such an object.'

'What about the Tooth?' Rachel asked. 'Could that have fallen too?'

'Now that,' Devon replied, 'is more of a mystery. The Church remains curiously reticent on the subject. I believe they wish us to forget about that machine altogether. Odd, don't you think?'

Sounds of both furnace and machinery grew louder as they approached the Poison Kitchens. The air was pungent, heavy with drifting ash from the funnels. A foul-smelling residue coated the planks underfoot: they kicked up clouds of it with each step. By the time they reached the main gates, Dill's feathers and clothing were filthy.

The Poisoner himself seemed undisturbed by the noxious air. He waved them through into a lobby which might once have been opulent, but had now been defiled by ash. Black footprints ruined its richly patterned carpet, aether lamps popped and fizzed on the walls.

Devon drew the kitchen porter aside, and opened the nearest side door for him. 'Down there, left, one hundred yards, left again, right, third door on the right, up the stairs, second landing, fourth door on the left. Supervisor's office. He will find you a mask and show you what to do. Got all that?'

The young man looked blankly at him.

'Shoo,' Devon said.

The porter hurried off.

'I do hope he lasts longer than the others,' Devon said. 'It takes an age to properly screen workers, and I have barely enough to man the forges as it is.' He led Rachel and Dill on through a different door.

Heat and noise engulfed them, and Dill's eyes widened. The chamber stretched into the far distance. Dozens of huge, barrel-shaped furnaces squatted in rows along the factory floor. Workers fed the fiery mouths from a line of coal hoppers that inched along rails running down the centre. Pipes as ample as temple spires rose from these furnaces and disappeared into a canopy of girders and catwalks high above. Narrower pipes snaked and branched around them like creepers, and valves blew jets of flame at intervals. Steam hissed and the furnaces roared, smothering the shouts of the workers, the constant scrape of shovels and the persistent slow rumble of the iron wheels of the coal train. Dill felt the floor shuddering beneath his feet.

'Fuel,' Devon shouted.

They followed the line of hoppers through the chamber. Sweaty, soot-faced men greeted the Poisoner with nods and the occasional grin, pausing further in their work when they noticed the angel. At each furnace door they passed, heat blasted Dill's face and wings, snatching loose feathers and sending them spiralling into the heights.

Through a door at the far end of the furnace chamber they entered the relative quiet of an equipment locker. Dill's ears still rang from the fuel room, and his skin felt raw.

Devon snatched a couple of strange-looking masks from a row of hooks on the wall and handed one each to Dill and Rachel. Tubes dangled like squid tentacles from their mouthpieces.

'To protect your lungs,' he explained, pulling on his own mask. 'We proceed through dangerous rooms now.'

The next room was half the size of the furnace chamber. Its floor dropped away immediately and they rattled along a catwalk above lines of open vats. Milky liquids bubbled within, curls of steam rose towards them. Squid-masked technicians in grease-stained smocks adjusted valves, inspected dials, while others stood on ladders to remove scum from the boiling liquids with their oar-like poles.

Devon paused to inspect the work going on below. 'Acids, alkalis and ammoniates,' he said, his voice slightly muffled by the mask.

'Weapons?' Rachel asked.

'The most basic. These components will burn lungs, skin,' Devon glanced at Dill, 'feathers.'

Dill eyed the contents of the vats through the scratched glass visor of his mask. The air he sucked through the fibrous tubes tasted sour and vaguely metallic. His legs felt unsteady on the rickety catwalk. It would be very easy for someone to lean over too far.

At the door to the next chamber, Devon paused briefly. 'Research room,' he said. 'Do not remove your masks, and please touch nothing.'

They entered a laboratory, smaller again in size than the previous rooms. Glass beakers and tubes crowded wide workspaces. The chemists here wore smocks as filthy and spattered as butchers' aprons. Engrossed in their work, they ignored the visitors, as they poured and measured, mixed solutions, and scribbled occasional notes in huge ledgers. Racks and racks of stoppered glass tubes filled an enormous wooden carousel positioned in the middle of the room.

Dill approached the carousel and noticed each tube held a few drops of red liquid.

'What are those?' Rachel asked, a moment later.

'Diseases,' Devon said.

Dill held his breath.

'Some induce fevers, rashes, influenza, jaundice, anaemia. We have solutions here to encourage infection, weaken bones, elicit welts and sores, or even precipitate sterility and hereditary mutation.'

'Sterility?' Rachel stood wide-eyed. 'Hereditary mutation?'

'This is still a new science, and mostly we use poisons. But some derivatives of what you see here have already been tested in the field.'

'Against the tribes?'

'The idea appals you?'

Her gaze moved across the racks. 'I knew about the poisons, but these diseases ... they seem cruel, unnatural.'

Devon laughed behind his mask. 'Nature is cruel – and are we not part of nature? Nothing we do can ever be unnatural, because our will is a product of nature, and thus natural.' He turned to Dill. 'What do *you* think? Do you object to the use of our knowledge in this manner?'

Dill said, 'I think that some things are best left to god.'

The Poisoner clapped his hands together. 'Of course,' he said, tipping his head. 'You are quite correct. Now, please, let me show you the core of my work.' He pulled some gloves from a drawer, similar to those the workers wore, and handed them to Rachel and Dill. 'If you would be kind enough to put these on, we will proceed to the poison rooms.'

The first room was not what Dill had expected. The smell of brine hung heavy in the air. Pale green light rippled across the floor from banks of aquariums set into the walls. Devon removed his breathing mask, as did Dill and Rachel after a moment's hesitation. They wandered before the tanks and gaped at the monsters behind the glass.

'The most deadly poisons,' Devon explained, 'are harvested from those creatures found in the seas of this world.' He stopped before a tank. Yellow and green banded serpents writhed within. 'Tap snakes, from the Ordan reef. One bite contains enough poison to kill half a hundred men.'

Dill watched the sea snakes wiggle back and forth above the sand. Unconsciously, he pressed a gloved hand against the glass. One of the snakes struck at it and he snatched his hand away.

'Here,' Devon pointed to the next tank, 'among this coral, if you look closely you might be able to discern a parrot octopus. He is watching us now.'

A large black eye, ringed with blue, peered unblinking from the coral.

'More intelligent than cats,' Devon said, 'and able to survive outside water for a short time. We caught this fellow making nightly excursions around the room, until we sealed him in. He had a taste for the hammer shrimp over in the feeding tanks.'

Dill glanced nervously at the floor around him, wondering what else might have escaped its tank.

They walked the length of the chamber with Devon stopping at each aquarium to explain its contents. Dill learned of the vicious blisters caused by creepfish spines, and the slow, painful deaths endured by fishermen bitten by widow eels caught in their nets. He marvelled at the pale, globular jellyfish with their ghostly showers of tendrils. There were huge slugs with mottled blue skin, various anemones, brightly coloured gelatinous things of indeterminable shape, and armoured creatures like centipedes bristling with spikes.

At the end of the room, Devon lifted a curtain and they ducked through to yet another area packed with glass tanks. This chamber was brighter, but smelt musty; the air choked with sawdust. Pillars of sunlight dropped from high skylights, revealing dark shapes hunched behind the glass. In one corner of the room, a shelved alcove held bolts of fine cloth, one of which lay spread over a nearby table.

'Arthropods,' Devon explained. 'Most of the poisons we extract here are less potent. However, they have their uses. A lingering death is sometimes more desirable than a swift one.' He glanced at Rachel. 'The incident with Captain Mooreshank on the Towerbrack Peninsula springs to mind.'

She nodded.

Devon went on. 'We are just learning to infuse spider poison into the silk of its cousin. Garments made from such fine material are beautiful but deadly.' He smiled. 'Profitable too, we hope.'

Another curtain led to the third poison room. Damp heat fell on them as they pushed through to a vast conservatory. Green light filtered down through towering ferns, and a light mist sprayed from pipes in the roof. The air was dense with rich, tropical smells.

'Flora,' Devon said. 'Touch nothing. Some thorns can pierce the protective gloves. Be careful of your wings.'

They edged through lilting orchids with waxy leaves, past creepers twisted around weeping trunks, vines spotted with pale flowers which hung like rope. Sweat trickled down Dill's neck.

'These plants come from the Fringes: Loom and the Volcanic Isles beyond the Yellow Sea,' Devon said. 'Some very rare specimens among them – very fragile.'

Something rustled amid a clump of leaves. Rachel reached for her sword, but Devon stopped her. 'A catrap,' he said. 'The plant senses our presence. They entice their prey near by shaking, to simulate the sound of a small creature moving through the undergrowth. Poisonous thorns around the base of the plant ensure that whatever predators come to inspect the noise do not leave. Dead creatures enrich the soil around catraps, and the smell of rotting flesh attracts yet more prey.'

'I've never heard of such a thing,' Rachel murmured.

Devon tilted his head and regarded her through the top of his spectacles. 'In nature, deceit is a common method of ensuring one's food supply.'

Beyond this conservatory, he led them into the cool interior of a high thin tower. A spiral of narrow steps protruded from the circular walls, rising to dizzy heights. Shelves cut into the stone followed the stairway upwards, each one packed with hundreds of murky bottles. To one side, a huge workbench brimmed with beakers, tubes and flasks of coloured liquids and powders. There were also mortars and pestles of various sizes, brass burners and clamps beside a stack of metal cages in which rats scratched and scampered.

'Here we combine and test our poisons,' Devon said.

'You use rats?' Rachel asked.

'Initially.'

Dill's eyes followed the staircase up and up. It seemed to have no end.

'How many poisons are kept here?' he asked.

'Why, all of them,' Devon replied, dismissing the

shelves with a wave of his hand. 'Now, my friends, I must conclude our tour, sadly. I have an important experiment to finish this afternoon.' He gave them a warm, red smile. 'But please, do not hesitate to return, should you wish to gain more intimate knowledge of my work.'

Some time later, Dill and Rachel sat on the platform overlooking the Poison Kitchens and watched the ash from its chimneys drift into the abyss. A faint, rhythmic clanking sounded over the divide. Rachel's legs dangled between the bars of the balustrade. She peeled large flakes of rust from its iron rails and sent them spinning into darkness. 'What do *you* think is down there?' she asked suddenly.

Dill gave her a puzzled look. 'Ulcis of course,' he said. 'The city of Deep.'

'You really believe that? Everything they say? The city of the dead? The Ziggurat? The Garden of Bones? An army waiting to reclaim heaven?'

'Don't you?'

'I used to.' She brushed a finger over the flaking ironwork. 'Now I'm not sure. Everyone seems to be waiting for something better, even if that means waiting to die. But that doesn't mean there *is* something better, does it?' She looked at him, then quickly away. 'The Spine act as the hand of god, but I don't think even tempered assassins can hear Him. The closer I get to them, my colleagues, the more uncomfortable that makes me.'

Dill swallowed. She hadn't even been properly trained? 'You didn't let them temper you?' he ventured.

She let out a long breath. 'God, don't you think I want them to? To be free of all this. It's like a physical pain.'

She pressed the heels of her palms against her forehead. 'But it's not up to me. My brother is head of the house now, and he won't sign the consent document. He wants to punish me because I can do what he never could. I can kill, up close, and live with it. Stick a knife in a man and watch him bleed.' She grunted. 'In a way that makes me even more of a monster than Carnival. They say she wounds herself after every kill she makes, hurts herself to ease her suffering.'

Dill frowned. 'Wouldn't that cause even more pain?'

'There are different kinds of pain,' Rachel said. 'Sometimes one can blot out the other.' She scowled at her bandaged hands. 'All my scars were given to me by others. I don't need to inflict my own, never have. So maybe I don't deserve to be tempered. We yearn for the needles because it's death without the fear of death.' She laughed: a hard, brittle sound. 'The Spine should be hunting me instead of her.'

Dill studied Rachel's bandages and felt uneasy. 'You fought her?'

Rachel shrugged.

'Where did she come from?'

'Straight from Iril, if you believe the priests. A demon sent to harvest souls for the Maze. Others claim she came from out of the abyss with Callis and the Ninety-Nine. When the angelwine finally wore off, she began killing to sustain herself.' She stared hard into the abyss. 'I used to believe those stories about her were exaggerated, I believed that Carnival killed but she didn't really take souls. I thought she was as mortal as you or me. But I've seen too many husks left after Scar Nights, and I've seen the way she moves: she's too fast, too strong. And her eyes . . . so much rage, hunger. Always black.'

'Can you stop her?'

'I doubt it.'

'Then why do you try?'

A bitter smile. 'I'm Spine.'

They were silent for a while. The flames above the Poison Kitchens roared intermittently, blazing brightly then diminishing. Fat gouts of smoke rose from the funnels, swelled and fell again as ash. Beyond, the sun was sinking towards the abyss rim. Through the haze of pollution, the sky looked bruised and sick.

Rachel detached another sliver of rust and threw it into the darkness. 'There have been expeditions, you know, down there.'

That surprised him. 'Into the abyss?'

'Secret ones. Unknown to the temple. People have stolen airships, made balloons, strange winged things, all sorts of contraptions. Gone down there.'

'What happened to them?'

'They never returned.'

Dill stared into the depths. Even here in the evening light, the darkness of the abyss unnerved him. Rachel continued to throw flakes of rust, watching them dance below like tiny leaves. Across the gulf facing them a siren sounded and a warship disengaged from its refuelling berth beneath the Poison Kitchens. It floated gently down, then nudged its way out of the shadows and into the wide gap, tugged by guide-ropes. He heard the distant sound of pulleys cranking and the shouts of dockhands. Then the great ship broke free and burned skywards with a deep roar, climbing steadily until it rose above the cranes and chains and pillars of smoke.

They watched the ship turn slowly, black against the sunset.

Rachel stood up and leaned out over the balustrade. Iron creaked under her weight. 'If I fell over would you catch me?' she asked. She lifted her feet, supporting her weight on her stomach.

Dill got to his feet. 'I can't fly very well.'

'*Would* you try to save me?' She leaned further out. The banister creaked again.

He took a step towards her. 'Please, it doesn't look safe.'

'Would you try, even if you knew you couldn't pull me back?'

'Yes.'

Rachel leaned back and put her feet on the ground, but she didn't turn to face him. 'Maybe you would,' she said softly.

13

THE LEAGUE OF ROPE

A single brand lent a ruddy glow to the rusted tin slopes and bleached wood of the League shantytown. Shacks hung skewed in their cradles, linked to the walkway by thin planks. Beyond the ropes, the lights of Deepgate dipped away and rose again far in the distance, broken only by the temple's silhouette.

Fogwill watched reflections curl over Captain Clay's black armour as the temple guard looked around in distaste. Boards creaked under the big man's armoured boots. 'Are you sure this is it?' he asked.

Clay wrinkled his nose and sniffed the air. 'Smells like it.'

Fogwill didn't need to be told. Something was rotting nearby. A dead rat perhaps? And Clay had insisted that he come out here without perfume. His cassock retained a trace, as the captain had pointed out with a scowl, but not enough to mask this unholy stench. 'Then you'd better go,' he said. 'I'll manage from here.'

The captain of the temple guard grunted. 'Adjunct, this is the Dens.' He leaned over his pike. 'This scrounger near strangled one of my men. Dirty great big ugly vicious bastard. Wouldn't trust him as much as a bag of cats.'

'Nevertheless, I shall speak with him alone. Your presence would anger him, *more*. I can find my own way back.' Fogwill suddenly realized what he'd said, and rather wished he hadn't said it.

Clay hesitated, then turned, shaking his head, and marched back along the boards, with his pike held sideways for balance. The walkway lurched with his every step; support ropes twanged and fretted. *Ropes, not even cables here.* Fogwill held on tightly and tried not to look at the darkness beneath the shacks on either side, but it was hopeless: the abyss pulled his gaze towards it. He closed his eyes.

When the walkway had settled and the worst of his nausea had passed, the Adjunct stood alone outside the box made of timbers and tin sheets that, apparently, served as a house. Its single gaping window showed no sign of life within.

He ducked under the street-rope that supported this side of the walkway and eyed the plank spanning the gap to the front door. It was about four feet across, with nothing but a couple of rotted ropes to hold on to: nothing else to stop one falling into the darkness. He couldn't see a net below. *There surely must be a net. Even here. It's the law.* That thought didn't reassure him as he tested the plank with his foot. It gave a sickening creak. Perhaps he ought to call over to the house for assistance? And thus reveal himself as the frightened whelp he was? *Very clever.* It might also wake the neighbourhood, and he didn't want this neighbourhood woken. There was no alternative but to cross. Fogwill took a deep breath and edged forward, gripping both swaying ropes as best he could. Even in the dim light he could see the white marks round his fingers where he had removed his rings. The plank bowed under his weight as his slippers inched towards the middle.

Those four feet seemed to take him as long as the walk from the temple, and when he reached the door he was shaking. It took all of his courage to release his hand from the security of the rope and knock.

There was no answer.

Fogwill cursed. He ought to have told Clay to wait for him. This was not a part of Deepgate where it was wise to linger alone after dark.

He knocked again, harder.

'Closed!' a gruff voice shouted.

Fogwill leaned closer to the door and spoke as loud as he dared. 'May I speak with you for a moment?'

There was no reply. Fogwill waited. He knocked again.

'Away!' the voice bellowed.

Fogwill flinched. *He's going to wake the whole street.* 'Please, it's urgent.' The other shacks remained dark and silent. Hanging above the centre of the walkway, a brand fizzed tar into its drum. He had lifted his hand to knock again when the door creaked open a fraction. No light came from within as he leaned towards the crack and whispered quickly, 'I must speak with you. It's about your daughter.'

'Bloody priest, leave me alone. Leech took her.'

The door slammed in Fogwill's face.

'No,' he protested.

Fogwill heard movement inside the shack, and the door again opened a little. He decided to press his advantage. 'I don't believe Carnival was responsible.'

This time the door swung wide and the ugliest face Fogwill had ever seen emerged from the shadows beyond. He stifled a squeal. The face – and yes it was a face, now

that he got a good look at it – peered up and down the
street then settled on him. It sniffed.

'You stink,' Mr Nettle said.

Fogwill's relief at stepping off the plank dissipated as
soon as the door closed behind him. Inside, he couldn't
see a thing. For an awful moment he was afraid he'd made
a terrible decision in coming here at all. If he was attacked
by this lout, he would be quite unable to defend himself.
Clay had warned him this man was known to be violent,
and he was certainly no friend of the Church. What if
Fogwill was stabbed? Or worse? God help him, he might
even be ravished.

Then Mr Nettle struck a flint, and an oil lamp brightened the hall. Standing in the narrow space edged by
pulpboard and tin sheets, Mr Nettle raised the lamp in
one fist and regarded Fogwill sourly.

The scrounger was huge. In his ragged dressing gown,
he stood larger than a fully armoured temple guard,
blocking the narrow hallway like a pile of builder's rubble.
His features were as rough and ill-defined as the hewn
stone before a sculptor began carving the details. His
flattened nose had been broken and set crooked, and
stubble as coarse as iron filings covered half his face, while
bruises covered the rest. Red eyes ringed with dark
shadows glared down at Fogwill.

From the tiredness in his eyes and the hollowness of
his cheeks, the man looked like he hadn't eaten or slept in
a week. He looked finished. *And* he stank like a dungeon.

'This way,' Mr Nettle growled.

The scrounger trudged further along the corridor, stepping over bundles of paper and boxes of bottles, then
turning his enormous shoulders sideways to get past a stack
of crates propped against the wall. The whole house shud-

dered as though it might fall apart at any moment. Nails jutted randomly from odd places where they had been used to patch scraps of wood and tin on to the walls. On closer inspection, Fogwill realized that the walls themselves had been constructed from junk. Here, one wardrobe door formed part of the side wall, while its twin served as part of the ceiling. There, an old mirror frame, the glass long smashed, filled a gap between two struts. Rusted pipes and broken ladders acted as joists to support this patchwork. Evidently Mr Nettle was no carpenter. There wasn't a straight join to be seen. And what was that? A shield? He recognized the design: *a temple guard's shield.* Fogwill edged through the space with his hands close to his chest, careful not to touch anything. He tried not to think about rats.

Empty whisky bottles had rolled down the slope of the living-room floor to gather against a faded advertisement for Whitworth's Honey Washing Oil – a product, Fogwill suspected, Mr Nettle himself had never used.

The scrounger cleared some boxes from an old chair, and piled them on the rest of the junk behind. He grunted, 'Sit.'

Fogwill perched gingerly on the edge of the seat, one of whose arm rests was nothing more than a splintered spike. This was not at all how he had imagined a scrounger's house to look. He had expected something more like an antiques shop: solid furniture, rare objects rescued from the nets, to be restored and resold. Not just paper and bottles, tin cans, bundles of rags. True, there were one or two unusual items that stood out from the debris: a marble clock with one hand missing, clearly not originating from this part of town; some large brass cogs that could easily have come from the Presbyter's aurolethiscope; several garish paintings of city scenes daubed on pieces of pulpboard nailed to the walls; but most of it was simply rubbish. It packed the room from floor to ceiling. How could someone live in this filth?

Mr Nettle put down the oil lamp and folded his arms, waiting for Fogwill to speak.

The priest smoothed his cassock, the plain black one Clay had insisted he wore. 'May I ask what your daughter did for a living?' he asked in his creamiest voice.

Mr Nettle grimaced. Finally he said, 'Painter.'

Fogwill cast his eyes over the paintings. 'She painted these?' They were particularly amateurish. *People actually bought these?*

Mr Nettle nodded.

'Excellent work,' Fogwill said hastily. 'She had a good eye.'

'Penny apiece.'

Fogwill wondered if he should buy one to help smooth things over, before he remembered that he'd left all his money back at the temple, so decided to change the subject. 'Mr Nettle, do you know exactly where your daughter was when she disappeared?'

In answer, Mr Nettle reached behind him and pulled out a ragged square of pulpboard. Fogwill saw it was an incomplete work, a first sketch, and quite as awful as the others. Nevertheless, there could be no doubt of the subject represented.

'She was working on this?'

'Found it in the nets down there. I searched there first.'

Fogwill studied the sketch. He recognized the neighbourhood. The chimneys and funnels of the Poison Kitchens rising in the background were unmistakable. This wasn't proof, of course. The implications were there, but it wasn't enough to warrant accusing Devon, even with Fogwill's existing suspicions. Carnival had killed in every part of the city. He had to ask next: 'Did she have bruises on both arms?'

The scrounger's eyes narrowed.

'Were her arms bruised?' Fogwill repeated.

Mr Nettle studied him for a moment. 'Aye.'

Our murderer. The scrounger hadn't kept her on ice all this time. Fogwill cast his gaze over the other paintings: different scenes from the city in the same few gaudy colours. Obviously the girl had had a weird affection for red and yellow, as they were the only colours used, whatever the subject. 'We've found others,' he explained. 'The puncture wounds are the same, but the bruises . . . Those are not Carnival's work. Carnival suspends her victims by the feet.'

'Who did it?'

'We don't know.'

The scrounger pushed his face even closer to Fogwill's. 'But you suspect someone?' His tone was a threat.

Fogwill saw that the muscles on Mr Nettle's arms had become as taut as the street-rope holding a house. He squirmed inwardly, but forced himself to meet the man's gaze. 'No.'

The scrounger's eyes stayed locked on Fogwill's for a long moment, the bruises on his face seeming to pulse.

Fogwill struggled to appear calm. He smelled whisky on the man's breath, and felt a trickle of sweat run beneath his own ear. Why had he dismissed Clay so readily?

At last Mr Nettle stepped back. 'Get out,' he said.

Fogwill crossed the plank in two strides and raced back in the direction of the temple, robe fluttering. The walkway buckled and tipped beneath his feet but he didn't slow. He didn't slow down at all.

Mr Nettle dressed quickly. He stuffed his scrounging tools into a backpack: rope, grapple, hammer, spikes, a small pulley, storm lantern and flints. He grabbed his water flask, a disc of hardbread, a pouch of raisins and a cord of pigskin, and threw them in with the tools. Then he tucked his cleaver in his belt, wheeled Smith's trolley out to the walkway, and began loading it with pig iron. The help he needed would be expensive. Maybe the iron would cover it, maybe not. It might cost him a lot more.

While he worked, a gust of cold air blew from the abyss and shook the League of Rope. Shanties swung and knocked together. Timbers boomed on pulpboard walls and nails scratched tin roofs. Even the Warrens were moving, down below. Gaslights shivered among the chains. Only the temple stood motionless, black and immense, windows like a jet of embers frozen high above the heart of the city.

The fat little priest had lied. Mr Nettle knew it in his gut. The Church suspected someone. He rubbed a hand over his sweating face, sighed slowly. *Not Carnival?* Maybe the priests would do something about it, maybe not. Didn't matter. Mr Nettle planned to do something first, whatever the cost.

Sorcery didn't exist. Everybody knew that. In taverns and grog-holes throughout the Warrens, folk dismissed the idea loudly, laughed heartily at the merest suggestion. But a careful listener might note how they dismissed the idea a little *too* loudly, laughed a little *too* heartily.

When the trolley was fully loaded, Mr Nettle spat on

the ground, steeled himself, and set off to meet the only man in Deepgate who could speak to hell.

The further Fogwill got from Mr Nettle's house, the more his nausea and vertigo returned. Here, as in all areas on the outskirts of the city, the distance between the great chains was at its widest; more of each neighbourhood being supported by a less substantial web of chain, cable and rope.

Everything wobbled, shook and groaned. Wood sweated. The smell was frightful. *Like a sick-house full of plague victims. This entire district is rotting, ill.*

Ropes threatened to snap. One cut would bring the whole nasty, ugly, filthy, smelly lot down into the abyss. With each step taken, Fogwill worried that it might be his last. Even those nets he could glimpse beneath the boards offered him little peace of mind. For the most part they were thin and frayed and looked too frail to support the weight of a dog, let alone his own portly frame. The darkness didn't help. Occasional brands gave the timbers a buttery glow, but for the most part Fogwill was left to stumble along under the weak moonlight, his hands never leaving the street-ropes on either side. So soon after Scar Night, the moon was still a slender crescent. League-folk rarely ventured out at night and the streets were empty, but the lack of louts and cutthroats was little consolation. The man he was going to see was more dangerous than any of them.

The crippled thaumaturge lived inside the Sparrow Bridge in Chapelfunnel. A towering wooden construction built upon a granite deck, the bridge spanned the abyss between Tanners' Gloom on the west side and the old coalgas towers on the east. Once open to the sky, and wide enough to allow two carts to pass side by side, Sparrow Bridge had formerly been a symbol of the district's booming coalgas industry. In years past, workers could peer over its balustrades and see a canal of air and chains plough deep into the Warrens, hedged on both sides by walls of good strong flint and trunks of smoke. But prosperity brings wealth, and wealth brings men, and men need to be housed. Now Sparrow Bridge towered to four storeys. Homes had been built above, stacked one upon the other like children's bricks and sewn up with chains bolted to any anchor available. Pinched roofs bucked across its summit in a ragged line. Forty or so families had lived in the bridge before Thomas Scatterclaw settled here. Carts still trundled through the long tunnel below the houses, loaded with leather for the Chapelfunnel market or steel from the dismantled coalgas yards, but now moving only one at a time, and only in the daytime.

Mr Nettle looked up at the bridge. Scaffolding clung to the outside of the houses, but it was sagging, the poles and ladders rotten. There were holes in the roofs where shingles had come loose. Broken windows fronted the abyss, all of them dark but one, high up, where a dull red light glowed.

'Iron is it?'

Mr Nettle turned towards the voice. The man emerging from the tunnel sat on a low, wheeled platform and pushed himself along with bandaged hands. As he drew near, Mr Nettle saw that his legs had been severed below the knee. Despite this, he remained powerful. Muscles bunched on his broad chest. His arms looked strong enough to break a horse's neck. Two deep scars, like sword wounds, running down his left forearm made Mr Nettle think he might once have been a soldier or a temple guard.

'Is it enough?' Mr Nettle asked.

'Depends what you want,' the man said. Wheels squeaked under him. 'But no, in the end it won't be enough.'

'That supposed to be a riddle?'

The man grunted. 'Danning is my name. Want to know what happened to my legs?'

'No.'

The other man grinned. 'You'll want to speak to Mr Scatterclaw. Upstairs. I'll take the iron.'

'Might be he can't help me.'

Danning shrugged. 'Not my problem. That's how it works here.'

The scrounger hesitated. Smith's pig iron was a fortune to someone from the League, enough to feed him for six months or more. If the thaumaturge was unable to help, Mr Nettle couldn't imagine any future for himself. But what if Scatterclaw *could* help him? That future might be worse than none at all.

'Can't make up your mind for you,' Danning said, 'but it seems to me you've risked plenty coming here already.' He smiled, but it was not a kind smile. 'Mr Scatterclaw knows you're here. And if Mr Scatterclaw knows, the Maze knows.'

Mr Nettle released his grip on the trolley.

Danning tilted his head. 'Door beside the red window.' He pushed himself over to the trolley, grabbed the handles and eased them back so that they rested on his wide shoulders. Then, grunting, he set off the way he had come, six wheels squeaking now.

The scaffolding wobbled the whole way up. Greasy ropes protested and soft planks dipped, but Mr Nettle reached the uppermost catwalk without incident. The Chapelfunnel canal curved away below him, broken by moonlit chains into narrow strips of abyss. Beside the door, red light sweated through a warped window, blurred red shapes inside. Mr Nettle stashed his backpack in the shadows and knocked.

A brusque voice issued from inside. 'He's here. Hide yourselves.'

The scrounger waited. He did not want to think about who or what Thomas Scatterclaw might be speaking to. Iril had opened many doors inside Sparrow Bridge.

'We have company,' Scatterclaw bellowed. 'Do you want to frighten him out of his wits? Get out of my sight. All of you. Hide!'

Mr Nettle listened at the door for a long time. He heard nothing further. No footfalls. Nothing. Not knowing what else to do, he knocked again.

A pause, then, 'Come in.'

The door revealed a wall of broken glass. Razor-sharp shards of every shape and colour had been glued to a wooden partition set a few feet back from the door. Eight feet high, this partition stretched away on either side to the edges of a long room. It formed a narrow corridor from which a dozen other corridors, also faced with broken glass, led off into the interior. A red lantern depended from the rafters, its light the colour of blood.

A maze? The thaumaturge had built a shrine to Iril. Mr Nettle stepped inside and closed the door behind him. The corridor was just wide enough to allow him to move sideways along it without tearing his clothes on the glass fragments. Mazes, in any form, were forbidden in Deepgate. Iril's demons drew power from mazes. Not two months ago, an Ivygarths silversmith had been dragged before the Avulsior for crafting a brooch, it was said, of such intricacy that it had been likened to Iril's corridors. But here was a real maze, a solid thing composed of wood and glass. The Church would burn it to the ground if they discovered it.

He edged along to the first intersection. Another corridor ran to a dead end twenty feet ahead. Six more branched off from it. Mr Nettle called out, 'Scatterclaw?'

'Over here.'

But the voice seemed to come from everywhere at once. Mr Nettle turned carefully into the sharp passageway and eased himself along, wary of losing his way. On one side he noted a crescent-shaped shard of glass, black in the red light, and tried to burn it into his memory. He decided on the third branch on the right.

A third lengthy corridor, at least forty feet long, with many more leading away from it. The scrounger frowned. From the outside, Sparrow Bridge did not seem wide enough to contain all this. He looked back, spied the crescent-shaped shard, then squeezed on between the treacherous glass walls and shuffled deeper into the maze. Something nicked his shoulder and he halted, felt blood trickle down his back.

'Stop! Stop! Stop!' Scatterclaw cried. 'Stay where you are, all of you. He is not lost. You are not lost, are you, Scrounger?'

'No.'

'Then proceed.'

Sweat ran from Mr Nettle's brow, but he dared not lift his hand to mop it. There was barely room to breathe in here. He sucked in his chest and moved on again.

Another opening led to another corridor and this one appeared to stretch for twice the length of the last. Walls of glass glistened blackly. Nothing made sense: the entire room could not be more than sixty feet wide. He glanced up and saw the lantern overhead. Had it always been hanging directly above his head? He was growing weary of this.

'Scatterclaw,' he shouted.

'Don't linger. They know where you are.'

'Who?'

No reply.

Mr Nettle cursed and moved on. He took a left, edged fifty paces, then a right. When he looked up the lantern was still there, directly above. Damn the thaumaturge. Wasn't it enough that he'd paid a wealth of iron to speak to the man? Now he was expected to crawl through this trap. He'd half a mind to climb the partition, get a good look at the place, or use his cleaver to shave away some of the glass fragments.

But Mr Nettle did neither. Thomas Scatterclaw was not a man he wanted to anger. Folks said he'd come across the Yellow Sea from a place where Iril was worshipped. They said he'd come here a hundred and forty years ago and his body had been grey and fleshless then. They said he'd pierced his lips, ears and eyes with splinters of gallows wood so that he could converse with demons, and that he'd had nails hammered into his spine to keep his gaze from heaven while he slept.

The scrounger waited for a dozen breaths, and then pushed on. A left then another left. Twenty paces. A right. Ten paces. Another right. Always the same wickedly sharp corridors, always the same blood-coloured lantern overhead. Had he been tricked? Was he to spend the rest of his life in here? He wandered for what seemed like hours, down corridor after corridor, glass inches from his chest and inches from his back.

Finally he stopped.

Ten paces ahead was an opening in the left wall. But this did not lead to another corridor; it opened into a wider space. Even from here he could see another partition a short distance beyond, but this time a wall without glass. Warily, Mr Nettle approached it.

Thomas Scatterclaw sat cross-legged in the centre of a box-like space, some twenty feet across and hemmed in by partition walls. A deep-red robe and cowl hid every inch of him, but Mr Nettle thought he saw bumps in the cloth on the man's back where no bumps should be. On the floor in front of him, a rusty kitchen knife and a plain, chipped bowl. The bowl was full of blood.

Mr Nettle grunted. 'You the thaumaturge?'

'Take the knife and open a vein.' Thomas Scatterclaw didn't look up. 'Add your blood to this – to the dead blood.'

'What for?'

'Do it quickly.'

'You don't know what I want.'

'No,' Scatterclaw said, 'but Iril does. Quickly now, there are demons in here.'

Mr Nettle glanced round. Nothing but the tired wooden partitions. No sounds, no creak of wood. The thaumaturge was trying to unnerve him.

'Now,' Scatterclaw snarled.

Mr Nettle picked up the knife, and without thinking any more about it, cut across the back of his hand behind his thumb. Blood welled and trickled over his hand.

'In the bowl,' Scatterclaw said. 'Hurry.'

Mr Nettle did as he was told.

Iril's priest appeared to shudder beneath his robe. He leaned forward, picked up the bowl, and Mr Nettle saw that his exposed hands were black and gnarled as though they had been burned, the fingers twisted around each other like tightly woven roots. Had the thaumaturge done this to himself too? Scatterclaw tilted the bowl under his cowl, and drank.

Disgusted, the scrounger watched the man drain the bowl and set it down.

'Do not close your eyes,' Scatterclaw said. 'Not for an instant. Do you understand? No more than a blink. They get in through your eyes but only if you cannot see them. They will try to sneak up on you, trick you. If they get inside you, you will never leave this maze. You'll stay trapped in here with them until Iril comes for you.'

'Who?'

'The Non Morai.'

Again Mr Nettle looked around anxiously.

'You'll see them if you look hard enough,' Scatterclaw said. 'And I advise you *do* look hard. Be thankful it isn't dark, for darkness makes them bold. All that trouble on Cog Island was caused by the Non Morai at night. Doors from hell attract them like flies.'

The light in the room appeared to thicken, until Mr Nettle felt as though he was straining to see through a red veil. Walls and floor and rafters turned a dark, dark red that was almost black. He heard movement behind him and whirled round. Nothing. Now he could smell an odour like spoiled meat. Something moved at the corner of his vision, as though trying to approach unseen, but when he swung to look, there was nothing there. Yet Mr

Nettle felt an aura of malice in that empty space, so strong his heartbeats quickened.

Thomas Scatterclaw breathed slow and deep, and then spoke in a glutinous voice that was not his own. 'How many are here?'

Behind him, Mr Nettle heard a chorus of whispers. *Eleven.*

He wheeled, saw nothing.

'And a living soul,' Scatterclaw said.

Ours, the voices hissed.

Thomas Scatterclaw, or whatever had taken possession of him, was silent for a long time, and then the cowl turned to face Mr Nettle. 'Your daughter is not with us. A living man has taken her.'

The scrounger's fists bunched. 'Who?'

'He is diseased. Hafe reaches for him.'

'Hafe?'

'The hell of the fourth angel. Halls of dirt and poison. Green ghosts, harrowcells and flowers.'

Mr Nettle frowned. The Maze, he suspected, was trying to confuse him. So it was with Iril. 'Who is he?'

Voices then swarmed all around Mr Nettle. *Close your eyes. Let us in and we'll tell you.*

For a heartbeat the scrounger almost obeyed. It seemed the most natural thing to close his eyes, to let the voices inside. But some part of him resisted. 'Who is he?'

The voices hissed, snarled.

Thomas Scatterclaw said, 'Devon.'

Smoke rose from smouldering censers around the Sinners' Well and hung in a fragrant pall between the severed heads. Nine of the twenty spikes were occupied: six men, two women, a child. Pulpboard signs proclaimed them blasphemers, Iril worshippers, or Heshette spies. All rooted out by the Spine, brought before Ichin Samuel Tell to be redeemed before the mob. Their bodies had been cast, still bleeding, into the abyss; the heads left as a reminder of Spine efficacy. Fogwill surveyed the scene through watering eyes and breathed through the folds of his sleeve. Was his man here? Was he too late?

Then, in the shadows, he spied the glow of a pipe. It lit up a narrow, dirt-streaked face, and then all was dark again. Fogwill approached his spy.

'Good evening, Adjunct,' the man said.

'Any developments?' Fogwill asked.

'No. He works late, as usual.'

'You managed to get away without any problems?'

The man sucked on his pipe till it illuminated ranks of narrow teeth, bony cheeks and a knife-thin nose. 'Left for a smoke, didn't I? Half the workers do it.' He grinned. 'Who was going to stop me? The furnace gaffer? He's scared of me. I still got my knife, and they all know it.'

Fogwill glanced over at the nearest head. Crows had already taken the woman's eyes and lips. He grimaced. 'Why did we have to meet here? I abhor this place.'

'I like it here.' Smoke leaked through the spy's teeth. 'The heads tell me things.'

Fogwill tried to swallow, but his throat was too dry. The man was a lunatic. 'What things?' he asked, despite himself.

'Secret things,' the spy said.

'Blood has been shed here,' the Adjunct said. 'It's dangerous. God knows what *things* might be lurking here.'

'The censers are blessed.'

'You can never be too careful.' Fogwill caught a glimpse of movement, and spun. A black shape, like a dog but much larger, loped away between the chains. 'Look, did you see that? What was it? A manifestation?'

The spy shrugged. Fogwill found the gesture oddly disconcerting. This man had once been Spine; not an Adept, but a common Cutter. The needle marks in his neck remained – evidence of the Spine masters' attempt to temper him. But these traces were augmented by tattooed knots – the indelible stains of failure. A common enough occurrence, for tempering was not always successful. Sometimes minds just broke.

Ejected from the sanctuary of the temple, damaged assassins did not survive for long. Society shunned them, and it was only a matter of time before some cutthroat, with sharper wits and drunken morals, took exception to them.

'You learn anything from the scrounger?' the spy inquired.

'His daughter disappeared close to the Scythe – in the Depression. The bruising indicates it wasn't Carnival's work.'

'Figures.' The assassin inhaled. 'Want me to go ahead?'

Fogwill nodded.

'If I don't find anything?'

'Report to me tomorrow morning.'

'And if I do?'

Fogwill hesitated. 'You know God's will.' And, there, the words were out, as simply as that.

I've just sanctioned murder.

★

Whatever had been inside Thomas Scatterclaw had now departed, leaving him collapsed and senseless. But the voices in the maze were growing louder, bolder.

Why not close your eyes? Just for a moment. The light is so bright.

The room *had* brightened, almost painfully so, but Mr Nettle had no desire to close his eyes. His anger gave him the strength to ignore the demons, if that's what they were.

Devon had killed Abigail. Devon was mortal. He could be made to suffer. What form of suffering, the scrounger didn't know, not yet. But he would see the Poisoner scream and beg for his life before the night was out.

We can help you. Close your eyes. Or break the lantern. Yes, smash it. We can help you if it's dark.

'Shut up!' He had to think. The thaumaturge's maze still trapped him and he had no idea how to get out of it. Didn't much like the thought of squeezing back through walls of broken glass with these demons at his heels. Better if he found another way.

There is another way. A safe way. Break the lantern and we'll show you.

Mr Nettle studied the room. The rafters were too high to reach, and the floorboards looked too solid to smash through. Maybe he could climb one of the partitions, step across the tops of them to the edges of the room? He cursed himself for having left his backpack outside.

Something cold touched his hand. He lashed out.

At empty air.

The voices wheeled around him, laughing.

Mr Nettle circled slowly. Movement everywhere, but he couldn't seem to get a clear look at whatever was moving, as though the air shifted and blurred around indistinct shapes. Shadows that weren't shadows when he looked; figures that evaporated, became whorls of grain in the partition walls.

Overhead, the lantern flickered and dimmed, and in that moment Mr Nettle glimpsed them: thin men with white faces and red grins. They were standing in a circle around him.

He ran to the nearest partition, grabbed the top of it, and hauled himself up.

Glass bit his fingers: the other side of the wood was evilly sharp. He hoisted one knee up and crouched on the top of the partition. The maze now looked smaller than it had appeared from below, not more than fifty feet square, but the complexity of it stunned him. Narrow corridors crammed together, running in every direction. Square spirals, L-shapes and S-shapes. Countless dead ends. And all laced with blood-red glass. Twenty paces away, the door where he'd come in; and beside the door, the room's single window. If he was careful, he could hop across the top of the maze to reach it. Slowly, he stood. The top of the partition was only two inches wide.

Cheat, the voices howled. *Cheat, cheat, cheat.*

Mr Nettle stepped across to the adjacent partition, wavered for a second. He sensed the air shift, *push* him, as though trying to throw him off balance, and he flung his arms out. For several heartbeats he stood there, knees trembling, certain he was going to fall. But he recovered his balance. Then a deep breath, and another step. The partition groaned, wobbled, and his insides lurched. His heart was pounding. The maze of glass glistened below him, like walls of teeth that seemed to grin, salivate.

Cheat, cheat, cheat. The demons' fury was palpable. Icy breaths caressed Mr Nettle's face. Unseen things thrashed around him. He stepped to the next partition. The wood cracked, but held. Mr Nettle swayed for a sickening moment. Corridors of glass tilted and pitched. He took another step. Another.

He was halfway across when the lantern went out, and plunged the room into darkness.

14

✝WO ASSASSINS

There was a knock at the laboratory door. Devon slammed the rat cage shut and raised his breathing mask. 'What is it now?'

A nervous chemist poked his head in. 'Sorry, sir, we need to know if you still want the aether tanks drained tonight. There's a ship due in from the Plantations in the morning. If we drain the tanks we'll need to recalibrate, and she'll be waiting for the best part of the day before we can refuel her.'

'Tradeship or churchship?'

'Churchship.'

'Drain the tanks.'

'What about the ship?'

'The ship can wait. I don't want any further interruptions tonight.'

'Very good, sir.' The chemist slunk away.

The Poisoner returned to the rat cage and peered down at the scampering creature. From his waistcoat pocket he plucked a small phial and shook it, squinting at the rose-coloured liquid within. He replaced his breathing mask, opened the phial and carefully drew a drop of the liquid into a pipette. This he mixed with a spoon of honey in a shallow dish and placed inside the cage. The rat scurried over and began lapping at the solution. Devon watched it anxiously.

When all of it was consumed he studied the rat for a few minutes. There was no visible change in its behaviour.

'Now,' he muttered, picking up a scalpel, 'I am afraid this is going to hurt.'

He held the blade over the rat, following it patiently as it bounded about the cage. Then he stabbed it in the back. The rat shrieked and tried to wriggle free, but Devon held the scalpel firmly in place. He pinned the creature down until it stopped struggling, then withdrew the scalpel and plunked it into a beaker of alcohol.

Devon waited, his breathing loud in the mask. Minutes passed. The rat twitched once. Blood leaked from the wound. Then nothing. Devon put a finger under its chest, rolled it over. The creature was dead.

He sighed heavily.

Devon pulled off his mask and dropped it on the workbench. His face was itching, his hair dishevelled about his ears. Carefully, he removed his spectacles and cleaned them before perching them back on the bridge of his nose. He glanced back at the dead rat in the cage. It was still a dead rat in a cage.

The Poisoner crumpled on his stool. Enough for today. He felt exhausted and still had that mess to clean up in his study. He was always tired these days. Over the years he'd found himself going to bed earlier and rising earlier, already worn out before the day began. His body seemed heavier, every task more laborious. He accepted the weariness, but the pain . . .

Some nights Devon woke in agony, clutching his chest,

as if breathing shards of glass. His wounds bled constantly. The poisons, fuels and sulphurs of the Poison Kitchens had soaked into his flesh and filled his bones like lead. There was no room inside for any more. He was dying.

The Saviour of Deepgate – poisoned and left to rot by the people I've saved. And for what? The populace despise me. My own chemists despise me. The Church despises me, for all that I've done for them. Who are these people? People whose survival was bought by my suffering. By my Elizabeth's suffering. Yet I endure this agony so that they can outlive me.

The hypocrisy enraged him. Everyone in Deepgate was waiting to die. Except Devon. They did not deserve their own lives, and yet they took *his*. But he wasn't finished yet. He'd take back what they'd stolen, and more. Only thirteen souls were required to make the angelwine potent. Had it required a thousand, Devon would have cut them from the city without hesitation.

Deepgate owed him.

It had been careless of him, he supposed, to leave the girl's body in his apartment, but he'd had no intention of venturing out on Scar Night, and he'd lacked the strength this morning to move the corpse. The prospect of lugging the body around made him feel even wearier. He would just dump it in the first dark gap he found over the abyss, then make himself some supper. Lately he hadn't been eating enough. A good supper would sort him out: perhaps steak with minted potatoes. He picked up the jar of honey from the worktop, wiped away some spatters of rat-blood, and stuffed it in his pocket – pancakes with honey for dessert.

To minimize any further contact with his chemists, Devon left by one of the back exits. Labourers filed in and out of the door in shuffling lines, going to and from the furnaces. Soot-blackened faces weary; clean pink faces despondent.

To Devon's dismay, he spotted a group of other chemists under the clock-tower gaslight. Above them, the clock sounded midnight with a brassy *thunk*. He recognized Danderport, a sprightly, eager nuisance with permanently moist lips and restless fingers, who was engaged in a fierce debate with some other crinkled, sulphurous little oiler.

Danderport beckoned him over. 'Sir, your opinion please.'

'What?' he snapped.

'The Tooth, sir.'

'What about it?'

Danderport gave him a limp smile, his fingers dancing. '*Adraki* aeronauts got a proper look at it as they rounded Blackthrone on the hunt for the *Skylark*. We were wondering if you had any thoughts about the method of its construction. My own theory is that the hull material may be vat-grown. Brent here disagrees.'

Devon considered this. The Tooth of God, as the priests called it, seemed too heavy to have ever moved without sinking deep into the Deadsands. Yet it had moved once. Deep trails of compacted earth still criss-crossed the desert in places, frequently vanishing under drifting sands only to become revealed years later. Whatever materials had been used in its construction were far lighter and stronger than anything they were currently familiar with.

'It is possible,' he conceded.

'Sir, perhaps a closer inspection of the Tooth might be possible at some point?' Danderport's voice seesawed. 'Merely an inspection. We wouldn't touch a thing.'

The Poisoner harrumphed. 'If Sypes agrees to it, I'll let you know.'

Danderport's face collapsed briefly before he turned back to his debate.

Devon's chores gave him a gentle tug. He left the chemists pugging Danderport's ideas like swill, and strode across the yard and out through the gates. It was late, he was tired, and he had a corpse to dispose of before supper.

In darkness Mr Nettle continued to balance on top of the two-inch-wide partition wall. He couldn't move, couldn't see the next partition or the labyrinth of broken glass below. But he sensed invisible shapes swirling around him and he could taste their rage. It was like a thunderstorm imprisoned within a bottle.

Without even touching him, the Non Morai tore at him.

Close your eyes. Close your eyes. Close your eyes.

'Piss off,' Mr Nettle growled. He pulled his cleaver from his belt and swiped madly at the air. The partition swayed and almost stole his balance.

The demons shrieked. *Close your eyes! Let us in!*

He saw them when he didn't look at them, always out of the corners of his eyes. Vague black shapes, darker than the surrounding gloom. Glimpses of long red teeth and long white fingers. Sharp nails. Whenever he tried to get a proper look at them, they fled, as if furious at his gaze. He twisted his head around frantically, trying to track them. They were everywhere at once, yet nowhere, moving so fast he couldn't be sure he saw anything at all. Now that his eyes were growing accustomed to the darkness, he spied the window in the far wall, a bleary grey square, and the upper edge of the partition nearest to it. He knew there was another partition in front of him, but he would have to gauge the distance across from memory. If he got it wrong he'd be down in the maze, and without the lantern light he'd likely stay there for good.

Something touched the back of his neck.

Mr Nettle flinched, twisted round. Shadows churned like a swarm of beetles, hissing.

Close your eyes. Stay here with us.

Hell he would. The scrounger tucked his cleaver back into his belt and stepped out into nothing.

The sole of his boot pressed against something solid. For a moment he balanced there, each foot on the top edge of a different partition, and then he stepped across.

Let us in!

Now he could make out a few faint lines: the tops of two or three partitions closest to the window. Glass glinted below. But he still had to cross twenty feet of darkness as profound as the Chapelfunnel canal. How could he even know if another partition ran parallel to the one he was on? Would he step into the space where one corridor joined another and tumble head first between two walls of glass? And if he fell, would he instinctively close his eyes?

There is no danger from us, the Non Morai crooned. *We want to help you. If you try to cross here you will fall. Move left a pace. Safer.*

Last thing he needed was to have *them* tell him which way to go. He took another step.

Felt nothing beneath his foot.

Fell.

Glass bit deeply into both shoulders and arms, gouged through flesh. His jaw slammed against the floor, the impact kicking the wind out of him. He couldn't help it: for an instant he closed his eyes.

That was enough.

Mr Nettle snapped his eyes open but it was already too late. He felt something *pushing* into him, like stale water being forced into his lungs. And he could taste it: the taste of airless pools and dead weeds. He clawed at the air in front of his face, tried to pull whatever was there away. But there was nothing. The rank fluid flooded his throat and lungs. Mr Nettle gagged, coughed, fought for air. Fear gripped him, and he scrambled upright and ran.

Glass walls ripped his shoulders to shreds. He ploughed on blindly, unable to breathe. Mr Nettle knew he was a coward. He'd always been one. He'd known it since his father, a huge man with weed-stained fingers, had held him by the scruff of the neck over the edge of Nine Ropes Bridge, over the darkness.

There's bottles down there.

Five years old and not knowing there was a net, he'd begged his old man not to let go of him. Then he was falling. Then came the net. He'd lain there for an age, sobbing and clutching the hemp strands, and when the tears finally stopped, he'd scrambled around looking for bottles. There had been none.

There never were any bottles, the Non Morai hissed, imitating his old man's voice. *Thought that net had frayed and wasted.*

Now Mr Nettle felt the same terror again: blind fear crushing his heart and lungs. He barged down the corridor. Sharp edges plucked constantly at his flesh. Blood sluiced over his arms. He didn't care, couldn't breathe, couldn't think. He was going to die.

He slammed into a wall.

Glass fragments shattered against his hands, shoulders, chest. Mr Nettle roared in pain, recoiled, and threw himself at the wall again.

Iril's shrine shuddered. The partition collapsed, crashing into the one behind.

Then he was climbing up and over a slope of glass. At the top he saw the window, only three yards away. He leapt, fell short. Arms wrapped around the top of the next partition; shards deep in his knees now. He dragged himself up, pulled himself over. The window was in front of him.

No! A whirlwind of screams, as the Non Morai clawed at his bleeding skin, their touch like freezing rain. *Cheat! You cannot leave the maze! You dare not!*

The door now forgotten, Mr Nettle dived through the window.

He hit the scaffolding outside in a shower of glass. The whole structure skreaked, tilted, and swung out over the Chapelfunnel canal. Glass tinkled off chains below. Mr Nettle lay still for a dozen heartbeats, afraid to breathe or move. Then, slowly, the pressure in his chest eased, he felt his lungs clear and his throat loosen. The stale taste in his mouth faded. He spat furiously . . . and breathed.

Every inch of him had been cut, his clothes were in tatters, the skin on his hands shredded. But he rose like a man released from heavy chains and gazed grimly out across Chapelfunnel to where the flames of the Poison Kitchens roared beneath a smiling moon.

The stench of blood in Devon's apartment forced him to open a window. He would have to get rid of the corpse

and air the room if he was ever going to enjoy his meal.
From a closet he grabbed one of the sacks he kept specially
for this purpose. Less than a dozen left now – he made a
mental note to obtain some more. Once the place was
cleaned up, he would get one of his men to deliver some.
He'd have to peruse the temple screening documents
again, find someone without a family.

Drained of fluid, the girl's body was relatively light, so
he didn't have much trouble piling it into the sack. For a
moment he wondered if he shouldn't dump it further away
this time. There were places without nets where the abyss
would swallow the evidence for good.

No. Devon wanted the bodies to be discovered. He
wanted the Presbyter, if that's who had helped him, to
witness the result of his assistance.

Do you see what I'm working on? Do you approve?

He took pleasure in the thought of the old man balking
in silence. Killing did not come easily, even to a man like
Devon. Despite the purity of his motives, he found murder
tiresome and disagreeable, even vulgar. Deepgate had
reduced him to this, a common cutthroat, and the city
had an obligation to share the burden it had imposed upon
him.

But most of all he wanted Sypes to break his insuffer-
able silence. What did the old man hope to gain from
Devon's work? Power? Immortality? Did he think Devon
would share the fruits of his labours so readily?

Is he really so afraid of death? Or is there something more?

The Poisoner rubbed his eyes. He would learn the
answers before long. Right now he had a body to dispose
of, and he was too tired and hungry to walk far.

But still his cautious side interjected: why court attention? If he was publicly exposed as a soul-thief, no one

could protect him. The Spine would see him hanging from the Avulsior's gallows. Therefore he would compromise, hide the body some distance away. The sooner he got the job done, the sooner he could get on with his supper.

Derelict buildings crowded the darkness. Whichever direction he chose, he had to carry his burden uphill. Twenty years ago this district had teemed with industry, but over the years the sheer weight of the many factories, foundries and warehouses had caused a degree of subsidence that left the neighbourhood sagging towards its centre. For the most part, adjustments had been made to keep the buildings level for as long as possible, but there was nothing to be done about the overstretched crosschains that had caused the slump.

To the west, on the axis side of the Depression, as this district had come to be known, the abyssal gap curved away from the Poison Kitchens and the neighbouring shipyards. Those who laboured there called it the Scythe because of its crescent shape. It started narrow at Drake's Flourmill, by the thirty-third chain, broadening to a width suitable for airships at Cotter's brickworks and the Fly Holes, where the nets had been damaged by suicides. From there the gap ran past Chapelfunnel where coalgas used to be made, Rin's Rivets, the Spinning Chambers and the hole where the Cistern Tavern had been, reaching the Poison Kitchens at its widest extent. Here bristled the spines of the main shipyards, Coulter's berth among them, still twisted and charred, where the churchship *Ataler* had burned five years ago. Hammers from Samuel North Rare Metals rang out beyond that, over the pounding from ore smelters, furnaces and clay pens. The Scythe narrowed again at the Breach, never repaired since a lesser chain had snapped and ripped a clay store clean in two, killing sixty-three men. It disappeared at the forty-seventh chain, Mesa's Chain, swallowed by workers' shanties that grew thick as fungus around its edges.

The Depression had once shaken with the roar and hiss of churchships, tradeships and warships, the hollers of porters, pulley gaffers and rope hands, above the groan of stressed cable. Now it slouched and crumbled in silence.

A few blocks back from this gap, Devon's own apartment had been converted from the top floor of what had once been Crossop's Rhak and Whisky Warehouse. Although not one of the essential industries that usually command wharfside locations, it had been prosperous in its day and it remained an imposing building. Due to its position in the dead centre of the Depression, it had stayed almost completely level during the subsequent subsidence, requiring only minor ratcheting of its load pulleys. Old Crossop had watched the businesses around him decline, quite literally, until he was one of the last, and then the last. Finally, the lack of tradeships docking at this part of the Scythe left him isolated from his suppliers, and he was forced to sell at a price that made him sputter and clutch his heart. What little stock was left fetched more than the building. Devon had bought that too. He enjoyed the odd glass of Rhak.

Devon had purchased the warehouse fifteen years ago, and even then it had been the only habitable construction for several blocks around. No windows overlooked his own, half-inch-thick steel doors kept intruders out, and the solid walls muffled any sounds from within, not that there was anyone around to hear. It well suited the Poisoner to have his apartments here.

So all directions were uphill and he had to make a choice. Using the docks for disposal meant somehow casting the body to avoid twenty feet of net, or a treacherous climb along a mooring gantry, neither of which prospects appealed to him. There was also the likelihood of someone spotting him from one of the crowded dwellings on the other side of the Scythe. A closer place came to mind.

By the time he reached the cusp of the hill, Devon's chest was on fire. He collapsed, gasping, pinned under the corpse that now seemed so heavy. These pains had been getting worse recently, and his lungs bubbled with acid. He spat, and noticed blood in his saliva.

They were draining the aether tanks over in the Poison Kitchens and the flamestacks erupted in silver blooms, painting the brickwork and iron and flat tar roofs of the Depression. Even here, ash from the distant chimneys snowed lightly. Most people would have found such air unpalatable, but Devon had grown accustomed to it: the burning of gases and oils was the taste of progress, raw and undiluted – a smell that should have meant power.

Not power. Chains.

He felt like shouting across the city.

Do you see how you've crippled me? The sacrifice I made to keep you safe . . . Do you care?

He beat his fist against the girl's body.

You are nothing but walking dead. All of you. Corpses yet to be cast into the abyss. I am the only living man in this city, and I am being slowly murdered.

That's what it was: murder. Deepgate was trying to kill him. Devon spat again and glared at his own bloody saliva. Murder? He'd show them murder.

At the end of the block a freight bridge spanned the gap between Blacklock's foundry, with its single, drunken chimney, and the receding arches which linked Smithport fulling mill to its warehouse.

There were nets below, but deep enough. He considered cutting through them. The climb down looked so difficult. *I am too weary for this.* By day the bridge's shadow would conceal the sack, and there would be few passers-by, if any, to notice the smell. Scroungers no longer scoured the Depression. The nets here had long since been picked clean.

Devon heaved the sack up onto the rusty balustrade and tipped it over. The net creaked below. For a long moment he looked down into the darkness. He had completely lost his appetite.

Mr Nettle knew what was in the sack. He'd known the moment he spied Devon leaving Crossop's warehouse. A week past, he'd pulled a similar sack from a net not far from here. On that day, he'd waited a long, long time before he cut it open.

Crouched hidden in a doorway in the foundry wall, he waited until Devon was out of sight. Then he sprinted to the corner of the bridge, hooked his grapple around the balustrade, and slid down into the net.

Darkness and silence all around. Mr Nettle lit his storm lamp. Ash caked the woven hemp, crumbled into the abyss under his lacerated hands. The sack lay directly underneath the bridge in the lowest dip of the net. With the lamp handle gripped between his teeth, he took his cleaver and sliced through the sack's fabric.

She was younger than Abigail had been, maybe fifteen or sixteen. Her hair darker, lips fuller. But, for all that, it might have been his daughter: her skin was now just as pale, her eyes just as empty. He took her hand in his and rested her head and shoulders in the crook of his arm. She was as light as a flower.

For a long time he held her, as he had held Abigail, rocking back and forth, feeling his breathing resonate through her. He wondered if anyone was looking for her. Was her father roaming the streets even now, calling out her name? What had her name been? Did the Poisoner know? Or care?

The cuts on Mr Nettle's hands, forearms and shoulders throbbed evilly, as though the glass from Scatterclaw's maze still tore at him.

He took a firm grip of the net, brought down his cleaver, and hacked through the hemp strands immediately around the girl. She slipped away into darkness.

Once he reached the surface again, he bolted back to Crossop's, hardly caring if the thunder of his boots gave him away. He arrived at the corner of the warehouse just in time to see the Poisoner disappear inside. The metal door shut with a boom. One, two, three locks clanked in succession.

Mr Nettle stepped out of the shadows and studied the building.

Light shone from an open window on the top floor. The drainpipe running close to it looked old, but there was no other way.

Da. Abigail's voice came to him from a distant, quiet part of his mind, but the shock of it still cut through his anger.

Not now, girl.

Da, don't do this.

Leave me alone.

It's murder.

It's justice.

Murder!

Her cry pierced his heart, and for a moment he stood there, uncertain. Murder? How could he *murder* a living, breathing man?

But was it murder?

What if the man you killed didn't have a soul? Was that a sin? And what if it was?

What if it was?

Blood began to pound in his ears again. He hauled himself up the drainpipe. Rust flaked under his hands, but the pipe held his weight. He climbed vigorously, ignoring the pain in his wounded arms and shoulders; desiccated brick crumbled under the scrape of his boots and sprinkled to the lane below. If he could reach the apartment before Devon, his task would be simpler. He didn't want to be caught climbing in, where he would be vulnerable. Better if he was already inside, and ready.

At the top he put a foot on the window ledge and balanced his weight between the ledge and the drainpipe. He peered inside.

Oil lamps warmed wood-panelled walls. Brass equipment, glass bottles, flasks. A desk and a broad, high-backed chair facing away from the window, and there, opposite, another chair with leather straps bolted to its arm rests. His eyes narrowed on that chair and the tubes looped around a metal stand to its side. He checked his cleaver was still secure in his belt, reached for the window frame to pull himself in . . . and stopped.

A puff of smoke had drifted up from the high-backed chair facing away from him. Someone unseen was sitting there.

Mr Nettle slunk back behind the window frame, his heart racing. How could the bastard get back so quick? That was impossible. Then who? An accomplice? He ground his teeth. The Poisoner he could handle. Two men might be harder.

He couldn't see anything around the wide back of the chair. This meant the smoker couldn't have spotted him either. If he moved quickly, silently now, he still had the advantage of surprise. Doubt held him back. Devon would arrive any second.

Hell with it.

He reached for the window again.

Just then, the door opened and the Poisoner walked in.

Devon froze. A factory worker was sitting in his chair, and the man was covered, head to toe, in soot. Such mess, quite frankly, was unacceptable here. 'Can I help you?' he asked.

The worker pulled out a knife, a cutter's blade. In his other hand he held up the manacles Devon had used recently on the girl. 'Bruises on the arms,' he said, then tipped his head at the letting chair and the blood-smeared tubes and flasks. 'Been stealing souls, have we?'

Devon's heart sank to his boots. *Have I been wrong all along?* He'd been unforgivably foolish and arrogant to assume it was Sypes who was protecting him. He said, 'There is a perfectly rational explanation for all of this.'

Silence ensued.

'Tell me,' Devon said, 'does Sypes intend to grant me a trial?'

A guarded look.

He doesn't know? Not Sypes then. But who?

'Fogwill,' Devon said, and saw at once the truth of it in the other man's eyes. The Adjunct had gone behind his master's back. He studied the would-be assassin carefully, and almost grinned when he noticed the tattooed knots, partially obscured by soot, on the man's neck. *A Spine reject, broken by the tempering process.* Devon felt a sudden twinge of hope. There was still a chance then. Broken Spine were notoriously unstable. This man would be a seething cauldron of ego and fanaticism. And, of course, quite insane.

Devon intended to stir things up.

'The Adjunct made a mistake sending you here,' he said. 'You are a zealot, but without tempering you lack the capacity for restraint. This makes you easier to manipulate.'

'Think you can manipulate me?'

'It ought to be easy enough,' Devon said lightly. 'All I have to do is anger you.'

The other man's teeth flashed. 'Your arrogance is astonishing,' he hissed. 'Do you so much want to die?'

Pathetic really. He just can't help himself.

'Actually, no,' Devon replied. 'Death is my opponent, and my work always sought to defeat him. Our forefathers almost succeeded in that a thousand years ago. You will remember the story of the Soft Men?'

The assassin's expression darkened. 'I remember their punishment.'

Devon smiled. 'They developed a process to extract the soul and bottle it. Do you know what happens when a man consumes the soul of another? I will tell you. When flesh becomes saturated with the only substance that truly enriches it, the balance between the physical and metaphysical shifts. Will, so empowered, is irresistible. Desire can extend life, strengthen the body, heal wounds. Physical ageing becomes a matter of whim.'

He took a step closer to the letting chair and to the metal stand supporting the tubes. 'This equipment is similar to what the Soft Men used. Thirteen souls are required to reach saturation point, a level of potency when the solution can be absorbed by a recipient. A single drop might sustain a man for many lifetimes; give him such control over his flesh that mortal wounds would become mere scratches. A man infused with angelwine is nearer, in every sense, to God.'

The assassin was now coiled like a spring, the knife gripped tightly in his fist. 'You'll not have your trial,' he snarled.

Devon plucked a small bottle from his coat pocket and held it up. Clear liquid sloshed within. 'Eleven unblessed souls.' He pulled the stopper and sniffed. 'Stolen from Ulcis, and no doubt hunted by Iril even as we speak. I wonder if the Maze can sense what it has lost.'

The assassin looked aghast, backed away. 'Replace the cork,' he hissed. 'Hide these souls before—'

Devon threw the contents of the bottle into the assassin's face.

The man howled and doubled over, spitting, dragging his arm frantically across his face.

Devon grabbed the metal stand and swung it hard. The blow threw the assassin across the desk. He smashed through beakers and test-tubes, and dropped to the carpet.

Pain clenched Devon's chest. He felt blood trickling beneath his bandages from freshly opened wounds. Wincing, he pulled another, smaller bottle from his waistcoat pocket and examined the pale-red liquid within.

'Room for one more?' He held the bottle to his ear then sighed, shook his head. 'Iril take me, I'm talking to a bottle of souls.'

And part of me almost expected a response.

He tossed aside the other, empty, bottle. 'Waste of good Rhak,' he muttered.

Broken glass littered the floor. Devon crunched through it as he dragged the unconscious assassin towards the letting chair. 'I am old,' he said, 'and sick. But, unlike you . . .' He heaved the assassin into the chair. 'I am alive. You, my friend, have been dead since birth.'

He tightened the straps around the man's arms and legs. 'Zealots,' he muttered. 'Too easy to manipulate.'

Mr Nettle was shaking as he perched outside the window and watched Devon bind the assassin to the chair. He watched Devon insert tubes into the man's arms. He watched blood flow into a flask on the floor. He watched it all, but didn't see. He was thinking about the angelwine.

Eleven souls.

Abigail's soul?

She was dead, her body lost to the abyss, but her soul had never been given to Ulcis or taken by Iril. Her soul was trapped in this world, in the Poisoner's elixir. Even now, there was still hope for her.

Could her soul be reunited with her body? Would she live again – not in the abyss or the Maze, but here in the city? With him?

Mr Nettle knew what he had to do.

He shuddered.

He had to let Devon complete his work. When the

angelwine became potent he would kill the Poisoner and take it. He would reclaim Abigail's soul from the man who had stolen it.

And then?

Somehow, he had to get her body back.

15

BOOBYTRAPS AND SNAILS

After three hours of restless sleep, Fogwill was up at dawn to greet the assassin. He paced before his cold, untouched breakfast, blinking tired eyes, twisting his rings this way and that.

By mid-morning there was still no sign of the man and he began to fear the worst. Noon came and went and the Adjunct found himself standing by the window, staring listlessly at the view. Louring skies pulled the horizon close, pressed down on the rooftops and soaked the colour from everything. Spine were not late. Even broken Spine did not fail to report.

He knew the assassin was dead.

But that was the least of his worries. The smallest criticism of Devon's work led to bouts of illness in the temple. What would the Poisoner do if he learned who was behind an *assassin attempt*? Fogwill winced. Slurry would be the least of it.

He had to act now, before it was too late.

So he sent runners to the Poison Kitchens to enquire after Devon, and instructions to Captain Clay to gather six of his men and meet him on the Gatebridge within the hour.

Clay trudged heavily out of the temple, his coal-coloured armour clinking, his face slumped under the grey weight of the afternoon heat. Six lethargic temple guards fell in behind him.

'Rain is overdue,' Clay said. 'The clouds are pregnant with it, but keeping it up there to torment us. A foul day – and I've a feeling things are about to get worse. If we're out here, I suppose you propose a march into the city.'

Fogwill mopped his brow. 'We are going to the Poisoner's apartment.'

'Bloody Hell,' Clay said, 'I knew it.'

The Adjunct chose to ignore this impertinence. Benedict Clay, for all his gruffness and bluntness, was a good man. 'The Poisoner did not appear for work this morning,' he said. 'I am concerned something may have happened to him.'

'And this requires six guards?' When Fogwill didn't reply, the captain sighed. 'Well,' he said, 'it isn't getting any cooler. We'd best make a start.'

The streets were quiet and those people they passed went about their business sluggishly, hardly finding the energy to glance up from the cobbles at the Adjunct and his retinue. The temple guards sweated in their armour and Fogwill sweated in his cassock. Even the chains seemed to sweat under the burden of the city. When they crossed the Scythe at Docker's Bridge, the air was turgid, with no hint of a breeze from the abyss, and Fogwill wondered if Ulcis himself was sweating down in the darkness below.

The Adjunct tried not to worry about what he might find in the Poisoner's apartment, but he couldn't help himself. If Devon had overcome the assassin, then doubtless he would have fled. And removed any evidence of his crimes? Almost certainly. Sypes would be furious. But would Devon's disappearance convince the Presbyter of his guilt? Fogwill wasn't sure. After all, he'd given the assassin free rein, told him to use his own judgement. That was like handing a lunatic a knife and telling him to go use it.

They reached the Depression by mid-afternoon. Under the faint red glow of the Poison Kitchens' flamestacks the district simmered. Hot, foul air pooled where the factories and warehouses slumped in a bowl. Brickwork sweated in a dripping haze. Flecks of ash alighted on chains and cobbles like feeding moths, and blackened the sweat on Fogwill's cheeks and neck. His handkerchief was filthy.

The door to Crossop's warehouse opened onto a gloomy stairwell. Clay growled, 'Don't like the look of this. What you want us to say to him if he's there?'

'Tell him I'm concerned, and I'd like a word.'

'That's it? We marched out here for that?' Clay huffed, and then ordered his temple guards to enter the warehouse.

That was the last time Fogwill saw any of the captain's men alive.

The explosion shook the Depression. Stones and bricks and timbers and mortar burst upwards. Smoke mushroomed from the roof of the warehouse.

Fogwill fell back with a jolt onto his rear, his ears ringing with the sound of the blast.

Clay grabbed him, was shouting something, and at first Fogwill couldn't hear.

'I said get away,' Clay cried. He yanked Fogwill's cassock. 'The debris, man! We'll be crushed.' The captain dragged him down the lane towards the doorway of a derelict factory. Fogwill slipped and stumbled, trying to remain upright. He glanced back.

The upper half of the warehouse was now missing. Flames curled up the inside of the walls and lapped at glassless windows. Black smoke spewed from the yawning gap where the roof had been.

Clay pulled him into the doorway just as the debris began to fall. Bricks shattered on the cobbles. Iron spars and burning timbers crashed into the lane or ripped through eaves and tore gutters free. Grit fell like rain.

Fogwill squeezed his hands over his ears.

The sky darkened. A dense pall of smoke was spreading over the Depression. Lit by the distant flamestacks, the expanding cloud seemed to smoulder at its extremities like molten basalt. There was a low, thunderous rumble, then Devon's former apartment collapsed inwards.

'Move!' Clay rushed back into the lane.

Bricks were still crashing down all around them. Fogwill hesitated.

Stones pinged against the captain's armour. 'The chains are going!' he shouted. 'Whole district's going to fall.'

The Adjunct looked back at the ruined warehouse. Heat from the fire slammed into him. Flames fifty feet high engulfed a knot of brickwork and chains that shifted and tightened under collapsing walls and chimneystacks. Even as he watched, those same chains were snapping, whipping everywhere.

Fogwill ran after Clay, wheezing.

They reached the end of the lane just as a mighty roar rocked the ground beneath them. The cobbles shuddered and bucked and Fogwill was thrown off his feet. He rolled like a barrel and struck a wall.

And then there was silence.

'Iril be damned,' Clay breathed.

The Adjunct picked himself up, dusted himself down, and looked back.

Crossop's warehouse was gone. Half a block of the Depression was gone. Where moments ago there had been factories and foundries, there was nothing but a vast hole, veiled in dust and smoke.

Clay grunted. 'There goes the neighbourhood.'

Angry storm clouds brought an early darkness to the city. Wet gales spun weathervanes, slammed shutters, and drove sheets of rain against the windowpanes in Presbyter Sypes's library.

Sypes sat at his desk with his eyes closed, rubbing his temples. 'How long had he been spying for you in the Poison Kitchens?'

Fogwill paced before the Presbyter's desk, his head low, and toyed with his rings. Every word Sypes spoke felt like a slap. 'Several weeks.'

'Does anyone else know about this?'

'No, I thought it best—'

'To undermine my authority?' Sypes's bony fingers tightened around his walking stick. 'Do you think I am too old, too weak, too confused to make decisions?'

'I was trying to be discreet.'

The old man's brows lowered and he pointed the stick at Fogwill. 'This is what you call discreet? Now your . . . *assassin* has vanished. Devon is missing. And I have a hole in my city large enough to swallow half of Sandport.'

'Let's send a unit of temple guard. And more Spine—'

'More!' Sypes's roar drowned the wind-lashed windowpanes. 'What do you expect to find – Devon signalling his whereabouts from a rooftop? A trail of corpses?' He slammed the stick on the desk. 'Yesterday I knew exactly where he was.'

'Yesterday you brushed my suspicions aside.'

A scowl. Fogwill stopped pacing.

'You *knew*? And you did nothing? You were prepared to allow the murders to continue? The *theft of souls*?'

Sypes avoided his eye.

'For God's sake, why?'

The old man's lips crinkled, as though he were chewing on something unpalatable. 'Come with me,' he said. 'There's something you need to see.'

They left the library and took one of the acolyte stairwells deep into the heart of the temple. At the bottom of the stairs Sypes lifted a brand from its wall mount and led Fogwill through a network of dank passages and cellars which appeared to be used for dry storage. Cobwebs clung to everything. After a while they came to a heavy metal door hidden behind crates. Sypes unlocked it and they descended another spiral staircase. Down and down, until Fogwill couldn't believe it was possible to descend any further.

'We must be below the Spine Halls now,' he said.

'Part of the old dungeons,' Sypes's voice echoed. 'Disused now. Here, help me with this door.'

At the foot of the stairwell, the Presbyter unlocked another ancient door, and Fogwill helped him drag it open. They were assaulted by the most frightful odour. Rotting meat? Fogwill harboured no such illusions. It seemed every time the Presbyter led him somewhere it was to see a dead body.

'Another corpse?' he ventured.

'Yes, well, sort of. I have it locked in one of the cells.'

Then the old man was off into the dungeons. Puzzled, and not a little apprehensive, Fogwill scurried after him. Rusted grates in the walls marked the entrances to dark cells. The smell grew worse. Sypes's brand guttered and plunged them into near-darkness.

'Useless thing,' the Presbyter muttered. 'Hasn't been tarred in years.' He halted outside one of the cells and beckoned Fogwill closer. 'Be careful. Don't get too close to the bars. It spits.'

'I thought you said it was dead.'

'I'm not entirely convinced.'

Fogwill peered into the cell. The torchlight did not penetrate far beyond the bars, and he strained to see. For a heartbeat he thought he discerned movement. From the back of the cell came the sound of a chain slithering over stone. He recoiled. 'What is it?'

The Presbyter grunted, gave an impatient wave of his hand.

Fogwill looked closer. As his eyes grew accustomed to the darkness, he made out a shape. A wing? 'It's an angel,' he breathed.

'Not quite,' Sypes said.

Then Fogwill saw what his master meant. The wing was attached to a shoulder, the shoulder to a torso, the torso to a leg, arm, neck, and head. Or most of a head. The rest of the angel was missing. It appeared to have been divided, roughly, in half. It was gnawing on something white and wet.

'This *thing*,' the Presbyter said, 'is Callis. Or part of him. The other half remains with Ulcis. Down below.' He rapped his stick on the dungeon floor.

'Darkness take me! What is it doing here?'

'What it's always done. Speaking the will of its master. Issuing orders.'

'It can speak?'

'It never shuts up. This is the first time it's been silent in a year.'

On cue, Callis spoke: 'Feed me.'

'No!' Sypes boomed. 'You've had enough.'

The sound of wet breathing issued from the darkness. 'Never enough,' the angel hissed.

Fogwill was stunned. This pitiful creature was Dill's ancestor, mutilated, left to rot in a dungeon for thousands of years. Then the angel's words sunk in, and he cast a wary eye at the Presbyter. 'What are you feeding it?'

'Anything except what it asks for.'

The Adjunct swallowed. 'But if this is Ulcis's herald, then whose bones stand in the Sanctum corridor with the Ninety-Nine?'

'Have you looked closely at those bones? They are of similar but not identical sizes.' The Presbyter shrugged. 'The skeleton is a composite. A rib here, a forearm there . . . Donated, no doubt, from the remains of the other Ninety-Nine.'

'But why? Why is Callis here? In this . . . cell?'

Sypes grimaced, and then addressed the angel. 'Tell him.'

The voice crawled back from the darkness, thick with malice. 'Feed me.'

'Tell him.'

A growl.

'Tell him! Or you'll starve for a year.'

'You dare deny me!' the creature cried. It dragged itself, panting, across the cell floor. 'Ulcis will not be denied. He is coming, priest. An army forged from the corpses of your fathers, bound to his will. We will take what is ours. Soon.'

'First it was merely requests,' Presbyter Sypes said. 'More souls, more souls. And it could croon so sweetly for something so hideous. But it then asked for more than we could ever provide. The Heshette are decimated. Who else is left to kill? When I couldn't engineer a way to meet its requests, it shed its veneer. Demands followed. Then threats. I do not take kindly to being threatened.'

'Good God!' Fogwill exclaimed. 'Don't you see? This urgency . . .? Ulcis is going to reclaim heaven. He's going to challenge Ayen. We need to prepare. We need to—'

'No,' Sypes said.

'What?'

'No, Fogwill, this monster speaks freely when it is hungry, and lately I've taken to keeping it ravenous. Ulcis has never intended to reclaim heaven. It's this world he wants. Our Church is founded entirely on a lie.'

The Adjunct gaped at his master. This was such a shocking thing to hear that for a moment he forgot his fear, and slumped against the cell bars.

'Get back!' Sypes cried.

Chain rattled.

Fogwill felt teeth sink into his calf. He wailed, tried to pull away, but the grip was ferocious.

'Release him!' Sypes roared. 'Or never feed again. I'll keep you rotting here for eternity.'

Snarling, the angel released its grip. Fogwill staggered back, pale-faced and shaking. Blood flowed freely from the wound and into his robes. He turned one way, then another, dazed and unsure. Soap – he needed soap. He had to get away from here, away from Sypes's words, away from the mutilated angel. He didn't want to know this. He wanted sunlight, a place to gather his wits. Somewhere where he could find his faith again and hold on to it tight.

Presbyter Sypes was shaking him roughly. 'Get a grip of yourself, man! I need you thinking straight.'

Chains scraping again at the back of the cell. 'Feed me! Feed me!'

On the fringes of the Depression, Devon sat on a deck-chair on the roof of an old, leaning tower that had formerly belonged to Jacob Blacklock, once a foundry owner of some means. The white parasol he had erected snapped in the wind, and offered him little protection from the driving rain, but he was enjoying the view all the same. Dark clouds mounded over Deepgate, lit by the blazing factories and warehouses clustered around the gaping rent in the city. Even from this distance, firelight reflected in his spectacles and the crystal flute of Rhak he held in his hand. He held the glass under his nose, sniffed the oily fumes, and then set it down. Old Crossop's stock had done a fine job in fuelling the fire. At least it had not gone to waste.

Now he had important work to do. Cautious of the sloping roof, he rose and walked over to the stairs that spiralled down into his new home. The Blacklocks had abandoned this tower after the demise of their foundry, when the supporting chains had been stretched to the point where the Depression was deemed unsafe, but Devon was not overly concerned. The tower had remained intact for so long, it was unlikely to collapse in the near future. Not that he had the luxury of choice.

Compared to his previous abode, the room he inhabited was simple. Piles of crumbled mortar banked the circular walls. Wind whistled through a shattered window. Recesses in the naked stone held some of his books and a guttering oil lamp. The rest of his books were in piles on the floor, except for a few he had used to prop the legs of his desk and chair to keep them level. Crates packed with essential equipment, clothes and food lay stacked to one side, each with the word *Crossop* branded into the wood. In the centre of the room stood the letting chair, and seven flasks of Spine blood.

Devon had explored this tower years ago on one of his winter strolls, and kept a note of the place. The Blacklocks had left behind a few simple pieces of furniture: a worm-riddled desk that would not have fitted through the narrow window or down the stairwell, and had not been worth the trouble of dismantling; an old bureau and coffer, similarly too cumbersome to move; and a barrel of lamp oil. The tower cistern was a third full, some ninety gallons or so, brackish but drinkable. But it had been a hard night's work bringing the rest of his equipment up the hill, and then up the stairs. The exertion had almost finished him. Still, once he was settled, he would be able to live here for several weeks without venturing far into Deepgate. Though he felt some regret at the loss of his fine furnishings and paintings – the delicate Clune mirror, and his set of leather-bound Bradenkas – he was not a man to dwell on his losses for long, and he set to work unpacking the remainder of the equipment. His situation, after all, was in some ways simpler now. His work at the Poison Kitchens would no longer interfere with his development of the angelwine, and disposal of the final body, whoever that turned out to be, need not be so arduous. The tower had a deep basement.

Once his apparatus was set up – the flasks, stands and burners arranged for extraction, purification and filtration – Devon sat at his desk and opened the bag containing his papers. He set the Soft Men's journal to one side and his own notes beside it.

Thirteen souls had brought the original elixir to saturation point. Devon had expected some sign of potency to become apparent before now but, to his dismay, there had been no indication yet of any of the reported effects. True, the notes were fragmented, inconsistent in places. The language was archaic, often laced with terms Devon did not fully comprehend, but from what he could gather, the effects had been remarkable.

After ingesting angelwine, laboratory rats recovered quickly from what would normally have been mortal wounds and poxes. Severed limbs were regrown, even decapitation was not fatal. The heads survived, alert, while the bodies continued to twitch and scratch inside their cages. If head and torso were reunited, they melded, and the rats became completely functional once more. By continuing to refresh saturated flesh with drops of elixir, lifespan could be increased indefinitely.

Devon flipped through the pages of his transcription. One thing beyond the lack of preliminary results troubled him deeply. The animals would succumb to fits of unbridled rage – and madness.

Angelwine-fed rats would attack, rip apart anything living they came into contact with. Frequently they would even attempt to harm themselves, gnaw their own limbs, as though seeking death.

Seeking release from unbearable trauma?

The elixir, however, would not be denied. Life prevailed. Any damage the animals wrought upon themselves soon healed. The only way to end the wretched creatures' torment had been to remove every last drop of their blood.

Further proof that life's energy is contained within the blood. The soul? A temple word. And, down in the abyss, what removes the blood from the dead before this energy dissipates? The god of chains?

Devon smiled. One day it might be worth finding out.

There were long gaps in the notes after the initial animal tests. Pages had been defaced, as though such knowledge had been too dangerous for even the Church to hoard. But there were hints: fragments scrawled in margins after Mr Partridge, Mr Hightower and Mr Bloom had taken a sip of angelwine.

Devon ran his finger along some of the clues he had been able to decipher: a few anguished sentences written by Mr Hightower before the Spine had come to claim him and his colleagues.

- *A tainted spirit or many, hidden in the broth, may bend the will of the riven collective.*
- *Murderers or blackhearts? Or goodly spirits, demented by the weight of thickened sin.*
- *Tempestuous is their wrath for our sins.*
- *Souls whisper from the veil. The sharpest knife cannot cut them out. Flesh heals. The voices pull me closer to Iril.*

Clearly the text implied that the extracted souls implanted in the new hosts were conscious. And furious. Devon dismissed this, albeit uneasily. He was dealing with metaphysical energies applied to physical matter, unconscious energies that could be utilized and directed by a conscious, living brain. He wasn't bottling ghosts.

Hightower, given his ardent faith, was simply struggling with forces he was unable to comprehend in anything but spiritual terms. He believed he was possessed.

Devon considered this. Hightower had obviously suffered terribly. The dementia was either a product of his conflicted faith, or side effects caused by pollutants in the elixir. The latter was more likely. Mindless rats, after all, had screamed too.

Back in the Temple library, Sypes had surrendered his chair to Fogwill and called for lint, alcohol and bandages. Now the old man was on his knees, attending himself to the Adjunct's wounds.

'The Soft Men's Journal took months to find,' Sypes explained, dabbing blood from Fogwill's calf. 'Amid all this . . .' He waved the red-stained wad of lint at the pillars of books behind him. 'This decay.'

Fogwill barely felt the Presbyter's ministrations. He could not stop shaking. A terrible cold had settled in his heart. In the tumult of his upended life, he groped for pieces that made sense.

Our faith, built upon a lie? Heaven is for ever closed. Callis, Herald to the Hoarder of Souls, little more than a ravenous beast. And our god . . .

The Temple of Ulcis rose above him, an impossible weight. Naught but cold, empty spaces.

What is *our god?*

'I could not understand the science, of course. Few of our chemists could.'

The theft of thirteen souls – for what? *Did you hope to turn Devon into a monster to rival Ulcis?*

Sypes bound Fogwill's newly cleaned calf in bandages,

tightly, forcing the Adjunct to wince. Then the old man rose, his face weary, his brow furrowed. 'Do you think it was an easy decision to make?' he snapped. 'Devon is the only man with the audacity to see something like this through. He loathes the Church!'

'You'd make him a god?'

'Not him, you fool! One sip of angelwine and he'd have turned as mad as a broom. We would have soon taken the elixir from him.'

Not you, Sypes . . . Darkness take me . . . Did you think you could hold madness at bay?

'Look around you, Adjunct!' Sypes lashed his stick at the codex pillars. 'Is there verity here? What truths are mouldering, buried under all these lies?' He hobbled over to the nearest pillar, unlocked a grate, and pulled out one of the volumes. 'Blackcake. Cannon. Forgotten words.' He began ripping out pages. 'No meaning here! And here . . .' – another grate, another book – '. . . Heathen cults. Barrows near Loom. What does that mean?' He threw the book to the floor, pulled out another. 'Ha! An account of the Battle of the Tooth. Lies!' The old man tore more pages free, tossed them into the air. 'All lies! It means nothing.'

The Presbyter stood, chest heaving, among the tumbling pages. Thin ink-stained fingers curled around his walking stick. 'The oldest books are dust, Fogwill. And *there's* the only verity. Time subjugates everything. Truth and lies become synonymous. In the end, nothing we think or do matters.'

'But you can't believe that. You'd oppose your own god, take angelwine and suffer madness? You'd risk the wrath of the Spine – to save us all.'

The old priest sighed deeply. 'The elixir was meant for

Carnival. A restorative to end her suffering. With angel-wine we . . .' He leaned heavily on his stick. 'It was the only thing with which we might have bought her aid.'

You wanted Carnival as an ally? Barely an hour ago the Adjunct would have found such blasphemy staggering. But now? *A tower of cards, this plan. One enemy employed to fashion the means by which we might recruit a second foe, the second to oppose the most dangerous of them all.*

Our own god?

The Presbyter must have caught Fogwill's expression, for he said, 'The god of chains is furious, Fogwill. He's coming for our souls, a dead army at his command, all mindless prisoners of his will. Who but Carnival could stand against him?' He rubbed his face, let out a long breath. 'The angelwine . . .? Devon must be found.'

Fogwill nodded slowly. 'Our forces?'

'Recall them,' Sypes said. 'We need them here . . . ready.'

'What will we tell them?'

Sypes shrugged. 'I haven't the faintest idea.'

Something strange was happening. For two days Dill had noticed the change, but as usual no one bothered to explain what was going on. Warships were returning from the outposts, more than he had ever seen gathering before. The Deepgate skies were full of them. And soldiers: units of men assembled in the Gatebridge courtyard each morning before marching into the city. Overheard snippets of kitchen staff conversation suggested some form of military manoeuvre was under way. The priests were rushing around, grim-faced, no time to speak to Dill. Even the mourners at the Sending appeared more agitated than usual and, in the Sanctum, both the Presbyter and Adjunct Crumb were wrapped in separate clouds of gloom.

The angel began to wonder if everyone in the city except him was privy to some secret. Was Deepgate expecting an attack from the heathens?

No doubt Rachel had been busy with her Spine duties, for he hadn't seen her since their tour of the Poison Kitchens. Yesterday, just as the sun broke through the crown of spires, he'd climbed the stairwells and ladders to emerge on the tower roof where she'd convinced him to fly. But she hadn't appeared. Not that he'd gone there to look for her; it was just that he had rather more time on his hands than usual, and he enjoyed the feeling of the breeze on his feathers, and the chance to get away from the close-lipped priests who shouldered by him on some important errand or other.

The snails were becoming more of a problem too. More of them than ever had been finding their way into his cell, and lately he'd taken to releasing them further afield. He walked for miles throughout the temple, planting one here, one there. He left them outside the priests' cells, one at each door, and in the Sanctum Corridor; he placed them on steps and on window ledges, and outside the school-room. Once he went to the Spine Halls with half a bucket of them, but it was dark down there, so he changed his mind and put them in the Blue Hall instead, under table napkins.

Today he had a full bucket, nearly a hundred snails, and was wandering the dusty passages near the acolytes' stairwells, looking for suitable places to deposit them, when a stooped, grey-faced priest struggled by with an armful of scrolls, shoving Dill's wings aside. 'Must you always get in everyone's way?'

'I'm sorry.' Dill flattened himself against the wall.

'Can't you bind those things up?' the priest snarled. He scurried on down the passageway, cassock swishing the flagstones underfoot, grey head shaking like a stone working loose from those around it.

The priest threw a dismissive final word over his shoulder. 'If you must collect snails, for God's sake don't let Fondelgrue near them.'

The kitchen? Dill hadn't thought of that. It would be warm in there. Perhaps the snails would like the heat and stay put. He snapped his wings out and stormed away, his feathers brooming dust from the walls.

I'll take up just as much room as I like.

So he raced through passageways and arches, wings spread wide, drawing them in only as he passed each of the wall-mounted torches. He left a trail of snails as he went.

By the time he reached the stairwell to the ivy-tower, his bucket was empty and he felt victorious. He hadn't yielded to another priest. Then again, he hadn't met one either, but that wasn't the point. He snatched up a brand and tore up the stairs.

A hundred steps higher the narrow windows began. Dill slotted the brand into an empty sconce, set down his bucket, and pounded up the rest of the stairs. If anyone was coming down, they'd just have to move out of his way.

The trapdoor opened on to endless blue sky. Underneath crumbling arches, the gargoyles sat hunched, facing outwards, indifferent.

Rachel wasn't here. Dill flopped to the ground.

No one had time for him any more. Why were they always in such a rush? If the city was preparing for an attack, shouldn't he at least be informed? Was he not still an appointed guardian of the temple?

He jumped to his feet, flapped his wings irritably. *Are you watching?* The windows in the surrounding spires were all closed, the priests too busy threading through the corridors inside, too busy weaving their big secret to notice or care. Dill beat his wings harder, lifted an inch from the ground, before he panicked and let himself drop.

But a door open an inch is still an open door. Right then, Dill decided to do something he knew was forbidden. He decided to teach himself how to fly.

His initial attempts were dire. Worried that someone would emerge from the tower, he found a beam of wood to secure the trapdoor. Even then, he fretted and paced for a while before he felt confident that nobody would suddenly appear. Each time he beat his wings and felt himself begin to rise, he would pause, nervously listening for someone climbing the steps below. Eventually, he plucked up the courage to rise a full foot in the air. Then three feet. Then six. But he always descended again quickly to press his ear against the trapdoor.

Turning became a problem. He found he could hold himself static in the air quite comfortably, but when he attempted to move left or right, forward or backwards, he would lose his balance, panic, and crash to the stone surface before he knew what had gone wrong. He could hover, raise and lower himself, but what use would that be except for replacing candles in the temple candelabra? How had Gaine done it? Dill had never seen his father fly, but knew the angel had flown with the churchships into battle in his youth. If only his father were here to show him.

Days passed. Dill returned each morning to the ivy-tower to practise. He held himself aloft for longer each time, hovering above the centre of the circular roof, with the stone gargoyles shunning him, yet mocking him, and he dreaded the turns he would try to make, and the inevitable tumble to the flagstones that would follow. His hands and knees were constantly grazed, his clothes always dusty and torn. Nobody seemed to notice. The temple staff remained preoccupied with their secret dilemma. Rachel meanwhile did not appear. Dill persisted alone.

And then one morning, it came to him.

He was hovering some six feet above the roof, hearing finches twitter among the arches, when he noticed a tiny flower sprouting from a gargoyle's neck. On impulse he decided to pluck it, and before he knew it had crossed the circle and was holding the flower in his hand. It felt like a trophy. He then moved back and left across the circle, towards another of the stone creatures. It now seemed effortless: he just thought of shifting in a certain direction, and it happened. His heart was racing.

The motions he made with his wings were so subtle he wasn't even sure what he was doing. He deliberately tried moving to the right and felt himself begin to fall, only just catching himself in time. No: too much thought. He had to relax, let his wings carry him effortlessly. The trick, he discovered, was not to *try*, but rather just let it happen. Slowly, he banked right and upwards, turning again to bring himself into the centre of the circle. Now higher this time; he ignored the physical motions of his wings and made a tight circle over the tower roof, then up, even higher, to the point where falling would injure him badly. With each new manoeuvre, his confidence grew.

He had it. He could fly.

Dill soared, laughing. He left the gargoyles and the broken arches far below and flew over wedges of pitched slate and chimneys, and out beyond the Rookery Spire. Deepgate stretched before him, soft with morning mist. He sucked in a deep lungful of sweet air, circled the spire, then flew back to gaze triumphantly down at the familiar ivy-tower. The gargoyles now looked tiny, earthbound and ugly, staring out with their fixed grimaces, oblivious to the angel above them.

And then he realized the trapdoor was rattling. Someone was trying to get out onto the roof.

A moment of panic nearly sent him plummeting, but he recovered and managed to control his descent. Dill landed safely, if not particularly elegantly. When he knocked the wooden beam away and pulled open the trapdoor, he was out of breath and shaking.

Rachel stepped out into the sunlight and eyed him suspiciously. 'What have you been up to?' she said. Her gaze travelled the length of his scuffed clothing.

'Nothing.'

'Why couldn't I open that trapdoor?'

He blushed, cheeks and eyes. 'I was . . . exercising.'

She focused on the scuffs on Dill's breeches. 'Exercising?' There was a hint of a smile on her lips. 'My brother used to say the same thing.'

Dill felt his eyes bloom pink. He turned and brushed some dust off his clothing. 'Where have you been?' he asked. 'I haven't seen you anywhere in the temple for ages.'

'I've been busy. All this trouble with Devon has left the military in chaos. No one knows which ship is to be refuelled where, which payload is bound for which deck. The warships and regulars in the garrisons have been recalled. There's even talk of reinstating the reservists.'

'What trouble with Devon?'

She regarded him strangely. 'Does no one tell you anything?'

Dill shook his head. He tried to look indifferent, but the last of his elation quickly dissolved into chagrin. 'No, I suppose not.'

So Rachel told Dill about the Poisoner's disappearance and the explosion which had killed the temple guards sent to search his apartment. Now a citywide manhunt was under way. Dill listened with a mixture of wonder and growing shame. The city was not preparing for an attack. The Church hadn't turned its back on him by failing to involve him. And yet he had broken temple law by learning to fly.

'He was making angelwine,' Rachel explained.

'Like the—'

'Exactly. The Soft Men. A bunch of extra husks turn up, the Church sends temple guards out to speak to Devon, and *boom*! Six armoured crispies and no sign of the Poisoner.'

'Has the Church—?'

'Yes, Sypes had to make a statement. If the Spine possessed enough emotion to get antsy, they'd be crawling over every chain in Deepgate by now. Angelwine!' She shook her head. 'There's even talk of digging up the Soft Men and asking them what we can expect.'

'Why would—'

'He's dying, and dying men get desperate.'

Dill frowned. 'Why won't you—?'

'Let you finish a sentence?' She paused. 'I don't know. Sorry. Go ahead, I won't interrupt again.'

Dill couldn't think of anything else to say.

16

MANHUN†

In the days that followed, the hunt for Devon showed no sign of abating. Every morning Dill made a circuit of his balcony and watched the airships patrolling low over Deepgate. The city sky buzzed with them. At night, their aether searchlights probed the darkest corners under the waxing moon, while Dill huddled in his cell among his candles and his snails and hoped that, just once, the searchlights would fall on him.

Taking the snails to the kitchen had been a bad idea. Fondelgrue had pounced on them and put them all in a bag. The fat cook had assured Dill that he knew a place where they would be happy, and where Dill would never see them again, but the angel wasn't convinced. He'd offered to go with Fondelgrue to make sure the snails were all right, but the cook had shooed him away and said don't worry, they'll be absolutely fine, very warm, very happy, now sod off. So Dill had found a new place to release his charges – the temple guards' armour room. There were lots of dark places in there for them to hide.

He'd just completed an evening snail-run to the armoury when Rachel burst into his cell and he dropped the book he was reading.

'They've got every temple guard in the city out there, knocking at doors, searching houses, questioning everyone, bloodhounds sniffing everywhere, and the third, seventh and ninth have been recalled from Sandport and the Plantation hill forts to join the search. And they've begun reinstating reservists, hundreds of them. There are more soldiers in the city than I've seen in years, and yet more are on the way. Have you seen the warships? Sypes has aeronauts out on the decks with sightglasses.'

She paused for a breath. 'The nobles are unsettled, and the common folk are moaning like kittens in a bath tub. They can feel a curfew coming, increased taxes. You should hear the talk in the alehouses and penny taverns. Why so many soldiers for a simple manhunt? And why the blazes should they have to pay for it all?'

'Will there be trouble?' Dill asked, still slightly perturbed that she hadn't knocked.

'Not from the forces,' she said. 'The reservists are happy to be earning wages again, and merchants and nobles can afford the extra levy. But the commoners might cause a problem: those who are happy enough for their souls to be saved, and willing enough to attend the executions, but don't care to dip into their pockets to feed an army of this size.'

She made her way to his balcony door and wandered outside. After a moment he grabbed his book and went to join her.

Shadows reached out from the western rim of the abyss, already cloaking a third of Deepgate. To the east, the streets and homes glittered: chains, roofs and chimneys turned golden in the sunset, glints of copper and bronze, windows bright as scattered gems. A dozen airships drifted above the city, like scavengers sifting treasure.

'It's full moon tonight,' Rachel said. 'Spine mark the occasion with a night of prayers to Ulcis. They pray the moon will not wane, and that Scar Night doesn't return.'

'*They?*'

She shrugged. 'Normally I feel easier at full moon, since Carnival keeps herself hidden. The streets at night are reasonably busy, people relax. But tonight . . .' A warship droned by, close to the temple. Rachel paused and watched it for a while. 'Tonight everything feels *wrong*. They're leaving farmlands unguarded all along the Coyle, recalling soldiers from as far north as the Shale logging camps and Hollowhill. Too many soldiers for a simple manhunt. Something else is going on. Presbyter Sypes isn't telling us everything.'

'An attack from the Heshette?'

'No.' She studied the warship a moment longer, then faced him. 'The Heshette haven't been a threat to the city for decades. What are you reading, anyway?'

Dill showed her the book: *Battle Flight Strategies for Temple Archons.*

She smiled.

'It's not forbidden,' he said. 'I checked.' But he still felt his eyes blush a little.

In the darkness of the den he had built in the nets below Devon's tower, Mr Nettle watched the warships pass overhead. Engines thrummed distantly; searchlights divided the night, moving incessantly, like the legs of strange aether gods.

A five-by-four tin sheet and three stout beams salvaged from the shell of a coalgas depository formed the makeshift roof. Rope tied it all together and secured it to the net.

The nets here were thick, as they were in all industrial districts, easily strong enough to support the weight of his shelter. He'd ventured out a few times in the past two weeks to stock up on supplies. With nothing to trade, and no time to go scrounging, he'd been forced to steal the food from carts at the Gardenhowe market. He'd filled his water flask from a worker's pipe near the Scythe, but hadn't dropped a halfpenny into the slot.

Mr Nettle's crimes gnawed at him – his mind kept returning to them like fresh scabs – but they didn't trouble him like his other dilemma. That one sat in his gut like a brick.

Twelve souls had been harvested – one more was needed. In order to make the angelwine potent, the Poisoner would have to bleed the life from another innocent.

And Mr Nettle would have to let him do it.

He clenched his teeth and turned over in the net, as though that would somehow ease the pain. Abigail was all that mattered. *Abigail, Abigail*: he said her name over and over in his mind, using it to drum other thoughts out. Now that he knew where her soul was, he had to let Devon finish composing the elixir. He had to do it, *for her*.

But Abigail's voice was always in his thoughts, and she wasn't happy.

What about the other souls? she asked him. *Will they be trapped inside me? Or will I be trapped inside them?*

He didn't want to think about that. How many people would she be?

The ropes beneath him stretched as he twisted over on his stomach and peered into the abyss. The journey down there would be difficult.

Impossible, Abigail insisted. *How are you going to climb*

*down? By rope? Are you going to use your grapple and spikes
all the way down to the city of Deep? Then what? Will you
walk into Ulcis's palace of chains and demand he release my
body?*

He didn't know. Everyone had heard the stories of the
folk who'd gone down there. And how no one ever came
back.

I'll find a way.

How?

I don't know. Maybe he could steal an airship, or scale
the edge of the abyss.

Steal an airship? She laughed. *Who do you think you are?
You're a scrounger, for god's sake.*

Leave me alone.

Then what about your soul? You are giving up eternity.

An image of Abigail came to him then: at six years old,
stamping her foot.

What *about* his soul? He had been damned from the
moment he decided to retrieve his daughter's body from
the abyss. The god of chains did not welcome intrusions.
There would be no salvation for Mr Nettle.

I don't care, he told her. And he realized that he didn't.
There was solace in damnation. If he was to let Devon
murder again, then it was fitting. Necessary.

He'll bleed them! Her anger made him flinch. *How can
you let him hurt anyone else? Someone else like me.*

Shut up!

A fist closed on his heart. How had he reached this
place? What forces had steered him? There had been no
choice in his life since Abigail's death. None. He wasn't
responsible – god was. God was trying to take everything
from him, trying to empty him. Trying to beat him down.

For a moment he despaired. In the dark of the nets beneath the tower and the city and the airships, he felt small, empty but for the echoes of Abigail's voice.

Then anger welled, filling the void inside him, pushing back at everything. Anger enough to support a city. He twisted fistfuls of the net, blood pounded in his ears, and he spat into the abyss. So what if another died? He wasn't holding the knife.

Don't!

He won't defeat me.

Abigail would be his victory.

He found himself breathing heavily, and he turned on his back, still clutching the net. The airship had drifted out of sight behind the tower, but another was rumbling closer from the south. High above, a light shone from the tower's narrow window.

Careless.

Recently, Devon had taken to leaving a light burning at all hours of the night. During their first sweep of the Depression, the temple guard had been unable to force the tower door, so had simply moved on when their bloodhounds had shown no interest in the place. But if Devon thought he was safe then he was a fool. That light would eventually attract someone's attention – especially in this neighbourhood. How could the Poisoner be so stupid?

A head popped out of the window and peered up at the sky. Spectacles glinted, disappeared back inside.

Mr Nettle moved a hand to the handle of his cleaver but kept his eyes fixed on the window.

Suddenly a hammering sound startled him. He sat bolt upright, listening. There was a pause, and then the sound repeated. There could be no mistake; someone was pounding on the door of the Poisoner's tower.

Carnival watched the airships above from the bough of an old stonewood tree. A bright halo shone through low cloud, but after this night the full moon would begin to wane. Two weeks until Scar Night and hunger had already begun to crawl back into her veins. An empty ache cloyed in her stomach, a discomfort that would build over the days to come – until the dark moon rose, and she died again.

She tried to ignore the sensation. The night was deliciously cool amid the scent of flowers from the garden beneath. Sweet-thorns, honeyweed and sprays of jasmine bordered the neat silver lawn around her tree, and brushed the ivy-dark walls beyond.

She often came to this place at night to clear her lungs, to sit up in the tree and listen to the whisper of leaves in the breeze. An old gardener arrived every day at dawn, unlocked the iron grate set in the north wall, locked it shut behind him, and then began his leisurely circuit of the flower beds.

Carnival rarely stayed out until such hours – when the light hurt her eyes – but once or twice she had watched the old man in silence from her perch. She found his calm devotion relaxing; the way he pottered around muttering to himself, hoeing and pruning, enjoying the still of the morning. This was the closest she ever felt to another person in the city.

She avoided the garden on Scar Night.

From his shabby appearance, she doubted he owned the plants he tended. This was a garden to display wealth, and if its owners ever visited this place, it was long after the sun had steamed the dew off the grass and forced Carnival back into hiding.

Now, with the night chilly against her skin and the fragrance of bark and flowers all around her, she gazed up and frowned as a warship thundered overhead, its searchlights cutting through the darkness.

How long was their search going to go on? In the beginning she had studied the airships with mild interest. Had she killed someone important the last Scar Night? The doctor hadn't seemed to be of particularly high social standing; could he be the relative of some general, some high-ranking priest? Every few decades, usually on the appointment of a new Presbyter, the temple would make a display of hunting her down. Nervous guards patrolled the streets, never looking too closely into the shadows. Curfews were instigated; the population were shown that *something was being done.* Usually the charade dwindled after a while, but *this* search showed no signs of letting up, and it was beginning to grate on her nerves. Those airships were so *loud* – she cursed every time one of them disturbed her rest. And she began to wonder if she was really the target after all.

The airship turned, low in the sky, its engines hacking and pounding as if its sole purpose was to annoy her. A searchlight swept over the garden, blinding her.

'Damn them!' She twisted her face away. The beam lingered briefly, bleaching the garden, before moving on again. Darkness swamped back over her.

Carnival gripped the branch tightly as her eyes narrowed on the airborne intruder. This was going to have to stop. If they were trying to find her, she was going to make it easier for them.

Lying in the soil below, she spied a three-pronged gardening fork. She leaped from the branch, snapped out her wings, and swooped low across the lawn, snatching up the fork as she passed.

Then she beat a path upwards towards the warship.

Mr Nettle glanced up again at the tower window. Devon had killed the light. Apparently he'd heard the knocking too.

'Too late,' he hissed through his teeth. 'They've found you, you old fool.'

Careful not to make a sound, he scrambled from his den to where the net joined one of the tower's support chains. A nest of rusted girders and heavy plates – broken and welded countless times – sank into the darkness below. With one hand on the stone for balance, he hopped from one chain to the next until he reached a place where he could get a clear view of the tower door.

It was dark, but Mr Nettle saw two armour-clad figures standing before the tower – temple guards armed with pikes. A bloodhound snuffled about their feet, all floppy ears and saliva. The closer man rapped his pike several times against the door. 'Open up,' he called. 'Presbyter's orders.'

Mr Nettle cursed under his breath. If he rushed the guards, it was doubtful he could overpower them both, and the sound would only reveal him to Devon. It was a hopeless situation. His left hand pressed firmly against the stone wall, the other clenched and unclenched on the cleaver handle. He could only hope that the guards hadn't spotted the light from the window, that this was a random search, and that the two men would give up and move on.

Then a voice from inside the tower made him catch his breath. 'Hold on, hold on, will you? I'm coming as fast as I can.'

Devon was coming down to meet them?

Thoughts tumbled inside Mr Nettle's skull. What was the idiot doing? Was he drunk or had he lost his damn mind? Had he decided to give himself up? Was Ulcis going to deny him the elixir too?

Abigail's voice remained thankfully silent. She knew him well enough to leave him to his despair. His head drooped, rested against the wall. God had beaten him.

A lock rattled, then Mr Nettle heard the tower door creak open a fraction.

'Who are you? What do you want at this time of night?' Devon sounded annoyed.

The bloodhound sniffed at the door for a moment, then resumed dragging its jowls around the guards' feet. Whatever scent it had been given, the Poisoner had managed to shed.

Evidently the guards could not see clearly to whom they were speaking. 'We have orders to search all the buildings in this area.'

'Orders? On whose authority?'

'Presbyter Sypes.'

There was a pause. 'No, I am sorry. That's quite impossible.'

The guards shared a look, stiffened, and levelled their pikes at the door. 'Why?' the first demanded.

'Because,' Devon said, 'it would lead to my arrest.'

And then Mr Nettle heard a sound: a rush of air. To his astonishment the nearest guard collapsed at once. The other staggered back a few paces and swayed dizzily for a moment, before he too dropped to the ground with a thump and clunk of armour. The bloodhound scampered away a few feet, and then turned, tail wagging and jowls swinging. It barked.

Devon stepped out from the doorway and looked up and down the lane. He held a metal canister with a flexible tube protruding from its tip. 'Two weeks,' he said. 'It took you two bloody weeks to get here. I was about to start putting up signposts.'

The bloodhound backed away, raised its head, and barked again, then edged forward.

Devon tossed it something from his pocket.

The dog slewed around, paws skidding, and slobbered down whatever had been thrown to it. Then it turned, strings of saliva swinging, and looked up expectantly at Devon.

Mr Nettle watched the Poisoner drag the guards inside the tower.

The dog followed, tail wagging.

The tower basement was dank and windowless. Metal panels bolted over the rotten floorboards boomed as Devon paced back and forth before his captives. Rats scratched in the crawlspace under the floor, pattered across the heavy iron foundations below. A smoking fuel burner set low on the wall cast long shadows as he walked, intermittently covering and revealing the bruises on the two guards' faces.

Devon had simply piled the unconscious men head over heels down twenty steep steps. It had been noisy, but relatively effortless, and he felt that minimum strain was important in his present condition. Their armour had protected them from the worst of the fall. Now somewhat bashed and scraped, it gleamed dully in the glow of the flames.

The men were groggy but awake; chained back to back around one of the girders supporting the weight of the rooms stacked above. One was young, soft-skinned, but broad as a wrestler; the other, probably his lieutenant, had the look of a worn veteran with too many cold morning patrols etched in his face. The dog was sniffing around the rear of the basement.

'How are you feeling?' Devon asked, his tone cheerful from habit. It was important to seem polite, important that the men felt – as much as possible given the circum-stances – that he was a potential ally whose actions were outside his control. But it was also necessary to cause friction between the pair from the beginning, for he had not the time or energy to interrogate them separately. Easier if he could turn them against each other. The more he learned about them, the more harm he could poten-tially cause them, and pain, after all, had always been at the core of Devon's work.

'My chest,' the younger guard gasped. 'I can't breathe.'

Devon nodded. 'You probably broke a rib when you fell down the stairs. I doubt it's serious, though, and I may have an unguent upstairs to ease the pain.'

The veteran squinted into the harsh light from the burner. 'Devon?'

'I have a dilemma,' Devon went on, watching both men carefully.

They waited in silence for him to go on.

He tapped a finger against his lips as he continued pacing. He sighed, wrung his hands, and then adopted a regretful, almost despondent tone. 'I'm afraid only one of you will live through this.'

Surprisingly, the veteran's eyes widened in fear. Perhaps cold mornings were all this man had suffered. The younger man's expression, however, hardened.

Good.

'What are your names?' Devon asked mildly.

A ragged breath escaped the younger guard's throat.

The veteran answered uneasily. 'Angus. And he's Lars.'

'The dog?'

'Fitzgerald,' the veteran added.

At the sound of his name, Fitzgerald lifted his snout a moment before returning to his explorations.

The rhythmic impact of Devon's boots on the metal floor panels rang out like the slow ticking of an iron clock. The echoes pressed back on them from the walls, and made the underground space seem even more confined. 'Any family, either of you?' he asked.

'What?' The veteran, Angus, winced. 'What do you want from us?'

Devon kept his face in shadow, between the burner and the guards. He did not alter his pace. 'Excuse my bluntness, but this has to be resolved before we can proceed. I asked you a question.'

Lars's head dropped and he screwed up his eyes. 'Wife,' he said. 'Two children.'

Angus was silent for a moment, then shook his head. 'I'm married. Four children.'

Devon noticed the tremble in his voice, and kept pacing, his shadow sweeping over the floor.

'He's lying,' Lars hissed.

Angus twisted against the chains, trying to see round at his comrade's face. 'Bastard,' he said.

Devon snorted. 'As I do not intend to spend any more time getting to know you,' he said, 'I'm not sure how best to resolve this dilemma.' He approached his captives and squatted on his haunches beside them. 'Perhaps I ought to leave the decision in your own hands.'

'They know where we are.' Angus looked like he was on the verge of tears. 'They'll come looking for us.'

Devon resumed pacing. 'My problem is that I need to enlist the help of one of you.' He turned to face both captives as he walked. 'But which one? All temple guard have access to the Sanctum, so that is not an issue. Lars, you sound somewhat the worse for wear, and yet I have already taken a disliking to your companion.'

Lars buried his head against his chest and breathed short, ragged gasps. Angus wrenched his shoulders forward against his chains. The rhythm of Devon's footsteps continued steadily.

'Let us go,' Angus pleaded. 'We won't report this.'

Lars lifted his head and clenched his jaws. His eyes rolled upwards and closed.

'I will make this simple.' Devon let out a long sigh. 'One of you is going to die here, in this tower. The other is going to work for me. I do not care which of you, so you can decide between yourselves.'

He stopped. His final footstep resounded for a heartbeat, then faded. 'Would you like a few more minutes to make up your minds?'

The warship reminded Carnival of an insect larva, some enormous maggot burrowing in and out of the clouds. Flashes of silver rippled over the craft's envelope where it caught the moonlight. Hot air from the cooling system fed fat ribs around the liftgas envelope to provide more accurate buoyancy control and allow rapid ascent with fast inflation. An engine powered twin propellers towards the rear, turning the ship in a slow circle as she watched. Valves clicked within. Beneath the bulk of fabric, portholes burned in the shadowy gondola. The bridge was up front, the crew berths, galley and engine room behind. Neat decks, wide enough for a man to walk along, jutted from both port and starboard sides and extended some distance behind the engine room where four aeronauts tended the searchlights stationed at each corner, adjusting aether flow and turning the mirrored bowls so that the beams swept over the city.

Carnival landed silently on the forward port deck, opened a door and stepped inside.

She found herself in a painfully bright teak corridor that ran from the engine room to the bridge. Brass-bordered doors led to interior rooms, their portholes now dark. Engines thundered and shook the rich red carpet underfoot. The air smelled of fuel and polish.

She strolled along the corridor and stepped forward onto the bridge.

The captain stood pin-straight in his uniform, all sharp white lines and silver buttons, and peered through the arc of windows above the control panel. A helmsman wearing a skewed white cap held a tall wheel in the centre of the bridge.

'Eleven degrees starboard,' the captain said.

'Aye sir,' the helmsman responded. 'Eleven degrees starboard.' With one eye on a compass to his left, he spun the wheel around several times, slowed it, and brought it to a stop.

Carnival closed the door behind her. The captain glanced over his shoulder.

For a moment he stared at Carnival as though her

presence was nothing more than an unexpected interruption. Then, abruptly, the colour drained from his face.

'Holding now,' the helmsman said. 'One, one, five degrees.'

A moment of silence filled the bridge.

The helmsman stared at the captain, and then turned to follow his gaze.

'Hell,' he said.

Carnival approached both men, relaxed her wings. Feathers brushed the roof and splayed across the floor. Her scars seemed to darken under aether-lights. Her midnight eyes thinned. 'No,' she said, 'just me.'

The helmsman edged a step closer to the captain.

The captain himself was rooted to the spot, his arms stiff at his sides, eyes wide, jaw thrust out like a bracket.

She stopped a few paces from the captain. 'I'm in no mood for slaughter,' she said.

Both men stared.

'What are you looking for? When is it going to stop?'

The captain swallowed.

'Are you going to answer me' – she bared her teeth – 'or do we trade scars?'

His eyes flicked over the lacerations on her face, and widened a little more. He replied in a hoarse whisper: 'Devon.'

Carnival tilted her head to one side and frowned.

'Deepgate's Poisoner,' the captain said. 'Head of Military Science.'

'Why him?' she snapped.

The captain hesitated, glanced at his helmsman, but the other man failed to notice, as Carnival occupied his full attention. 'Angelwine,' the captain said. 'Devon has been making angelwine.'

Carnival blinked.

'The temple's been finding husks,' the captain explained. 'I mean . . . more husks.'

'Where?'

'All areas of—'

'When?'

'Other nights . . . not just—'

With a crack, her wings were open. She took a step forward and leaned closer to the captain, her eyes as narrow as knife blades. 'This . . . Devon, he bleeds them?'

The captain's jaw was so rigid, his lips barely moved. 'Aye, he—'

The door crashed open. Carnival wheeled, her wings slicing the air, to see aeronauts pouring into the bridge, short swords already unsheathed. The first man through the door paused, stumbled and almost fell when he saw what awaited him. Behind him, two more broke sideways to avoid a collision, then they too halted. As more followed, they spread out slowly, blocking her escape.

A line of eight men now stood frozen behind their steel and gaped at her.

Carnival snarled.

One bulky, grizzled man by the starboard corridor door regained his senses first. From the pips on his collar, he was the executive officer. With his eyes locked on Carnival, he addressed the captain in a low and steady voice. 'We heard through the com pipe.'

She sensed the captain and the helmsman moving away to the perimeter of the bridge.

'Orders, captain?' the executive officer demanded.

As Carnival flexed her wings, a gust of air blew over the men confronting her. Her feathers stretched in a ragged curtain almost to the side walls of the bridge. From her toes right up to her furrowed brow, the scars criss-crossing her entire body began to itch. She felt the old wounds on her face tighten, writhe.

'Gods below,' an aeronaut murmured, backing away.

'She can't escape,' another boyish aeronaut said. 'There are eight of us, and armed.' But his sword trembled in his hand.

The older officer looked to the captain for orders.

'Kill her,' the helmsman said.

The aeronauts paused, uncertain.

Carnival's eyes smouldered. She drew in her wings and crouched low, tensing her muscles to pounce. Tendons bulged in her neck, pushed against the rope scar around her throat. Slowly, she slipped the gardening fork from her belt.

Eight men took an involuntary step backwards.

'I'm in no mood for slaughter,' she said. 'Leave.'

'Kill her,' the helmsman snarled.

A sword lanced through the air towards her. Carnival caught the blade in the prongs of the fork and twisted. It thunked into the wall of the bridge and stuck there quivering. 'Leave!' she cried. 'Now!'

'Kill her!' the helmsman screamed.

As one, the aeronauts rushed her, their swords thrust forward.

Carnival sucked in a long breath and held it. And then she leapt with such force that two of her attackers instinctively jerked their swords back in alarm, their eyes closed.

But Carnival's leap carried her straight up, smashing through the ceiling as if it was paper, and into the envelope directly above.

Gas hissed and billowed around her. A thin skeleton of metal hoops joined by narrow struts ran the entire length of the warship, tapering into the far gloom at each end. Carnival twisted around, still clutching the fork. She could cut her way out anywhere.

She flew upwards.

The prongs tore easily through the taut, distended fabric. She half climbed, half clawed her way up through, and then she was out into the cool night air.

She breathed.

Below her, the envelope rippled as liftgas poured from the expanding gash. The warship tilted sharply, dropped away. Its propellers screamed, driving the gondola even faster towards the streets below. The aeronauts on the aft deck were clinging desperately to the guard-rails, unable to move. One of them slipped away, crying out before the propeller silenced him.

Carnival watched the warcraft plummet. The gondola struck a row of townhouses, punched a hole through the roofs. There was a flash—

—and a ball of fire bloomed skyward. The warship envelope blew to pieces, shredding the townhouse roofs nearby. Windows shattered for blocks around. Slates spun out in high arcs. Scraps of flame billowed high above the city.

As the roar of the explosion reached Carnival's ears, an updraught punched her higher. She rode it, her great wings spread wide, her eyes mirroring the flames below.

'Maybe I was in the mood after all,' she said.

17

ANGELWINE

The Poisoner did not rush his preparations. This procedure was too important for mistakes. He cleaned the collection flasks and tubes carefully, reverently, then steeped the distillation cylinder in alcohol and rinsed it four times before he dried its woozy yellow glass inside and out with compressed air. The syringes were disinfected next in the same manner, and then laid out in sharply glinting lines on a steel tray. He even took the opportunity to give a quick polish to the metal stand he used to support the draining tubes. Everything must be perfect. If a priest had been to hand, he'd have had the equipment blessed, perhaps.

When everything was ready, he poured himself a large glass of Rhak and raised it in a solitary toast.

'Presbyter Sypes,' he said, and knocked back the contents in one gulp.

There was an enigma. The more he thought about it, the more certain he became that the old priest had deliberately helped him, and that the Spine assassin he'd killed had been the Adjunct's instrument.

The fat man went behind your back, didn't he? And now that I've been forced to flee, you fear the angelwine is lost to you. Did you plan to take it from me? What did you hope to gain with it? Power? Immortality?

Devon had to know the truth. And for that he needed the assistance of a temple guard.

There was also the issue of the city-wide search for him. Soon the two guards would be reported missing. It was time to acquire some leverage.

But first, he had work to do. He began to gather his flasks, cylinders, tubes and syringes into a deep, sterile trencher.

Just then he heard a distant boom.

Devon snuffed the lamp, drew back the heavy drape he'd placed over the window. Nothing to be seen. He climbed the drunken stairwell to the tower battlements.

Airships were converging on a blazing fire far to the east, possibly in Merrygate. Devon counted the search-lights and smiled.

One less of them for me to worry about.

Anything might have brought that airship down: aeronautical incompetence; an arrow from some disgruntled commoner; a Heshette saboteur. Or was Carnival finally tiring of the search? The Poisoner didn't care right now. He had a man's soul to steal.

When he reached the basement, Devon saw at once who the final soul in his elixir would be.

Angus glared at him from a sweat-soaked face, his eyes red and brimming with pain. Evidently he had been trying to struggle free, for the chains around his chest had scratched and dented his breastplate. He flinched at each of Devon's approaching footsteps. Behind him, Lars slumped in his chains, unconscious. Fitzgerald still snuffled around the dark corners of the room.

Devon squatted before Angus. 'Your companion

appears to have passed out. Did you manage to come to an agreement in my absence?'

Angus spoke slowly, clearly desperate to keep a measure of conviction in his voice. 'Lars was in too much pain. He agreed . . .' He lowered his eyes. 'We both agreed, I'll help you.'

'If your friend was conscious, would he tell me the same thing?'

The guard nodded stiffly.

'Shall I revive him? Let him confirm that decision for himself?'

Angus blinked away drops of sweat. 'No need,' he said. 'He agreed.'

'Still,' Devon remarked, 'it seems an unusual decision. He has a family who will miss him and you apparently do not.'

'Too much pain,' Angus hissed through his teeth.

'Why should I believe you?'

Every muscle in Angus's face and neck was tense. A sheen of sweat plastered his grey skin. For a long moment he held Devon's gaze, then finally he said, 'Please.'

Devon tapped a finger against his chin while he studied the veteran. Eventually he nodded. 'Angus, you are exactly the sort of fellow I need. I do believe I can use you.' He turned to the trencher and began unpacking equipment.

'Alive?' Angus asked.

'What?' As Devon glanced back at him, he thought he saw the chained guard fumble to conceal something behind his back. 'Yes, yes,' he said. 'Alive.'

Mr Nettle crouched in the dark net and waited – and waited. High above him, the tower's single window remained dark. Eventually he stood up, shifting his weight as the hemp sagged under him. If he could hook the battlements with a grapple, the slope of the tower would make it an easy climb.

And then what?

He couldn't squeeze through the narrow window. He needed another place where he could watch the door and wait for Devon to appear. The Poisoner couldn't stay in his tower for ever.

So he decided to abandon his den and find a place in one of the burnt-out shells on the opposite side of the alley.

From the broken pipes scattered over what was left of the floor, he guessed this had once been a clay pen, but fire had long ago reduced the interior to a blackened skeleton. Chains and cables kept the outer brickwork intact, while the lower floor sloped dizzily towards the open abyss. Almost the entire upper floor had collapsed, but a narrow platform of spiked beams and floorboards protruded from the side facing the alley and offered Mr Nettle a place where he could hide and watch.

He slung his grapple over a broken rafter, pulled himself up, and settled by the window. A few splinters of glass still jutted from its frame.

As the night dragged on, Mr Nettle crouched among rain-damp wood and piles of rubble, afraid even to light his storm lamp. The smell of rot and ash soaked into his clothes and skin, and stayed there. Stars blinked through the lattice of beams above. No more airships passed overhead, but he heard the distant tremble of their engines from another part of the city. One of them had crashed earlier. None of his business.

Across the lane, the tower kept its secrets in silence.

After a long while the bars of sky visible overhead began to lighten. Angles of wood and rubble stood out more distinctly against the charred brick. The hum of airships faded with the sounds of dawn: birds chirruping, distant shouts and muted clanging from the shipyards.

It grew hot, humid, as morning laboured towards afternoon under a leaden sky. Mr Nettle shifted position, trying to ease the numbness in his joints. He rubbed tired eyes, then pulled out the flask of water and handful of raisins that were all that remained of his provisions. Both tasted of ash.

His head slumped with fatigue. His clothes, thick with grime, grated against countless small wounds. He cricked his neck and tried to get comfortable. The weight of the cleaver against his leg reassured him.

Murder isn't something to be relished. Abigail sounded exhausted.

He was too tired to argue.

Gods how he needed a drink. His gut ached for it. To pull himself back he gripped the handle of the cleaver tightly in his lacerated fist. Something was bothering him: it gnawed at the back of his mind like a rat he could hear but not see. It was something important the Poisoner had said; something Mr Nettle had since forgotten.

Whatever it was would come to him in time. With some effort he released his grip on the cleaver and slumped back away from the window. The loose bricks all around ground more ash into his clothes. His hands and nails were black from it.

The bastard couldn't stay in there for ever.

All afternoon the sun made no appearance, cast no shadows. The air stayed thick and humid, almost smothered the distant pounding and clanking from the

Scythe shipyards, the shouts of workers, and the occasional chime of bells from the temple.

Mr Nettle blinked sweat from his eyes, closed them for a moment, distantly aware of the drone of engines.

Something was wrong. Mr Nettle was suddenly inside Devon's apartments. In his hand, a Cutter's blade – an assassin's weapon.

Devon sat there grinning, his head a hideous tapestry of broken skin.

The Poisoner held up a small bottle, in which blood-coloured liquid roiled and sighed, lapping the glass in slow waves, and Mr Nettle realized there were whispers coming from the fluid, faint moans and cries of grief. This was wrong too: the angelwine had been clear. No, that had been a trick – a bottle of Rhak. He wasn't thinking clearly. This here was the true elixir.

The Poisoner spoke, but no sound came from his lips.

Mr Nettle closed on Devon sluggishly, as though wading through chest-high water. He tried to stab the Poisoner, forcing his arm to the motion. But the knife was gone, his hand now empty.

A silent laugh from Devon, cold amusement in his eyes.

Mr Nettle backed away, felt the window sill behind him. He turned, dragged himself out into a darkness so complete it felt like the abyss itself. Somewhere overhead an airship buzzed like an angry wasp. He reached for the drainpipe he knew was there.

Nothing. Just brick, black and soft with ash.

He felt the Poisoner's hands on his back, pushing, and suddenly he was falling. The buzzing of the airship filled his head ... and, somewhere distant, Abigail screaming.

He woke with a jolt. Darkness, ash, engine noise. For a few heartbeats he sat confused, trying to clear the fog from his mind, and then he remembered where he was. He sat bolt upright and peered again out of the window. The alley was empty, faintly silver under moon-drenched clouds. The tower door was still shut.

Mr Nettle wiped his eyes. He must have slept late into the night. The search for Devon had obviously returned to this district. An airship thrummed somewhere nearby, out of sight.

Was Devon still inside the tower?

An image from his dream flitted back to him. How the knife in his hand had disappeared.

Suddenly he was fully awake and swamped with dread. The nagging doubt at the back of his mind had resurfaced: the forgotten implications of Devon's conversation with the assassin. He realized he wouldn't be able to kill the Poisoner after all.

Once the angelwine was potent, Devon would take a sip. Mr Nettle had accepted that. There would still be enough left to restore Abigail. But he'd overlooked the effect it would have on Devon. Like a dirge, the Poisoner's words came back to him.

Mortal wounds would become mere scratches.

How could he kill such a man?

Now, before it was too late; he had to stop Devon *now*. He had to reach him before he took a sip of the angelwine. Mr Nettle surged to his feet.

The tower door opened.

A temple guard stepped into the lane, his battered armour full of pools of moonlight. His face was shadowed by his helm but Mr Nettle recognized him from before. Over his shoulder he carried a shrouded corpse, in his hand his dead colleague's helmet. The bloodhound loped out of the tower beside him, sniffed the air, and then set off in the direction of the temple.

One of the guards had survived.

So Devon was dead.

Mr Nettle's heart thumped with too many rapid questions. The angelwine? Was it potent? Could it still be in the tower? Or would the guard take it to the temple? Either way, he had to find it – quickly, before the priests destroyed it. Mr Nettle slipped down from his hiding place and went to search the tower for his daughter's soul.

If he hadn't already abandoned god, he would have prayed.

18

✝ROUBLE IN ✝HE SANC✝UM

Dill woke, gasping, from a nightmare of blood and scars. The echo of a hollow, wicked laugh faded to the sound of bells clanging. His brow was slick with sweat, his chest tight. One of his wings lay curled under him, numb where he had twisted in his sleep. He rose slowly, winced as needles of pain stitched his crumpled muscles.

While he brushed his feathers flat, he tried to shake that evil laugh from his mind. Carnival had haunted his dreams more frequently of late. The lacerations on her skin were always fresh, always inches from his face, the darkness in her eyes a mocking challenge.

Always black. How could an angel sustain such rage? For so long . . .?

He shivered despite the warmth of his cell.

Morning brooded behind the stained-glass window. Mountains of grey cloud had rolled in with the dawn and threatened more rain. The air hung heavy as a damp curtain.

Dressing himself was like struggling into armour. His black velvet jacket and boots were criss-crossed with snail tracks – not that it mattered. With Devon still at large, perhaps still looting souls for his angelwine, and Scar

Night drawing near, no one would pay Dill much attention. By the time he was done dressing he already felt
tired. He sheathed the sword at his hip, and trudged off to
work.

Borelock was already waiting for him in the Sanctum
corridor. The priest muttered something vague about the
damned weather and handed the reins to Dill, but said
nothing more about the toppled relic. In front of the
soulcage the twin mares drooped their heads, their coats
already shining with sweat. Dill flicked the reins and they
huffed and clopped away with an air of resignation. Even
the skeletons above appeared to slouch in their chains.

The temple doors opened on to a flat grey-white heat
that forced Dill to blink and turn away. A heavy silence
hung over Gatebridge. Behind the gathered dead, the
mourners shifted in their heavy robes. One of the guards
barked an order, and the others moved slowly to load the
soulcage.

It wasn't until Dill had wheeled the soulcage round and
brought it back into the darkness of the corridor that he
noticed the temple guard who accompanied him. At first
Dill thought the man must be injured. He walked unsteadily, hunched over, and he carried his pike more like a
crutch than a weapon. His armour was dented and
scratched. He must have sensed the angel peering at him
for he glanced up, and Dill then saw the sickly pallor of
his skin, the dark crescents under his eyes, the pain barely
concealed.

Dill turned away, ashamed and embarrassed. This man
had claimed his right to accompany the dead. Someone
he mourned must be inside the cage.

For the rest of the journey Dill kept his eyes averted.

He tried to slow the horses to make it easier for the man to keep up. But the mares, long used to this task, chose their own pace. The guard, however, somehow managed to follow just a few steps behind, the clink of his armour punctuating the rhythmic creak of the soulcage's wheels.

There was no breeze to cool the Sanctum. Deep in their iron hedge, the candles wavered briefly as the doors swung shut behind the departing horses. Presbyter Sypes slouched at his lectern while Adjunct Crumb sat crumpled in a chair at his side. Both men stared at the floor.

Sweat plastered over his face and panting in the heat, the guard dragged the chain over to attach to the soulcage. Dill climbed on top of the cage, ready to adjust the hook. He wondered which of these shrouded bodies the guard mourned for. Would the guard even recognize it?

The angel reached down to receive the chain. But the guard did not hand it up to him. Instead, he did something astonishing.

He lifted his pike, aimed it at Dill, and demanded, 'Give me the key.'

Dill stared in amazement.

Presbyter Sypes straightened. 'Guard?'

'The soulcage key. Give me it,' the guard growled, pressing the sharp tip of his pike into Dill's chest.

Pain nipped Dill between his ribs. He recoiled but the guard pressed even harder.

'Now!'

Dill tossed him the key.

Presbyter Sypes rapped his walking stick on the flag-stones. 'What the blazes is going on?' Adjunct Crumb had risen suddenly from his chair and stood beside him, pallid and wide-eyed.

The guard unlocked the soulcage and climbed in.

'Get out of there,' the Presbyter hissed. 'What do you think you're doing?'

The guard was tearing open one of the shrouds.

'Guard, have you lost your senses?'

Dill peered down through the soulcage bars. The man was grabbing handfuls of cloth and pulling them loose from a corpse.

The corpse stood up.

Dill jerked away in horror and nearly fell off the cage. The corpse's skin was red and peeling, its eyelids slack. Wisps of white hair curled around blisters, above ears that looked torn and chewed. Worst of all, it was still bleeding.

The cadaver shed the rest of its shroud, then took out a pair of gold, thin-rimmed spectacles from its waistcoat pocket and perched them on its nose.

Then Dill recognized it.

'What a day.' The Poisoner hopped down from the cage. Nothing of his grin belonged to his face: it was a grin wholly owned by the skull inside. 'Even the dead are sweating.'

Presbyter Sypes and Adjunct Crumb both gaped.

The guard reclaimed his pike as he followed Devon out of the soulcage. He staggered two or three steps, his gaze sweeping dizzy circles across the floor.

Adjunct Crumb found his voice first. 'You've decided to give yourself up?'

Devon uttered a curse, his red lips peeling back from skeletal teeth. 'Does that seem remotely likely, Fogwill? Is there no link between your mouth and brain? Are you wholly unconnected inside?' The Poisoner mopped his brow with a soiled handkerchief, causing blisters to burst and to leak fluids.

'Soldier!' Presbyter Sypes shook his stick. 'Arrest this man.'

The guard clutched his pike with whitened knuckles. He inclined his head towards the Poisoner and hissed, 'The pain . . . I can't . . .'

'Soon enough, Angus,' Devon replied. He turned to the Presbyter, who was edging closer to the bell-pull that would summon the temple guards. 'He won't help you, Sypes. Move an inch closer to that rope and I'll have him spit you where you stand.'

The Presbyter halted and whispered, 'What have you done to him?'

'He has already betrayed his comrade in order to live. Betraying the Church came somewhat easier.' There was a note of sorrow in Devon's voice. 'Faith, like iron, is strong but brittle. It can support great weights of doubt and yet a small amount of pressure in just the right place will snap it.' He made a motion like a hammer tap. 'One only has to witness Ichin Tell's . . . performances to see how easily suffering can shatter faith. Too much of it destroys the man, too little merely strengthens the resolve and extends the whole process.' He grimaced at the guard, as though he found the sight of him distasteful. 'This unfortunate fellow suffers from a painful infliction which can either be eased with serum or allowed to proceed on its natural course. He serves me because he wants to live.'

'He won't save you,' the Presbyter said to the guard. 'For God's sake help us now and save your soul.'

'*There's* a bargain to die for,' Devon sneered. 'Even now, you promote faith over belief. Believe me, Sypes, the fate of your soul matters less when every drop of your blood is screaming out for another hour of life. Just look at him!'

The guard winced.

'I had hoped this would not prove necessary,' Devon said, his expression hardening. 'The poison inside him is rare and expensive. But I was forced to use it, wasn't I, Angus?'

Angus nodded like a berated child.

'A concealed knife!' Devon said, indignant. He looked at Presbyter Sypes as though he expected the old priest to share his own disapproval of such an action. 'This man attempted to murder me the moment I loosened his chains.'

The Presbyter frowned. 'I imagine you have that effect on many people. So what do you want?'

Devon's spectacles glinted in the candlelight. 'What do I want?' He regarded Presbyter Sypes for a few moments. 'I want to show you a miracle.' From his waistcoat he produced a syringe full of blood-coloured liquid. 'You know what this is?'

'Don't do this,' the Presbyter said. 'Not here. Let's speak in private.'

Devon rolled back his sleeve. 'We'll speak, Sypes, but later.' He glanced at Fogwill and then at Dill. 'This requires temple witnesses.' He brought the syringe to his arm and slipped the needle under his skin. 'Of course, I had intended to find a smoked glass bottle for it, or gold-laced phial, something more appropriate . . .' A tiny amount of liquid disappeared into his vein. 'But ultimately a common syringe seemed more practical.' Devon removed the needle and held out his arms like a showman. 'Now watch.'

'Mad as a broom,' Presbyter Sypes muttered.

If anyone had asked Dill later to recount the subsequent events there in the Sanctum, he would have been unable to say exactly what had happened or in which order they had happened. Events, as he remembered them, unfolded with the speed of a dream.

A flurry of expressions – bliss, wonder, and pain – crossed the Poisoner's face. But that visage changed from moment to moment and made each expression seem to belong to a different man. Skin paled from red to pink to white then tightened across Devon's forehead and underneath his eyes. Blisters shrank, their fluids retreating back inside his flesh. Weeping sores dried and healed. The bleeding stopped. Devon stood before the abyss aperture with his arms outstretched and said, 'I can *feel* them inside.' His eyes brightened with each heartbeat and he searched the floor wildly. 'All of them, I can hear . . . their voices.'

With the attention of both Presbyter and Adjunct fixed on this transformation, and Angus folded over his pike, staring into some faraway place, only Dill noticed the man climbing out of the pit behind Devon. A grapple-hook appeared first on the rim, then a bandaged hand, then another hand, and then the largest, ugliest man Dill had ever seen dragged himself up and into the Sanctum. He wore torn rags that exposed a hundred lacerations. Dirt, blood and stubble had turned his face into a vision of Hell. His eyes were burning with hate.

The newcomer pulled a cleaver from his belt, raised it.

'Mr Nettle!' Adjunct Crumb cried, suddenly aware. 'The scrounger!'

Devon wheeled drunkenly, arms outstretched.

The massive muscles of the scrounger's arm bunched, ripping apart seams in his filthy rags. He brought the weapon down with a ferocious swing.

The cleaver severed Devon's right hand at the wrist.

Blood sprayed everywhere. The hand, still firmly clutching the syringe, dropped to the floor.

Devon gaped at his wrist as arcs of blood jetted from the stump. He seemed about to say something, then closed his mouth and stood there, just blinking, for a dozen heartbeats, before finally he clamped his good hand over the wound. Blood sluiced between his fingers, spattered on the Sanctum floor.

Dill had never seen so much blood.

Mr Nettle picked up the severed hand and held it up like a trophy. The syringe glittered red in the candlelight. 'Abigail,' he said.

Devon roared and threw himself at Mr Nettle, slamming into him. Both men fell sprawling to the floor. The hand flew upwards in a high arc towards the pit.

Mr Nettle rolled aside and was on his feet instantly. He scrambled, crawled, slipped across the bloody floor, after the hand.

He was too late. Hand and syringe fell into darkness.

Angus had been slow to react but now he rushed towards the scrounger, raising his pike. Mr Nettle had his back to him, standing on the edge of the abyss, numbly gazing down.

The temple guard put all of his weight behind the impact. The blow connected with a crack. Mr Nettle tumbled forward into open space.

In a heartbeat he was gone, swallowed by the abyss.

'No!' Devon cried. He ran to join Angus at the edge of the pit, still clutching the stump of his wrist. Both men stared down into the darkness.

Dill felt his eyes crackle with unknown colours.

Suddenly the Poisoner twisted away, face sour, and

stormed back to confront Adjunct Crumb and the Presbyter. 'Another of your assassins?'

'Not ours,' the Adjunct said quite calmly. 'I believe you
murdered that man's daughter.'

'Ignorant savage,' Devon spat, 'I merely displaced her
soul.'

'I think,' Adjunct Crumb said, 'he might have preferred
her soul to remain where it was.'

Devon ignored this. He was studying the stump where
his right hand had been. Blood glistened wetly but had
stopped spurting from the wound. 'It matters not,' he
said. 'Look how it heals already.' He brandished the
damaged arm.

Dill saw that it *was* healing. New skin was growing over
the wound even as he watched.

'Angus, we're leaving now,' Devon said. 'Sypes is coming with us. If he resists, put a hole in him.' He returned
to the soulcage, rummaged among the shrouds, and pulled
out a leather travel bag.

The temple guard nudged the Presbyter away from the
lectern with the point of his pike. 'What about the other
two?' he asked.

'What do you think I am?' Devon said. 'A common
murderer?' He gave a small shrug. 'Deepgate needs to
know what has happened here. I don't think it would serve
me well to slay Ulcis's last archon. The god of chains
might take that personally. And as for the fat man,' he
frowned at the Adjunct, 'no finer fool could rule in Sypes's
absence. Lock them both in the soulcage.'

Pike wavering, Angus steered Fogwill and Dill into
the soulcage, locked the door, and tossed the key
into the shadows. He then urged Presbyter Sypes towards

the door, while Devon lifted his travel bag and followed
them.

Adjunct Crumb stumbled over the shroud-wrapped
bodies at his feet and fell heavily against Dill. He shouted
after Devon, 'You expect to simply walk out of here? The
city is full of armed men looking for you.'

Devon let out a long and weary sigh. 'I believe the
search has now reached the outskirts of Deepgate. And I
have suddenly developed a lack of confidence in your
soldiers' weapons.'

As they reached the doors, Devon winked back at Dill,
who was busy helping the Adjunct to his feet. 'Well
fought, archon,' he said.

For the first time, Dill remembered the sword sheathed
at his hip. His eyes flared red.

The Sanctum doors closed with a boom.

A bolt snapped shut, the sound of it a knife in Dill's
heart.

19

A DANGEROUS PLAN

'He was wounded, had one guard with him, and the Presbyter at the end of a bloody pike,' Mark Hael exclaimed. 'So how, in the name of a hundred archons, could he have just disappeared?'

The young aeronaut captain stood stiffly to attention while his commander paced back and forward before him. 'We think he stole an airship,' he replied.

Fogwill sat motionless at Sypes's desk, as precisely placed as an ornament, his jewelled fingers steepled under his chin. His scarlet cassock swept to the floor in dark cascades and oozed lavender scent. The Codex pillars rose above him; piles of stone and marble still littered the floor around the incomplete one, the Adjunct noted. More than two weeks had passed since he'd last been here and he'd yet to see a single mason on the scaffolding.

Definitely paying them by the hour.

Clay, the captain of the temple guard, slouched in the chair opposite and watched this interrogation with a bored expression, his eyes as dull as nailheads in pitted stone. He wore a smoke-coloured cloak over his armour, fastened at his neck with an iron brooch bearing the temple guards' insignia.

Commander Hael frowned. His own uniform was ghostly white and edged with gold. 'You *think* he stole an airship?' He stopped pacing. 'We either have a missing ship reported or we don't.'

'One warship is unaccounted for.'

'A *warship*?'

The young man kept his gaze level. 'The *Birkita*, a heavy-deck. She was in for rearming – full arsenal. The crew were due to board after this morning's Sending.'

The commander hissed. 'So he's armed to the teeth.'

Fogwill waved Mark Hael back to his seat and leaned across the desk. 'What I would like to know is how they managed to get to the docks without being seen.'

The aeronaut met Fogwill's eyes. 'We have a report of a temple guard escorting two mourners away from the bridge. We assume it was this man Angus. Of course the mourners' faces were hidden, but—'

Clay barked a laugh. 'Everyone's to blame. What do we do about it?'

Fogwill rubbed his temples. He could feel a headache coming. He just wanted to be alone, away from these brusque men. 'Which direction did the airship head?'

'North.'

'Thank you, you may go.'

The aeronaut glanced at Hael, who nodded.

'Commander.' The young man saluted, turned sharply and marched away.

Clay leaned further back in his chair. 'He simply walked out of the temple,' he said, never one to miss the obvious.

'An erudite observation, Captain Clay,' Fogwill retorted, more angry with himself than with the captain of the temple guard.

The Adjunct had spent an hour trapped in the soulcage

with a silent, brooding Dill before Borelock had wandered into the Sanctum dragging a cleaning bucket. Borelock had blinked once in surprise, and then rushed to release them, whereupon Fogwill had roused the temple guard, who sent runners to summon Captain Clay and Commander Hael. The Presbyter had not passed the Gatebridge, they had assured him, and so Fogwill had set them to scouring the temple, after dispersing the remaining mourners. It was already midday and only now did it appear that Devon had fled Deepgate entirely.

'We ought to send the armada in pursuit,' Clay suggested.

Fogwill bristled, twisting a ring on his finger. 'Commander Hael, how long before his ship runs out of fuel?'

'She was fully replenished,' Hael replied stiffly, 'so a week, eight days at most. Depends on the weather, the winds, and how hard Devon runs her.' He looked down at Fogwill with marked distaste, unable to disguise his contempt. 'What does Devon want from the Presbyter?'

Fogwill met his gaze squarely. 'Answers.'

'To what?'

The priest hesitated to reply. Sypes had been adamant that none but the two of them should know of Ulcis's intentions. How could an army, a whole city, be ordered to fight the god they had so long worshipped? Everything had rested on their recruiting Carnival. And now it seemed they had nothing to offer her. Instead they had an army of the dead preparing to swell its ranks by force, a kidnapped Presbyter, and a lunatic loose in a warship.

'He's not the only one looking for answers,' Hael said. 'This manhunt's been a sham from the beginning. Our plantations are open to attack all along the Coyle. We've barely men enough to guard the tradeship ports at Racha and Clune. Both the *Jasmin Eulen* and the *Marisa* were fired upon by raiding parties when they last docked. And we'll have a thousand reinstated reservists looking for pay before Scar Night. Who, may I ask, are we preparing to fight?'

Fogwill said nothing.

'I demand that you—'

'Commander,' Fogwill interrupted. 'Do not presume to issue demands to me in my own temple. Devon's intentions will no doubt become clear before long, and until they do I want the army here and on full alert. The Poisoner has a fully-loaded warship at his disposal, and the angelwine may already be changing him in ways we cannot predict.'

Hael's eyes turned as hard as the buttons on his uniform. Fogwill tried not to find pleasure in the commander's irritation, but it wasn't easy. Hael was a bully, and Fogwill had always despised bullies.

'I doubt the angelwine will make the slightest difference to him,' Clay drawled. 'Devon was nuts to begin with – just putting that stuff in his veins is proof enough. Never trusted him. Wouldn't go near Fondelgrue's pies for a week after Devon had been sniffing round the kitchens.'

'Thank you, Captain.' Fogwill unfolded his hands. 'Commander Hael, you said he took the warship north into the Deadsands. But why north? What will he find there?'

'Nothing,' Hael admitted. 'Scattered Heshette camps, sand and petrified forest – and Blackthrone. Most of the oases are poisoned. Anyway, the Heshette will be more of a threat to him than they are to us.'

'Then why should he go there?'

Clay tapped one finger against the side of his forehead. 'Mad as a bag of crabs.'

But Fogwill still wasn't convinced. Devon had some plan. Devon always had a plan. 'Very well,' he said, 'ready the armada for pursuit.'

After the others had gone, Fogwill sat alone at Sypes's desk, thinking. Carnival, it transpired, already knew of the angelwine's existence. According to some navigator who had survived a recent airship crash, the captain of that vessel had told her everything he knew.

Only now the angelwine was gone, lost to the abyss.

But she wouldn't know that.

The floor of the *Birkita* trembled as she burned her way north over the Deadsands. Her engines thumped steadily. Devon stood with his hand and stump resting on the great wheel and squinted through the curvature of windows at the front of the bridge. An orange sun sank into the west, throwing long shadows across the dunes. The teak and brass of the control deck glimmered in the warm light. Dozens of gleaming com-trumpets sprouted from the deck and the walls on either side. Banks of fat round dials displayed pressure, airspeed, altitude, direction, and innumerable other refinements the engineers had added to his original design. Devon assumed those readings he couldn't fathom to be unimportant. *An airship is a bag of gas. It goes up, down, forwards and backwards. It moves at a certain speed, in a certain direction. What else is there to know?*

A dusty breeze from the air ducts above the windows stirred his wispy hair. Ahead, the knuckled peaks of Blackthrone shone bronze beneath a sky rippled with pink and blue.

'Your man is absent,' Presbyter Sypes rasped. 'Has he abandoned you? Or couldn't you find his serum in time?'

The old priest hadn't moved from the chair Angus had found for him in the captain's cabin and set in the centre of the bridge floor. The black folds of his cassock all but swallowed him: only his head was visible, even gaunter than usual and bobbing slightly, like a turkey's, as he spoke.

'Did you have a pleasant nap?' Devon asked.

'Have I been asleep?'

'Constantly.'

'It's the heat.'

'It will become cooler once the sun has set. Angus is in the engine room, and blissfully full of serum. If I had to man the engines I would miss this wonderful view, and if you controlled them we would all be dead.' He turned the ship's wheel a fraction. 'Although at least then I wouldn't have to listen to your interminable snoring. There's wine, on the floor by your chair, if you're thirsty.'

Sypes found the bottle and raised it to his lips with shaking hands. The wine appeared to steady his nerves. 'Men of my age don't make good travellers.' He made an effort to focus on Devon. 'How's your hand?'

Devon lifted the stump where his hand had been. New skin covered the wrist. 'If that lout hadn't knocked it into the pit that hand would be back on my wrist by now. Then I could have used both of them to throttle him.'

'He seemed a resourceful type.'

Devon snorted. 'Not resourceful enough to have sprouted wings.'

'I understand you murdered his daughter?'

'I think we both share the blame for that, Sypes.'

Sypes lowered his eyes.

The Poisoner studied one of the dials on the control deck, then turned the wheel a few degrees. 'I wonder what your ghosts down there made of this morning's new arrivals. My hand and a fool assassin plummeting after it.'

The wrinkles on Sypes's face gathered. 'They're normally dead before they reach Ulcis's lair.'

'Lair? Rather a strange choice of word.' He glanced at the old man. 'Less distance for his soul to travel, I suppose. How long would he fall, do you think, before he hit bottom?'

Sypes did not reply. The warship shuddered and banked to one side. The bridge creaked ominously. Sypes nodded towards the distant mountain, slightly askew through the forward windows. 'You expect to find allies at Blackthrone?'

'Allies? No, slaves.'

Sypes's laugh turned into a hacking cough. 'You think the Heshette will ever do what you tell them?'

'I am an optimist.'

'They'll kill us all.'

Devon held out his stump. 'They can try.'

The old priest furrowed his brow. He reached for the wine bottle to stop it toppling. 'They'll destroy this ship the moment she lands.'

'Probably.'

'The angelwine,' Sypes grumbled, 'you do realize it's already turning you insane?'

The Poisoner merely smiled and turned back to stare out of the window. Blackthrone glowed at an odd angle in the last rays of sunlight. Devon muttered a curse, then spoke into the engine-room trumpet jutting from the control deck. 'Angus, purge the starboard ribs by . . .' he glanced at a dial, '. . . eight hundred gallons or so.' He turned back to Sypes. 'You see the way the mountain shines? Blackthrone ore – sapperbane they used to call it. There must be millions of tons of the stuff there. The strange thing is, we haven't ever found another source outside this mountain. Not one. I believe Blackthrone is not a natural mountain, but part of something that fell from the sky aeons ago.' Devon shrugged. 'That is why so little grows in the Deadsands. The mountain is poisonous to this world.'

Sypes's gaze flicked to the horizon and back to Devon. 'So you've decided to rekindle your interest in metallurgy?'

'I am interested in all sciences – most recently in forbidden sciences.' Devon noticed the way the Presbyter avoided meeting his eyes. 'No more skirting, Sypes. Why did you help me?'

Sypes had sunk further into the chair. For a long time he gazed out of the window, his eyes hooded. Finally he spoke. 'This was never supposed to happen, this man-hunt.'

'Fogwill,' Devon said.

Sypes nodded wearily. 'Once the Soft Men's journal came to you, I knew you wouldn't be able to resist attempting a distillation. The pains you suffer, the damage the poisons have wrought on you . . . Here was a way to end your suffering. Your physical suffering at least. I'm sorry the knowledge came to me too late to save Elizabeth.'

Devon's expression darkened. 'Don't say her name, Sypes. You haven't earned that right.'

'I'm sorry,' the old man wheezed.

Devon's anger faded. 'You didn't trust me enough to approach me directly?'

'Of course I didn't.'

'That at least makes sense.'

'When the angelwine was ready, I would have known by your appearance. It would have been a simple matter then to take it from you.'

Unconsciously, Devon raised his severed wrist to his chin. The skin felt new, tender, but there was no pain. He realized he was still wearing all the bandages under his suit – over the years he had grown so accustomed to them, he barely noticed them any more. But of course he could shed them now: the suit would be too large for his unswathed body. He almost smiled. 'You wanted the elixir for yourself?'

'No, for Carnival.'

He trusts her *over me?* In a way, the idea amused Devon. There was something profoundly satisfying about having achieved that level of infamy. 'The Spine would love you for that,' he remarked.

'It was a risk.' The Presbyter took another sip of wine. 'A sour balance. With angelwine in her blood she would no longer need to hunt victims to sustain herself. That would mean an end to Scar Night – thirteen sacrificed to save countless more. But now those same souls feel like links in a chain around my neck.'

The bridge lurched sharply to one side, metal protesting in incremental groans. Something twanged behind its walls, like a rope twisted too tightly. Devon grabbed the com-trumpet. 'Angus, I told you to purge the starboard . . .' He plucked up a second trumpet connected to the control deck by a length of flexible pipe, and held it to his ear as a tinny voice erupted from it. 'Yes . . . No . . . make it a thousand gallons now . . . Starboard . . . No, the

right one . . . Yes, the thing that looks like a stopcock . . .
What? I don't know, just turn the damn thing a couple of
times . . .'

A few heartbeats later the *Birkita* righted herself with a
hiss and a shudder. The horizon became more or less level
again, before it started to tilt in the opposite direction.
Devon reached for the trumpet again, but the bridge
levelled almost immediately.

The Poisoner turned back to the priest and eyed him
for a few moments. Sypes's explanation seemed thin.
Would he so readily sanction the theft of thirteen souls
just to end the bloodshed on Scar Night? That went
against everything the old man and his Church purport-
edly stood for. Surely in his god's eyes there could be no
worse crime? There was more at stake here. *He's afraid of
something, holding something back. He was even prepared to
risk the wrath of his god over this.* Any way Devon thought
about it, he couldn't get past that. *Is he afraid of his own
god? Or whatever he perceives to be a god?*

'Tell me,' he said. 'What really lies at the bottom of the
pit?'

'The dead – and Ulcis.' Sypes's answer came too
quickly.

Devon snorted. 'An ousted god, devoid of his throne,
who presides over an army of ghosts? I cannot accept
that.'

Sypes took another long draught of wine and replaced
the bottle on the floor. His hand was steadier; it lingered
to make sure the bottle stayed upright. 'You don't believe
in Ulcis?'

'I believe something resides down there. But a god?
No.'

'Your wife believed—'

Devon sensed Sypes was trying to distract him, but he could not control his anger. 'Elizabeth is dead and rotting, you old fool,' he said. 'Only the maggots got to her long before she died. Those same pit-worshipping maggots I gave my own health to protect. Now tell me what you know; I'm losing patience.'

'You plan to torture me?'

'What?' Devon was startled to find he was gripping the old man's arm, hard enough to hurt him. He released him. 'Of course not,' he said. 'No, no, of course not.' What was wrong with him? These outbursts were unlike him. A fog seemed to have settled in his head. He wasn't thinking clearly. The angelwine – the side effects the Soft Men had reported? No, it would pass, as the voices had passed.

Had there been voices?

After the elixir had entered his veins, he'd been convinced he heard them – the voices of everyone he'd displaced: whispering, crying, screaming. But now? He couldn't remember.

'I'm surprised at that,' Sypes said. 'You always claimed the efficacy of suffering could not be undervalued.'

'I think your heart would give out if I so much as shouted at you.'

The Presbyter laughed uneasily, a laugh that soon turned into a fit of coughing. He groped for the wine bottle, knocked it over. It rolled away, spilling wine across the deck. Devon retrieved it and handed it to him. Sypes drank deeply. When the worst of the coughing had passed he said, 'If you're planning to get me drunk—'

'God forbid, and suffer more of your snoring?'

'Then?'

Then what? What *was* he going to do? He'd had the

answer moments ago, he felt certain. But now he felt
confused. He tried to concentrate, to find his way out of
the fog shrouding his thoughts. Where was he? Where was
Elizabeth?

Elizabeth . . .

Lying on her bed weeping. Dying while he watched in
impotent grief. A life leached away until there was nothing
left. First her looks, her energy, and then finally her hope.
She had cried like a child and nothing he had contrived
could save her. Devon felt a phantom fist clench at the
missing end of his arm. The city took everything eventually. He knew what he had to do.

'The dead,' he snarled, 'do not reside at the bottom
of the abyss. They are gathered above it. Pilgrims are
brought to Deepgate to feed before they're butchered –
souls harvested to sustain whatever is down there. Is that
life?'

'What would you know about life?'

Devon roared, 'My blood and sweat have kept the rest
of you safe! You crippled me, ruined me. You took her
from me. You murdered her!'

'You are no longer crippled . . .' Sypes was floundering
now, his face flinching as though he expected Devon to
strike him.

'What is this?' Devon thrust his stump at Sypes. 'You
couldn't take enough of me. You never will. The masses
find who they need, and then *consume*. A flat-eyed, bovine
hunger. And all of you dead, festering under your skins,
waiting to become fodder for your faith.'

He took a deep breath. Before today, such an outburst
would have racked his lungs with pain. But not now. His
blood thundered in his veins, vigorous, fresh. He'd
wrenched his life back from the city. But it wasn't enough.

How could it ever be enough? Deepgate owed him more than it could ever repay.

'Whatever foul thing lies in that pit built the Tooth of God to cut the ore from Blackthrone and forge the chains, and then it slunk down into the abyss for three thousand years – to feed. A god?' He sneered. 'No, a parasite, like the rest of you.'

Sypes's eyes narrowed.

'You will tell me exactly what is down there.'

'What do you plan to do?'

Devon smiled thinly. 'I'll get its attention. I'll cut the chains.'

Sypes spluttered.

'Why not?' Devon said. 'Aren't you all going down there eventually? Isn't that the point of your lives? Why not send everyone down at once?'

Even the mottled spots on the Presbyter's scalp seemed to pale. 'You would murder everyone in the city?'

'Murder?' Devon cried. 'I'm giving them what they want!'

The young aeronaut's gaze had been snared by the shining brass of the aurolethiscope; he did not look at Adjunct Crumb as he spoke. 'Thirty heavy-decks have been dispatched after the *Birkita* under pushed compression. They'll unravel a flag line back to us as they go.'

'Fascinating,' Adjunct Crumb replied. 'And ultimately meaningless. Dill, do you have any idea what this man has just said?'

Dill didn't and he admitted so.

The aeronaut glanced at the Adjunct and started again. 'The heavy-decks—'

'Heavy-decks?'

'Loaded warships. Lime-gas, incendiaries—'

'I see. Please continue.'

'—are pursuing the *Birkita* under pushed compression. They've twin-lined the engines and upped fuel pressure by—'

'All right, all right, I don't need to know all the details. So they've tinkered with the engines to make the ships go faster. But what was all that nonsense about unravelling flags?'

'Ships will detach at intervals from the main fleet and remain static to form a flag line.'

'A flag line?'

'A communications line.'

'Ah!' The priest looked pleased. 'Why didn't you say so to begin with? Now go, shoo. The angel and I have important matters to discuss.'

When the aeronaut had disentangled his attention from the observatory workings and had left, Adjunct Crumb beckoned Dill closer to the aurolethiscope. 'Honestly, these people have the most complicated way of saying the simplest things. It's a wonder Deepgate's navy functions at all.' He reached up into the machine and began adjusting things. 'Now, if I remember, Sypes did it this way. We need to plug phantom-glass into the prism cupola' – he slotted something in – '. . . and twist the gloom filters round to prudent obreption.' He twisted something shiny. 'That's it. Now we ought to be able to see them. Would you like to see the dead?'

Dill approached the aurolethiscope warily, conscious of his wings intruding in the tiny observatory, afraid of knocking something over, and also painfully aware of the gloom all around. The darkness seemed to compress

around him. He could feel the weight of the temple
pressing down, squeezing blood to the pit of his stomach,
and he had to struggle to keep his breathing calm.

The observatory desk was buried under wax-sealed
scrolls, bone quills, glass pyramids of red, green, black
and blue ink. Further scrolls, in leather tubes, packed the
shelves all around. A glass-fronted cabinet held on display, like surgeons' tools, the elaborate devices for adjusting and calibrating the aurolethiscope. The machine took
up so much space that the room itself might have been
just a part of it, a hidden space within its workings. The
lens column towered to twice his height, and all the surrounding cogs, struts and foils crowded the dim arched
ceiling.

The Adjunct squeezed to one side of the desk, his
sleeves at chest level to avoid the candle flame. A cloud of
perfume wafted out from him, like sugared summer fruits.
'Now, look through here,' he said, 'and tell me what you
see.'

Dill leaned over the desk and peered into the eyepiece.
The lens reflected his grey-white eye as he moved closer
until he saw nothing but complete blackness.

'Can you see them?'

Dill looked harder, trying to make out any change in
the uniform darkness. 'I . . . It's hard to tell.'

'Give your eyes a moment to adjust.'

He scanned the void before him. Still nothing. He
might have been studying a sheet of black paper. He felt
the shadows in the observatory reach closer, felt his pulse
quicken. 'What do they look like?'

Adjunct Crumb huffed. 'Try adjusting the focus. The
handle to the left of the eyepiece. That's it.'

Dill cranked the handle. Above, he heard the brass

skeleton click into motion. *There.* He stopped. For half a heartbeat he'd glimpsed movement in the void. Tiny lights. He edged the handle back a fraction and the lights appeared again, very faint, twinkling.

'You see them?'

Two, three lights. They drifted slowly through the darkness, changing shape, occasionally winking out and on again. 'I see them,' he breathed.

'The souls of the dead,' the Adjunct said.

Dill strained to see more clearly, trying to discern the shapes of people in the lights. But they were too distant, just pale shifting glimmers. *If only Rachel could see this . . .* He watched the ghosts until they moved out of sight. Even after they had disappeared, he kept his eye to the glass for a long time, hoping they would return, but he saw no more.

Eventually Adjunct Crumb placed a hand on his shoulder and gently moved him aside. 'You're lucky to have seen them, very few people have – especially at this time. Normally they only appear around the time of the Sending.'

'They welcome the new dead?'

Adjunct Crumb appeared to suppress a wince. 'So we believe.'

Dill gazed at the eyepiece of the aurolethiscope and wished the Adjunct would let him take another look, but the priest settled back into the chair and regarded Dill thoughtfully. 'We have enemies all around us,' he announced.

'The heathens?'

'Certainly,' he hesitated, 'but I fear we now have a new enemy, a more dangerous one.'

Dill nodded. *Is this why he summoned me? They need my*

help against Devon? Rachel had already told him all the news: how the Poisoner's angelwine had driven him insane. Now he was loose in a stolen warship brimming with weapons, and the city was preparing for the worst. Abruptly Dill felt breathless, squeezed between excitement and fear.

'Do you remember the oath you swore to serve and protect the temple?' Adjunct Crumb continued.

The ceremony had occurred on his tenth birthday. Standing on the brink of the abyss, with a million candles shining in the Sanctum walls, Dill had pledged his allegiance before Presbyter Sypes, Adjunct Crumb and Gaine. They had named him temple archon and presented him with the old sword that now hung at his hip. 'I'll do anything you ask,' he said.

Adjunct Crumb looked into the eyepiece of the aurolethiscope. 'Tell me, what do you know of Carnival?'

'The Leech?'

The priest frowned. 'She's been called many things,' he said. 'Although I'm not sure I approve of "*The Leech*". A commoners' term if ever I've heard one.'

'She's a monster, a soul-thief,' Dill said. 'Rachel told me about her.'

'That's as well. I know we sometimes keep things from you, but it's for your own good. An angel should not be unnecessarily burdened with life's cruelties.'

But an archon should be told about the temple's enemies.

'Carnival would make a strong ally.'

Carnival?

'She . . .' Adjunct Crumb turned the aurolethiscope handle round idly. 'I know what she's done in the past. She's a tormented creature, but I fear now she may be the lesser of two evils.'

Dill was speechless. How could Devon be worse than Carnival? How could *anyone* be worse than Carnival?

The Adjunct kept turning the handle, this way and that. He didn't appear to be concentrating too hard on the view. 'Carnival is a demon in every sense, but she's a demon that we know, even if we don't understand her.' A ruby on his finger sparkled in the candlelight. 'I am not proposing we forgive her, but,' overhead the cogs clicked, 'beyond Scar Night, life goes on.'

'Why would she help?' Dill asked. 'I thought she hated us.' He'd almost said: *hated you.*

The aurolethiscope settled to silence. Adjunct Crumb leaned back and folded his fingers beneath his chin. 'We have something she desperately needs.' He went back to watching the abyss. 'It has come to my attention that she is aware of the existence of Devon's angelwine.'

'But it's lost. It fell—'

'And she must never be made aware of that fact. If she learns we no longer have it, our advantage becomes worthless.'

'What do you want me to do?'

Adjunct Crumb was turning the handle again. The whole machine ticked, clacked and whirred. 'I want you to deliver a message to her,' he said.

Dill's wings twitched involuntarily. He felt his eyes frost in fear. 'Me?'

'It will be easier for you to find her. You can fly.'

'But, I've never flown before, I don't . . .' The lie crushed his voice to silence. Pulses of white and green ran alternately through his irises. Fortunately the Adjunct did not turn away from the aurolethiscope to notice them.

'It's about time you learned. It must happen quickly, and Rachel can help you. I want you to find Carnival before next Scar Night and deliver an offer to parley. Tell no one about this, do you understand? *No one.*' He paused. 'Dill, it has to be you. She'd kill anyone else I sent after her. Commoners are her prey. Spine forever hunt her. Priests send the Spine after her. She loathes the aeronauts. Only recently she brought down a warship for no apparent reason. Most of its crew lost their lives.'

Dill could scarcely breathe. Battle-archons had faced Carnival before. He'd read about them in his books: archons who had already fathered many sons. The Church would never have risked their deaths otherwise. Few survived, and none had escaped uninjured.

'She'll kill me,' he said.

'No,' Adjunct Crumb said. 'I think she'll listen to you.'

'Why?'

'You'll be unarmed.'

20

CHANGES OF HEART

A heavy headwind buffeted the *Birkita* as she rumbled on through the night, whistling through her air ducts and strumming support cables. The warship was an orchestra of eerie midnight sounds. Stars crowded the darkness beyond the bridge windows. The Deadsands were blowing below in a shapeless silver gauze.

'It would be faster to walk,' Devon grumbled as he raked through his bag of poisons. But he didn't trust Angus enough with the engines or himself with the controls to set their speed at more than two-thirds full power. Which meant his pursuers must be gaining.

'I am in no hurry to reach Blackthrone,' Sypes said. The old priest had not risen from his chair since he'd settled there, and Devon was beginning to wonder if they'd have to carry him out of the airship seated on it after they landed.

'You wouldn't be,' he sneered.

'Nor am I in a hurry for you to find a suitable poison.'

The Poisoner grunted. With the warship's creeping progress against the wind, he'd lost patience with Sypes's reluctance to talk. The thump of blood in his own heart had grown stronger. His skin had tightened around his muscles. His teeth felt scoured clean, hard; eyes quick and restless. The angelwine was still transforming him, driving him. Why shouldn't he torture the priest? He had to do something positive before this damn wind blew them back to Deepgate. 'Not this one,' he muttered, placing one bottle on the control deck. 'Nor this.' He set another bottle aside.

He pulled out a small green phial, read its label, and shook his head.

Was there nothing in the bag he could use? Nothing here that wouldn't kill the old man outright? He needed something that would cause pain but not push the Presbyter into shock, coma, or worse. Snake venoms, fungal spores, extract of dogweed and blushlily, widow eel pigment; he set them all aside.

'Damn your heart,' he said.

Sypes stirred in his chair behind him. 'Found anything yet?'

'I'm working on it.'

'Any more wine? Or perhaps something to eat? I'm famished.'

'Give me a minute.'

The Poisoner lifted out the last bottle and frowned, then tipped the lot back into the bag and let out a long sigh. 'What would you like to eat?'

'Whatever is easy. I don't want to be a burden.'

'There are some pickled clams in the galley, a yard of salted pigskin. Or cuttlefish – dry, I'm afraid.'

'The clams would be fine.'

Propellers thrummed loudly as Devon pushed open the bridge door. Wind tore at the portholes. He locked the door behind him and then strode along the starboard companionway, sliding his hand along the smooth brass guide-rail.

Pots and pans swung from hooks in the dark galley. Barrels had been stacked against the far wall, most of them empty now or with a few salted scraps at the bottom. The shelves were mostly empty too. All of the fresh fruit and meat had been eaten and the *Birkita* had not been restocked after her last tour. Devon found the pot of clams he sought in the larder and stuffed it under his arm.

Perhaps he ought to torture Sypes the old-fashioned way? He could tie the old man down and find a knife. A lit taper might also be effective. The loss of a few fingers or an eye under anaesthetic would be no great risk to the Presbyter's health so long as he staunched the bleeding and kept the wounds clean. There would be bandages and lint somewhere aboard. He could even cut the priest's balls off. Devon winced at the thought. Some things he would rather not see. Conventional torture was unsophisticated, unpalatable, he decided. It lacked finesse.

But was he prepared to wait, while Deepgate's armada pursued them? Earlier he had stood on the aft deck to watch distant lights lift through the pall of smoke above the city. He had enemies behind him, and yet more foes waiting in the wasteland ahead. The Heshette would not welcome his arrival at the Tooth of God. Something told him his threshold of pain would be tested in the clash to come.

He shrugged the thoughts aside. Right now he had other concerns. Sypes's continuing silence infuriated him. The old goat was terrified of something. So much so that he'd flouted Church doctrine and gone to almost inconceivable lengths to buy Carnival's aid.

Why?

Unanswered questions troubled Devon. Sypes knew what was really down there, and if Devon was going to send all of Deepgate down to its maker, he wanted to know who that maker was.

A god?

He could not believe it: the temple had been built on faith and fostered with lies. But how could ignorance be the foundation for any system of order? Devon detested any deference to the supernatural. Were supernatural forces not simply natural forces yet to be explained? Blood contained energy which could be harvested to extend life. Gods, demons, devils and ghosts did not come into it. Everything had to be defined in terms Devon could comprehend. For a man of his brilliance, this was vital.

Thoughts still stewing, he left the galley and wandered the narrow companionways towards the accommodation section, with the pot of clams under his arm.

Perhaps he should learn to be more patient, for time was one thing he now had in abundance. Sypes would talk in the end. When the old man saw his beloved city about to fall to its doom, he would tell Devon what he desired to know.

The captain's cabin was only marginally larger than the crew bunkrooms, but richly finished: polished hardwood veneers, etched glass, carpets soft as molten gold. Bottles of Rhak, whisky and wine gleamed in the drinks cabinet.

There was no white vintage to be found, so Devon selected a light Duskvalley red that would, if not complement the clams, at least not overwhelm the flavour.

He was reading the label when the ship pitched forward and he was thrown against the cabin wall. The Duskvalley slipped from his grip. Bottles and glasses clinked and smashed and tumbled across the floor. The drone of engines rose suddenly to a shriek.

'Blood and chains,' he muttered, levering himself upright. 'I'll kill the old fool for this.'

Devon scrambled out of the cabin, leaning heavily against one wall. The starboard companionway sloped downwards to the bridge. He half ran, half slid to the end of it and slammed against the bridge door. Through the porthole he saw Sypes leaning over the control deck, gripping the elevator rudder levers in his hands. A sand-storm filled the bridge windows. Devon fumbled with his keys till he found the right one, and unlocked the door.

It stayed firmly shut. The priest had lodged his chair beneath the handle.

'Old fool!' Devon shook the door, pounded on it.

Sypes wheeled, frowning.

Using the handrail, Devon struggled back up the sloping companionway and took a right, cutting along the midship companionway to the port side. His shoulder thumped against the wall. The *Birkita*'s engines were screaming and stuttering now, the air vents clogged with sand. When he reached the port companionway, its angle was so steep that he had to slide along the deck on his backside till his knees cracked against the alternative bridge door. Again he rattled his keys, tried one, then another. Finally he unlocked the door.

It wouldn't open. Sypes had moved the chair and slid it under the handle of the portside entrance.

'Open this.' Devon kicked at the door.

Sypes ignored him. Sand fumed behind the bridge's forward windows. The slope of the companionway was becoming steeper – too steep to climb back up it. The old man had angled the airship's elevators, flooded the aft ribs and emptied the forward ones, letting the weight of the bridge drag them nose down.

'You'll kill yourself!' Devon screamed, and kicked with both feet, again, again.

The door opened at last and he fell through it.

Sypes didn't turn as Devon hit the control deck beside him. His white-knuckled hands held both elevator control levers fully forward. Angus's voice chattered wildly through the engine-room com-trumpet. Cables stretched and groaned under pressure. Wood creaked. The sandstorm parted and dunes loomed behind the windows.

Devon threw the priest aside, twisted valves to flood the forward ribs, and slammed the elevator levers back.

Nothing happened.

Behind the glass, the dunes drew nearer. Tufts of withered grass shuddered in the wind. Rocks and petrified trees cast stark shadows under the warship's aether-lights. They were only a hundred yards from the ground, then ninety yards, eighty.

The warship's nose lifted slightly.

'Faster,' Devon growled. With one hand and one stump he jammed both levers as far back as he could, then shouted into the com-trumpet: 'Angus! Increase fuel pressure. We need more hot air up front *now*.' He twisted to face Sypes. 'Where the hell did you learn how to operate an airship?'

'It's just a bag of gas,' Sypes explained from the floor. 'How hard could it be?'

The Poisoner snarled, went back to the controls.

Dunes approached. Sixty yards away, fifty, forty.

The nose crept a little higher.

Devon saw ripples of sand through the haze, wind-etched curls and waves beneath the limbs of petrified trees. Thirty yards. Air hissed from the forward ribs as they stretched almost to bursting under the increased pressure.

Twenty yards.

Stone branches raced past the window like grasping claws.

The *Birkita* levelled. She started to climb.

Devon eased his grip on the controls.

Presbyter Sypes picked himself up from the floor and nodded at the pot still wedged beneath Devon's arm. 'You forgot the wine,' he said.

'He told you to do what?'

'To find Carnival and deliver a message.' Dill's eyes were still white after his meeting with Adjunct Crumb, but he didn't care. Rachel was long used to the sight by now.

'Why?'

Dill explained.

'He wants to *bargain* with her? Recruit her to go after *Devon*? That makes no sense.'

'He said I'd be safe with her as long as I was unarmed.' He paused. 'He took my sword away.'

She looked at him in astonishment.

'He said nobody had ever faced her unarmed before.'

'With good reason. I wouldn't want to face her without every weapon available in the Spine arsenal.' She sat on the sill beneath Callis's window and flexed and stretched her wounded hand absently. The bandages were off now but her skin still looked red and swollen.

Dill had only just learned about Rachel's fight in the planetarium. The Spine had reported to the priests, and one of them, a fellow called Primpleneck with a lazy eye, had related the story to a temple guard called Paddock. The story spread through the ranks of the temple guard until the kitchen staff got to overhear their conversation at breakfast. The stewards told the cooks who told the maids and the potboys, who in turn told the cleaners who, having no one else to tell, gossiped to the stable staff. At least that's what the dung-shoveller had said when he accosted Dill outside the stables this morning.

'Oh that,' Dill had said to him haughtily. 'I heard about *that* ages ago.'

He'd stalked off and begun an extra long snail run afterwards. There were so many unexpected places to hide the slimy little things, when you really put your mind to it.

'I won't let them,' Rachel said.

'What?'

'It's too dangerous. I won't let them send you.' She stood up. 'I can't be expected to protect you under these circumstances. They assigned me to be your overseer, so I'm going to oversee you now. I'll speak to Fogwill, demand he calls this whole thing off. I'll get your sword back for you.' She shook her head. 'I can't believe they'd risk you. Don't they realize who you are?'

'The last archon.'

'No . . .' She frowned. 'That's not what I meant. I meant . . .' She appeared to be struggling to find the right words. 'I meant that you're the only part of this whole rotten mess that hasn't been spoiled or corrupted. You are the heart of the temple . . . the heart of Deepgate. They need you more than they can possibly imagine.'

Dill felt his eyes change colour. It wasn't a colour he recognized at once. He hadn't felt it since his father had been alive.

Rachel was already walking to the door.

'Wait,' he said.

She didn't stop. 'It's a bad idea, Dill. It's lunacy. I don't know what Fogwill thinks he's doing.'

'Please, I want to do this. Let me go.'

She halted. Perhaps something in his voice had given her pause. She said, 'I don't know.'

But Dill knew. Here was the moment he'd waited for his whole life: the chance to do something for the temple; the chance to be an archon worthy of his ancestors. Here was his chance to shine. Even without his sword he felt more like a temple archon now than he'd ever done before.

21

DILL AND CARNIVAL

Scar Night was still ten days away and the waning moon rose huge and bloody out of the Deadsands. It lost its colour as it climbed, becoming sharp and bright until it shone alone in its own circle of night, as if shunned by the stars. Deepgate sparkled below, a thousand blinking points of light. A freezing northern wind tore through the city, whistled and howled through the chains. Cables shivered and sang. Webs of iron trembled and chimed weird, discordant notes.

All around him, Dill thought he heard distant screams.

A cold night, and colder still on the rooftop where the angel cowered. The chill of the slates crept bone-deep into his fingers; his breath misted before him; and still he didn't move. The darkness pinned him.

Where to start?

One direction seemed as unwelcoming as the next. Adjunct Crumb had told him to stay high and keep moving. 'She'll find you,' he had said. Dill's hand sought the hilt of his sword, grasped nothing but air. They had taken it, he remembered.

The Adjunct was probably asleep by now. The temple's dark outline cut a ragged shape behind Dill, a few faint lamps glowing beyond the stained glass, like fading embers. They were probably all asleep by now – even Rachel. Only Dill himself was awake. Awake . . . alone . . . and outside.

In the dark.

How long had he been out here? It must have been hours now. He hadn't felt his eyes change colour since he'd left the temple. They had turned white at that point and they were still white now.

Where to start?

Frost laced his feathers, his arms and legs were numb. Sleep tugged at him despite the cold and dawn could not be far away. But he didn't dare move.

A falling star darted across the south. Was it the fourth or fifth he'd spotted tonight? *Ayen has been busy, then: another companion banished from the sky.* He watched it glimmer and die.

Stay high and move.

Move.

He had to move, or he would freeze.

His chain mail scrittered as he stood up and spread his wings. Adjunct Crumb had given him the armour, which had once belonged to Gaine. Its tiny links were wrought from ancient steel, once light and strong, now corroded and heavy with rust. It soaked in the cold and seemed to clamp it over Dill's heart. He took another deep breath. The night smelled of metal. Dill took a step forward, then another, his feet slipping on the icy slates. Beyond the edge of the roof a labyrinth of streets spread out before him, brilliant in the moonlight, like leagues of chain-shattered ice. Dill paused there for a long time, buffeted by the wind, and listened to Deepgate's haunting music.

Move. Or freeze.

He leapt from the roof.

Cold rushed over him, rippled through his shirt and breeches, blew back his hair; it slipped beneath his collar, across his chest, and stole his breath. He followed the course of a cobbled street, beating his wings, once, twice, and then letting the icy air carry him forward. *Steady and calm.* Once, twice, keeping the rooftops a level distance beneath him. Steeply-pitched slate rose in frozen waves above the narrow lanes. Shadows gathered between pools of gaslight.

As he flew he watched those shadows, as the Adjunct had told him to, alert for movement. *Carnival can see in the dark*, the priest had warned. *Don't let her take you by surprise.* There were shadows everywhere. Was she hiding there below, watching him now? He pulled himself higher, sucked in gulps of biting air.

Once, twice, he beat his wings, every stroke taking him further from the temple, further from safety.

And if she was airborne? Would he hear her approach? What if she was behind him? His heart clenched and he twisted round to look, fumbling for his missing sword, certain he would find Carnival reaching for him with those scarred hands and eyes like knife cuts. But there was only the outline of the temple, the cold stars. His fist opened, releasing its grip on . . . nothing.

The lane jagged its way deeper into the city. Solid doors, shuttered windows, iron chimney grates. Shadows clung to everything. *Too many shadows.* He started to fly faster, his chain mail dangling from his chest, his shirt billowing beneath it. Again and again he beat his wings, shoulder muscles tightening, feathers glowing around him like blowing sheets of snow. He focused on the rhythm of motion and tried to drive all other thoughts from his head.

Below, the lane sank below a pendulum house suspended from one of the foundation chains. Dill left it
behind and sailed up over the chain, in a wide arc that
would bring him back around the temple. He would spiral
outwards until he reached the rim. *And then?* He prayed it
would be dawn by then.

Steady and calm.

The moon looked down, a bright eye, and Dill imagined other, hidden eyes watching him from below: eyes in
the darkness under the eaves, and in the darkened windows, eyes in the temple, and eyes peering between the
chains, staring out from the abyss below.

He swung around the temple, high above the weathervanes of Lilley, and saw the gap cut by the Scythe and the
funnels of the Poison Kitchens beyond. Industry crammed
the banks of the Scythe, shrouded in amber smog. Flamestacks bloomed and lit the bellies of smoke clouds. Steam
curled around tangled pipes. The iron skeletons of gantries
and cranes and docking spines reached up through the
fumes. He looked for airships but saw none. Most were
away hunting Devon in the desert, he realized, and he felt
even more alone than before.

Dill flew on towards the flames, towards the light.

He left Lilley behind and soared over Ivygarths. Chains
webbed everything: a garden of gnarled trees; a leaning
tower with a light burning in the top window; an inn with
a wooden goat hanging above the door. There were no
people out; no sounds but the air rushing by, the clink of
his armour and the beat of his wings.

It grew warmer near the Scythe, so Dill decided to rest
a while and shed the cold from his bones. He landed on a
flat, tarred roof overlooking the abyssal gap, where the
sour-sweet smell of coalgas lingered. Foundation chains

stretched over the Scythe as though floating on a still black lake. Factories crowded the far shore and disgorged ash into the gusting wind. Jets of steam hissed and whined among smoke and flames, while a deeper, booming sound arose from the Poison Kitchens.

At least it was warm and bright here. Heat from the flamestacks reached across the gulf and warmed his face and hands, melted the frost from his feathers. His rusted chain mail shone red-gold.

'Ironic, isn't it?' said a voice from behind, a woman's voice. 'They pollute their own god's burrow.'

Dill froze.

'Relax,' the woman continued. 'I'm in no mood for slaughter.'

'Finally he's moving.' Clay squinted through the sightglass they'd set on a tripod before Fogwill's window. 'I thought he'd become frozen to that rooftop.'

'We're likely to freeze in here if you keep that window open much longer.' Fogwill shifted in his blanket. 'Nothing more dangerous than a chill draught at night.'

Clay grunted. 'I can think of a few other things.'

Fogwill scowled and pulled his chair closer to the fire. He picked up a poker and stabbed at the embers. 'Which way is he heading?'

'South.' The captain of the temple guard seemed not to notice the cold as he hunched over the sightglass in his worn leathers. 'Hell's bloody balls, he looks like a lame dove dragging such a big empty scabbard. What did you make him wear it for?'

'I didn't. He insisted.'

'Poor sod.'

Fogwill replaced the poker and cleaned his hands with a square of linen. 'I wouldn't have sent him if I didn't think it was safe.' He did his best to sound like he believed that.

'Plenty of chilly draughts out there,' Clay grumbled, shaking his head. 'This plan of yours is madness.'

Fogwill felt inclined to agree, but what choice did he have? He hadn't even been able to tell Clay the real reason behind this attempt to parley with Carnival. He couldn't tell *that* to anyone. Hence the lie that Carnival would be offered Devon's angelwine in exchange for the *Poisoner's* death. Nobody but Fogwill need know Carnival's real target. Dill himself had been easy enough to convince. Now that the Church had two immortal enemies, wasn't it reasonable and apposite to turn them against each other? But others were more sceptical, so Fogwill had contrived a way in which he might speak to Carnival in complete safety. He would set a trap. Mark Hael, apparently thrilled at the prospect of putting Fogwill and Carnival in the same room, had gone off to make the arrangements. Clay, by contrast, had just stared at Fogwill for a long moment and then abruptly walked away, muttering curses.

Fogwill shivered inwardly on recalling the captain's reaction. He threw the square of linen into the fire. 'I would have hoped Commander Hael would be here by now with news from the Poison Kitchens.'

'That place has been in chaos since Devon disappeared. No one else knows how to get anything done. I wouldn't be surprised if half the armada set out with barrels of butter in their deck cages instead of lime-gas.'

'Perhaps I should go and check on the preparations myself.'

'Won't do any good. He'll be here soon enough, when

it's all set up. Aye, aye, the angel's fumbling at his scabbard now. Might be he's seen something.'

Fogwill moved to stand up. 'Carnival?'

'Nope. Chill draught probably.'

The priest slumped back into his chair.

Clay twisted the tube of the sightglass and breathed a curse. 'Damn focusing,' he muttered. 'Got him again, still heading south.'

The fire shifted, crackled. Fogwill placed another log on top and watched the flames curl around it. He plucked another square of linen from a box by the hearth and cleaned his hands again. 'We ought to have trained him with the guard,' he said, 'like we did with Gaine. But Sypes didn't see the point. Not with the heathens scattered and our fleet growing in strength. He assumed the war would be over soon. An angel should become a symbol of peace, he told me, not war.'

'Never trusted Gaine,' Clay muttered. 'Swear his eyes turned dark every time he looked at me.'

'That's why we *could* trust him,' Fogwill said. 'Archons can't hide their emotions like ordinary men can.'

'Damn creepy if you ask me. What about Carnival – reckon her eyes change colour too?'

'She's no angel. Well . . . no temple angel.'

'Was one once, or so I've heard.'

'That's Warren gossip.'

Clay struggled again with the sightglass focusing ring. 'The last archon to come from the abyss, they say. Her eyes have been black as pitch since she bloomed, and that was three thousand years past. Some folk think she takes the blood to replace—'

'Captain . . .'

'Just saying . . .'

Fogwill wrinkled his nose. Once Clay got started it was difficult to shut him up. 'They say a lot of things in the alehouses of Deepgate. Like she's seven feet tall with seven heads and seven tongues.'

'Seven tongues?' The captain turned, grinning.

Fogwill closed his eyes.

Clay returned his attention to the sightglass. 'Soldiers on that airship saw her well enough. Navigator survived the crash with most of his skin intact. Nearly had her, he said. Hemmed in with swords, but she broke right through the roof and cut her way through the . . .' He waved a hand.

'The envelope. But she didn't attack them directly.'

'Outnumbered,' Clay said. 'Should have had her then. Navigator said she had teeth like a wildcat and unholy eyes.'

'She didn't attack because it wasn't Scar Night.'

'Tell that to the men lost in the crash.'

Fogwill stared into the fire and said nothing.

The sightglass tapped against the window frame. Clay turned away. 'That one's out of sight,' he murmured. 'Round the other side of the temple.'

'Let's close the window then. It's freezing in here.'

Clay stole another disapproving glance at the billows of silk pinned up to adorn the ceiling and the vases of flowers arranged around the study before he finally shut the window. He pulled up a chair and joined Fogwill by the fire. The study heated up quickly. They sat in silence for a while, warming their hands and listening to the crackling wood.

'I've been thinking,' Clay said.

Fogwill raised a sceptical eyebrow.

Clay grumbled something under his breath.

'I'm sorry?'

'Nothing. I've been thinking about what Devon wants with the Presbyter.'

'Yes?'

'What if the whole thing was a sham? What if they were in it together?'

Fogwill picked up another square of linen and wiped his hands, although this time they didn't need cleaning. 'Together?' he said in a high voice. If even Clay had stumbled on the truth, then what about the Spine? 'Absurd. Sypes would never sanction such a thing. It contravenes Church law. Goes against the will of god. Really, that's quite—'

'But what if god is dead?'

'Dead?' Fogwill stopped cleaning his hands. 'You think god is dead?'

The captain shrugged.

'Are you a man of faith, Mr Clay? Do you believe in the soul?'

'Of course,' the captain replied gruffly.

'I've seen them,' Fogwill said. 'I've seen the soul-lights with my own eyes. Believe me, the ghosts are down there, and if they exist then Ulcis is very much alive. Sypes also watched the dead. He spent every hour of every night peering into the abyss, worrying what they were up to.'

'I can understand that,' Clay yawned. 'Never trusted no ghosts either.'

'Have you ever seen a ghost, Mr Clay?'

The captain shifted in his chair. 'Not as such, but I heard this story once—'

Fogwill raised a hand. 'This is not the place to discuss it.'

Clay blew through his teeth. 'Whole thing is a waste of time. She won't parley.'

'I don't suppose you trust Carnival either.'

'Damn right. Something unnatural about her.'

A smile found its way to Fogwill's lips. 'You think there's something unnatural about an immortal, scar-ravaged, blood-sucking angel who steals souls during the night of moondark? Whatever could be unnatural about that?'

Clay was thinking about it.

After a moment Fogwill laughed. 'No, Captain Clay, I can't think of anything either.'

An hour passed before Mark Hael appeared. He had with him a chemist who wore a grease-stained apron and a breathing mask still slung around his neck. The man's arms and head were bare, his skin scrubbed raw. Even his lips looked peeled. He sniffed the air and surveyed the room gleefully.

Fogwill couldn't help but notice the soot stains on the commander's uniform and the smudges left by both men's boots on his Loombenno carpet.

'This is Coleblue,' Hael said. 'He set up the gas tanks in the Sanctum.'

Coleblue tramped more soot into the carpet and rubbed his red hands together briskly. 'I can't guarantee it will work. We've tested it on birds, yes, pigeons, sparrows, doves, same respiratory system we think, faster than ours, more sensitive, but you never know.'

'What did it do to these birds?' Fogwill asked.

'Killed them fast.' Coleblue snapped his fingers. 'Like miners' finches, quick quick.'

Fogwill eyed the chemist's boiled skin. A sharply unpleasant odour hung about the man that reminded him of gasoliers. 'What would happen if *I* breathed it?'

Coleblue's eyes narrowed. 'You don't want to do that,

no, no, not too many breaths anyway. Carnival will be more sensitive to the poison, yes. As you surmised, she ought to be incapacitated more quickly than you. But it's best you hold your breath and leave the room as soon as it has been released.'

Clay grunted. 'The gas in that airship didn't bother her much.'

'Liftgas doesn't burn lungs like this. You can't breathe liftgas, no, but then she knew it was there, knew not to inhale.' Coleblue looked from Clay to Fogwill. 'She won't even smell this until she drops.' He smacked his hands together.

'I hope I won't have to use it at all,' Fogwill said. 'It's merely a precaution.'

'Don't like the sound of it,' Clay said. 'Risky.'

Fogwill's brows arched. 'You don't much trust gas, Captain, do you?'

'Never trust anything you can't see.'

'What about air?'

'Especially air.'

With a slight shake of his head the priest turned back to the chemist. 'Where did you hide the valve?'

'Under the lectern,' Coleblue said. 'Twist it anti-clockwise to release the gas. The Sanctum will be flooded in seconds. We can go there now and I'll show you.'

'Fine.' Fogwill rose. 'I'll be back shortly, Clay. Will you keep an eye out for Dill?' He followed Hael and Coleblue to the door, then stopped. 'Mr Coleblue, what would happen if Dill breathed the gas?'

'Nasty.' Coleblue snapped his fingers again. 'Quick quick.'

★

She means to kill me.

Dill couldn't have reached for his sword even if he'd had it with him. His limbs were frozen, his blood dead in his veins. His thin armour felt like loops of heavy chain draped around his shoulders, the empty scabbard like an airship anchor.

Carnival stood with her wings half outstretched, hunched slightly as though ready for flight.

Or ready to pounce?

The feathers were hues of dark grey, flecked here and there with brown and black. She was lean, with muscles tight as wire coiled around slender bones, and as gaunt as a Spine assassin. Her mouldy leather trousers and vest might have been ten hundred years old. Tangled black hair hung like a torn net over her face, partly obscuring her scars. *So many scars.*

Old scars cut through ancient scars. Thin white lines criss-crossed her cheeks, her forehead, her chin, her bare arms, leaving no part of her skin unmarked. Knife scars, all of them but one: a gouge like a rope mark looped her neck. She fingered it idly as she studied him, her head tilted to one side, as if she'd never seen his like before. And yet beneath the scars she might have been pretty. She looked no more than a year older than him. Without her scars she might have passed for a temple angel – had it not been for those eyes.

Carnival's eyes were as black as the abyss, darker than the rage of a hundred archons; cold and empty as death. Fires from the Poison Kitchens burned deep in them and seemed the only glimmer of life there.

'I hate it here,' she said.

'It's cold . . .' Dill said. 'But warmer . . . by the fires.'

They stared at each other for a long time. Booms and

random clanks from the factories drifted with the ash across the Scythe and filled the night.

She was eyeing his empty scabbard. Dill noticed a small iron fork tucked into her own belt. A gardener's tool?

Carnival sniffed. 'This air is foul.'

He nodded.

'Poisonous.'

He nodded.

'You like to inhale poison?'

He shook his head.

'Come with me.'

It wasn't a request. She turned and walked away, and Dill followed.

She took to the air and glanced round at him once. Her teeth flashed and then she was off in a graceful, powerful arc, wings pounding, quickly gaining height. With his heart hammering, Dill pulled himself up after her.

Carnival led him north. Dill struggled to keep up, but the armour dragged him down. His wings lashed the air and his lungs burned. The scabbard kept knocking against his leg and he now wished he'd never brought it. But he'd needed something to remind him he was a temple warrior. It had mattered at the time; now it felt foolish.

The city below was a blur. Houses and chains and streets rushed by. Dill's eyes were fixed on Carnival. Her wings cut through swathes of stars, the wind whipping her long black hair. She beat her wings once for his every two strokes, and still the gap between them widened.

'Wait!' he yelled, but the wind stole his cry. Gritting his teeth, he forced his exhausted muscles to keep moving.

And then, abruptly, Carnival stopped. She dropped like a stone towards the rooftops. Dill began to follow, but halted when he saw where she'd landed. It was a walled garden, dark as a pool of tar. Only a small patch of its lawn shone faintly in the moonlight, criss-crossed with shadows from a naked tree planted in the centre, and from the mesh of chains stretched between the neighbouring townhouses. Sheer darkness crouched around the lawn itself. Dill circled above, a tight pain cramping his chest. All of the blood seemed to have drained from his wings.

'What?' Carnival shouted.

To catch his breath, Dill landed on a thin chain above the garden. Iron creaked; the chain shifted. He lost his balance, toppled, and suddenly he was lying on his back on the lawn, gasping and looking straight up at the stars.

Carnival grunted. 'Deftly managed.'

Dill rose shakily. The garden didn't seem as dark as it had looked from above. Sprays of flowers and ivy-strewn walls bordered the lawn, while a wrought-iron gate led to a cobbled lane beyond. All around him the air was fragrant with night roses. He flexed his wings tentatively: nothing appeared to be broken.

Carnival seemed as relaxed as earlier. 'I dream of you,' she said.

Dill blinked.

'I dream of all the angels.' Again she regarded him in that curious way. 'Why do you think that is?'

'I don't know.'

'I never know the names, but I know all the faces. Old and young. Sometimes I dream of them among corpses and sometimes I dream of them dying. Then they leave me for ever, and I dream of their sons.' She paused. 'Do you dream of me?'

A memory stirred – creaking chains, scars, fresh blood. 'Sometimes,' he said.

'What is your name?'

'Dill.'

'You know my name.'

Dill merely swallowed.

'The temple sent you.'

He managed a nod.

'Why?'

Adjunct Crumb had told him what to say. He'd talked eloquently about peace and understanding, about hatred and fear and forgiveness. Dill had spent hours learning the speech, but under her gaze the words failed him. 'I . . . They . . .' he began.

Carnival didn't seem to hear him. She stared through him with those night eyes of hers. 'I like this garden,' she said. 'An old servant used to tend these plants for rich owners who never come here.' She grabbed a sprig of jasmine and rolled the white flowers in one scarred palm. 'I think he once sensed me watching him from high in the tree. I heard his blood quicken, saw his muscles tense. Do you know what he did?'

Dill shook his head.

'He carried on tending his flowers, pulling weeds from the earth, pruning back the roses and ivy, never looking up at the tree, all the time his heart beating like a drum roll. When he finished he trimmed the grass with his shears, then gathered it all in his barrow and took it away, like he always did.

'I've been here every morning since. He never came back.'

'They want to parley,' Dill managed at last.

She laughed: a high, savage laugh that lifted the hairs on the back of his neck. He took a step back.

Carnival stepped closer. 'What do they think I need from them? Peace? Absolution? Will they promise to rein in the Spine?'

Dill backed further away.

Carnival advanced. 'A place in the abyss for my soul and all those inside me?' Lances of moonlight cut across her eyes. The scars constricted beneath her tumbled hair. 'Or blood? Am I to get first pick of the dead, before the temple dumps them?' She bared her teeth. 'Or will they give me a sword, make me an *angel* like you?' She pressed a finger into his chest, leaned closer until her face was only an inch from his. 'I don't believe in angels.'

Dill felt his wings press back against the garden wall. 'Angelwine,' he blurted.

Carnival stopped. Her teeth were clenched, her hair wild about her face, but the fire had left her eyes. 'It's a trap,' she said.

'No.'

'They want to kill me.'

'No,' Dill said. 'I mean, yes, but . . .'

'They think I don't remember,' Carnival said. 'They think I've forgotten the planetarium so soon. They think I remember nothing!' Her expression turned to fury. 'That Spine Bitch, she should have burned, should have . . .'

Rachel? She means Rachel. He tried desperately to pull her away from her anger. 'They want you to come to the Sanctum at dawn. Adjunct Crumb will speak to you there alone. No soldiers. No Spine. He'll make you a deal.'

She snorted. 'Tell him to go to hell. Do you think I'm insane?'

Dill didn't answer that.

'There have been other traps,' she snarled, 'a long time ago. Different places. Scores of places.' Her breaths were coming faster, her eyes furiously searching the ground. 'Places where the Maze came in my wake. And blood. I think . . .' She slammed her palms against her sides. 'They know I can't remember. They—'

'*She'll* be there,' Dill said.

'Who?'

'The Spine,' he said, 'from the planetarium. I can arrange it.'

Carnival froze. She glared at him for a long moment before her scars relaxed into a terrible grin. 'You can arrange that?'

Dill felt as though he'd stepped from the city straight into the abyss. He nodded.

'Your eyes,' Carnival said.

Dill hardly heard her. All his life he'd wanted to do something right, to make the Church proud of him. He'd wanted to stand tall among the ranks of his ancestors. But now he wished he could take back everything he'd said and done. A memory came to him of Rachel leaning over the balustrade at the Scythe.

If I fell over would you catch me?

At that moment Dill realized who he was. Not a temple warrior like Callis. Not worthy enough to be called an angel. He was a coward and a betrayer, and his eyes were burning as green as his friend's.

'You don't fear me any more,' Carnival said.

He met her gaze sharply. 'No.'

'Just wait,' she growled.

22

✝HINGS GO WRONG

Devon leaned against the *Birkita*'s aft-deck rail and watched the dawn. He'd allowed Angus a few hours' sleep before they attempted to land, in the hope that he might be fresher and less likely to fumble the descent. The Heshette would be watching and it was important the craft's landing did not appear to be uncontrolled. Sypes was still on the bridge, but now tied to his chair, snoring off the wine he'd drunk earlier. The old priest seemed unable to stay awake for any length of time, as though his mind sought to hide its secrets under a blanket of sleep. Devon himself felt no desire to rest. The angelwine was fire in his veins. It burned and itched and kept him sharp. He wondered if he'd ever need to sleep again.

But he knew it was changing him in other ways. His temper flared at nothing and his anger, once unleashed, was difficult to rein in. After Sypes's attempt to destroy the airship it had taken a supreme effort of will not to strangle the old priest. It seemed to Devon his consciousness was thin, but swelling like the skin of a thundercloud.

Over what? Does this anger come from my own subconscious or from the angelwine itself? Could the elixir harbour residues of hate? The thought was ludicrous – a soul was not aware or conscious; nothing more than energy to fuel the flesh – but he still felt uneasy.

He leaned out over the rail and let the desert wind cool his face. Deepgate lay far south across the pink dunes, hidden beneath the horizon, with only a haze of smoke to betray its position. A cloud of silver motes hung in the sky between here and there, and seemed not to move, but the warships would be burning after him with all the speed they could muster. Aether-lights flickered between them as they passed messages back and forward. To the north, Blackthrone rose sharp and serrated in the morning light.

Even from this distance the mountain looked unnatural, like something carved by ancients: the knuckles of a massive bronze fist punching through the foothills around it.

The desert here was virgin, free of the caravan tracks that scarred the lands around Deepgate. Endless ripples and curves of sand swept by, blown into drifting plumes by the wind and broken only by plains of boulders and groves of petrified trees.

Devon estimated he would reach the foothills within the hour. He'd let his captives continue to sleep until then; if for no other reason than that he might enjoy the peace of the morning undisturbed. *And then the tribes?* It would be the first test of the angelwine, of what he had become. Perhaps he should just keep going, fly over Blackthrone and on to the horizon? What new lands would he find out there? The Deadsands stretched as far as Dalamoor in the far north, a hard desert settlement in the shadow of arid, nameless mountains. Those missionaries who took that road rarely found their way home: victims of thirst or of the Heshette. Survivors brought back stories of wicked cults, bandits, parched farmlands and hidden pools of slipsand.

Those who travelled east and followed the green banks of the Coyle, south of the river towns, fared better. Three hundred and seventy years ago, Arthur Drum had been the toast of Deepgate when his skiff returned unmolested, with news that the Coyle spilled into the Yellow Sea. Further expeditions skirted the coasts and found little but mud and stilt villages inhabited by savages. But then, ninety years ago, the great salt captain Donald Bosonson had set out straight across the water. He returned a year later with fewer than half his men alive, and with grim tidings. Lush but uninhabited islands, the Volcanic Isles, peppered the south, but if there was an end to the Yellow Sea it lay beyond the reach of the largest ships.

Winds permitting, airships could travel faster, but the weight of fuel limited their range. Only the largest could reach the Coyle delta. And for what? A thousand leagues of sucking mud and salt vipers. There were still occasional sea expeditions to the Volcanic Isles, but they brought back little to justify the expense and the Church was keen to curtail them.

His conservatory had been stocked with plants from these rotting green lands, his aquarium with specimens from the poisonous brine that had claimed so many sailors.

So it is with life: everything is poison. Everything decays, is consumed, and gives birth to yet more hunger and decay.

Once more he gazed south across the Deadsands, into the far distance where the Yellow Sea churned somewhere beyond the horizon. Nothing but sand and scrub plains and petrified trees. Civilization blossomed in only one place in this wasteland.

Civilization? The word tasted sour in his mouth. *The hunger in that city is palpable, the need to suck the marrow from anyone who can keep their dead hearts beating for another moment. But there is another hunger evident: one that reaches up from the abyss. A hunger for souls.*

He would soon give Ulcis a feast of souls.

The port companionway door creaked open and Devon turned to see Angus step out. The guard had discarded his armour, revealing the boiled leathers he wore underneath. Dark lines marred his sickly white face. 'I need more serum,' he said, in obvious pain.

His intervals of need were getting more frequent. Angus would not last much longer. Devon nodded and pulled the serum bottle from his waistcoat pocket. He gripped it in the crook of his arm while he filled the syringe.

Angus was staring at the bottle. 'There's not much left,' he said.

'There's still enough.' Devon held the syringe in his teeth while he tucked the precious poison back into his pocket.

'Enough for what? Another day?'

Twelve hours in fact. Angus had grown resistant to the treatment more quickly than Devon had anticipated. The guard might have been useful in piloting that great land machine, the Tooth of God, back to Deepgate. Now it seemed Devon would have to rely entirely on cooperation from the tribes. An uneasy prospect. 'Enough to last until we get back,' he insisted.

'And if there isn't?'

The Poisoner smiled as he slid the needle into the guard's arm. 'I can end the pain – in other ways.'

Angus closed his eyes and shuddered as the serum took hold. Sweat broke from his forehead and he sucked in a sharp breath. Then he opened his eyes and sneered, 'The Poisoner's mercy. You chain me to your side like a dog and then offer my death as a reward.'

'You desire pain?' Devon asked.

'I want life.'

'Life is nothing but degrees of pain and hunger. Why cling to such suffering? Like everyone else, are you not simply waiting to die?'

The guard snorted. 'There's more to life than waiting for death.'

'What? To breed? Create more snapping mouths to carry your hunger for another generation?'

'You don't like women?'

He remembered Elizabeth on her deathbed, lingering, while the poisons took her further away from him. She had not been able to open her eyes or speak. Devon had gripped her hand tightly, causing them both pain. She had moaned, and he had squeezed her hand until he wept. At that moment pain was all he had left to share with her.

Angus said, 'When that stuff runs out, I'm going to kill you.'

Devon studied him briefly, then turned away and stared out at the lightening sky, still thinking of Elizabeth. For the first time since he'd taken the angelwine, he missed the pain. 'We'll be landing shortly,' he said. 'Then *everyone* will want to kill me.'

Rachel was still on the top balcony of the Rookery Spire when she received the summons. It was the highest point in the temple and gave her the best view of Deepgate. Just an hour ago she'd watched Dill finally leap from the rooftop and take to the air, but she'd soon lost sight of him in the vast moonlit city. Since then she had spent most of the time pacing back and forth while she shuttled a throwing knife between the fingers of one hand. In her other hand she still held Dill's sword. She'd retrieved it from Fogwill for safekeeping.

The messenger who approached her was overweight and gasping for breath. There were more than two thousand steps to the top of the Rookery Spire. 'You're . . . to . . .' he clutched at his chest '. . . come to the Sanctum.'

'Me?' She was mystified.

He nodded.

'I'm the last person they want there.'

'Adjunct Crumb . . .' He leaned against the balustrade. '. . . will explain. The angel . . .' He paused to suck in another gulp of air.

'What about him? What's happened?'

'He's . . . back now.'

'Already?' Rachel's grip tightened around Dill's sword. 'Has he been harmed?'

The messenger managed to shake his head.

Without waiting to hear more, Rachel flew down the stairwell and raced through the passages of the temple. She felt like kissing Dill's sword. Perhaps it wasn't as useless at it appeared. Apparently the weapon's absence from Dill's scabbard had just saved the young angel's life.

When she reached the Sanctum, Dill and Fogwill stood there waiting. There was no sign of Carnival, however. Fogwill was in a flurry, and Dill kept his head bowed. When the angel glanced up, she saw that his eyes were green.

What's he done to be so ashamed of?

'He's refusing to leave,' Fogwill said. 'Refusing a direct order from his superior! He simply will not budge. Now

that you're here, perhaps you can talk some sense into
him. I don't want to have him removed by force.'

'Where's Carnival?' Rachel asked.

'She'll be here any moment.' Fogwill glowered at Dill,
whose head dropped even lower. 'Meanwhile we have a
bit of a problem.'

Dawn poured into the bowl of the city, as if chasing
Carnival through the streets. She flew hungrily, almost
recklessly between the chains, skirted pendulum houses,
over and under bridges, and tore down lanes scarcely
wider than her wingspan. Dead leaves stormed behind
her. A shutter opened, then slammed quickly shut again,
but Carnival didn't give it a second glance. She was
thinking about the Spine bitch and what she was going to
do to her.

Of course it was a trap. She didn't care. There had
been other traps before the one in the planetarium, other
places where they'd managed to hurt her. Some dark part
of her mind recalled this: memories she'd buried deep
because to reach for them made her want to scream. It
didn't matter now. However much they wounded her,
she'd injure them back a hundred times more, a thousand
times. She'd bring Iril right to their doorsteps and damn
them all to its corridors.

The bitch would be first.

Mist turned the Warrens into a soft puzzle of chains.
Carnival plunged on through, drinking the fresh, wet air.
People moved beneath her but she paid them no notice.
They could wait until Scar Night. Only the Spine bitch
wouldn't have to wait; she'd made that woman a promise.

And now, today, in the dark reaches of the temple, she meant to carry it out.

When she reached the Gatebridge, she paused. The mist was thinning. A pale sun shone through and endowed the great building with a golden halo. To reach the Sanctum she would have to go underneath. She hesitated, thumping her wings to keep her level, and looked down into the abyss. The rope scar around her neck constricted until she gasped.

What was she so afraid of?

Carnival couldn't remember. Was it their god? She didn't believe in gods. Gods were the inventions of men. Men fashioned gods to carry the burden of their own guilt. Men killed because they were afraid, and forgiveness made the killing easier. Without absolution, men suffered.

On every part of her body Carnival's old scars flared anew. She knew all about suffering. Teeth clenched, she swallowed hard, and dived.

Spikes and ribs of dark metal crowded the base of the temple. Iron loops as large as city blocks held the foundation chains in a ring. There were countless apertures leading into the massive building, all linked by a great confusion of chain-bridges and cables. Spine normally used these to enter and exit the temple unseen. But now it was morning and there was no one to be seen. Dew coated the metal and fell away in rusty drips. Carnival flew on beneath, snarling as the rope scar around her neck started to burn like a garrotte.

A lantern hung from a wider aperture in the centre of the temple. When she reached it she forced herself to wait. She could hardly breathe, but she waited and listened and sniffed the air. For a while there was nothing but the sound of dripping and the smell of rust, and then she heard voices.

Rachel didn't blame him. If it took her own presence here to get Carnival to come and listen to the fat man's ridiculous plan, then fine. That was, after all, her job. But how could she get the message into Dill's wooden skull? He had his stupid sword back now and stood there with his eyes glowing as green as spring, and he would not leave the Sanctum. He refused to leave her side.

His stubbornness was more than likely going to get him killed.

'I'm going to call Clay,' Fogwill warned, 'and get him to drag you out by the scruff of the neck. How would that look, Dill? A temple archon ejected like a drunk from a penny tavern.'

Dill still did not reply.

Rachel felt movement in the air and looked at the aperture leading into the abyss. Nothing visible, but she kept her gaze there while she spoke to Dill. 'Fogwill's right. This thing is between her and me. You did the right thing. You don't have to prove anything.'

Dill said nothing.

Fogwill was pacing before a thousand candles set deep in the iron-thicket walls; his footsteps echoed back from the vaulted ceiling. He approached the lectern, threw up his hands, and turned away. 'You can't be here, Dill. You'll ruin everything. I'm going to tell you one last time: *leave.*'

Dill didn't move.

Rachel was watching the aperture intently now. All of her nerves were on edge, every instinct screaming. She heard nothing, but she sensed *something*. Cold seeped into the Sanctum through that hole. A few of the candle-flames in the walls wavered. Her hand slipped to one of the bamboo tubes at her belt.

'Do you have to fidget with those things?' Fogwill snapped. 'They make me nervous.'

Rachel kept her hand where it was.

Fogwill started pacing again.

Another gust of air came from the aperture. Candles guttered; half of them blew out.

Carnival rose from the abyss with a powerful sweep of her wings. She held herself aloft for a dozen heartbeats, glancing around, before her gaze fell on Rachel. 'I made you a promise,' she said. Her smile was predatory, the freshest scar on her face.

Rachel shrugged. As gently as she could, she began to loosen the plug from the bamboo tube. But she stopped as Dill began backing towards her, his hand around the hilt of his sword.

Dill!

She should never have given it back. But he'd looked so desperately unhappy without it, and she'd thought he would just take it and go when she asked him to. Of course that had been before Adjunct Crumb had told her what he'd done. She placed a hand on Dill's arm, stopped him from drawing the weapon.

Fogwill had frozen mid-step and stood with his mouth open.

For God's sake, speak to her.

Carnival landed lightly on the edge of the aperture and folded her wings and then her arms. All of her attention was fixed on Rachel, who noted the iron fork in the angel's belt with dismay. However impotent the weapon looked,

she knew better than to dismiss it. The last time they'd
fought, Carnival had been unarmed and blinded.

'I . . .' Fogwill was sweating. 'We . . . have a proposal
for you.'

Carnival ignored him, her dark eyes still focused on
Rachel.

'A trade.' The Adjunct edged closer to the lectern, to
the gas valve.

Don't you dare. Not while Dill is here. But Rachel
couldn't move to stop him. She might alert Carnival to
the danger. Or worse. The mood in the Sanctum felt
brittle as glass. Any move on Rachel's part was likely to
shatter it.

'You are aware,' Fogwill began, 'of the restorative
qualities of angelwine – the elixir first used by Callis to
bestow immense strength and longevity upon his warriors.'
He swallowed. 'You are also probably aware that a distillation of this elixir now exists.'

Carnival grunted, but the Adjunct's statement at least
earned him a glance.

She is tempted. But the priest's careful choice of words
had not escaped Rachel. *This is a dangerous game you're
playing, Fogwill. And to what end? There's something more
here than meets the eye.*

The fat priest leaned insouciantly against the lectern, a
posture so contrived it made Rachel clench her teeth.

'By our laws, a blasphemous potion,' Fogwill went on.
'It should never have been distilled. Nevertheless it now
exists, though it has been removed from Devon's hands –
and it would be of immeasurable benefit to you. So, a
trade? The angelwine for your assistance in a small
matter.'

Carnival merely glowered at him.

Fogwill practically wilted. Sweat shone on his wide forehead. He reached a hand behind the lectern, casting a fretful glance at Rachel and Dill, then swallowed. 'We'd like you to kill someone for us.'

Someone? Why are you still hedging, Fogwill?

Carnival reacted bitterly. 'You expect me to kill for *you*?' she hissed. 'Do you think I'm a fucking assassin like this bitch, to be bought?' She wheeled on Rachel and scars gathered on her brow. Her eyes had narrowed to murderous slits. She snapped out her wings to their full length and beat them, again, again, until a gale blew around her. On every side, candles blew out. 'It's getting darker, Spine.'

Fogwill had his hands up. 'Wait, hear me out.'

Rachel yanked the bamboo container free from her belt, pushed her thumb against its plug.

Carnival advanced, dragging a storm behind her.

'Leave her!' And suddenly Dill was between them, his sword wobbling in his hand.

'Dill!' Rachel yanked him aside.

Carnival attacked.

She came so fast, Rachel barely saw her move. One heartbeat the assassin was upright, the next she was thrown across the Sanctum with brutal force. She slid twenty feet on her back and came to a halt inches from the wall. The bamboo tube rolled away into the shadows.

'I said leave her!' Dill swiped at the scarred angel.

Carnival diverted his blow without taking her eyes off Rachel. She caught the blunt blade in her fist, jerked it aside, and then punched Dill in the face. He dropped like a puppet whose strings had been severed. Wings thundering, Carnival came after the assassin again.

Rachel leapt to her feet, unsheathed her sword. She

had to act *now*, while there was still some light in the Sanctum. She ran at her adversary, swung the blade up over her shoulder, feigned a down-cut . . .

Carnival moved to intercept the sword.

With her bare hands . . .? She thinks she's that *fast? Shit, she* is *that fast.* But Rachel had no intention of attacking with her blade just yet. At the last moment, she slid both legs forward and dropped onto her back on the polished marble floor, turning her charge into a reckless slide. Carnival recoiled from the manoeuvre, but too late. The Spine assassin collided with the angel, taking Carnival's legs out from under her.

It was an unorthodox tactic, but effective. Carnival tumbled over head first, wings thrashing, as Rachel skidded to a halt six feet beyond. *Great, but she won't let me attempt that one again.* The assassin rolled over onto her stomach, and slipped her loaded blowpipe from her belt. Still lying on the floor, she put the weapon to her lips, and blew.

Somehow, the scarred angel had landed on her feet. She spun around, snatching the poisoned dart from the air with appalling ease. Then she put the blunt end of the needle-like missile in her mouth, and sneered. Now she advanced again, pounding her wings, chewing on the dart as if it was a toothpick. 'You think you can poison *me*, Spine?' she growled. 'What else have you got? Throwing knives? Acid powders? Are you too scared to use your sword?'

Dill was crawling on his hands and knees beside Carnival, reaching up to her, wheezing. 'The angelwine . . . I'll tell you . . . where it is. The Church no longer has it . . . Just leave her . . . please.'

Abruptly the gale blowing through the Sanctum died.

Carnival spat out the dart, grabbed Dill's throat, and hoisted him upright. 'Tell me!' she hissed.

Dill gasped, 'It's . . . lost.'

'Where?'

'The abyss . . . Devon's syringe fell . . .'

She released him abruptly.

Dill crumpled to the floor.

Only a scattered handful of candles remained lit. Webs of shadow from the iron-hedged walls shivered around Carnival. Rachel returned the blowpipe to her belt, and got shakily to her feet. Adjunct Crumb still stood at the lectern, his face ashen.

Then the scarred angel cracked her wings apart and rose into the air. Shadows towered behind her, dark and huge as thunderclouds. For a long moment, she stared hard into the abyss, candle flames glittering in her eyes. With a snarl, she drew her wings back in.

'No!' Fogwill cried. 'Listen to me!'

Carnival plunged into the void.

'Gods!' Fogwill rushed to the door and pulled frantic-ally at a bell cord. 'A disaster, a disaster. If she finds that syringe we have nothing. Why did you tell her, Dill? Why?'

Rachel rubbed her shoulder and winced. 'What the hell does it matter anyway? Let her have her goddamn potion.'

At that moment Captain Clay and Mark Hael burst into the Sanctum. Rachel's brother surveyed the scene. 'What happened? Where is she?'

Fogwill explained.

'Last we'll see of her,' Clay said. 'Good riddance.'

The Adjunct kept pacing, this way and that in nervous circles. He dragged his hands over his scalp repeatedly as though he still had hair. 'No,' he protested. 'We have to find the syringe before she does. It's all we have left now!'

He stopped pacing. 'Dill, you have to go – you have to stop her, now, before it's too late.'

'He's not going anywhere,' Rachel said.

But the fat priest ignored her. Pacing again, while his hands traced patterns in the air before him like jewelled butterflies, he muttered to himself, 'She won't kill him. She didn't harm him before. He'll be safe while he's unarmed.'

'You'd send him to Deep, *unarmed*?' Rachel said, shocked.

'He'll need light,' Fogwill said, 'a storm lantern.' He turned to Clay. 'Fetch a lamp.'

Clay hesitated.

'A lamp! He needs a lamp.'

The temple guard captain nodded, then left the Sanctum.

Rachel placed a hand on Dill's shoulder. 'You don't have to do this,' she said, then to Fogwill, 'You can't make him do this. You'll send him to his death!'

The Adjunct's pace faltered. 'I don't have any choice!' he snapped. As he gazed at her, Rachel saw the truth of it in the ghostly pallor of his skin, the pleading, pain-filled eyes, the bitter, crushing weight of his decision etched into every line of his face.

God, Fogwill, you're suffering. But why? What can't you tell us?

But his look had been enough to convince her. 'All right,' she said. She marched over to the rim of the aperture. 'If he has to go down there, then I'll go with him.'

Mark Hael snorted. 'Been learning to fly, dear sister?'

'He can carry me.' She peered into the darkness, then swung to face Dill. 'You're strong enough.'

Dill lowered his sword until the tip of the blade touched the floor. The gold hand guard gleamed dully in the candlelight. Somehow it was dented. 'Rachel,' he said, 'I don't know . . . I can't . . .'

'You can,' she said.

'Can what?' Captain Clay had returned with a storm lantern, a frown creasing his grizzled brow.

'My little sister insists she wants to go with him,' Mark Hael explained.

'Here, lad.' Clay's expression remained grave, as he placed the storm lantern in Dill's free hand, closing the angel's fingers around the handle. 'It's well full of oil – the best we have. Burns bright. There's extra wick and flints stored in the base of it too, case you need them.'

Dill's wings slumped. He stared at the lantern for a moment, then raised his eyes to meet Rachel's. They glowed whiter than she'd ever seen before.

'I'll protect you, Dill,' she whispered. 'I promise.'

'Rachel, this is insane.' Her brother strode towards her. 'We don't have time for this.'

Her eyes held Dill's. 'I trust you,' she said. 'Catch me.'

'Rachel!' Mark Hael lunged for her, too late.

She had stepped back and disappeared into the abyss.

A brittle silence. Dill's heart momentarily ceased to beat. Adjunct Crumb froze. Mark Hael and Captain Clay did the same. No one moved.

And then a shriek of joy came from the depths. 'The bitch nearly hit me.' Carnival's laughter echoed through the high chamber.

Suddenly Dill felt himself being wrenched forwards. The aeronaut commander had grabbed his chain mail and was forcing him towards the edge. 'Help her,' he said. 'Go!'

Dill struggled against the man's grip, his heels slipping on the polished floor. 'No, I . . .'

But Mark Hael dragged him forward effortlessly. 'You must.'

The dark void drew closer, utterly cold, utterly dead.

'Please.' The angel's eyes were now blazing white. He would have screamed but he couldn't find enough air in his lungs to expel. His wings lashed uselessly, too weak to halt his progress towards that terrible darkness. His hands were flailing, both lantern and sword swinging wildly.

They were standing now over the edge. The abyss reached up to him, a rising well where every one of Dill's nightmares lurked. It sapped the last of his strength, seemed to drain his life away. His knees buckled. His stomach lurched. 'I can't,' he protested feebly.

'Save her!' Mark Hael yelled, and shook him.

Dill stared into the abyss. She was lost to him and he hated her for it. He hated her because there was nothing he could do to help her. He knew that if he stepped into that darkness he would die. The void below was everything and nothing: an emptiness that encompassed his whole life. It would consume him utterly. How far could Rachel have already fallen? Did it matter? He could not hope to save her. He was weak, clumsy and foolish, a liar, a betrayer, and a coward – the antithesis of everything an archon should be. He was *nothing*.

Yet she trusted him.

Dill stepped into the darkness.

PART THREE

WAR

23

✝HE ABYSS

Blackthrone rose in layers of jagged escarpments and wrinkled gullies, gleaming hot and blistered in the sun. Veins of yellow and green trickled around scattered glints of crystal. The quarry at the base of its southern slope had bitten deeply into the mountain itself, opening a gaping crescent of metal cliffs. House-sized boulders and hills of scree broke against the base of the grinning rock, but they were like so many pebbles and mounds of grit in the shadow of the Tooth.

The Tooth *towered* over the quarry. Yellow streaks marred its smooth white hull. Sand drifts a hundred feet high smothered the base of one side and partially obscured the river-wide trails in the packed earth behind. A dusty scoop like an enormous jawbone jutted from the front, beneath rows of cutting wheels on retracted mandibles. High above the cutters a strip of windows flashed violently, and higher still blackened funnels punched up from the roof, wrapped in gantries and stairwells.

Devon eased the ship's wheel around. 'Now that,' he said, 'is one big tooth.'

Presbyter Sypes's eyes fluttered open, then closed again. He resumed snoring.

Signs of habitation were evident below. Work had been done to clear some of the sand around the vast machine, to give access to the shade below the hull. Trails led up the surrounding sand drifts and disappeared into a line of rag-covered holes a quarter of the way up one side. Rope ladders hung from holes higher up, but the Heshette themselves were keeping out of sight. Devon knew better than to assume that they were unaware of the warship's presence.

He spoke into a trumpet on the control deck. 'Purge the ribs, Angus, slowly. We're going down.'

After a moment a hiss issued from the envelope overhead and the *Birkita* began to descend.

Devon spun the wheel to bring the warship round in a circle above the quarry. A clutter of stretched-hide roofs and poles came into view, packing the shade between the far side of the Tooth and the cliff wall. Animal tracks pocked muddy earth around them.

A spring? Of course, Blackthrone traps the rain.

But still nothing grew in the poisonous earth. The machine was just a temporary home to the Heshette and their animals, a harsh oasis between the seasonal plains around Dalamoor and the bandit villages west of the Coyle.

The warship descended, and Devon swung her away from the cliffs to bring them back around the Tooth's crown.

'More lift, Angus,' he said into the trumpet.

Another hiss. They dropped two fathoms.

'I said lift, man. Not purge. Lift.' Devon's voice was steady, but the vibrations from the engine shook his hand on the wheel. The quarry floor unfolded below, rose quickly to meet them.

The cliffs loomed closer. Devon throttled the starboard propeller and wrenched the rudder hard to port. The warship rolled slightly and began to nose away from the rock. Cables pinged overhead.

'*Lift*, Angus.'

Angus's voice came through another trumpet. 'Drop dead.'

'Unlikely,' Devon said. 'I would walk free from any crash. This course of action will do nothing but kill you and the priest.'

A barrage of tinny obscenities erupted from the engine-room trumpet. Another hiss, and suddenly they were dropping even faster.

Damn him to hell.

The ground came up at them. Devon nudged the front of the envelope away from the cliffs. Through the portside windows he saw massive funnels rising quickly past. They were now between the Tooth and the rock face, falling too quickly to manoeuvre safely past the huge machine.

'Lift, Angus, or you'll never see another drop of serum.'

Angus did not reply. Devon swung the wheel hard to starboard. He slammed both elevator levers back then cranked the propellers full.

Engines rumbled, then roared. The bridge shuddered. To port, the shadowed hull of the Tooth rushed upwards. Cliffs hemmed them in to starboard. Clouds of dust billowed through the front ducts. Devon coughed and blinked furiously, trying to see through the bridge windows. The ground was close, rising. He felt the bridge tilt.

'Last chance, Angus,' he shouted. It might have been into the wrong trumpet – he didn't look, didn't care. They were going to crash. He had to level the ship. He cut the propellers, forced the elevator controls forward.

Dust choked the forward view, a storm caught between two rising walls, dull white on one side, sharp, ragged rock on the other.

A heavy grinding sound from behind. A loud crack. Ropes fretted, twanged. Wood snapped, splintered, and they hit the ground with a bone-breaking crunch.

Devon's chin smacked hard against the wheel. The bridge windows shattered in an explosion of glass and dust.

The warship settled with a series of long creaks and groans. The gondola listed to one side, and came to rest with a final hiss.

Devon cut the engines and turned to check on the Presbyter. Sypes's chair had slid across the floor and rested against one wall, but the old man was still slumped there, snoring lightly.

'Incredible,' Devon muttered.

Bleating noises forced his attention back outside. Through the falling dust he saw goats bucking and kicking among piles of broken wood and torn hide. Chickens fluttered and squawked, scattered feathers everywhere. The *Birkita* had landed on the Heshette animal pens. A cockerel hopped through the bridge window onto the control deck and cocked its head at him.

'Bother,' Devon said. He shook Sypes awake.

The Presbyter blinked and rubbed his eyes, then squinted at the cockerel. 'Good landing?'

'We're down, aren't we?'

'Not the best start for your proposed alliance,' Sypes said. 'I urge you reconsider. The Heshette will murder us on sight for this.'

Devon grunted, picked up his bag of poisons, and left

to survey the damage. Angus, if he was still alive, could stay where he was and rot.

Extricating himself from the wreckage proved to be a lengthy process. Devon picked his way through the shattered pens, dragging aside sun-bleached poles to clear a path. Frightened goats clambered over each other as they struggled to escape, bleating incessantly.

The *Birkita* was in poor shape. The gondola listed at a shallow angle. Splinters of teak formed a jagged line where the aft deck had buckled. The starboard propeller hung loose and the port one had sheared, a foot shorter on both blades where it had collided with an outcrop of rock. Three of the four main aether-lights were smashed. But, incredibly, the envelope was still intact. It rested against the hull of the Tooth, hardly reaching an eighth of the way up the giant machine.

The Tooth rose like a pale citadel, its sheer walls tapering to scorched funnels high above. Underneath, rows and rows of massive wheels sat in shadowed tracks among piles of crushed rock. Fine lines had been etched into the hull in endless whorls and curls.

Some sort of ceramic? Three thousand years and there is hardly a mark on it. Light too, or the whole thing would sink into the desert. The refuse of a civilization so much more advanced than our own, abandoned here like a broken shovel.

Devon walked the entire length of the machine, looking for a pattern in its hull etchings, some clue as to how it had been assembled. He was so caught up in his observations that when he reached the scoop at the front he was startled to find the Heshette there waiting for him.

They looked like figures sculpted from sand. Sun-faded gabardines hung shapelessly about them. Dust-coloured scarves wrapped their faces. A dozen men assembled in the sunshine beyond the shadow of the Tooth, mostly armed with hunting bows and spears, but there were other weapons: clubs, bone axes, long knives, hooked swords, and bandit rapiers – weapons scavenged from a hundred conflicts.

Only the shaman stood out from the group. His long beard hung below the folds of his scarf like a frayed and knotted rope adorned with feather and bone fetishes. In one gnarled fist he clutched a bleached wood staff as tall as himself.

This is the man who shapes the minds of the tribe, who fuels their hatred. This is the man I need to convince.

The tribesmen were approaching. Devon flexed his shoulders, squared his jaw, and went to meet them. This was going to be difficult. And, he suspected, it was going to hurt.

After a dozen steps he found out just how much.

There was no parley, no negotiation, no trade of insults. There was only pain.

An axe slammed into his chest. Devon landed on his back.

The man who'd thrown the axe didn't shout or run. He didn't break his stride. The scarf around his head hid whatever expression of hate or satisfaction he wore.

Devon pressed fingers to his chest and they came away bloody. He wrenched the axe free and stared in disbelief at the blood glistening on the sharpened-bone blade. Then he struggled to his knees. 'Now look here,' he said.

None of the Heshette uttered a word. But the weapons came hard and fast.

A stone glanced off Devon's temple. A second axe drove high into his shoulder and opened half his neck.

Arrows hissed. One struck his thigh, another tore a strip from his cheek, another pierced his stomach, another ripped through his ear, another grazed his scalp, another thumped into his lung. Something heavy smacked against his skull and the world reeled.

Devon was confused. He wanted to shout *stop*, but a second stone struck him clean on the forehead. As he crumpled, the Tooth's massive hull slid across his vision like a dirty, bone-coloured sky.

Still the blows rained. Metal and stone struck him, ripped him, beat him back into the sand. He heard constant thuds all around. A spear entered his groin. He grabbed it and pulled himself upright, tore the weapon free. Knives thumped into his shoulders, his belly, his chest, his neck, and he was looking up at sky again. Something broke a rib: he heard the bone snap, clear and loud in the desert silence. He tried to stand, but a heavy weight cracked into his arm and the force spun him round.

Devon turned back. The Heshette were raising and aiming bows, picking up rocks. He looked down at his ruined body. Flesh hung in strips from bloody wounds. A shard of bone pierced the flesh at the back of his arm. Blood darkened the sand at his feet. His breaths came wetly. He opened split and swollen lips, ran his tongue over a loose tooth. Fluids gurgled inside him when he tried to speak. A knock to the head blurred the vision in his right eye. He reached up and found the shaft of an arrow there, jutting from the eye itself. He snapped off the shaft. Behind his skull, he located the tip, grabbed it, and pulled it through.

Small pieces of his brain clung to the wood.

The pain crept almost tenderly upon him, like an itch

he wanted to scratch. It circled the tips of his fingers and trembled on his skin. He sucked in a breath and the pain found him, and tore at him. It howled in his blood and his skull and his tongue and his teeth. It clamoured and clawed behind his eyes and screamed in his ears.

Devon began to laugh.

Darkness. Dill could see nothing. He couldn't see his out-stretched hands or his chain mail rattling against his chest as he dived deeper. He plummeted with his wings folded tight against his back, a scream lodged in his throat. Cold air rushed up at him, streamed through his fingers, ripped tears from his eyes. He screwed them shut but it made no difference. Everything was black. With every heartbeat he was falling deeper into death. He opened his eyes again and let the tears flow freely.

'Rachel!' he cried. The void swallowed his voice before it even reached his ears.

Fear begged him to stop. The abyss couldn't go on for ever; he would hit the bottom sometime. But he had no choice. If he stopped he'd be just as alone in the dark and Rachel would surely be lost. And he couldn't go back – not without her.

I trust you.

In his mind he saw her face. The image stirred in him a desperate hatred: hatred of himself, hatred of the Battle-archons who had gone before him. Hatred of everything they had been and he wasn't. He screwed his eyes shut again.

He dived and dived, and screamed and screamed, 'Rachel! Rachel!'

The abyss sucked him under like tar; it filled his lungs,

leached into his flesh and his mind until it became everything. Dill's terror was absolute.

Catch me.

How could he catch her? She was falling somewhere below, or above, or a foot to his left or right. How could he expect to find her in this? He was blind. And she was dead. She had been dead the moment she threw herself into the abyss.

I trust you.

Those words were wrapped around his heart and wouldn't let go. They would still be wrapped around his heart when he died. Dill opened his eyes, tears trickling from the corners, and stared into nothing. Rushing air forced his lips open and he screamed again. An army of ghosts waited for him below. Would her spirit already be among them? Would he see them before he felt the slam of rock that ended his own life? And then?

What then?

There would be no priests to bless his corpse. Ulcis would offer him no salvation, no place in his army. Would the Maze come for him? Could it reach into the city of Deep to claim him? Or would he lie for ever in the darkness, broken and forgotten?

He would never see his father again. The thought struck him like a fist. Dill furled his wings even closer to his back and extended his fingers and dived and dived.

'Rachel!'

Above the torrent of air he thought he heard a distant voice.

'Rachel!'

Had he heard anything at all? How close was he to the end? Had he merely heard the wails of ghosts, warning him? Calling to him to stop his descent?

'Rachel!'

A voice called back from below. It might have been calling his name – but he wasn't sure – somewhere off to his left. He checked his dive, banked in that direction. One hand moved to the storm lantern at his belt, the other gripped the hilt of his sword until it stung.

'Rachel!'

'Dill.' The voice seemed to echo across eternity.

He swept towards the sound of it, not daring to hope, his mind full of the pounding of blood and mocking darkness.

'Dill, here, below you!'

Dill flexed his wings to ease his descent. Air dragged at his feathers. He didn't understand. She couldn't still be falling; she couldn't possibly see him to call out. But it sounded so like her.

Or her ghost? *Am I already dead? Did I hit the bottom?*

'Dill, left, above you, thirty yards.'

Above? He snapped his wings open and let the uprising air pull him to a stop.

'Rachel?'

'Above you, to your left.'

'Where are you?' he pleaded. His voice disappeared into the dark.

'Light your lantern.'

It took an age to locate the lantern at his belt. Then he fumbled for the spark wheel, beating his wings to keep him level, not even knowing if his eyes were open or closed. After three tries the lantern brightened. His hands, belt and trousers became illuminated. The sword guard gleamed gold. Rusted steel links glistened at his chest. But there was nothing else visible. All around him the blackness of the void stretched on, untouched by the light, and seemed even denser than before. His chest began to tighten; his breathing came quicker. 'Rachel?' he called.

'I see you!' she cried. 'Above you, not far. I'm here.'

In a daze, Dill followed the sound of her voice.

Rachel had one arm around Carnival's shoulders, the back of her knees supported in the crook of the angel's scarred arm.

Carnival's wings thumped with sluggish force. She bobbed slightly, supporting Rachel as though she weighed nothing. 'Turn down the lantern,' she hissed.

For a moment he was too shocked to comply. He just stared.

Carnival's jaw clenched. Her lips drew back from her teeth.

Dill dimmed the light.

'She saved me,' Rachel said. 'She saw you diving after me. She told me where you were.'

Carnival's face was a shocking white: even her scars seemed to have paled. But her eyes remained cold and empty. 'Dark here, isn't it?' she rasped. Her voice sounded as though she was suffocating. 'There's a ledge over there' – she jerked her head – 'where you can rest.'

They flew there in silence. By the light of his lantern, Dill saw Rachel glance back at him over Carnival's shoulder, and smile. His heart stuttered.

A narrow rim of metal, the ledge jutted from rock as smooth as glass. Vertical ribs of the same metal, an arm-span apart, stretched away on either side. Dill landed a few feet from the others. His sword struck the ledge with a hollow peal.

'The abyss must narrow as it descends,' Rachel said,

her voice strangely hollow and metallic. She peered down into the depths, then lifted her head to gaze above. 'I think this wall slopes inwards.'

For the first time Dill looked up. Deepgate shimmered far above, faint wisps and pearls of light, like sunlight filtering through a clutch of jewellery. 'How far down are we?' he said.

'Half a league at least,' Rachel said. 'Perhaps more.' She placed a hand on the abyss wall. 'This surface . . . is melted.'

Reflections from his lantern shone deep in the rock. Dill's reflection peered out at him, like another angel trapped in glittering black ice. Pale, forlorn, it reminded him of the archons in the temple tapestries.

Carnival left them and moved to perch some distance away, out of the lantern light, her footfalls soundless.

Once they were alone, Dill sat down beside Rachel and whispered, 'What about her? What are you going to do?'

'She could have let me die.'

'Why didn't she?'

'I don't know, Dill. She won't speak to me. There's something different about her, something . . . deeply wrong with her. I've never seen her like this before.' She lowered her voice. 'I think she's terrified.'

'Can you stop her before she reaches Deep?'

Rachel's hands curled around the lip of the ledge she sat on, and her eyes seemed to dull. She said flatly, 'I can't fight her like this. Here. We have to wait.'

'Until when?'

'Until we reach the bottom.'

'But if Ulcis finds us?'

She shrugged. 'There's nothing else I can do.'

Dill leaned back, feeling his feathers brush the abyss wall. A thousand tons of darkness crushed him. Deafening silence. He closed his eyes, trying to shut it all out, but that only made things worse.

I could take you back; I should take you back up.

She wasn't supposed to be here. Dill had been ordered to recover the angelwine, not Rachel. If he'd been stronger, braver, she wouldn't be here at all. She'd jumped because she'd known Dill couldn't face the abyss on his own. She'd jumped because he was a coward. And now his cowardice had put her in danger again.

'Thank you,' Rachel said, 'for coming after me.'

Dill could not find his voice.

'Are you all right?'

'I'm . . . sorry I didn't catch you,' he said.

'No,' Rachel placed a hand on his arm, 'I'm the one who should be sorry. I was so furious with Mark and Fogwill, I didn't stop to think. How could you ever have found me down here in this darkness? I realized that the instant I jumped.' She stole a glance at Carnival. 'I thought I was dead.'

Dill turned away so that she couldn't see the light of shame in his eyes.

'I jumped,' Rachel said, 'and suddenly it dawned on me what I'd done. I called and called until my voice was hoarse. She caught me. One moment I was falling, the next I was in her arms. At first I thought it was you.'

Dill pulled his arm away from her grasp.

She moved closer, but did not reach out to him again. 'At least you tried.'

They sat in silence for an age. Dill's mind replayed the events in the Sanctum over and over again. He watched

Rachel slip away. *Catch me.* That brittle moment when no one breathed, then her brother was grabbing him, dragging him towards certain death.

Dill had hesitated. Even the weight of darkness couldn't crush that memory.

Rachel whispered, 'You were so brave.'

Dill could not look at her. He didn't hear Carnival approach, but her voice cut through his thoughts with a welcome sharpness. 'I can't see the bottom.' Face tight and pained, she clutched at the rope-scar on her neck as though the rope was still there. Her voice was hoarse. 'Can you carry her now, or must I?'

'I can do it, I think,' Dill said.

'Then do so.'

They stood up and the assassin wrapped her arms around his neck. Her touch sent a shiver through him.

Carnival was watching them, dark eyes unreadable, her scars a map of hate and murder.

Each scar a life. She's made a mask for herself. But perhaps there's still an angel hidden somewhere deep beneath those scars. She knew I would never reach Rachel in time. She could so easily have let her fall to her death. But she didn't.

'Thank you,' Dill said, 'for saving her.'

Carnival spoke without emotion. 'Don't thank me, angel. I don't know what's down there or how long it will take me to find the Poisoner's angelwine. But I do know one thing.' She looked at Rachel and hunger flashed in her eyes. 'This bitch still has blood in her veins.' She smiled. 'And Scar Night is coming.'

24

UNEASY
ALLIANCES

The Heshette shaman spoke from behind his scarf. 'If we remove your head from your neck, cut off your arms and legs, and divide what's left into small enough pieces to feed to the goats – will you die then, do you think?' His accent was Dalamoor, the clipped speech of camel herders. Bones in his beard clicked together as he leaned forward.

Devon sat in the sand and tried to reach with his left hand an arrow stuck behind his left shoulder. He'd already pulled out the others, and they'd *hurt*. The axes had been less painful to dislodge but had left deep gouges in his chest and neck. He'd had to push the severed flesh together again to help it knit, but his wounds *were* healing. He no longer bled. The pain in his skull had subsided and the vision was clearing in his once ruined eye. He looked up at the scarf and said, 'I really don't know.'

The shaman struck him hard in the throat with his staff. Devon fell back, gagging. He spat blood and sand and wrenched himself back to his knees, driving his stump into the ground. The other tribesmen stood in a circle around the pair of them, faces hidden by their own scarves, weapons ready.

'That . . . course of action,' Devon said between breaths, 'would be . . . bad . . . for both of us.'

'Worse for you, I think,' the shaman said. One of the tribesmen laughed.

Devon finally got hold of the arrow and yanked. It came out with a spike of pain that forced his teeth together. 'Aren't you even curious as to why I'm here?' He dropped the arrow onto the bloody, sand-crusted pile before him. There were a dozen there already, bone-tipped and fletched with vulture feathers.

The shaman tugged at his beard. 'We'll need a saw to do this right.'

'I have come here to offer you something,' Devon said.

'The arms and legs first, I think,' the shaman continued.

'Will you parley?'

'And then the head. If he still lives we can position the head to give him a better view of the more delicate cuts.' The shaman turned to one of his men. 'You, fetch a saw.'

'Yes, Bataba.' The man bounded off under the Tooth's hull, towards the rear of the machine.

'Sharp or blunt, whichever you prefer,' Bataba called after him.

The man grinned back.

Devon's shoulder itched as the arrow wound closed and healed. Another of the savages had upturned his poison bag and was sifting through the coloured bottles, sniffing at their glass stoppers.

'I recommend the red one,' Devon said to him. 'Yes, that small one.' He turned back to face Bataba. 'Is my heightened constitution of no interest to you?'

'It presents me with a challenge,' Bataba conceded.

A score of men had already surrounded the *Birkita*'s gondola and, growing confident they were not to be attacked from within, were edging closer. In moments they'd find Sypes.

'I can offer you something far more rewarding than my death,' Devon said.

'Your death will be sufficient, Poisoner.'

'You know me?'

'Did you think Deepgate was entirely free of our spies? We learned of the Church's manhunt days ago. And now skyships pursue you here. But you are a fool to have come to us.'

'We share an enemy.'

Bataba snorted. 'Thirty years of poison and disease and you seek an alliance?'

The Heshette were inside the airship now, shouting and smashing everything they could find. One of them gave a shrill ululation, and moments later Sypes was dragged through the aft port door and thrown onto the deck. As the old priest sprawled face down on the buckled wood, Devon winced. 'You ought to be more careful with him,' he said. 'He's as frail as he looks and worth a considerable sum in ransom. This priest is Deepgate's Presbyter.'

Bataba watched the Presbyter pick himself up. 'A token of your faith? Or are you a token of his?'

'Kill him if you wish.'

'You think I require your permission, Poisoner?'

Devon did not reply. By now the tribesman had returned with a rusty saw – painfully blunt. He felt nauseous.

Everything now rested on his offer.

'Listen to me,' he said. 'I came here to *end* this war, to end the decades of bloodshed. I came here to offer you victory. I can give you Deepgate.'

Bataba turned slowly, his face still hidden by the scarf. Blood matted the tokens sewn into his beard. 'You are a liar and a murderer. Every word you speak is poison. We will ransom the priest, but not you.'

Devon spat more blood into the sand. 'Then you're a fool,' he said. 'Do you think our sciences end with me? There are others to take my place. And how much do you think you'll get for him? Look at him, he's almost dead. Just keeping him alive will be a struggle. The temple will prevail without one crippled old priest. I'm asking for your help to end this war.'

Bataba hefted the saw, studied the dull serrated blade. 'This will cause a great deal of pain,' he said flatly.

Devon snorted. 'A waste of your efforts. Pain, as you can see, means little enough to me.'

The shaman looked up. Slowly, he unwrapped the scarf from his head.

Devon's breath caught. Half the shaman's face was darkly tanned and smooth; the other half was a ruin. The left eye was misty grey, the right nothing but a red welt. Burns like reptile skin swept up from his neck and over his sunken cheeks. His right ear was missing. Black tattoos spiralled through the burns, through the wrinkled mess of his missing eye, and narrowed to points on his cracked and blistered scalp. Clumps of hair still sprouted from the unburned side.

'Yes,' the shaman said, 'little enough to you.'

*

'We should turn off the lantern,' Rachel said, above the whoomph of Dill's wings. She hugged his neck with one arm, while her legs wrapped around his midriff.

'No.' Dill held the lamp close, like a mother holding a baby.

'We need to save the oil.'

'I . . .' He could think of nothing to justify his need, other than the truth.

'He's afraid of the dark,' Carnival growled, banking close by.

Rachel studied him for a moment then rested her head against his shoulder. 'We can keep it lit a while longer, then,' she said.

'No.' All at once, the light seemed as much of an enemy as a friend, both easing and exposing his fear. 'You're right,' he said. 'We need to save the oil.'

With trembling fingers, he extinguished the lantern.

Darkness slammed in.

They flew down deeper and deeper into the abyss. The dark formed a solid wall around them, broken only by the faintest knot of light above. Deepgate was smaller, more distant every time Dill looked up. He felt Rachel's breaths against his neck, her chest rising and falling against his own, and he tried to match her breathing. But, as much as he tried, he took two breaths for every one of hers.

Only Carnival could see in this gloom. Occasionally he heard a wing beat off to one side, or felt the air stir as she circled them. Her plan had been for them to keep close to the gently sloping wall, but without light Dill had no way of knowing where it lay. With every turn he made, he feared he would bruise a wing against the rock. He strained his eyes, trying to distinguish forms in the dark, until they were weary.

The air grew warmer, denser. Sweat broke from his forehead and matted his hair; breathing became laborious. His armour rubbed against him, stifled him, and trapped the sweat on his back. A dull pain took root in his neck, then reached out tendrils into his shoulders and crept down his spine.

Unseen, Carnival sailed around them effortlessly.

After a while Rachel asked him, 'Do you need to rest?'

'I'm all right,' he mumbled. Dill's thoughts were elsewhere.

The city of Deep lay somewhere below, legions of ghosts wandering its cold streets. Were they now looking up from the darkness? Did they still yearn for Ayen's light? Oblivion seemed a kinder fate than millennia without light at all.

Rachel shifted against his chest. The scabbard on her back bruised his arm where he gripped her. A movement in the air told him Carnival had glided past again. He waited a few moments before he whispered in Rachel's ear. 'Do you think she meant what she said? About . . . about why she saved you?'

He felt Rachel stiffen.

She said, 'Perhaps that's why she's so afraid. When Scar Night comes she'll need a living soul if she's to survive.'

'Can you resist her?'

Rachel merely shrugged.

As they circled deeper into the pit, Rachel grew steadily heavier in his weary arms. Her weight forced him to beat his wings constantly to keep their descent gentle, and his shoulders began to cramp under the strain. His shirt clung to his back like a blister, the chain mail grated his skin in a hundred places. The heavy sword twisted his belt and the hilt dug into his side. They breathed in each other's damp breaths as Rachel's heart pressed against his own.

Down and down, for what seemed like hours.

There was nothing in that interminable dark by which to gauge their progress, but the thickening air, the mounting pain, and the building heat. Dill was about to suggest that they rest a while when a sudden realization gripped him. He pulled up, halting their descent.

'What is it?' Rachel asked.

'Carnival. She's left us?'

They listened, heard nothing but their own breathing and the beat of Dill's wings.

'I'll light the lantern again,' Rachel said.

'But she'll see us,' Dill said. *And you'll see me.*

'She can already see us without it. We need to know if the bottom is close.'

Dill held the lantern while Rachel spun the flint wheel. Even at the lowest wick, the light was blinding.

'Can you see anything?' Dill asked.

'Nothing.'

Darkness swallowed the light completely. They hovered for a while in the vast silence.

'You look exhausted,' Rachel said. 'Let's get over to the side.'

'Which direction?'

'I don't know. If the abyss continued to narrow as we descended it can't be far away.'

He nodded.

'Go slowly,' she warned.

After they had flown a short distance, the abyss wall appeared before them, glittering in the dark. Either he had chosen the correct direction by instinct or the abyss was much narrower here. Rachel unhooked the lantern and held it up. The rock face was warped and blistered, like melted black glass. Their reflections flowed over its uneven surface, faces stretched and contorted into pale, phantom-like forms.

Dill shuddered. *Are we now ghosts? Is this finally the realm of the dead?*

'There's another ledge below,' Rachel observed.

The metal perch was wet. Water seeped from a crack in the rock face and gurgled along tiny gullies so that drips hit the ledge with eerie chimes. Rachel cupped her hands and tasted the water. 'It's fine. Cold.'

When they had slaked their thirsts they found a place further along the ledge which was relatively dry. Dill dangled his legs over the edge and stretched his neck, wincing at the pain. 'How far do you think we've come?'

Rachel looked up. 'I can't see Deepgate clearly, but it seems brighter up there. It must be late morning by now.'

Far, far above, faint curls and lines of light scarred the apex, impossibly distant. He returned his gaze to the depths. Nothing. 'Maybe the abyss goes on down for ever.'

Rachel raised the lantern and edged a few steps further along the ledge. She paused, squatted down. 'Dill, this ledge isn't flat. It rises at a shallow angle.' She squinted along the metal ridge. 'I wasn't sure the first time we stopped, but now I am. It's steeper down here. It must follow the abyss wall in a spiral.'

'A path down?'

She lifted her head. 'Or a path up. The top of it must be hidden somewhere under the abyss rim.'

'Why?'

Rachel shook her head. 'I don't know, but this

shouldn't be here. The metal' – she ran her hand along the edge – 'is rusted, but it wasn't further up. This section of path is older, perhaps decades older.'

'Can we follow it down?'

The assassin peered below. 'I can't see any sign of Deep. If the city exists there, it's unlit, or it could be leagues still further down. We might keep walking for days.'

An entire city, kept in eternal dark. Dill's heart cramped at the thought. *All the darkness in the world gathers there, is trapped there.* He shuffled closer to the lantern. *And the oil will run out soon.* Suddenly he felt like he was drowning, slipping deeper into a lightless ocean. The desire to just break for the surface overwhelmed him. He stood up, shaking, gulping air.

'Dill?' Rachel was by his side. 'Look at me!' She grabbed him, pulled him round to face her. 'I won't let anything bad happen to you.'

Dill couldn't breathe.

'Look at me! I won't leave you. You're safe.' She lifted the lantern between them. Her eyes were bright, full of concern. 'There's plenty of oil left, plenty of light.'

Gradually the pressure in Dill's chest eased, his shaking subsided. 'I'm sorry,' he said. 'I feel so ashamed.' He tried to turn away, break her grip, but she held him tightly.

'Don't be,' she said. 'Everyone is afraid of something. Look at Carnival – why do you think she avoids the daylight?'

'I'm a temple archon,' his voice broke, 'but I can't do anything right. I can't use a sword, I can hardly fly.' He closed his eyes trying desperately to conceal his shame. 'I can't even manage the soulcage horses. And this darkness . . . it terrifies me! I'm a coward. I'm nothing.'

What would my father think of me? And you, Rachel, what would you think if you knew how I hesitated? There was no escape from his shame. He met her gaze, and misery swamped him.

'You *are* facing the dark, Dill. Look how far you've come already. Gods below, you're braver than me.'

'But you can fight.'

'You think that's brave?' A pained smile. 'There's nothing honourable in Church-sanctified murder. A Heshette heathen is still a human being. A traitor is still a human being.' The hurt in her eyes shocked him. 'Before the Spine gave me to the rooftops, I hunted Heshette spies and informers, sometimes mercenaries and pilgrims who'd fled the city. In Hollowhill and Sandport and the Shale Forest. I don't know how many – it frightens me to remember. But I murdered them because I was afraid not to. Once you're part of the Spine, you obey or become a threat yourself.'

For a long moment they stood in silence, leagues of empty darkness above them, immeasurable unknown depths below, and it seemed to Dill that they were the only two people left in the world. Angel and assassin, alone here but for their warped, wraithlike reflections deep in the black stone.

Is this how the abyss sees us? Grotesque parodies of the people we once hoped we'd become? His own reflection mocked him with its cruel honesty. In the mirrored stone he saw an angel he barely recognized: older than his sixteen years, yet malformed, stretched thin by longing only to be corrupted by the hard edges of reality, debased by fear.

He tore his gaze away.

Is this all I am? Please, Ulcis, give me the strength to

change. Give me courage, for Rachel's sake. More than me, she needs someone to protect her.

He remembered Carnival. How much had she been shaped by brutal truths? Yet Carnival had no illusions about who she was or who she might become. Suddenly Dill understood her. Her scars were self-inflicted. *She hates herself, damages herself to keep some deeper part intact.* Dill's heart clenched at the realization. Carnival's soul wasn't scarred and ugly: it was pure. And she guarded it fiercely.

Her scars were armour.

Carnival and Rachel . . . bitter enemies. And yet so similar.

He searched for her in the depths. *Where is she? When Scar Night comes, who will kill who?*

Rachel seemed to read his thoughts. She released him, her eyes veiled. 'Perhaps Carnival decided she didn't need us after all.' She didn't sound like she believed that.

Water dripped steadily, beating a tiny rhythm on the metal: a narrow trail from Deep to Deepgate. *For whom was it constructed? Will this path be walked by the dead?* Dill sniffed: the air held an odour that he found familiar but couldn't place. For some reason it reminded him of dreams he'd experienced – dreams of battle. 'Can you smell something?' he asked.

'Like what?'

'I don't know. It just smells odd.'

'It's warmer down here. The air is stale.'

Maybe that was it. He took a deep breath, then frowned. *No.* There was something else, something that made him think of war. In his dreams he was always flying, brandishing a sword or pike or spear, his armour gleaming, a painted shield strapped to one arm. The more he thought about it, the more the smell reminded him of—

Weapons?

Did forged metal have an identifiable smell? Dill shook his head. What else could it be? Something he associated with weapons, armour and war . . .

A movement down in the darkness caught his attention, a whisper of air. Carnival emerged from the void. She wore a savage grin and her black eyes were shining.

'I've seen the bottom,' she said. 'This you have to see.'

25

THE TOOTH

Inside the Tooth, Bataba led the way, his long white staff poised horizontal at his side. Devon followed, with two Heshette at either shoulder. Both had removed their scarves to reveal the grim expressions on their broad, darkly weathered faces. Presbyter Sypes's walking stick tapped along behind them. The rest of the tribesmen had stayed to loot the airship and beat Angus. Devon didn't care: the temple guard was of little use to him now.

The corridor they were passing through had the appearance of being carved from bone or ivory. Tusklike pillars buttressed the hull, where sunlight lanced in from air vents to strike the opposite wall in hot, white slats. Sand crunched on the hard tiles underfoot. A writhing mass of pipes extended overhead, smooth and pale as sand-adders. Everywhere Devon looked, he saw the same faint whorls of etching that covered the hull exterior.

But the Heshette had turned the vast machine into a city. Smoke lingered, thick with the stench of sweat, dung fires and spice. Dark-skinned women peered from behind curtains of hide draped over internal doorways. Devon caught glimpses of clay urns, woven rugs, horse tackle and vulture claws. Squalls of ragged children pushed past, shrieking and running ahead, banging bones against the walls.

At the end of the corridor, Bataba lit a taper and they clattered down stairs into a vast, cool gloom. A forest of bone-white piston shafts reached into the dim heights around a line of engines like monstrous vertebrae. Banks of dials glittered on the far wall, under enormous glass vats full of dark red liquid.

Not blood? But that ripe smell . . . iron?

Devon tried to get a closer look, but the Heshette urged him onwards. Beyond the engine room they were ushered into another long, narrow corridor. More tusklike pillars tapered in to a pinched ceiling. Doors on either side held ceramic identification plates. *Reclamation, Seeding, Separation, Base Ignition, Second ignition, Crew One, Crew Two, Discipline.* Hieroglyphs had been stamped beneath each word, strange curled symbols like knots of snakes.

The passage snaked on through the heart of the Tooth, passed swollen bulkheads and gaping holes which blew moist air at them. *This whole machine has been fashioned to resemble something organic. The purpose? To inflict awe in those who would see it – to disguise the mechanics.* Smoke from Bataba's taper curled across the ceiling and left a patina of soot on the already smudged walls. Eventually they reached the end and climbed a narrow, oddly canting staircase to where a hatch opened into a bright space above.

The bridge looked like the inside of a seashell. Smooth walls, ribbed with bony protrusions, swept seamlessly up from the floor to coalesce at a low, rippled ceiling. Desert sky bleached a line of windows opposite. The glass had an odd gelatinous quality that tinted the light in pink and yellow whorls. Beneath the windows was an intricate skeletal contraption like a sculpture made from the bones of a thousand tiny creatures. Glass veins glittered inside, full of red fluid.

The fluid was moving, pumping.

Devon peered closer.

Something inside. Contracting. Expanding. Steady. The inhalation and expulsion of air. A draught – from moist-lipped, calciferous vents.

The machine appeared to be breathing.

The Tooth is alive? A mechanical heart, lungs, blood? Brain? No, no, this design is deliberate. The technology replicates, approximates life. These walls – not bone. Ceramic? The veins – no, not veins: pipes – full of oil, not blood. Hydraulics. The draught? A cooling system. Still operational after three thousand years? Why not? A human body can be altered to survive indefinitely. Why not a machine? Given enough fuel . . .

The Heshette shaman addressed one of his men. 'Fetch the council.'

The man nodded and turned to go.

'Except Drosi,' Bataba added. 'Leave him be. The journey from his room would only tire him.'

Presbyter Sypes jabbed his stick at the sighing contraption. 'This device,' he said. 'Why does it appear to breathe?'

'The bone mountain sleeps,' the shaman growled. 'Ask no more questions, priest.'

'In other words,' Devon said, 'he doesn't know.'

'Silence,' Bataba snarled. 'Or I'll have both your tongues out and spitted.'

'This zeal to cut things off,' Devon said. 'A tribal custom? Or a personal perversion?'

Bataba glowered at him.

One by one, the Heshette councillors arrived. Seven men in total assembled: four greybeards and three younger men who carried themselves with the arrogance of warriors. They were dark-skinned, wearing gabardines; scarves around their necks. All of them were disfigured in some way. Chemical burns and ineffectual tribal healing had turned faces into fleshy swamps. The eldest blinked rheumy eyes. One of the warriors, with a forked beard and lean scar-whitened arms, gave Devon a dangerous look, then shifted his hand to the hilt of the curved knife roped to his waist.

'Later,' Bataba said.

The warrior grinned.

Devon shifted his gaze from one savage to the next and decided it would have been better if his poisons had managed to sterilize the Deadsands completely.

Finally the man who'd left to summon the council returned. He supported an ancient cripple who brandished a wooden crutch.

The cripple was using his crutch to hit his helper's arm. 'Leave me be, goat. I can manage.' He squinted through weeping, wood-smoke eyes. 'Where's Bataba? Ayen's boiled balls, what does that one-eyed *shoka* want now?'

The shaman straightened. 'I've summoned the council, Drosi.'

'Half-breed! I'm sick of your meetings. Drag me down here like a snake-tickler's beggar whore sent looking for *kathalla* and pipe-water? In this heat, too!'

Bataba spoke to the man supporting Drosi. 'Adi, there was no need for you to trouble the councillor.'

Adi gave him a helpless glance.

'Leave me out, would you?' Drosi said. 'You loose-fluted bastard! Might be old but I'm not stupid. Think you can have your meetings without me now? Think I don't know what's going on? I was running this council when you were still sucking your mother's teat.'

Most of the other councillors shifted uncomfortably. Devon did his best to hide a smile.

'Drosi,' Bataba growled, 'we have prisoners.'

The old man waved his crutch at the shaman. 'Don't use that tone of voice with me, you puckered sack of *harsha* balls. I remember when—'

'Dark worshippers. Enemies of Ayen.'

'I don't give a shrivel what—'

'Councillor!' Bataba rapped his staff on the floor. 'This man is the Poisoner of Deepgate. The other is Sypes, head of the black temple, breeder of carrion angels, feeder of the outcast god.'

Drosi stopped waving his crutch. He chewed his lip. 'Never heard of them.'

Bataba's voice lowered. 'We've been fighting the war against them all these years.'

'War? What war?'

'The war with the chained folk, the outcast's children.'

'When was this?'

'You fought in it yourself.' The shaman paused. 'For a decade.'

Drosi screwed up his eyes and bobbed his head. 'We won that. We won that war, I remember. Now you make fun of an old man.' He spat at the shaman's feet.

Bataba spoke carefully. 'The war that took both your sons, twelve years past.'

Drosi leaned heavily on his crutch. He muttered something under his breath then turned to Adi at his side. 'Bran, fetch your brother, lad. I've had enough of this nonsense.'

Adi fidgeted. 'Councillor, I'm not your son.'

'Don't be ridiculous.'

'Councillor, I am Hoden's son, Adi. Cousin to your third wife, Deniz.'

Drosi shook his head and scrunched up his eyes again, his lips forming unspoken words. He peered at Adi then scowled at the councillors around the room.

The forked-bearded warrior spoke. 'Go home, old man, back to your *hamaruk*. We have work to do.' His accent was softer than the shaman's, closer to that of the river town traders.

Devon looked more closely at the man's knife. The blade was slightly curved, the steel etched with designs imitating those on the Tooth's hull. A score of lines marred the grip. *A bandit habit, this marking of the grip: each line likely represents an opened throat.*

'Curb your arrogance, Mochet,' said one of the elder councillors. 'The shaman did not give you leave to speak.'

The warrior called Mochet frowned.

'Shit stickers,' Drosi said. 'Not one grain of wit between the lot of you.' He smacked Adi again with his crutch. 'Come on, Bran, we're not staying here.'

With Drosi muttering all the way, Adi helped the old man from the room.

When they were gone, the shaman cleared his throat and addressed the council. 'Now, each of you . . .'

A scratch at the door.

'Come,' Bataba said.

The door opened and a face appeared, a young man, his skin aflame with suppurating sores. 'Shaman,' he wheezed, his voice ragged and moist.

Damage to the lungs in this one, I know the poison. And the sores? Gull-pox. He'll be dead in a month.

The pox-faced youth went on, 'The outcast guard in the skyship has lost his mind.'

'Explain.'

'He won't stop screaming, raving like a madman. He froths at the mouth and tears his own flesh.'

'You were too harsh with your sport?'

'No, shaman, he welcomes our blows and howls for more. We have restrained him.'

Bataba looked inquiringly at Devon.

'He'll die soon enough,' the Poisoner said.

Sypes's brow furrowed. 'You can't just abandon him.'

'He's of no more use to me.'

'That's—'

Bataba interrupted. 'What's wrong with him?'

'He poisoned the man.' Sypes jabbed his stick.

'Have the healers look at him,' Bataba said to the youth at the door.

'Easier just to finish him off,' Devon said.

The shaman's eyes narrowed. 'My men enjoy their sport, as you yourself will find out.'

Sypes fumed above his stick. 'For God's sake,' he said to Devon, 'at least give him something to ease his pain.'

'A knife would do the job just as well.'

Mochet spat. 'The Poisoner treats his own as he treats the Kin. You've called us here to decide the method of his death, Bataba?' His forked beard glistened with oil. 'The men are saying he took a dozen arrows in his flesh, plucked them out and laughed at us.'

Devon met the young warrior's eyes, then gave him a small nod.

'Cut him,' said an elder councillor, a man with onyx skin and misty eyes. 'These folk believe hell comes for spilled blood, so let him watch the sand drink his own.'

'A thousand cuts,' said another stocky young warrior. 'And let's make them fight each other.'

'Look at the priest,' Mochet snorted. 'Poor sport, I think. Unless we took the Poisoner's other hand off. Or an arm. Or remove his eyes?'

Bataba said, 'He'll die soon enough, Mochet, but that's not the reason I've summoned this council. We must decide if we can use him first.'

'I'd use his ribs for a spear rack,' Mochet growled, 'his eyes in lizard traps, and a foot for my hunting hounds to chew on. Those are the best uses for him, shaman.'

Devon was beginning to believe the Heshette must hoard entire rooms of the severed limbs of their enemies. He smiled patiently and thought of his own eventual uses for warrior body parts.

'He wants to offer us a deal,' Bataba said.

A moment of silence.

'I've a deal for him.' Mochet brandished a fist. 'And if he doesn't like that, I've a better one here.' He drew his knife.

'Put the knife away,' Bataba said. 'We'll listen to what he has to say.'

Mochet lowered the knife but didn't sheathe it. 'You expect us to bargain with this worm?'

There were muttered protests all round.

'Have you forgotten what he's done to us?' Mochet's beard was dripping oil like sweat. 'Have you so soon forgotten the poisons and the burnings? Did you not see the ways our warriors died? The sicknesses? What is it you think you'll gain from him? A new eye, perhaps? I say we run him through. Here. *Now.*' He took a step toward Devon, muscles bunching behind the outstretched knife.

'Stop,' Bataba commanded.

Mochet halted.

'I have not forgotten the past,' Bataba continued. 'But I will not neglect the future. The Poisoner has fled Deepgate. Skyships hunt him. He has sought us out as allies.'

'His skyship crashed,' Mochet said. 'We all saw it.'

Devon regarded him coldly. 'The airship landed,' he said, 'as smoothly as my incompetent companion could land it.'

Mochet scowled his disbelief.

Bataba gazed at each of the council members in turn. 'He claims he can give us the city,' he hissed.

'A lie,' Mochet said.

The shaman folded his arms across the multiple fetishes in his beard. 'Let us hear him and then decide. If his reasons for aiding us are weak, Mochet, you'll enjoy your sport today.'

All at once Devon had the attention of all the councillors.

He removed the spectacles from his waistcoat pocket and cleaned them while he considered his words. The angelwine had restored his eyesight, but it was an old habit. In a way he missed having to wear them. More than his death was now at stake here. If he failed to convince these men, he would endure an eternity among their imaginations. He replaced the spectacles in his pocket and took a deep breath.

'I do not give a damn about any of you,' he said. 'I do not give a damn about your beliefs, your culture, or your little war.'

A circle of Heshette brows lowered.

'To me, you are ignorant savages – little better than

animals. As far as I'm concerned, you can all live in this bone mountain for ever, or drop dead from gull-pox. I don't care.'

Mochet's jaw had clenched. The tattoos on Bataba's face twisted into new shapes. Sypes was watching the men's expressions carefully. As was the Poisoner.

Apparently they believed him.

'The only people I hate more than savages like you are those walking corpses in Deepgate and their puppeteers in the temple.' He fixed his gaze on Sypes. 'The Heshette worship Ayen, the goddess of Light and Life, and so have at least some limited understanding of what it is to be alive. In Deepgate, life is forfeited at birth; an entire culture waiting to die, eager to be consumed by the darkness beneath their feet.' He snorted. 'Or that's the theory. In truth, those maggots cling to their existence with savage tenacity, devouring anything, anyone, in a desperate frenzy for one more miserable day of waiting for the end.' He forced his words through clenched teeth. 'Their hypocrisy is staggering. My wife died to feed their insatiable hunger for life. The Poison Kitchens claimed her, as they almost claimed me. Two of us, people who wanted more than this non-life they promote, who were not content to become food for their god, destined to be used up and discarded by those mindless masses who yearn for the pit.'

Devon felt like striking the old priest then. He felt the elixir thumping inside him; it whispered to him, darkened the edges of his vision. The councillors seemed to fade until only Sypes existed: a haggard old priest hunched over his walking stick, more dead than alive.

'I will cut your rotting city down for no other reason than to give your people what they want. Will they flee, priest? When the abyss reaches out to them, will they turn away?'

Presbyter Sypes met his stare. 'There are innocents in Deepgate, children—'

'Let their parents evacuate them,' Devon snarled. 'If they do not, then the crime is theirs . . . yours. The Church fostered their absurd faith – not me.'

He saw from the Presbyter's pained expression that the old man understood that. But Sypes hadn't lost his faith; he still believed in Ulcis. Devon knew then, with utter certainty, that his suspicions had been correct. The priest *was* afraid of his god. Suddenly he realized why Sypes had endeavoured to have the angelwine made for Carnival. It was such a ridiculous idea, he had never before considered it. The priest had actually hoped to convince Carnival to stand against his own god. Whatever waited in the abyss had clearly become a threat.

'Tens of thousands will die,' Sypes said.

'They'll die happily,' Devon hissed. 'I'm giving them what they desire, what they deserve.'

But what will rise from the abyss? Devon could not wait to find out.

The shaman interjected, 'How do you propose to accomplish this, Poisoner?'

Anger bruised Devon's vision, pulsing and fading, and for a long moment he stared in confusion at the tall tribesman, trying to remember who he was. He finally shook his head clear. 'I'll awaken this machine,' he said, 'this bone mountain as you call it, and bring it to the abyss to cut the city's chains.'

One of the councillors muttered, 'The outcast god would be crushed, its keepers destroyed. Shaman, what retribution from Ulcis?'

Bataba's brow furrowed in thought. 'Ayen will protect us.' He nodded. 'She will sanction this.'

'The Poisoner is a liar,' Mochet hissed. 'This is a trick.'

'He has betrayed his own people,' Sypes said. 'He'll betray you too.'

'They were never my people, Sypes.' Devon's voice sounded strange even to his own ears, as though he had spoken in a chorus of whispers. 'They were never people to begin with. They've always been *dead.*'

Bataba rapped his staff on the floor. 'Council, you have heard him. What is your decision? Do we delay our sport, ally with this man? Or do we finish this now? Deepgate's skyships burn closer.'

'Kill him,' Mochet demanded.

But the other six were uncertain. They muttered among themselves. Eventually, an elder councillor approached the shaman. 'We will delay our sport. For now.'

Devon breathed deeply. 'Good,' he said. 'But before we begin, there is something important I must do for you.'

'What's that?' Bataba asked.

'Save your lives.'

Through the viewing windows on the bridge of the *Adraki*, the armada stretched ahead over the Deadsands towards Blackthrone, like a long curving bank of steel clouds. Sunlight flashed across the great silver balloons and sparkled on the brass of the gondolas beneath them. Fogwill might have found the sight impressive, even inspiring, had he been able to look up from the bucket between his knees. The bridge lurched, a tremor ran through the carpet under his feet, and he retched again.

A whistle sounded and Commander Hael put his ear to

a trumpet fitted to the portside wall. After a moment, he responded into another trumpet. 'Aye, flag that news back to the *Kora* and the *Bokemni*.' He turned to the captain. 'Fourteen degrees starboard. Stretch the formation to day-range limits. I want Clay notified of any developments.'

'Aye, sir,' the captain nodded to an aeronaut seated on his left, who relayed the message via a third trumpet to the signalman on the aft deck.

The aeronaut commander turned to face Fogwill. 'They've spotted movement around the Poisoner's ship. The heathens are evidently busy.'

'Cannibalism . . . or repairs?' Fogwill asked between spasms.

'Hard to tell,' Hael said. 'The advance fleet is still circling high, beyond arrow range.' As they had been for most of the day.

The rest of the armada was strung out between Black-throne and Deepgate, forming a continuous line through which information could be flagged back and forwards between the warships hovering over the stricken *Birkita* and those over Deepgate, where Captain Clay was busy organizing the regulars for a march across the desert.

News of the *Birkita*'s sudden plummet to earth had reached the city just after dawn, whereupon Mark Hael had ordered the formation to hold as was while his own ship, the *Adraki*, was rigged for flight. The *Birkita*'s prox-imity to the Tooth of God could mean only one thing. She'd been holed. Devon wasn't going anywhere in a hurry. Now that the winds had changed in their favour, Hael would be able to reach the crash-site in just six to eight hours. He had elected to command the attack personally.

But Hael was not known for restraint when it came to

unleashing ordnance, and Fogwill, desperate to see Sypes returned unharmed, had insisted he accompany the commander. With Carnival now off hunting angelwine, and Dill vanished, perhaps even dead, Fogwill's brief moment of command had put the city in greater peril than ever. The Adjunct needed his old master back in charge of things. Clay had tried to talk him out of the excursion, of course – the temple guard captain did not trust airships. But Fogwill had been adamant. After all, he'd assured himself, they'd be safely above arrow range. What was the worst that could happen?

The contents of the bucket sloshed between Fogwill's trembling knees. His stomach bucked again as the warship shuddered, thrumming a discordant rhythm in every one of the priest's nerves.

'A fine breeze, Adjunct.' Mark Hael was grinning. 'Perhaps Ulcis himself has sent it to aid us.'

Fogwill groaned. The same wind had been blowing fiercely since they'd left Deepgate three hours ago. Devon's own ship had been forced to crawl through the night against a northerly gale, but the wind had swung to the south with the arrival of dawn and the *Adraki* had been able to thunder along the armada's stationary flagline at triple Devon's speed. They were closing fast.

Provided the *Adraki* didn't tear herself to pieces in the process.

Mark Hael didn't seem to care. He'd ordered the engines to be cranked up full and appeared to relish the screaming wind, the pitching and thumping of the bridge, the groan of over-stressed cables.

And he'd claimed Devon wasn't going anywhere in a hurry.

Fogwill just wanted to get off. He wiped his mouth

with the back of his hand. The talc had all smudged off by now, revealing his unhealthy pallor to all.

'You don't look well,' Hael commented, his grin even wider. He appeared to thoroughly enjoy Fogwill's discomfort.

'Why do these things sway about so?'

'Air currents. We're pushing the *Adraki* hard. You'd feel better if you kept your eyes fixed on the horizon.'

But the Adjunct kept his gaze pinned to the bucket. 'Standing makes me feel dizzier. How much longer must I endure this?'

The commander drummed his fingers on the control panel. 'Another five hours. The advance fleet vessels are massing. We'll circle and look for signs of Devon and Sypes once we arrive. With any luck the Shetties will have done away with the Poisoner for us.'

'Sypes must be protected,' Fogwill said. He then put his head in his hands and began to retch again. The stench from the bucket brought tears to his eyes.

'If those savages have him, it's already too late,' Hael continued, unconcerned. 'I know them. They won't keep him for ransom.'

Fogwill looked up. His throat felt raw, saliva dribbled over his chin. 'We need to . . . get the Presbyter back,' he managed.

Hael grunted. 'There's nothing I can guarantee. I don't have enough men for mud-work, so a landing would be pointless.'

'What *do* you suggest we do, then?'

'What we normally do.' Hael stared out across the desert, the buttons on his uniform glinting in the sun. 'We'll gas them. This many ships against one Shettie stronghold should clear out most of them. Then Clay's regulars can march out and mop up.'

'But Devon may survive.'

'Where's he going to go?'

After some discussion, Dill and Rachel had decided to abandon the spiral path – a route too slow and treacherous for them to keep pace with Carnival. Clasping her in his arms, Dill flew carefully, cautious of reaching the bottom of the abyss too abruptly. They kept the lantern burning low as they descended, and strained to see through the humid darkness, searching for some sign of Deep itself or the ghosts down below.

But whatever awaited them still remained hidden.

Carnival wouldn't as much as hint at what she'd seen during her earlier reconnaissance. She circled them impatiently but kept her distance to stay out of the lantern light. Whenever Dill caught a glimpse of her, he saw nothing in her eyes but a glint of savage humour, as if she were savouring some cruel joke.

He knew better than to press her for answers. Not that he was overly keen to hear what she might say. Her malicious eagerness for them to reach the bottom unnerved him.

In the silence Dill heard his blood drumming in his ears. Rachel's arms were heavy about his neck, her breath hot against his cheek. The antique steel of his mail shirt began to feel like pig-iron, becoming heavier until it felt like carrying the weight of a city on his back. And every-where now, that smell.

Of war.

Of weapons.

Feebly, he shook his head. He couldn't place it, and yet some part of him knew what it was – the pungent odour howled to be recognized.

War. Weapons. *Something . . .?*

Rachel interrupted his thoughts. 'Listen,' she said, 'can you hear it?'

Dill listened hard.

A tapping sound, metallic, very faint.

'What is it?' he said.

'I don't know,' she murmured.

Deeper into the abyss, and gradually, the strange clamour grew louder. It reminded him of the Poison Kitchens – the familiar distant sounds of industry, factories and forges. The odour intensified too but its cause still eluded him.

There. Just for a moment he thought he spotted a grey shape in the void beneath them. He pulled up sharply.

I know this. A shiver of fear brushed up his spine.

Rachel sniffed, frowned. 'That odour – what the hell is it?'

Dill peered down. 'I thought I saw—' He broke off. 'Maybe it was nothing.'

But as they continued to drop, the blackness below began to lighten. Further vague outlines appeared, dissipated. Down to one side he spied a dim smudge like a pall of almost invisible smoke. He tried hard to focus but could not define its shape. Was it just an outcrop of rock? Had he seen anything at all?

'Dill, look up there,' Rachel hissed. 'A storm is blowing over the Deadsands.'

He lifted his head and his breath caught. From down here, Deepgate appeared to be no larger than his fist, but the distant city seethed. Glittering clouds of dust and rust fell from the agitated chains and neighbourhoods so far above, while spikes of sunlight punched through in countless places. An angry corona surrounded the outline of the city itself – and in the very centre, a bright ring flared around a black speck. *The Church of Ulcis.*

'It's brighter now,' Rachel murmured. 'The sun is high. It must be close to noon.'

'It looks so far away,' Dill said.

Deepgate seemed as distant as the sun, and as unreachable.

Gazing up, he didn't notice the ground approaching until they were almost upon it. When he glanced down, he saw what looked like a steep, chalky slope rushing towards them. Beyond the lantern light, the slope sank away into the distant gloom.

'Dill!'

'I see it!' He thrashed his wings to slow their descent. Sudden wind whipped at Rachel's hair.

'My God, Dill, look!'

Dill couldn't understand what he was seeing. Where was the city of Deep? The buildings, streets, gardens? Where were the soul-lights? The army of ghosts? Where was Ulcis?

What *was* this?

He landed hard. The ground surface gave way beneath him, cracking, snapping. He lost his footing and tumbled wings over heels, pitching Rachel into the dark. Hundreds of hard edges jabbed him, punched the wind from his aching chest. The sword hilt pummelled his ribs. The lantern threw dizzy circles of light. Desperately, he thrust out his arms to slow his fall, but his hands sunk into something crumbly and he slid forward again. Thick, sour dust choked his lungs.

Weapons? War?

Dill came to a halt, face down, in a cloud of dust. He groaned and lifted his head.

Bones.

He was lying on a mountain of bones. Femurs, fingers, clavicles, ribs, spines, as far as he could see – an impossible slope of dry and shattered skeletons. Fleshless hands reached up from gullies and mounds of brittle remains. Screes of skulls and teeth shifted, trickled and rattled further down into the dark.

Dill had sunk to the elbows in broken bones. He coughed, blinked.

That smell.

Not of weapons or war, but of the Sanctum corridor, the Ninety-Nine: the long-dead archons that inspired his dreams of battle.

He rose unsteadily, smacked bone-dust from his clothes.

But these were not the bones of angels, but of people. Thousands of people. Millions. Discarded in this pit, heaped like the feast-pile of an eternal banquet.

Rachel scrambled down to join him, sending a further landslide of bone fragments down the slope.

Dill couldn't speak. He stood gawping at the crumbling mountain, gasping in the chalky air, still searching in vain for some sign of Deep. But there was nothing here. Only bones. Three thousand years of bones.

And, from the darkness all around, the continual sound of hammers striking metal. Of industry.

Or forges?

'Dill?' Rachel shook him gently. 'Are you all right?'

'I don't understand.' He looked at her. 'Where are the soul-lights? The ghosts?'

As she shifted her weight, something snapped under her foot. 'These are old bones,' she said. 'Ancient. Further up, the remains are fresher. But there's no flesh, no shrouds.' She picked up a smaller bone that might have been a finger and examined it. 'There are marks on it, scratches. The flesh has been scraped away, picked clean.' She glanced up. 'The sun's moved on. It will grow darker again soon. We should get off this . . .' She let the sentence die. 'We should get to the bottom.'

A sharp rapping sounded from further up the slope. Carnival was sitting there on a pile of skulls, her raven wings outstretched. In each scarred hand she clutched a long bone, using them like drumsticks to beat on a skull between her knees. 'Not the best idea,' she drawled, her eyes brimming with malicious glee. 'That's where they're coming from.'

Dill spun round. At first he saw nothing but darkness, then gradually he became aware of the lights.

The dead were coming.

26

ATTACKED

Rags, he'd instructed, and rags they fetched. There was no shortage of rags in this godforsaken hole. They tore strips from blankets and strips from gabardines, soaked them in mud and set to work stuffing them into every vent in the Tooth's enormous hull. This would minimize the effect of the gas the armada was sure to use on them. Scarves were also collected and set aside, ready to dip in urine and then cover their faces. The Heshette women were already gathering buckets of the stuff. The urine, Devon had explained, would help counter the poisons they might breathe.

It wouldn't, of course, but the opportunity to have these savages breathe their own piss was too good to miss.

Bataba oversaw the operation with stern diligence, while a dozen sour-faced Heshette escorted Devon outside. All carried spades. Devon clutched a lamp, a hammer, a nail and a stub of a candle in his one hand.

'Only twelve of you,' he said as they stepped through the door and into the blinding force of the desert sun.

'Wouldn't want you to leave before the fun starts,' Mochet snarled. He wrapped his scarf around his head.

Devon huffed. 'As if it were possible to man the engines

and simultaneously navigate! An airship cannot be flown single-handed.' He cringed at his own feeble joke. 'And I feel hurt that you would expect me to flee such fine company.'

'I expect you to shut up.'

Devon squinted through his own scarf, one he imagined was full of lice. The stained gabardine Bataba had given him smelled of smoke and dung.

Deepgate's advance armada had arrived at a position to the south of them, almost five hours ago. Since then they had been massing, stretching their communication line, bringing more ships forward for a concentrated assault. Seventeen warships now, with more on the way. When it became apparent they were in no hurry to attack, Devon had decided to use the extra time to his advantage.

Sightglasses flashed on the warship decks, but from that distance the aeronaut spotters would be unlikely to make out much detail. Devon kept his stump hidden in the sleeve of his gabardine nevertheless.

They think we've merely crashed. Once their advance force is ready, they'll dump lime-gas and incendiaries all around the Tooth, smoke out as many of these savages as possible for their crossbows to pick off. The Poisoner nodded to himself, satisfied. *They think they have all the time in the world. Which means they think Sypes is already dead.*

Flanked by Heshette, Devon slipped and skidded his way down the sand drift before passing into the shade underneath the Tooth's hull. Vast, earth-clotted tracks loomed over him, large enough to allow the group to clamber between their cogged wheels and reach the remains of the animal pens and the stricken warship on the far side. Goats had been crowded into a makeshift corral to one side where they bleated and pushed each other. Bells tinkled.

The *Birkita*'s gondola had been totally stripped. Looters had ripped teak planks from the aft deck and stacked them in piles. Rope and cable lay in coils beside heaps of pots and pans and kitchen utensils. Furniture was strewn everywhere. Plush chairs, richly veneered cabinets, tables and bookcases listed in the sand. Four Heshette warriors had found the captain's drinks cabinet and now squatted in the sand, wasting fine wines down their bearded throats.

Inside, Devon almost lost his balance when he reached out with his stump to grab the door frame. Cursing, he made his way along the corridor towards the engine room. Sand mounded the decks and – ridiculous as the notion was – he wished that Fogwill could have been present to comment on the mess. It would have been the last complaint that giddy plum ever made.

They found the tanks of liftgas stored in a cage in the engine room. Pipes from two of them led up to valves accessing the envelope above. Twin axles protruded from the rear of the engine, through gearboxes, to the propellers on the aft deck. Oil glistened like sweat, hydraulic tubing veined the walls. A network of further pipes spread from vents in the engine and disappeared into channels on either side of the room, to feed the airship's ribs with hot-air. Devon set down his equipment and breathed a sigh of relief; everything appeared to be intact.

'Find some tubing,' he said to Mochet. 'As much of it as you can. You can strip these, and these. Drain the fluid and run lines from these other tanks into the hot-air pipes. Here, here and here, as many as you can. Just cut the metal and wrap the joins tightly. It doesn't have to be perfect.' He surveyed the room. 'We'll need strips of cloth, lots of them. And as much ballast as you can shovel aboard. Sand and rock will do; anything heavy.' He looked Mochet up and down. 'How much would you say you weigh?'

Discoloured teeth split Mochet's beard. He threw his spade at Devon's feet. 'Dig, Poisoner.'

So Devon shovelled sand into the port corridor along with eight of the Heshette, while Mochet and the others laboured inside. One-handed, the work was awkward for Devon. Most of the sand ended up in the faces of his comrades. Occasionally he waved his stump at them in apology. He was a cripple, couldn't they see? The sun blazed directly overhead, falling between the Tooth and the quarry wall, ruthlessly devouring any shade and cooking the sand under his ill-fitting moccasins. Through the gauze of his scarf he peered into the white-hot sky, expecting the armada to appear above the upper edges of the Tooth any minute. But there had so far been no calls from the Heshette lookouts.

Grudgingly, Devon went back to work. When he'd put aboard as much ballast as he could stomach, he hopped back into the gondola to check on the progress inside. Two of the Heshette diggers exchanged a glance, then threw down their spades and followed him.

'Don't worry,' Devon said as they muscled up beside him. 'I'm sure Mochet can take care of himself.'

They followed him anyway.

The men inside had almost finished connecting the tubes to the hot-air pipes. Mochet leaned against a support strut and toyed with his knife while he watched the progress with hooded eyes.

'Busy?' Devon asked.

Mochet grunted. 'Push me harder, Poisoner, and my knife will test the limits of your blood's endurance. Your very existence is an insult to Ayen.'

'You speak for your goddess, then? Is your shaman aware of that?'

The warrior bared his teeth, but did not reply.

Devon gathered up the equipment he had assembled from the Tooth and stepped back outside the engine room into the midship companionway, with Mochet hounding him.

'Hold this to the deck while I hammer,' he said, giving the nail to Mochet. 'At an angle – like this.'

Mochet obeyed. 'Miss your aim, Poisoner, and I'll use the hammer on you.'

Devon struck the nail partway into the wood, then pushed the candle on top of it so that it stuck out at a shallow angle from the floor. Then he opened the lamp and eased oil over the wax, just an inch from the wick. Next he took the strips of cloth the Heshette had found, soaked them in lamp oil, and made a long fuse which he fed back into the engine room. He doused the floor and walls around the fuse with the last of the oil.

When he was satisfied, he turned to Mochet's men. 'We need to open the valves now, gently. Let the gas flood the ribs. Open all of the tanks, but not too much. Just a few turns, until you hear the hiss.'

All of the Heshette heard him clearly, but Mochet relayed the instructions regardless. They twisted open the valves on the liftgas tanks and withdrew into the companionway.

'Now,' the Poisoner said, 'light the candle.' He handed Mochet a pouch of flints. 'I'll wait outside.'

The warrior seized his arm. 'No, Poisoner. You'll stay until it's done.'

Five minutes later Devon glanced back at the *Birkita* from the shadow of the Tooth's hull. Her ribs were slowly filling out; he hoped it was fast enough.

Bataba met them inside. A wet scarf covered his face, and he offered another damp rag to Devon.

Devon sniffed it. 'You have enough of these for everyone?'

'We do.'

'And one for Sypes?'

Bataba nodded.

'Excellent.' The Poisoner rubbed hand and stump together. 'You can keep that one. I'll risk the gas.'

Chalk-faced, Fogwill gripped the control panel on the bridge of the *Adraki*, fixed his eyes on the tilting horizon and concentrated on keeping what was left in his stomach still in his stomach. His throat felt raw. How could there be anything left? He had already vomited far more than he remembered having eaten, and even brought up things he wasn't convinced he had eaten. Abruptly, his insides lurched and something rumbled further down.

The airship captain glared at him, a veteran whose eyes held no sympathy for the Adjunct's delicate condition. Fogwill tried to smile back. He wasn't keen to use the ship's commode unless there was no alternative. Mark Hael had taken some delight in informing him how it worked.

Blackthrone baked under a parched sky. Eighteen warships had now gathered above the Tooth, turning slowly to the west as the wind changed. Vents above the bridge windows blew a hot, metallic breeze that failed to dry the sweat from Fogwill's brow. Engines droned on all sides like persistent flies. At the sound of a whistle, Hael put his ear to one of the com-trumpets on the wall.

After a moment he said, 'We're now approaching the *Birkita*. She's been stripped. A group of Heshette were spotted fleeing back inside the Tooth.'

'The Presbyter?' Fogwill ventured.

The commander relayed this question and waited for the reply: 'Too far away to tell.' He turned to the captain. 'Flag the armada to hold steady above the *Birkita* at four hundred feet windward, maintain formation, and keep us within signal distance. I want two-thirds payloads of lime-gas fused and ready to drop at my command, full complements of crossbowmen in position, and incendiaries primed for a cook-up when the bastards split. Keep me informed of changes in wind direction and speed.'

Fogwill swallowed. 'This gas . . . is fatal?'

'Depends how much of it is breathed,' Hael said.

'Then I'm afraid I can't allow you to use it.'

The commander shrugged. 'It's the best way to flush them out. That thing down there looks too solid for incendiaries.'

The Tooth did look impenetrable. Fogwill had heard of the machine, but had not seen it until now. Few people had. It towered over the quarry cliffs behind it, shimmering in the harsh light. Dark holes pocked its dazzling-white hull; sand drifts smothered its base on the nearest side; smoke-scorched funnels crowned its tapering summit. Skeletal arms at the front held massive columns of cutting wheels over a huge, dusty scoop.

Fogwill studied it with awe. This vast machine was in truth a holy relic, abandoned by Callis nearly three thousand years ago after construction of the foundation chains. It had last moved under the direction of Ulcis's Herald himself. He remembered that crippled angel locked in the temple dungeon, and swallowed hard. Three thousand years. How many souls since?

Missionaries who had seen the machine spread fervent rumours that it possessed some vestige of divine awareness. Looking at it now, Fogwill found it hard to give credence to those rumours. The Tooth was impressive, yes. But sentient? Hardly. And yet the machine did seem to evince some latent power, as though it was waiting, watching from those openings in its hull.

My imagination. It is the Heshette who are watching us.

The Adjunct shuddered, but was unable to shake off his unease. Something else was bothering him. The Tooth looked altogether too . . . complete. Too unmarked.

Too ready.

'Why would Devon come here?' He spoke his thoughts aloud unintentionally.

'Water. It's one of the few oases in this region we haven't poisoned.' Hael sneered. 'A holy site.'

'But he would easily have been able to reach the Coyle, taken a skiff downriver. Why would he fly against a headwind, and straight to the heathens?'

'He was avoiding the Coyle garrisons. Sandport, Racha, Clune are inimical ports for a fugitive. No doubt he expected to find the Tooth unoccupied. The Heshette are nomadic, and infrequent visitors to Blackthrone.'

Fogwill shook his head. Devon wasn't stupid. There had to be another reason. He looked down at the Tooth, at the massive blades that had cut sapperbane from the mountain so long ago. Thousands of tons stripped from the mountain, processed, and forged into chains. Abruptly his unease grew to fear. 'Would your gases and incendiaries be able to stop that thing if it was moving?'

The aeronaut commander turned slowly. He appeared to consider this for a moment, then shook his head. 'He wouldn't be able to operate it.'

'This is Devon we're talking about, remember?'

Hael grunted. 'The Poisoner missed his one good chance to flee. He's a fool – or already insane.'

'A fool who evaded a citywide manhunt, kidnapped the Presbyter, and stole an airship from under your nose.'

Evidently the commander did not like to be reminded in front of his men. 'We have him now,' he growled.

Fogwill couldn't tear his gaze from the machine's cutters – sharpened cogs powerful enough to shred sapperbane. And chains? *Darkness take me, I know what you are planning, Devon. Sypes . . . forgive me, you would understand what I must do.* He turned to the warship's captain. 'Start the attack now.'

'Belay that order,' Hael said. 'Do not presume, Adjunct, to issue commands aboard my ship.'

Fogwill hitched himself up straighter on his stool. 'I am your superior in the service of the Church, Commander.'

'Not aboard this vessel.'

'Then,' Fogwill lowered his voice, 'I humbly request that you relay a message for me back to Deepgate. I believe that *is* within my rights aboard this vessel.' He didn't wait for Hael to acknowledge him. 'Tell Clay to wake up the regulars and sober up the reservists. I want every last one of them dragged naked from the whorehouses if need be, and as many more volunteers or conscripts as he can find. They are to be armed and ready for a ground assault against the city. The cavalry divisions are to be re-formed, every ex-military beast that's lugging coal is to be found and requisitioned. Then I want him to scour the Poison Kitchens for whatever those chemists are hoarding, and have the lot brought to the abyss perimeter and scattered in piles, ready for deployment. I want the sappers brought out of retirement – pay those bastards whatever it takes – and I want them undermining the Deadsands towards Blackthrone as though they were digging another abyss. And then I expect the city's carpenters and smiths to drop everything and to undertake new contracts for the temple. We need heavy offensive ordnance, mangonels, scorpions, siege engines, whatever they can come up with. Tell them I want weapons powerful enough to stop a god.'

'Siege engines? Mangonels? Scorpions?' Hael's tone had become mocking. 'Words from old men's tales – how are they to build such things?'

'Our history,' Fogwill said. 'We warred before. A hundred years ago, two hundred. With the river towns, bandit strongholds, on the fringes of the Deadsands.'

'History?' Hael snapped. 'Deepgate has no history. Sypes has it all locked up in his damn books.'

'Then they can use their brains for once. Just look at that thing. We'll need to breach it like a citadel. Instruct Clay to get everyone working right *now*, day and night. I don't care what the cost is. We have a war on our hands.'

Grudgingly, Mark Hael relayed the message through a trumpet to the signalman.

'Now, Commander Hael.' A hollow ache had taken root in Fogwill's chest. The Presbyter would understand, approve, but still . . . *I'm sorry Sypes.* 'When do you suggest we attack?'

The commander got no chance to reply.

'Sir!' the captain said, 'the *Birkita*'s lifting. She's running.'

Fogwill leaned across the control panel to see the warship rise from behind the Tooth.

'She's coming up fast,' Hael said. 'He's flooded the ribs with liftgas. Close on her. Instruct the men to ready grapples, and flag the other ships to burn high, staggered to strike if *we* miss.' He sprinted towards the port companionway door, turned back once and spat, 'So much for your war.'

The *Birkita* had cleared the funnels of the Tooth and was rising close below them. Streams of ballast sand poured from her gondola. She was turning as though out of control.

This is wrong.

Fogwill shot a questioning glance at the captain and navigator, but both men were too busy to speak to him. So he stumbled after Hael, still clutching his rumbling belly.

What was the worst that could happen?

Outside, the wind tore at Fogwill's robes. The *Adraki*'s engines thundered. Hael's aeronauts were cranking tension into the grapple gun springs at each corner of the aft deck, fitting barbed iron shafts into the barrels, adjusting sights and oiling spools of cable. Propellers hacked the air and massive rudders slammed sideways as the *Adraki* turned to intercept the Poisoner's ship. Air rushed into the warship's ribs and abruptly the deck lurched. Fogwill was caught by surprise. He staggered towards the port rail, arms flailing. One of his slippers fell off. The rail rushed closer, a white void beyond.

Hael caught him by the neck of his robe. 'Get inside,' he growled, 'before you kill yourself.'

Fogwill's knees were shaking. 'Let that ship go,' he cried. 'Devon isn't aboard. It's a trap.'

Then his head swam and he retched.

Mark Hael grimaced and stepped away, releasing him. Fogwill slumped to the deck as the commander strode over to the rail. Two granite-faced aeronauts scowled at him from their positions at the grapple guns.

'Ready port grapples,' Hael called out. 'Bow gun, target the aft deck. Put a line across it if you can. Aft, get ready if he misses – go for the envelope. On my mark.'

Fogwill saw the *Birkita* rise above the deck rail, a hundred yards away.

'Fire.'

With a loud crack, the bow grapple shot from the gun and arced across the space between the airships. Cable fizzed from its spool.

The grapple struck the *Birkita*'s aft deck and lodged in the wood.

'Contact!'

'Winch!'

Two aeronauts pumped hard at the winch behind the gun, red-faced, muscles straining. The cable began to lose slack.

Mark Hael was nodding sternly. 'Bow gun ready! Aim low in the envelope. Let's steal a little of her breath. And . . . Fire!'

A second crack sent the bow grapple lancing through the air. It missed its mark and shattered a window in the *Birkita*'s gondola.

'Contact. Low from target.'

'Winch.'

Aeronauts cranked the second winch. Both lines became taut.

Hael plucked a com-trumpet from the gondola's rear wall. 'Bring us parallel. Swing ballast arm portside, spill sand and purge ribs on stress. We're going to pitch. Prepare to tow.' He turned back to his men on the deck. 'Lance those lines and bring her in.'

The starboard winchmen rushed to the port side and unstrapped long poles from the deck rail. The poles were ten yards long and hooked at one end. They snagged both lines and pushed. Cable groaned.

'Slack!' one shouted. The winchmen released pressure. When the poles were horizontal, they bolted the ends to fixtures in the deck.

'Winch!'

The cables strained taut again. The *Birkita* bobbed as they drew her closer. Mark Hael glanced down at Fogwill sitting on the deck and explained, 'To stop the lines cutting our envelope when she rises above us.' He grinned. 'We've got her.'

The *Birkita* exploded.

Fogwill saw the aeronaut commander turn slowly against a sky of flame. Something knocked Fogwill sideways and everything went dark.

Someone was screaming quietly behind the ringing in Fogwill's ears. 'Down! Down! Down!'

Iron pressed into Fogwill's cheek. A rail? Sand beyond. Pressure crushed his shoulder. The Deadsands reeled beneath him.

Distant voices.

'Holed!'

'I don't care, I don't care.'

'The cable!'

'Portside.'

'Where?'

'His leg – stop the bleeding.'

'I don't know.'

'Bow.'

'Where?'

'Leave it!'

'No. It's all gone. All of it.'

Fogwill gripped the rail. Sand and rocks and brass and white sky swung all around him. The deck moaned and shuddered.

'Cut – just bloody cut it!'

He looked at his hand. Blood spattered his powdered skin. How white his skin looked against the blood. This was wrong. He didn't like this dream. Blood smeared his rings too. Their gold and gems were filthy. He would have to wash them when he got up. He turned his head, pain shooting through his neck. Planks of teak sloped at a steep angle, pinning him to the rail. More blood ran over the wood in little trickles towards him, towards the hem of his robe. He tried to move, but his hands stung. His muscles gave up, he was too heavy. The approaching blood was going to soak his robe, ruin it. A propeller screamed nearby. Wind whipped at him.

'Both of them. *Now.*'

Fogwill sought the voice. Mark Hael lay on his back, gripping the port hatch, eyes frantic. Blood there too. It soaked the aeronaut commander's white uniform utterly. No way for an officer to be seen. Whatever would Fogwill's mother have said? And what was wrong with Hael's belly? A metal barb jutted from the wet cloth there. A grapple? That shouldn't be there, Fogwill thought with a kind of detached curiosity. He ought to say something to the commander, tell him about the grapple. He tried to speak, but the howling wind stole his words.

He examined his rings again; the seastones and rubies glinted under the blood. He rubbed at the gold. It would clean: soap and water would do the trick. The captain would have some handy inside. But the hatch was far up the sloping deck. He would have to crawl over all the blood to reach it.

'I can't stop it. The port propeller's gone.'

Fogwill wished the aeronauts would stop yelling. Their shouts and the rip of the wind and the buzzing of the propellers were giving him an awful headache.

Pinned by the grapple, Mark Hael was trying to see inside the hatch. Iron barbs protruded absurdly from his belly. 'Cut the stern,' he rasped. 'Pull the fucking tubes out.'

There weren't any tubes. Just a grapple. Surely the commander could see that? But he wasn't looking at his belly. He was still twisted round, peering inside the airship.

Sand stung Fogwill's eyes and he blinked. He looked back beyond the rail. Dunes were rising towards them fast. Too fast. They ought to slow down.

'Slow down,' Fogwill whispered. Nobody heard him. Mark Hael's attention was elsewhere. They were really going to have to slow down. He had to tell the captain that. He pushed at the rail digging into him but it was useless. He was too tired. His shoulder throbbed. His hands felt badly swollen. He blinked again, trying to clear sand from his eyes. Stinging tears flowed over his cheeks. His slippers. Where were his slippers? He searched around frantically. The desert rushed closer. Sand and rock surged towards him. He couldn't see his slippers anywhere.

The dead crept from the darkness and surged up the mountain of bones. The lights that Dill had first taken to be souls were instead licks of flame curling around tapers clutched in bony fists. These were not ghosts; they were men and women. Some looked as thin as the skeletons beneath their feet; others were tumescent, their flesh shades of grey and blue. All wore rags. All looked hungry.

An army of them.

Dill dimmed his lantern.

'Too late,' Carnival hissed. 'They've seen you.'

More were coming. They flooded out onto the bone mountain behind the others and, as Dill's eyes grew accustomed to the gloom, he realized from where.

The city of Deep had been hacked out of the abyss wall, where torrents of dark sculpture rose to staggering heights, façades of writhing figures and tormented faces. The lower third of the city swarmed with distant lights. Flames moved behind carved muscle and sinew; they crossed arched spinal bridges, down stairs like spirals of black bone, and out onto the slopes composed of human remains. Walls of skulls screamed silently from the rock-face. Tapers winked through eye sockets and tooth-framed doors, as figures slipped behind. Fluted pillars supported great stone spheres, cut into impossible orgies of flesh, wings, teeth and bones, representations of countless angels feasting.

Deep shuddered to the pounding of metal.

Rachel was at Dill's side. 'There,' she pointed. 'The sounds are coming from there.'

Flames glowed deep within the dark city. Silhouettes of figures working. Red-hot metal and flashes of steel.

'Forges,' she said. 'They're making weapons.'

A tide of torchlight poured out from the city and scaled the bone mountain. They moved lithely, disturbing little, shadowed eyes fixed on the three interlopers. Tongues darted between bloodless lips as if tasting the air. White, grey and blue flesh slid beneath grease-stained rags. Knives and swords glinted.

In awful silence, the horde climbed closer.

'What are they?' Dill breathed.

'I think they're dead,' Rachel said. 'Or were.'

'We should leave.'

'Not yet.' She had a distant look about her. 'Remember what we came for.'

Carnival picked up a skull, examined it, then tossed it away with a grunt of indifference. The skull bounced and tumbled down the slope, where it landed a few feet from the nearest of the advancing army. The line of men and women paused, then began to climb again, faces now twisting into snarls.

'Great,' Rachel said. 'You've pissed them off.'

'So?'

'So, there's an army of them, and three of us.'

Carnival shrugged. 'As armies go,' she said, 'it's not so big.'

Ten yards below, one man raised a hand, and the closest of the horde, thirty or so ragged figures, halted behind him. They fixed their tapers among the bones at their feet with slow deliberation, never shifting their gaze from the intruders. All had produced bone-handled blades. Hundreds more climbed the slopes behind, fanned out to flank them in a wash of fire and steel.

Dill caught the scent of burning fat. From the corner of his eye he saw Rachel stiffen.

The man who'd raised his hand focused milky eyes on Dill and spat, 'What you want here?' His voice was a wheezing rasp, as though his throat had been punctured. His teeth had been filed to points.

'Who are you?' Rachel asked.

He gave her a cursory glance, then returned his attention to the angel. 'What you want here?' Behind him, the others were still spreading out, unhurried and silent, blanketing the slope as far as Dill could see.

Dill's knees weakened. He knew his eyes would be as pale as those of the man who'd addressed him. Had any reply come to mind then, it would have been unable to escape his constricted throat.

'None of your damn business,' Carnival said.

Rachel flinched.

The man bared his needle-sharp teeth. His gums were swollen and bleeding, but the blood looked old, black. The knife in his hand came up, and for a heartbeat Dill thought he was going to throw it.

Dill would have taken flight then if his muscles weren't quivering so, but he forced his leaden legs to move and he shifted position to stand between the needle-toothed man and Rachel. She stopped him with a hand and the faintest shake of her head, the muscles at the corners of her eyes tightening.

The knife wasn't thrown.

Carnival wiped her hands on her leather trousers. 'That's not pitch they're burning.'

Needle-tooth's cloudy gaze slid towards her. He barked a command back to his followers in a language Dill didn't understand. The army stirred behind him. A series of calls bounced back through the masses, and faded like echoes.

'Outcast,' Needle-tooth said to Carnival. 'Scarred bitch. He knows you're here. Wants you alive.'

Carnival smiled dangerously.

'Do I need to remind you,' Rachel murmured, 'we are out-numbered?'

'*You* might be,' Carnival said.

Dill tried to ease himself in front of Rachel. Again she stopped him. A bone beneath his foot snapped and he swayed while catching his balance. Further down the slope, there was movement. Items were being passed forward. Nets?

Needle-tooth sneered at Carnival. 'Freak.'

Carnival's scars darkened. Her wings snapped out, lightning-quick. She snatched the fork from her belt—

—and charged into the army.

Dill didn't see the net until it was almost upon her. Carnival, however, was quicker. She veered, with astonishing speed, and dived.

Needle-tooth was catapulted back, black blood geysering from his now truly punctured throat. He crashed into three followers with the force of a battering ram, and all four fell into the ranks behind. Two dozen men toppled. The net meanwhile landed on bones, sixty feet beyond Carnival.

She crouched, hissed.

Rachel was eyeing Needle-tooth's body. 'He isn't getting up,' she whispered to Dill. 'He's just been killed – *again.*'

Carnival pounced. And there was a storm of blood.

Dill had never seen anyone, human or angel, move so

fast. Carnival leapt, spun, wings extended flat above her, legs windmilling. Blood flew in arcs from three more throats before she landed. Crouching again, she paused for half a heartbeat, then, like a crossbow bolt, plunged into the nearest knot of opponents. Knives flashed. Carnival ducked inside one, two, three strikes . . . snaked through a flurry of limbs, her fork flickering . . . and suddenly there was open space around her.

A ring of fresh corpses crumpled onto the bones.

'Shit,' Rachel said, 'she's just warming up.'

Figures kept massing around Carnival, but she was already moving again. She flitted over the powdery slope as though she weighed nothing. She leapt again, punched her fork upwards between ribs, and into the heart of a wild-eyed woman, then withdrew it at once so as to catch a savage down-cut from a man to her left, stopping his knife between the iron prongs. An elbow shattered his face, then the fork licked out and he recoiled screaming.

The horde roared with bloodlust. Scores of frenzied men and women pressed closer, clawed towards her over the corpses of their fallen, snarling, hungry. Carnival wove among them, a dark whisper, and killed with a speed that continued to leave Dill stunned. Steel clashed with iron, again, again, again. Flesh ripped, blood sprayed, and howls filled the abyss.

And still they came, relentlessly, in savage waves. They threw themselves against Carnival's fury, only to be cut down. Carnival did not falter or slow. She whirled and spun like a fever nightmare. Lines of blood trailed behind her fork. Her hair flew wildly about the scars on her face. Blades sparked and clashed. Her dance was measured, precise; a methodical slaughter that Dill found abhorrent to watch. She didn't bother to fly; she didn't have to.

None were her match in speed or strength. Corpses fell on corpses, and soon the mountain of bones was strewn with the dead and the dying.

Now the horde began to hold back, uncertain, while Carnival stood on the summit of a pile of twitching corpses. Her wings unfurled suddenly like thunderheads, and her night-eyes thinned. She licked blood from one scarred arm and spat. 'Dead!' she roared. 'No souls!'

Dill had never seen an army flinch before.

Carnival beckoned them closer. They hesitated.

'We have to get out of here,' Dill said. '*Now.*'

'No,' Rachel said. 'Look at this place, Dill! The bones, the forges, the path up to the surface. And look at *them*! Fogwill risked everything to buy Carnival's help, and now I know why. Don't you see, these aren't the ghosts in your Codex stories. These *things* have no souls. This is wrong, *evil*. It isn't supposed to be like this. This is hell.'

'You can't stand against her. Nothing can stand against *that.*'

'Not in a fair fight.'

A guttural call went up from somewhere below and suddenly the air around Carnival was full of knives.

The scarred angel seemed to flex, sidestep, twist. Her fork still moved so fast Dill couldn't see it. Sparks showered around her: a hundred rapid steel concussions. The onslaught drove her to her knees, but her fork was still blurring, sparking, batting away the knives.

Silence suddenly.

Carnival stood.

She was wounded. Two of the knives had found their mark. One lodged in her thigh, the other beneath her armpit. Blood welled, trickled down her side, spattering the bones under her feet.

She grinned.

The army charged in triumph. A visceral howl, and they surged forward as one.

Dill moved to help her.

'No.' Rachel gripped his shoulder. 'Don't go near her when she's like this. She'll kill anything that gets close.'

Once more Carnival sprang to meet the oncoming horde. A vicious swipe sent the nearest two warriors reeling, ripped open. She drove her fist into a third one's face. His head snapped back and he collapsed at her feet.

More rushed in to flank her. Carnival dived beneath another net cast towards her. A withered, grey-skinned man snagged his foot in a ribcage. Carnival tore past him, slashed him open from groin to neck. She rolled, grabbed a skull and shattered it against the forehead of another assailant.

A score of knives flashed through the air. Metal clashed as Carnival's fork knocked them away. All but one, which lodged deep in the nape of her neck. She staggered back, roaring in pain.

And then they were all over her, pressing forward recklessly like wild beasts, punching and kicking and clawing at each other to get to her.

Still she cut them down. She whirled among them, stabbing, slashing. Bodies sank all around her, or fell away screaming, clutching severed veins. But yet more poured in, wave upon wave – a frenzied howling mob, scrambling over the dead and wounded.

Carnival was about to be engulfed by sheer weight of numbers, when she took to the air and kicked skywards. But a net snagged her wing. She shrieked in anger, twisted to tear it away, lost height. Another net engulfed her. A rope jerked back and the net closed tight. Trapped, she landed hard among the bones.

Her wings thrashed inside the net. She attacked the thick rope with her fork, but it would not yield to the blunt iron. A white-haired warrior drove his knife in towards her. Carnival's fork turned it aside, then ripped back up along the blade into his fingers. He screamed, and the knife withdrew. A fist slammed down. Carnival's fist slammed back and the man toppled, gurgling, his jaw smashed open. Then they had the net surrounded, kicking, pummelling. Too many now. Those behind snatched up bones from the remains on the slope and moved forward.

They were still beating her long after she'd stopped moving.

Dill cast his eye over the mounds of fresh dead. The mountain of bones had acquired a new summit. Blood covered everything.

'Can you still fly?' Rachel murmured.

'We can't leave her here,' Dill said.

At the sound of his voice, men turned; all bruised and bloody skin with shattered teeth. Blades shifted in knuckled fists. Sinewy muscles bunched under rags. Sneering, they began to climb towards him.

Rachel shook him. 'Dill! We have to go, *now*!'

For a moment he stared at her, confused. Carnival was still down there, helpless. She didn't deserve to die like this. He was weak, terrified, but he was still a temple archon. He had to do something. His hand closed around the handle of his sword.

'Dill!'

'I—'

Something punched him hard in the chest. He staggered back, winded, and collapsed. 'Wha—? Rachel?'

Her face had paled, her eyes wide open, staring. 'Oh my god. Dill? Oh my god.'

Dill looked down, to see his old chain mail had split open like paper. A knife was buried to the hilt in his chest. He reached for it.

'No!' Rachel screamed.

But the blood was already spurting from his heart, dark as death. It was the last thing he saw before he died.

27

IMPRISONMENT AND SABOTAGE

There were disconnected moments of lucidity. Chains scraping. Constant pain. Air inhaled like broken glass. Hammering metal. Glimpses of iron bars, roaring flames, seared rock, melted rock. Manacles. Black and yellow bruises, soft as rot. Bolts snapping. Rattling keys. Fat cauldrons frothing, sucking, stinking. Blood and meat. Rusted hooks heavy with slabs of butchered flesh. Shards of light on steel – hacking, hacking.

Darkness.

Then cold, hard eyes. Teeth. Scars.

And screams, terrible screams.

At some point Rachel realized the screams were coming from her own throat.

Someone was cradling her head, gently.

'Drink.'

Foul water sluicing over her parched lips.

Pain.

She was gagging, spitting.

Drowning . . .

*

. . . light from somewhere.

'Don't die on me, bitch.'

Get away from me, bitch. A Glueman with long, greasy hair, folding himself into the shadows, eating. *Scar Night is her night . . . The dark of the moon . . . One soul.*

'Who?'

Intolerable pressure on her chest. *'Leave me alone!'*

'Drink.'

'Dill?'

He was smiling, waving his lantern, rainbow eyes and feathers glowing softly in a golden sunset. He snuffed the light. Day snapped to night.

Catch me.

'The pain!'

Scars flared in the dark, then withdrew, leaving her alone with the pain.

Rachel woke, choking, heaving for air. A river of nails brushed against her skin. Dried blood crusted the corners of her mouth like rust. Tongue swollen, dry.

'Dill?'

She lifted her head from rough stone, and gasped. Renewed pain drove spikes into her neck, along her spine, into her stomach. Cracked ribs? Something clawed at her ankle. She reached down. Found more blood. A manacle.

'I'll light the lantern.' A woman's voice; a voice she knew.

She heard a flint wheel turn.

Tangles of dark hair did little to cover the bruises on Carnival's face. Her scars seemed fresh and full of blood. The angel narrowed her eyes as the lamp glowed. They were in a stone cell with an iron grate for a door.

'They threw this in here with us,' Carnival said, as she lifted the lantern and shuffled over to Rachel. A length of chain rattled across the floor in her wake. One of her wings slumped at an odd angle. 'Water too. And food.' Her tone was clipped, angry. 'You don't want to eat the food.'

Rachel tried to speak, but her throat felt full of blisters. Only a weak guttural sound escaped her.

'Look at you.' Carnival spoke through gritted teeth. 'You're almost as pretty as me.'

'What . . .?' Rachel swallowed. 'What happened?'

Carnival merely grunted.

Rachel tried to remember the fight. Images of blood and skull-like faces crowded back to her, indistinct, blurred. At once the blows she'd received seemed to cry out anew, pinched by the memory. She winced. She'd killed . . . how many? Clearly not enough.

Carnival was rubbing the manacled flesh at her own ankle. Rachel stared numbly at the manacle for a moment before she realized it was connected to her own by a length of chain. A feeling of sick dread took hold of her.

'Dill?' Suddenly she remembered his pale, panicked face, his eyes white as sunlit snow. 'Oh my god, what happened to Dill?' He'd looked so completely alone. But the army had reached her then, and she'd been forced to turn and fight.

'In the cell opposite,' Carnival said. Something in her tone, a hint of pleasure, made Rachel feel uneasy.

Groaning, the assassin pushed herself upright, her legs shivering in protest. She picked up the lantern and staggered over to the iron grate, chain scraping after her. The lantern illuminated broken flagstones beyond the cell, and bars opposite, a mirror of their own. A passageway divided the two cells, stretched away into darkness on either side. 'Dill?' she called.

No answer.

'Dill, please, are you there?'

Carnival spoke from the edge of the lantern light. Her face was hidden by shadow but she sounded like she was smiling. 'There was a lot of blood.'

'Dill!' Echoes of Rachel's voice receded down the passageway. Only the *tap, tap, tap* of dripping water answered. Anguish swelled in her stomach, engulfed her. She felt as if she were drowning in it. She collapsed to her knees and gripped the iron bars as though they could keep her afloat. *Please, god, let him be alive.*

Suddenly Rachel didn't know who she was praying to. Ulcis? There seemed to be no hope of salvation down here.

Carnival said, 'They'll gut him soon enough.'

'How can you say that?' Rachel snapped. 'He might still be alive!'

'He doesn't heal,' Carnival said, 'not like *me*.' Her last words were thick with venom.

My poor Dill. Rachel thought of him flying around the temple spires, laughing, his stupid toy sword banging against his hip. She thought of the stupid, useless, chain mail they had given him. His stupid bucket of snails. Tears prickled the corners of her eyes and she hugged her knees to her chin, dragging the chain closer. 'I was supposed to protect him.'

'From those *things*?'

'From you.'

Carnival snorted a laugh. 'He's safe from me now.'

'He wanted to help you,' Rachel said, 'after you'd been

injured. He tried to move so he could stand at your side. But I stopped him.'

Carnival said nothing.

Silence stretched between them. Rachel studied Carnival. Carnival peered back from behind her tracery of scars. The chain between them lay still, heavy on the cell floor. The angel's expression was blank, just a scrawl of ancient knife cuts. But was there a glint of something predatory in her eyes?

Finally Rachel asked, 'Why are we still alive?'

'Someone down here doesn't like you,' Carnival said flatly.

'How long till Scar Night?'

'Soon.'

The assassin found the flatness of Carnival's tone more disturbing than her anger. Anger could be steered, antipathy and malice were malleable. A glimmer of emotion might have offered a pathway, no matter how narrow, through those scars. But this detachment seemed absolute, as if its purpose was to separate Carnival from her hunger.

To protect her.

Rachel felt a twinge of pity. The angel had spent millennia constructing her defences. But they weren't enough. Rachel had seen Carnival lapse into fury too many times.

She can't detach herself completely. Darkness take me, even now she's still trying. But it won't hold. And so . . . the rage, the scars. How long now was it until Scar Night? Seven days? Six?

Carnival appeared to read her mind. 'Three days,' she said.

Rachel's hand went to her belt.

'They took your weapons,' Carnival said.

In Carnival's eyes, Rachel thought she saw misery.

There was a problem with the Tooth.

It didn't work.

Callis, that pseudo-mythological feathered fop, had seen fit to sabotage it, and if Devon ever found himself in the Sanctum corridor again he meant to drag the angel's damn skeleton down and show it what a mortar and pestle was for.

He was starting to hate the confinement of the Tooth's bridge. Three days in the sun and the stink of the dead saturated everything around him. A score of ropes tied to the base of the skeletal control panel disappeared through an open window. After the crash, there had been that many survivors from the *Adraki* for the Heshette to hang. For a desert people this method of execution might have seemed unusual, but the mimicry of the Avulsior's stage was not lost on the Poisoner. The Heshette didn't seem overly concerned with the smell, but then they didn't have to remain in here every hour of every day.

He opened the primer valve, an artefact like a boar's tusk, and pulled back the first ignition lever – a slender, rib-like appendage. Blood – no, oil – surged within the controls.

The floor vibrated slightly, then stopped.

'Darkness take me!' Devon swung a fist at the mound of controls, only to strike himself on the leg with his stump, when the fist turned out to be no longer there. He slammed the lever back and pinched the bridge of his nose. If that shaft had broken, it would take a full day to repair. He almost spat. They didn't have much time before the armada returned, reloaded, for a fresh assault.

Not that it would be any more effective than the first attack. The Tooth was well sealed against gas, impenetrable to crossbow fire, and shrugged off incendiaries as effectively as a rock. But the Poisoner was not about to suffer more of the Heshette and their damp-rag-wrapped faces. That joke had soured as quickly as the air around him.

What's more, the main city force would soon be assembled and ready to march against them. Heshette scouts reported massive construction work under way in the Deadsands, on Deepgate's northern perimeter. They were building weapons: catapults, scorpions, rams and siege-towers, cannibalizing half the League of Rope in the process. If he didn't hurry, there wouldn't be much left of the city for him to destroy.

And there was Scar Night to consider. If he could attack when the population were afraid to venture out, so much the better. Moondark would breed unease, dissension – if not mass desertion – among the reservists.

Devon left the bridge and trudged down the corridors to the engine room, where a hundred tapers burning among the piston shafts and walls of gears showed him the awful truth.

The propeller shaft they'd stripped from the *Adraki* had jumped from its mount.

Big Beard and *Bigger Beard* were straining against the steel mountings they'd fashioned to fit the bony depression in the ignition engine, trying to push the shaft back into place. Bataba had assigned these two to work for him. They had some clucking, unpronounceable camel-herder names, but Devon wasn't interested. *Big Beard* and *Bigger Beard* summed up their talents well enough. Wearily, he approached them. 'What happened?'

Bigger Beard glanced over his shoulder. 'It came out.'

'I can see that. Did the main engine turn?'

Bigger Beard gave him a blank look.

'The pistons, man. Did they move?' Devon sighed. 'These . . . pillars, these.' He pointed with his stump.

'No.'

Devon inspected the damage. The securing bolts had sheared. Steel did not meld well with this strange ceramic, and at the speed required for the ignition engine to fire the primary, their hotchpotch assembly was too eager to fly apart. Not a disaster, provided they could find some more bolts in the wreckage of the two fallen warships. He sent the Beards out to look.

Despite the setbacks he was getting there. Apart from this one shaft that Callis had removed like a key, the engines appeared to be intact. Enormous crystal vats held fuel enough, he supposed, for a journey around the world. The external lights – apparently a derivative of aether – were functional, although most of the internal lights had succumbed to the rigours of Heshette infestation.

But without main power, and with the hull air vents stuffed with rags and mud, the inside of the Tooth was like the inside of a labourer's sock. Devon stole a taper and set off deeper into the machine, haunted by the echo of his boots. Lately he had been thinking more about Sypes's refusal to speak. The old man was terrified not just of his god, but of anyone finding out his secret. Now Devon thought he understood why.

Toppled buckets and shreds of cloth littered the passages, which stank of urine. The mess hall was mouldering, the galley a cave of rusted sinks and taps. A single bottle of brown fluid stood on a shelf like something feared or revered, but the pots, pans and cutlery had long since disappeared into the Heshette hovels.

At last he came to the crew quarters, a maze of inter-connecting tunnels riveted with small, identical doors, each stamped with a hieroglyph. An air of rot suffused the place, as though after all these centuries the crew were still locked within. He found Bataba's guard asleep outside the makeshift cell, snoring like a warship. Devon kicked him. The fat man woke with a start and wiped drool from his bearded lips.

'You're supposed to be watching him,' Devon said.

'*Bara Sahbel!*' the guard cried. 'I do not take orders from you.' He heaved his great bulk upright with a series of greasy exhalations. 'You do not visit this prisoner without the shaman.'

'Fine. Go fetch him.'

The guard looked like he was about to argue, then he grumbled something in a dialect Devon didn't understand and trudged away, still half asleep, but willing, it seemed, to take orders from almost anyone. Devon meanwhile ducked inside the cell.

The smell made his eyes water. A slop bucket lay on its side in one corner. Sypes was naked and curled up opposite, eyes closed, the smashed remains of his walking stick scattered about him. His skin seemed devoid of muscle or flesh, draped like loose cloth over a jumble of bones, bruises darkening every inch of him. A heartbeat passed before Devon saw the shallow rise and fall of the old man's chest, the tremble in his ink-stained fingers, and realized that he was still alive.

'We'll be on our way soon,' Devon said, righting the slop bucket before he squatted down beside the priest.

Sypes did not open his eyes.

'There's no hope of rescue now, Sypes. No further need for your silence.' He paused, then spoke again in a whisper. 'Your god is rising, isn't he? But Ulcis isn't what your Church would have us believe. That's why you're so afraid.'

'I wanted to protect them.' The old man swallowed. 'I wanted to free Deepgate from her chains.'

'The only way to do that is to break them.'

'No,' Sypes said, 'you're wrong, Devon. Even chained, the city flourishes with life. Why can't you see that?'

Devon sighed. 'I once said how I was the only living man in Deepgate. I meant that everyone else takes, consumes, for no other reason than to feed the blood that feeds the abyss. That's not life, it's a hunger – as mindless as a poison or a disease. But I was wrong to claim *life* as mine alone. You and I stand each at the apex of twin pyramids, Sypes. Religion and science. There's nothing beneath us but snapping mouths. But there's life in you too, old man.'

'I can't accept that as a compliment. You're too arrogant. Besides, you're insane.'

Devon smiled. 'Can I get you anything to relieve the pain?'

'No. The pain is no more than I deserve after all I've done to them. If I die, it will be some comfort.'

'That reeks of martyrdom, Sypes, which doesn't suit you.'

'If I'm a martyr, then it's one to my conscience, not my god.'

'I fail to see the difference.'

Silence fell between them. Finally Devon said, 'Tell me about Ulcis. Who is he really?'

'He's Ayen's son! A god!' The outburst triggered a coughing fit.

'All right.' Devon raised his hand. 'Let's not kill ourselves over semantics. Sometimes I think we're both looking at the same thing through different ends of a sightglass. Our perceptions differ, but whatever we are trying to perceive doesn't change.'

Sypes drew a long ragged breath. 'Ulcis,' he said, 'consumes the souls of the dead and leaves them empty. The lucky ones remain as vessels for his will. As long as he exists, they linger . . . like walking husks. Others suffer an even worse fate.' He winced. 'Better to wander the Maze than to be used like that, to be stripped of everything that makes us human.'

'That,' Devon said, smiling, 'depends upon which god a soul is used to empower.'

Sypes snorted. 'Even Ulcis himself would struggle to match your arrogance. You think thirteen souls make you his equal?'

'I find that comparison demeaning. He is, after all, a parasite.'

'After the first holy war, his army grew too large to sustain itself. Without sustenance the dead rot. He could not swell their ranks and continue to . . . feed them. And so he has since allowed them to feast for a long, long time. For three millennia, the god of chains has waited, growing powerful on stolen souls while his slaves fed on his leavings.' The old man shook his head. 'Now they are coming, and they will harvest our world for their master. Oblivion awaits us all. If you cut the city down, you'll do nothing but aid him.'

Sudden convulsions gripped the priest. His body curled

up like a fist, eyes screwed shut, fingers clenched, and coughs racking his emaciated frame.

Devon crouched and seized hold of the Presbyter's shoulders until the worst of the tremors had passed. Then he pulled a handkerchief from his jacket pocket and, having no clean water to dampen it, pressed it into the old man's hand. Sypes clutched it like a lifeline.

Devon felt suddenly sorry for the Presbyter. Like all the city's priests, his faith was anchored in that pit. He hoped Sypes would survive to witness the city fall. It would be a kindness, for only then would he see the truth. The dead did not walk. There was no army in the darkness beneath Deepgate's chains.

'I'm getting you out of here,' he said.

'No,' Sypes gasped. 'I don't care any more. Help the temple guard instead. Ease his pain.'

Devon had forgotten about Angus. 'He's still alive?'

Sypes nodded. 'I heard that he's deranged, like a rabid dog, biting, and scratching himself. They've had to restrain him.'

'You!'

Devon turned to see Bataba standing in the doorway. 'What are you doing?'

'Interrogating the prisoner,' Devon said.

'You too are a prisoner.' The fetishes in Bataba's beard formed a crooked ladder up to his chin, under the welt across his ruined eye. 'What were you talking to him about?'

'Matters of faith – issues we don't see eye to eye on.'

The shaman bristled. 'Leave the priest. You are coming with me.'

★

The hatch swung open on to the full fury of a cinderblock sky. A blinding-white stairwell coiled up towards the sun. Below, the Deadsands hissed and shimmered.

'Up!' the shaman said.

Devon climbed.

On the roof of the huge machine it was worse. Soot-blackened funnels bisected the sunlight into searing slabs of white so painfully dazzling as to leave impressions in the eye. Blackthrone blazed, its serrated cliffs skeined with flashing copper, hot mineral seams, and incandescent crystal.

Bataba led him to the precipitous edge of the Tooth.

On the desert below some sort of game was under way. Horses jostled and thundered amid dust clouds, their riders swinging long, hooked poles. Every so often one of them would strike at the ground and send a fist-sized knot of rags hurtling through the air.

'*Kabarah*,' the shaman explained. 'They are contesting for the fat priest's jewels.'

Shrilling loudly, a handful of men spurred their mounts after the makeshift ball.

'An army is gathering against us,' the shaman continued. 'Soon there will be little time for games.'

Beyond the improvised pitch, the wreckage of the two airships lay strewn across the desert. Old women still picked through a shattered gondola, bickering over finds. From this height Devon could not tell which ship it had belonged to. Strips of silver from the envelopes fluttered in the sand like party decorations.

Bataba's gaze did not shift from the game. 'They do not trust you,' he said. '*I* do not trust you.'

'I can't imagine why,' Devon said.

'You have no respect for life.'

Devon snorted. 'You are just as keen as I am to go to war.'

'For different reasons, Poisoner. We seek to pull a thorn from Ayen's side, to crush her outcast son and those in this world who sustain him. But you—'

Renewed shouts went up from the riders below. Someone had hit the knot of rags into a roughly marked area of the pitch. A small boy picked up the bundle and scurried back with it to the centre.

'You,' the shaman continued, 'do not flinch at murdering thousands to revenge some perceived injustice to yourself.'

'Don't tell me you don't long for justice for your own people, for the decades of war that have decimated your tribes.'

'I won't deny we feel outrage. But our purpose is higher. We fight because it is Ayen's will.'

'And if Ayen does not exist, has never existed, then what difference is there between us? My motivations at least are founded on belief rather than simple faith.'

'Another reason we do not trust you,' the shaman growled.

Devon felt like pitching him over the side, but he took a measured breath and swallowed his anger. He was growing accustomed to the angelwine's violent demands. It seemed his consciousness had deliberately tightened around the seething knot inside him. His anger still flared when he least expected it, but he was gaining control.

A horseman struck the knotted bundle and sent it arcing towards the edge of the pitch. The other players surged after it, their mounts raising fresh plumes of dust.

Bataba said, 'The skyship survivors told us how the fat man roused the chained city against us. An army to rival the greatest in history, they said. It is fitting. Yet when I saw his perfumed corpse wrapped in silks, he seemed more woman than man.' His gaze returned to the game. 'We did not expect to find he had balls.'

A shrill ululation went up from below. Another rider had apparently scored. Devon felt faintly nauseous.

At that moment the Tooth shuddered. The roof vibrated and then settled into a steady, rhythmic booming. Curtains of built-up sand hissed loose from the funnels.

'It is time,' the shaman said, 'to go to war.'

28

ULCIS

In the darkness of her cell, Rachel had no means with which to judge the passage of time except the tick of water in the passageway beyond the grated door, and the ripening odour coming from the opposite cell.

She had given up calling for Dill.

She hunched against the damp stones, the corners of her eyes flinching at each tiny, hammer-blow drip, and tried not to think about anything other than keeping still. Whenever she shifted position, the manacle bit deeply into her ankle and the bruises on her face and chest throbbed angrily. Her throat was parched, her stomach cramped like a fist. She'd thrown away the bowls of meat their captors had left and flung curses down the passageway after them. No one had appeared to collect the bowls. There had been a jug of water, too, but it was empty now. She was thirsty, but so was Carnival. And Carnival would drink first.

For a time Rachel tried to *focus*, to send her mind far away – to the smoke-mist forests of Shale, to Spiral Hill in Clune with its whitewashed houses and terraced gardens daubed with children's colours – to the places she used to dream about as a girl. She tried desperately, throwing herself into these forced dreams. But the images were always elusive. Inexorably, the chain at her ankle pulled her back.

She had extinguished the lantern to conserve oil. In the darkness she thought she spied her cellmate's shape, but that might just be a trick of her eye. Carnival had remained wrapped in sullen silence for hours. Only the sound of her breaths reached over the space between them. They were short, shallow, and hungry.

'Carnival?'

No answer.

'How long now?'

The reply came through clenched teeth. 'Why should I warn you?'

Carnival's detachment from her own hunger had cracked. Now anger welled through to fill the gaps. She had become irritable, introverted, drawing inwards like a coiled spring.

'A day?'

'Less.' A lash of air buffeted Rachel as Carnival whipped out her wings and drew them back. The angel inhaled sharply, then rasped, 'Try the bars again.' Her voice was tense. 'Try . . . hard.'

Rachel rose unsteadily, aches and pains brawling for attention, and felt her way along the wall to the iron grate. The chain slithered over the flagstones behind her. Her hand closed on one of the bars, then she jammed her shoulder against the metal frame and pushed, straining her muscles until she cried out in pain.

The iron did not yield.

Breathless, she slumped to the floor. 'It's hopeless.' She pounded a fist against one of the bars.

Carnival's breathing quickened audibly.

'Why?' Rachel said. 'Why leave us here like this? If they wanted to watch you kill me, then where are they?'

'Not them,' Carnival hissed. 'It.'

'Ulcis?'

'I don't know,' Carnival snapped. 'Stop talking, shut up!'

Rachel pulled herself upright. She gripped the bars again and wedged both feet against the lintel. With every ounce of her strength, she heaved.

Nothing.

Gasping, she tore herself away. 'If we both try . . .'

Carnival growled.

'*Help me!*'

Rachel sensed movement. A scuff, a rattle of chain. Suddenly a hand gripped her wrist.

How did she . . .?

'Don't,' Carnival hissed in her ear, 'order me.'

'You're hurting me.'

'Yes.'

Rachel's breath felt thick in her chest, the darkness around her impenetrable, seething with malice. She reached for her sword, then paused. They had taken her sword, of course – and her knives, darts and poisons. Even the bamboo tubes with the horrors they contained. Without her weapons she felt naked.

Finally the pressure on her wrist eased. She heard Carnival move away, dragging her end of the chain to the far side of the cell.

'Can I ask you a question?' Rachel said.

'No.'

'Have you ever given a rat to a beggar?'

'*What?*'

'Forget it.' Rachel rubbed her swollen ankle, then

continued, 'I met this blind man once, a Glueman, who said you'd given him a rat and told him it was lamb.'

'You believed him?'

'No . . . I don't know.'

'Why not?' Carnival snarled. 'I've done worse. I've killed beggars and drunks and whores, nobles and soldiers and children.' She let out a low hiss. 'Even Spine.'

'You must have been lonely.'

Silence.

'Talk to me.'

'You think that will save you? It won't.'

'Fine.' Rachel fumbled for the lantern, spun the flint-wheel. 'If you're going to kill me, I at least want to see your face.'

The cell brightened. Fingers of shadow reached into the passageway beyond the grate. Carnival twisted away and hid her face from the light.

'If you won't talk,' Rachel said. 'I will.'

'I don't give a damn.'

'As long as I bleed when the time comes?'

Carnival flinched.

Rachel swallowed a pang of regret at her outburst. She foundered for a moment, trying to find a place to begin. At last she said, 'My father was a good man. No tears there. My mother died when I was eight, we don't know why. She got sick. Life twists like that.'

'Shut up!' Carnival snarled. 'Do you think I want to listen to this?'

'I don't care.'

Carnival sank into silent fuming.

'Our family has a townhouse in Ivygarths. A garden with a scraggy tree and a pond full of weeds. Nothing grand. I played with the other officers' children. We scrumped apples, terrorized ants, made the smaller boys eat newts – the usual stuff.'

Carnival had drawn herself into a knot, her face buried in her knees, arms wrapped around herself.

'Father was always away with the navy, always on some *perilous* campaign for the temple, for god. You don't much like aeronauts, do you?'

Carnival didn't even look up.

'He'd bring back presents. Dolls for me and pots of talcum from the river towns for mother. Painted soldiers for Mark. I'd sit on his knee and listen to his stories about exotic places. Dalamoor souks, monkey bandits, Racha gem-traders with cutthroat smiles. Thaumaturges from distant lands, if you can believe it. Men whose lips had been pierced with gallows-wood, men who knew Deep by a different name.' Her shoulders slumped. 'More than anything, I wanted to go with him when he left again. I wanted to be part of his stories.'

Carnival seemed to relax a little. Rachel realized she was listening.

'When the Spine accepted me I didn't hesitate. I joined because I wanted him to be proud of me, and because I wanted to experience my own stories – to share that part of his life with him.' She regarded her manacle distantly. 'That's why I grew to hate him.'

'Because he wasn't proud of you?' For once Carnival spoke without bitterness.

'No, because he didn't tell me what it felt like to kill. He *knew*, and he didn't tell me. After I came back from the Lowland Warrens, there was a wedge between us. We both recognized it but neither of us spoke about it. We hardly spoke at all after that.'

Carnival was silent for a while, then raised her head

and spoke angrily. 'I remember *this*.' Her finger traced the rope scar on her neck. '*My* first memory.'

'How old were you?'

'I don't know!' The angel took a shuddering breath. 'I was hanging by a rope from a foundation chain, sacks of rocks tied to my feet.'

Rachel winced. 'Who did that to you?'

The angel shrugged.

'You remember nothing? Nothing from before?'

'My name.'

'How did you get loose?'

Carnival's cold detachment was back in place. 'I chewed through the rope.'

Chewed? Oh gods . . . how?

'It took four days.'

Rachel didn't know what to say, and an uncomfortable silence fell between them. Outside the cell the water beat fierce, soulless notes. For a long time Rachel sat there listening. She thought about trying to loosen the bars again, but she was now so tired. Would she recognize when the end came? Would she see the moment when Carnival's defences shattered and the hunger took over? Did she want to know? Perhaps it was better just to sleep, to end it now.

Rachel remembered a voice from a dream she'd once had.

Don't die on me, bitch.

But she could no longer recall who the speaker had been. Her eyelids flickered.

An army of angels filled the dawn sky, their golden armour and steel alight like bright rain falling from the sun.

Turbulent sand boiled over the desert, dragged in the powerful wake of their wings. Rachel stood on the crest of a dune and watched the army converge on something half a league to the east – a small dark shape, a winged figure moving through the Deadsands. It was crawling on its hands and knees, crippled by the weight of what it dragged behind. Chains. Hundreds and thousands of chains.

Rachel.

She looked up.

Dill's sword sparkled gold, but his eyes were as white as his wings. He was being pulled away from her, struggling against an invisible current.

Wait, she shouted. *Come back.*

But the angel was already growing distant, merging into the ranks of his ancestors. They massed around him, all bronzed muscles and heavy armour plate, sneering, mocking him. Dill cried out. He was trying to tell her something.

What is it? What?

She almost heard him.

Rachel jerked awake, startled by a sudden conviction that Dill was still alive; that he needed her.

Bars of shadow reached over the rough floor and the coils of chain. The cell was illuminated.

From outside.

'Who are you?' Carnival crouched in the centre of the cell, gazing past her, furious.

'God,' a deep voice answered.

Rachel wheeled.

The god of chains was a landslide of flesh. Muddy skin cascaded in great overlapping slabs down from his tight-stretched pate to his bowed calves. He was naked, male it seemed. The only evidence of his gender remained his voice, overhangs of fat obscuring any more obvious proof. And he was winged. Huge wings, like eruptions of grit, poured from the hillocks of his shoulders. Large as they were, Rachel suspected this creature had not flown in many years.

'Pathetic,' Carnival hissed. 'Makes sense your god would look like this. No wonder Ayen kicked him out.'

The god ignored her. He raised his lantern and leaned closer to the bars, breasts shifting like continents, and swung eyes the colour of ancient blood towards Rachel. 'You are Spine,' he rumbled, 'but untempered. Why?'

'So much for omniscience,' Carnival sneered, her anger palpably keen to take strides along this new avenue.

'Are you Ulcis?' Rachel asked.

'Answer my question.'

'Answer mine.'

The god's mountainous visage creased in a hundred places. 'I am Ulcis,' he said.

'I am untempered,' Rachel explained, 'because my brother would not allow it.'

'That matters not,' said Ulcis. 'The Presbyter hid this from me. Why?'

Sypes? The old man was in contact with his god? Was hiding *things from him?* Warnings sounded in her head, and she felt suddenly unwilling to entertain this god further. 'Ask him yourself.'

Ulcis studied her a while longer with hooded eyes, searching, as though he was trying to peel away layers. When at last he spoke, his voice was an earthquake, 'You are not the first to come seeking answers, mortal. Life and death, the eternal question—'

'I'm not seeking answers,' Rachel broke in. 'I'm looking for a syringe.'

'Have you seen it?' Carnival said.

The god bristled. His great bulk gathered. Boulders of flesh rolled as he straightened. Furrows enveloping his eyes, he swung to face Carnival, prodded a fat finger in her direction. 'You, freak, why are *you* here?'

Carnival padded up to the bars and spat in his face.

A tremor ran through him. 'You don't remember me,' he boomed.

She spat in his face again.

'You don't remember anything –' the fat god wiped spittle from his jowls and his eyes began to glow – 'do you, Rebecca?'

Carnival's scars turned blood red.

The light in Ulcis's eyes seemed at once to deepen, to intensify. Darkness gathered around him, and compressed to form chains growing from his shoulders and wings. Chains that reached into the cell, and enveloped Carnival. Sounds issued from those chains: the voices of ten thousand souls.

Rachel felt the air turn deathly cold.

'Remember?' the god said to Carnival. 'Remember your mother, the mortal whore? A bone-crawler like the others, but so pretty, even in death when she began to rot. I gave her back her soul so that I might enjoy her suffering more.' He sneered. 'But you took it with you when we ripped you from her womb. You stole it from me. You will remember now, child – your first kill?'

Carnival gasped, tried to pull away, but the wraith chains held her tight.

'Now.' Ulcis's voice was thunder. 'Remember my rope.'

Carnival lunged for him.

Rachel heard bones snap as the angel hit the iron grate.

The god recoiled. In spitting fury, Carnival clawed the air in front of him.

'Now you remember, daughter,' Ulcis said. 'The rope? My gift to you, savage little Rebecca. My little carnival freak.'

Devon felt like he rode the shoulders of a god. Perched on the chair before the control bank, he snapped a lever back and the bridge responded with a powerful shudder. A deep rumbling shook the walls and floor. The Tooth lurched forward, engines thumping, into the Deadsands. Sand sprayed from either side of the forward scoop like crashing waves. The massive tracks ground and crushed everything in their path.

'An outcrop of rock,' Bataba warned, pointing. 'Look there! You must steer west.'

'Nonsense,' Devon shouted over the booming engines. 'This thing could flatten a mountain.'

'Show me. The cutting arms.'

Grinning, Devon twisted a valve open. Fluids pulsed within the trembling control bank. Air hissed from moist vents. He gripped a bony protrusion and slid it back. A ferocious grinding noise came from below, and a great jet of pulverized rock flew skywards. The bridge shook again, and the Tooth's cutters lifted into view, in a blaze of spinning cogs.

But the shaman had turned away. He was looking at a sack Devon had deposited in one corner of the bridge. Dark stains seeped into the burlap from its contents.

'Where are your men?' Devon asked. 'I thought they would be here to see this.'

'Up on the roof.'

'I see.' Devon eased the handle back a notch. The Tooth growled. Cutters bit deeper into the dunes, till geysers of sand sprayed up and over the bridge windows. The setting sun soaked through it like blood. 'Ah,' Devon said. 'My apologies, shaman. I believe I meant to move this handle the other way.'

'Careful, Poisoner.' Bataba's gaze remained pinned to the sack.

Devon slotted the handle back into place, then nodded at the object of the shaman's attention. 'I made Sypes a promise,' he explained, 'to ease the temple guard's suffering.'

Angus had been in a terrible state. The poison in his veins had pushed him to the very limits of endurance, even to the brink of insanity. But still he clung to life with a tenacity that Devon found both astonishing and repulsive. The Heshette healers had retreated, leaving the poor man restrained so as to prevent him from tearing at his own flesh. Devon became curious: he wanted to see how much Angus could endure. But he'd promised Sypes to help, so he had compromised.

'You were forbidden access to your poisons,' Bataba said.

'My chemicals were not necessary,' Devon said. 'Merely a saw.'

The shaman looked back at the sack, at its lumpy, seeping contents. 'What did you do?'

'I stopped him from scratching himself.'

The Tooth climbed a low rise in a series of jolts that jarred Devon's teeth, and then settled back into the dull thumping of engines as it picked up speed and rumbled down the slope on the other side.

Twilight deepened. The Tooth ploughed on into the Deadsands, swaying gently. It crested dunes, devoured rock beneath its tracks. Stars winked on. Scar Night's dark moon would soon be rising unseen: its very absence from sight an ominous portent of the blood to be shed before dawn. After a time Bataba left to join the other councillors on the roof.

Devon felt invigorated. He leaned over the array of controls, feeling the pulse and throb of the great machine in every muscle, and surveyed the landscape ahead.

To the south, aether-lights flickered in the night sky.

Decoys.

Devon pulled a lever and a web of metal mesh slammed down in front of the windows. The first attack would come long before the main armada reached them. Deepgate had one black warship, the *Whisperer*. His own idea. Silver-coloured ships were too easy for archers to spot at night. The *Whisperer* was a fast-strike vessel, slender and swift, its gondola stripped of crew quarters, grapples and docking pulleys, and every other non-essential fixture, to make room for its bulkier engines and extra payload. Out of aether contact with the main fleet, it would be somewhere close overhead, riding high currents on an interception parabola. And if the aeronauts' now acting commander, Hael's second-in-command, was as predictable as his predecessor, an attack ought to occur at any moment.

On cue, a distant boom sounded overhead. A fizz, as firelight lit the ground all around the Tooth for an instant and threw stark wells of shadow across the dunes.

Incendiaries.

Another boom, followed by more fizzing, and the desert

flickered orange and red. The Tooth thundered on regardless.

Two drums thudded into the sand ahead, spewing lime-gas. Devon lowered the cutters. The first drum shot into the night with a *pang*; the other exploded into shrapnel. Fragments of metal smacked against the lowered grille. Smoke brushed the windows. Two more drums of gas landed some yards to the left, upwind of the Tooth. Devon banked the machine windward and shredded them like dry leaves.

A hail of missiles glanced off the hull, followed by the concussions of more incendiaries.

All around, the desert burned.

Devon was whistling, rapping a knuckle against the control panel in tune, when the bridge door burst open and Bataba stormed in.

'A black skyship,' he snarled.

Devon regarded him disdainfully. 'You cannot expect me to anticipate everything.'

'We lost four men.'

'*I* didn't tell them to sit up there.'

'Four men, Poisoner – a score more with burns.'

Devon shrugged.

'You didn't know about this black ship?'

'I did not.'

'You are lying.'

'Have I not saved you once from a gas attack? Did I not bring down the *Adraki*, and then coax this machine into battle? And am I not about to crush the ground forces of Deepgate? All for you, shaman, so why would I lie?'

Bataba glowered at him. 'Anything else we ought to know? Your usefulness has all but run out.'

'If I think of anything, I'll let you know.'

Tension gave way to uneasy silence as the Tooth crawled up another steep dune. The rest of the fleet had finally arrived. Silver envelopes converged overhead, shining dully amidst furiously flashing aether-signals. At the summit Devon eased back the throttle. A vast sweep of lights glittered in the desert ahead.

'Deepgate troops,' Devon murmured.

'How many?'

'All of them.'

By the light of their broken lantern, Rachel saw that Carnival had been crying. She shuffled over, taking care not to shine the light directly in the angel's face.

Carnival hid her scarred cheeks in her hands. 'Leave me alone.'

'You didn't remember him?' Rachel asked.

'Leave me!'

Rachel flinched. 'I'm sorry.'

'I don't want your sympathy! Save your breath, bitch. It won't save you. Nothing will save you.'

Rachel had to hope otherwise. By forcing Carnival to remember, the god of chains had sought only to hurt his daughter. One look at him had been enough to shatter three millennia of defences, to reopen her deepest scars. It had left her vulnerable, but, Rachel suspected, it had also exposed her heart.

Carnival hugged her knees. A tracery of cuts engraved her arms. One wing hung crooked from her broken shoulder; the feathers limp and matted with grime.

Rachel squatted on the floor beside her. She picked up a handful of the chain links and let them drop. 'It's Scar Night right now, isn't it?'

'Yes.'

'You're going to kill me.'

A pause, then, 'Yes.'

'I'm sorry, I'm sorry. I'm sorry he's your father. I'm sorry for everything.' And she *was* sorry. Sorry her own life had ended up like this. Sorry Dill was dead. Sorry her father was dead.

When she thought about the old man, it was always the same image: him returning home from some campaign, a solid, earthy man in a starched white shell of a uniform, silver buttons liquid in the light of the hearth. She remembered his comical frowns as Mother fussed around him, babbling on about the books she'd read, the gossip from the officers' wives club, Mark's scuffles with the authorities at the academy. And she remembered her father's face when she told him she'd joined the Spine: the grim line of his mouth, the wounded look in his eyes.

You could have stopped me. Why didn't you stop me?

Rachel looked down at Carnival, at the lank black hair strewn all around her ruined face, the broken feathers in her wings, the rotting leather vest, patched a thousand times and flecked with ancient mould. Carnival was curled up tight, making herself small, childlike. Her thin scarred arms wrapped tightly around her knees, like bandages.

'Talk to me,' Rachel said softly.

Carnival was weeping again. 'Leave me alone! You're trying to save your own worthless flesh.' Carnival raised her head, teeth clenched, thin dark eyes swamped with tears. 'You think I give a damn about you? You're nothing to me. You're meat. Meat!'

'You can fight this.'

'Fight this?' A pained laugh. 'Fight this!' The angel spat out the words. 'You ignorant bitch!'

'Your life didn't begin with that rope, and it didn't end with it.'

'It should have been a chain!'

'Stop feeling so sorry for yourself.'

At once, the tightness left Carnival's face. Tears now flowed freely over her scars. She dropped her chin to her knees again, and took a deep, shaky breath. 'I hate this.' Anguish tapered her voice. 'I hate them – you. I'll kill them. You. All of you. Everyone!' She wailed. 'Get away from me! Get the hell away from me!'

Rachel touched her shoulder. 'Rebecca.'

Carnival slapped her away, hard. 'My name is Carnival!' she screamed.

'I'm sorry, I—'

A key rattled in the lock of the cell door. Rachel whirled round.

A giant stood behind the bars, dressed in filthy robes, his bulk filling the doorway. At first she thought Ulcis had returned, but then she saw that this man was built more solidly than the god, a mass of dense muscle. Bruises and stubble shadowed his face. Human bones strapped to his left leg formed a rude splint, while more, longer bones had been lashed together into a crutch on which he leaned. He fumbled with keys in his massive hands. The door creaked open.

'Abigail?' he said.

29

THE SCROUNGER

Mr Nettle's heart soared as his daughter picked herself up from the cell floor. She approached him warily, her face shadowed by the overhanging lid of the lantern at her hip. He felt like rushing over, scooping her up in his arms, and holding her tight.

He said, 'I'm taking you home.'

'Balls you are.'

Abruptly his elation collapsed. This girl was too short, too slim, too fair. She moved lithely, with a grace Abigail had never possessed. And she wore the leather armour of a Spine assassin.

The assassin lifted her lantern and regarded him with shocking green eyes. Her face was skeletal. Bruises marched in a line from her neck to one side of her forehead. 'Who the hell are you?' she asked.

'You're Spine,' Mr Nettle said.

She studied him, her expression pinched. 'I'm Rachel Hael.'

Mr Nettle scratched the scabs amid his stubble. 'You dead too?'

An odd look. Maybe this Spine didn't know she was dead. He'd heard of ghosts like that, the ones who never settled easily in Deep, the ones who resisted. Often they didn't realize they were dead. *In denial*, League folks said – but, then, what did those bastards know?

'You seen her?' he grunted.

'Who?'

'My daughter.' He leaned his big face closer. 'She won't be with *them*.'

Abigail would have fled once she'd seen those ghouls there on the bone mountain. He figured she'd be hiding down here in the tunnels below Deep, among the dead angels and their broth kitchens. The daft girl liked angels.

Rachel Hael dropped her gaze to his splint, the bones he'd found and tied to his wounded leg. Pain racked the flesh there as though she'd touched him. He shifted his weight and the crutch creaked.

She asked again, 'Who are you?'

'Nettle. Is she here?'

The girl looked puzzled. 'Are you one of Ulcis's servants?'

He flinched at the name. The fat god was down here somewhere, sliding down the tunnels like a wall of mud, watching everything. Hungry. And Mr Nettle had lost his cleaver. He spat, 'No.'

'Then what are you doing here?'

Was she stupid? 'Abigail,' he explained. 'I'm looking for her.'

'I don't know who she is. Are you from above? From Deepgate?'

'Aye.'

The city was only a dream now. It seemed he had fallen for days, or even years. He must have slept as he fell, or maybe that's when he'd died – he couldn't be sure. He'd woken when the angel bit him. Scrawny, evil-looking thing in dented armour, it must have caught him near the bottom. It had dropped him quick enough when he'd yelled and smashed a fist into its face.

Then he'd been lying in a crater of bones, dead as dead, with a bloody great bite-mark in his leg. Abigail hadn't spoken to him since then, hadn't told him where she was hiding. She was probably afraid *they*'d hear her. Or she was sulking.

His ribs felt tender from the fall, and his leg hurt like a tooth-puller had been at it with his tongs. Maybe it was infected: he didn't know, didn't much care. So he'd fixed it with a makeshift splint and gone off in search of his daughter. She was down here somewhere, and so was the syringe that held her soul. He'd find them both – dead or not, he was still a damn fine scrounger.

'How did you get here?' she asked.

'I fell.'

She stared like she didn't believe him.

'Where did you get the keys?'

'Scrounged them.' *Stole them.* This was his own voice in his head now, and for that he was thankful. Abigail would be furious with him if she knew – just like her mother. He wouldn't tell her about stealing keys, or any of the other things he'd done since he'd died.

The murders.

'Quiet,' he murmured to himself. 'Can't kill the dead.'

Someone sniffed, and then another voice came from the shadows: 'Is it human?' This one had wings.

Scars.

Mr Nettle recoiled. He looked for a weapon, saw none, so he hefted his crutch instead. His unsupported leg screamed in protest. He ignored it, ploughed forward.

'Wait.' The Spine pushed him back, strong for such a little thing. 'She won't hurt you.'

'Don't count on it,' Carnival muttered.

He growled.

'I recognize him now.' The scarred angel rose from the ground. 'My drunken assassin. Lost your cleaver, beggar?'

Mr Nettle went for her.

A tearing pain in his leg stopped him dead. The assassin had a foot pressed hard against his injured thigh. He swung a punch at her—

—and found himself on his back, gasping.

'Enough!' This time Rachel Hael had him pinned to the ground, her heel digging into the cords in his neck. He tried to grab her, but she dug her heel in deeper. 'I said, enough! Darkness take me, there's plenty down here for you both to piss on without pissing on each other.'

Mr Nettle noticed that her ankle was manacled to a chain. He twisted his neck, so his eyes followed the links. His grunt was almost a laugh: one bitch chained to another.

The Spine let him up again, handed back his crutch. 'What happened to your daughter?'

'Killed,' he said, keeping one eye on Carnival. 'Poisoner bled her. Need to find her before she gets herself in any more trouble.'

Assassin and angel exchanged a glance.

'The dead angels here,' Mr Nettle said, and his eyes narrowed on Carnival. 'They're even worse than you.'

Carnival folded her arms.

Rachel Hael looked uncomfortable. 'Your keys, will they open the other cell?'

The opposite cell, when he opened it, was dark, cold,

and stank of violence. Blood had been spilled here, lots of it. Mr Nettle shifted forward, on his crutch, to see better. 'Abigail?'

Behind him, the assassin raised her lantern.

White feathers matted with blood were scattered all across the floor. Mr Nettle bent down and started stuffing them into his pockets. You could sell feathers. Folks made pillows and warm jackets from them. And there were piles of them here, even though filthy. He'd have to clean all the muck and blood off first, but that didn't matter. They were still worth scrounging.

Then he noticed the corpse in the corner.

The angel lay broken on a bed of straw, like it had been thrown there, its skin black and swollen, mouth and eyes gaping in frozen terror. Its wings had been ripped to shreds, as though a pack of dogs had been at them.

But there was a sword.

Mr Nettle moved over to take it. That was worth more than all the feathers.

The Spine stopped him. 'Don't,' she said, her voice sounding strangely thick. She hunched down beside the angel and rested a hand on its forehead.

'Dill?'

Mr Nettle grunted, and went back to gathering feathers. Over his shoulder he saw the assassin prise the weapon free from the angel's grip. 'They didn't take his sword,' she said; then, angrily, 'They didn't even take his sword!' Then she laid the weapon on the angel's chest. She didn't once turn round.

There were more feathers than Mr Nettle could collect. When his pockets were full, he staggered upright on his crutch. 'There's no more cells after these,' he said.

Carnival was eyeing his swollen pockets, her lips peeled back from her teeth like she wanted to rip out his throat. Mr Nettle clenched a fist around the bones that formed his crutch. But the assassin stepped between them again. Her eyes were moist. 'Let's get out of here,' she said.

'Sword's worth money,' Mr Nettle said.

'Touch it, scrounger, and I'll break your neck.'

Mr Nettle gave the weapon a final, longing look before heaving himself painfully towards the door. A sword was no use to him anyway, not down here, not against all these dead things. Especially against the angels, a sword would be no use at all.

'Need to find Abigail,' he said.

'She's gone,' Carnival snarled. 'Forget her.'

'No.' Mr Nettle towered over the scarred angel. He was twice her size. 'She's here. She's all alone.'

Rachel Hael took his arm. 'I'll help you look for her,' she said. She glanced at Carnival, and quickly away again. 'But first we need to find a way to cut this chain. And we need weapons.'

Mr Nettle turned back to the sword.

'Not that,' Rachel said. 'Leave it – it doesn't belong to us.'

The scrounger grumbled. *Women.* No point even trying to figure them out. 'Storeroom down the way,' he said. 'Might find something there.'

They left the cells behind them and hurried along a rough passageway hewn from naked rock. The lantern threw wild shadows ahead of them, like fleeing wraiths. Carnival sprinted up front, still dragging the chain. One wing slumped from her broken shoulder. Mr Nettle hobbled on his crutch behind, trailing feathers. Rachel followed last, still lost in thought.

Anger curled around her memory of Dill lying broken and alone in his cell. Why hadn't their captors taken his sword? It struck her as irreconcilably cruel. By ignoring the weapon, they'd diminished him.

And yet, even now he was dead, she hadn't been able to take the sword herself – blunt as it was, it would have been better than nothing. But prising it from his dead grip had made her feel as cruel as those who'd so readily dismissed it. She cursed her dream. For a moment she'd felt sure she could save him.

She wondered what Carnival was now thinking. The angel – or demigod, if that's what she was – stormed ahead of them as though she meant to tear apart the city of Deep with her bare hands. After that battle on the mountain of bones, Rachel didn't doubt she was capable. It had taken an entire army to stop Carnival then. But now it was Scar Night.

And the scrounger? For his sake she hoped they didn't find his dead daughter.

The lantern guttered: barely a drop of oil left. Unless they stumbled upon some illuminated tunnels soon, only Carnival would be able to see. The chain between them rattled like a death cough.

The passageway climbed sinuously through a hive of smaller tunnels and crawl-spaces. Dank currents of air whispered around them, carrying sounds so faint Rachel wasn't sure she'd heard anything at all. Once she thought she heard someone sobbing, another time the chopping of knives. But always in the background, like a pulse, the hammering of metal in the forges. There were faint odours too, which were sickeningly familiar, but she forced those out of her mind and concentrated on keeping her footing on the weeping rock. After a while the passage levelled, and then, abruptly, it opened into a cavernous space.

It was a storeroom of sorts, stuffed with piles of mouldering detritus: furniture, bedsteads, bolts of cloth, crates and trunks full of random objects, stone trenchers and sinks, broken pottery, baskets of bottles, and more bottles containing everything from beads to teeth.

'Look for tools,' Rachel said to Mr Nettle, 'and weapons.'

'Quickly,' Carnival growled.

They set to work rummaging through all the rubbish, most of it smashed up or useless. Years of offerings, Rachel assumed, from the Avulsior's ceremonies way above; payment for the privilege of watching pilgrims redeemed. There were examples of workmanship from every quarter of Deepgate: once-fine garments, wrought iron, ceramics, children's toys, wooden sculptures, all heaped here into piles and left to rot.

Mr Nettle found the poppywood chest.

Rachel could barely have lifted the heavy crossbow, let alone used it effectively, but the scrounger hefted it easily in one massive arm and grinned at her.

'Smith's,' he explained.

'Belonged to a friend of yours?' she asked.

His grin faded. 'Aye.'

There were three bolts with the weapon: a hunting crescent, a burner, and a poisonsong wrapped in oilcloth – though no markings to indicate which type of poison.

'Craw plague,' Mr Nettle said.

She noted the way he watched Carnival from the corner of his eye as he spoke. Rachel gave him the hunting tip and carefully fastened the others to her belt. Chances were, the plague-bolt was dry – although still able to pierce – but the burner was worth more than any treasure.

'Should be hammers too,' Mr Nettle said, peering into the chest. 'Smith had hammers in here.'

'They've been taken. I suppose hammers are worth more to people living underground than a hulking great weapon like that.'

After all, what were they going to shoot at down here?

Rachel could have spent hours sifting through the storeroom for further weapons, but a look at Carnival's expression drove her to urgency. After she'd fitted a fresh cord to Nettle's crossbow, wound the windlass, and loaded the hunting tip for him, they set off again.

Tunnels branched and branched again until it seemed like they were negotiating the hollow roots of a tree. Carnival kept always to the widest passages, her wingtips scratching the rock on either side. It grew warmer, and gradually lighter, until Rachel spied fires burning in a chamber ahead.

'Turn off the lantern,' Carnival hissed. 'Don't you smell it?'

Rachel sniffed. Someone was cooking meat.

She realized the same smell had been there for some time. And then she realized she was salivating. Bile rose in her stomach at the thought. She glanced at Mr Nettle. Had he noticed too? Did he know what the smell meant or had his mind blocked out such a possibility?

What will the truth do to him?

Carnival went striding ahead.

'Wait,' Rachel whispered.

Carnival ignored her, and the chain between them grew taut. Cursing, the assassin took off after her.

Liquids gurgled and frothed within huge, steaming cauldrons set around the edges of the cavern. The rock walls were seeping, and blood-coloured with the heat and light from coals burning under massive grates. A heavy butcher's block occupied most of the available space between the cauldrons, its wooden surface deeply stained and gouged. Mercifully, there was no sign of any meat.

Carnival stood peering into one of the cauldrons. 'Scrounger,' she said, squinting against the light.

'Don't.' Rachel grabbed her arm.

The angel grunted.

Mr Nettle joined them. He scowled at the nearby cauldrons, but did not appear interested in their contents.

He can't face the truth. His mind isn't capable of accepting it. Or maybe he's just too damn stubborn. She wondered how long he'd already been down here, and what he'd eaten to stay alive.

Two stout doors led out of the opposite end of the cavern. One of them would doubtless be the cold room. Rachel studied the floor and saw grooves in the dirt suggesting that a number of heavy objects had been dragged through the smaller of the two doors.

Carnival approached this same door.

'Wait!'

But just as Rachel reached out to stop her, the larger door opened. And *something* clambered through.

The thing had to stoop low to squeeze its wings through the doorframe, moving its fleshless limbs in a series of crooked jerks. When it saw them, it dropped the bone it had been gnawing, straightened its misshapen body somewhat, and narrowed sulphurous yellow eyes. One side of its mouth drooped open to reveal a single pointed tooth. Between its white lips, a sliver of a tongue lolled like a bloodworm. Even here, in this already fetid air, the stink from the creature was overwhelming. Whatever it was, it was *rotting*.

Rachel then realized it was an angel – or had been once.

30

THE PALACE OF CHAINS

A thousand campfires shivered under Scar Night's dark moon. Dunes extended in frozen waves before them, till it seemed to Devon that he was looking at a city built on the distant shore of a sea. He eased the throttle of the Tooth and let the machine rumble to a halt. Sand showered down past the bridge windows.

So many fires. Every legion of Deepgate's regulars and reservists warmed themselves in readiness for the onslaught. Unseen, he realized, the seventh and ninth cavalry divisions would be off to the sides, moving into a position to outflank them. And up there the warships. Devon counted more than thirty, burning like comets among the stars. The *Whisperer* had emptied its payload. Somewhere overhead, it would be flying back to Deepgate to rearm.

Bataba kept squinting through the forward windows, alternately scratching the scar of his right eye and tugging at the fetishes in his beard. 'We are Ayen's fist,' he grumbled. 'This war should be fought under her light.'

'Not much we can do about that,' Devon said. 'Unless your goddess sees fit to raise the sun early.'

The shaman grunted.

'How do you want to do this?' the Poisoner asked.

'Just mow them down.'

Devon feigned surprise. 'I thought the Heshette looked their enemies in the face when they killed them.'

'In daylight, yes. But this fight is on the outcast's terms.'

'They'll send someone out to parley.'

Bataba continued to eye the horizon.

Devon stifled a yawn. 'As you wish.' He hitched a lever and the Tooth lurched forward to meet the assembled armies.

Bataba turned his back on the night as the Tooth eased over into a dip. 'What can we expect?' he asked.

'A bumpy ride.'

'Anything else we should know about?'

'The third through fifth divisions, the sappers, they'll have undermined the ground between. Tunnels, trenches of pitch, that sort of thing. Expect more explosions, but I doubt they've had time for any serious excavation. So that shouldn't be a problem. They'll have cobbled up some siege-towers, heavy ballistics and such, but nothing powerful enough to stop us. As long as we keep moving, they'll have a hard time breaching our hull in significant numbers. We should be safe until we reach the abyss. Their reservists, for all their zeal, haven't fought or trained in a decade.' He paused. 'My main concern is Spine saboteurs. Ichin Tell will have assassins hidden here and there in the sand, whose job will be to get inside while our attention is diverted. Look out for grapples from below.'

'I will post lookouts.'

'Better to set an ambush for them,' Devon said. 'Allow them an opening and let them come in. But be ready to close it again on them quickly.'

'Don't tell me how to fight, Poisoner. We've beaten their likes before.'

'In desert skirmishes,' Devon agreed, 'but you've never faced numbers like this. Almost every living man who ever held a sword for Deepgate is out there now.'

Bataba seemed not to hear him. He turned away as the Tooth began to climb out of the depression. 'I'll fetch the council,' he said, and then left the bridge.

When they reached the crest of the next dune, Devon saw a group of horsemen riding out to meet them, the temple standard rippling gold and black in the light of a dozen brands. A trumpet sounded shrill beneath the roar of the Tooth's churning engines. Devon kept the same course and fed power into the cutting arms. Cogs of the weird metal spun and sang, and threw off arcs of sand. The approaching riders broke formation and skirted the huge machine. As the trumpet blared again, Devon jammed the throttle forward in response.

Deepgate still lay hidden below the horizon, but huge fleshy columns of smoke rose from the city, as though every furnace was ablaze in forging weapons. The sky above was painted in colours of oil and coal and fire. Churchships dotted the billowing smoke like red blisters.

A last line of defence perhaps? Had Clay armed the temple armada too? The Poisoner wasn't overly concerned. By the time the churchships engaged him, the city itself would already be lost.

After half a league, the horsemen regrouped and rode back towards the waiting army.

Presently the council arrived on the bridge. They were in no better mood than Bataba, at least half of them with fresh burns from the *Whisperer*'s attack. None concealed their contempt for the Poisoner. They gathered around, brandishing their tribal knives in plain view, until their scowls were drawn to the distant lights.

'We've set bowmen at the vents on both sides,' Bataba explained. 'Barrels of tar from the wrecked skyships stand ready in dawn and dusk corridors. These saboteurs will find scaling our walls no easy task.'

Devon wasn't convinced, but he left his concerns unvoiced. 'Just keep one eye on the sky,' he reminded him.

Bataba ignored the jibe. He was studying the landscape before them. The Poisoner turned to follow his gaze. They were closer now, close enough to see units of troops clustered around the campfires, and mounted soldiers milling behind. Armour and shields flashed. On higher ground to the southeast and southwest the skeletal silhouettes of wooden towers, mangonels and scorpions waited before the abyss.

'The outriders have returned,' Bataba said.

The horsemen had broken through the infantry and reined in before a group of command tents situated behind the bulk of the army.

'At least we know where Clay is,' Devon observed, 'or wants us to think he is.'

They didn't have long to wait after the outriders had delivered their report. Buglers echoed commands through the lines of troops, and the armies of Deepgate rippled into motion.

Hundreds of banners split aside and streamed to east or west. Rear cavalry units moved into flanking positions. Reservist infantry assembled into blocks between them, bristling with spears and pikes. Lines of pitch fire tore through the sand before ranks of archers and arbalests. Aether-lights flared in unison high above, and Deepgate's warships started to converge, moving into position for a concentrated assault.

The plain before them now levelled. Rocks popped and crumbled beneath the Tooth's tracks, reduced to dust in the face of the great machine. Engines thundered. But to Devon these noises seemed distant, blanketed by a heavy silence in his mind.

He waited. The Tooth rocked and juddered, slowly building speed, flattening everything in its path. Caravan tracks criss-crossed the desolate ground before them like old wounds. The stars seemed to wink in approval. Deepgate's fire-lit trunks of smoke grew nearer.

Still he waited.

Soon enough the warships arrived, and the battle began.

A colossal boom like a thunderclap sounded overhead, followed by a prolonged crackling. The desert flickered orange and red. Gouts of flame fizzed past the bridge windows and blackened the glass. Phosphor smoke seethed in their wake. But the Tooth shrugged off this attack as though it were summer rain.

Boom, crackle, fizz.

Two hundred yards ahead, a second shower of fire fell from the night sky.

'They have missed,' the shaman said.

'No.' Devon knew what was coming.

All at once, the Deadsands burst into flame. For a quarter of a league to either side there was nothing but a lake of fire.

'The ground is on fire!' Bataba cried. 'Go around! Go around!' He groped for the control levers.

Devon elbowed him aside, and maintained his course, driving the Tooth straight for the flames. 'Calm yourself.

They want us to hesitate here. They want to steer us aside. Spine will then try to board.'

The shaman's face had paled. Sweat beaded his furrowed brow and trickled down across his tattoos. He rubbed at the scar around his missing eye as if it were a fresh wound.

'Afraid of fire, shaman?' Devon shouted over the mountainous rumble of the tracks and the roar of approaching flames.

'We'll roast alive!'

'Only if we stop.'

The Tooth ploughed on into the inferno. Smoke churned and boiled beyond the bridge's forward windows. Embers streamed upwards in spiralling torrents. There was a *snap*, and one of the windowpanes cracked from side to side.

'This is madness,' the shaman hissed.

'Keep calm!'

But smoke was now pouring through the cracked window, billowing across the ceiling. Bataba hunched beside Devon and breathed frantically through his headscarf. Tears streamed from his remaining eye. The Heshette councillors retreated, coughing, to the rear of the bridge.

'Seal that crack!' Devon yelled. 'If they drop gas now . . .'

Bataba relayed the order to a runner waiting by the door. Moments later a tribesman appeared with a tub of thick, grey bone-gum. Flinching back from the heat, he set to work sealing the damaged window.

The Tooth surged on, even deeper into the flames.

Devon started to sweat as the temperature rose, the throttle feeling slick in his palm. His lungs rejected the poisonous air, and he vomited, wiping his mouth on his sleeve. Men were barking orders in the corridors behind them. After plugging the window the tribesman staggered back, gabardine smoking. A runner appeared, muttered something quickly to the shaman, and disappeared. 'A unit of Spine has landed on the roof,' Bataba said. 'They tried to get in through the rear stairwell. They have been repelled.'

A frantic tapping sound came from somewhere behind, then a shout, 'Bolts!'

Steel barbs rattled against the forward grille like sheeting hail. Further explosions shook the bridge as the warships renewed their bombardment.

Boom, crackle, fizz.

Smoke blotted the view of the Deadsands completely. Tongues of flame licked the scorched glass. The heat grew intolerable. Devon kept the throttle hard forward, squeezing every ounce of power from the Tooth's labouring engines.

Bataba was on his knees, gasping. 'We're burning.'

'The tar they dropped on our hull is burning,' Devon replied. 'It will burn itself out soon.'

But the shaman had a fevered look in his eye. 'We have to turn back,' he cried. 'Try another path.'

'No,' Devon said. 'We're not stopping. We're almost through.'

'Turn back!'

'Control yourself. Look!'

Through a break in the smoke they saw Deepgate's army marching. A forest of spears. Armour and shields flowed towards them like a tide of molten metal. The blackened bones of mangonels and scorpions stood out against the fire-lit smog behind. Even now, siege engineers were igniting the payloads on the mangonels, winding tension into the great bows of the scorpions. Closer, riders surged in from the flanks and loosed crossbow bolts that pinged and shattered against the window grille.

And then they were out of the fire, and into cool, dark sand. Drums began to beat a low, steady rhythm.

Boom. Boom. Boom.

A bugle piped. The scorpions unleashed their spines. Iron-tipped shafts smashed against the hull a heartbeat later. Devon felt the throttle shudder in his grip.

'Runner!' Bataba yelled.

'Dawnside breach,' came the frantic reply. 'The hatch is off.'

'Fix it!'

'Don't touch those shafts,' Devon shouted above the din. 'If they aren't on fire, they're saturated with poison.'

The shaman shouted the order but a second barrage from the scorpions drowned out any acknowledgement. Drums pounded; deeper, faster.

Boom. Boom. Boom.

The tar on the hull had almost burned away. Through the charred glass Devon saw a boiling sea of armour, of spiked and visored helms, glittering swords and shields. Spears rippled as far as the horizon. Banners of black and gold snapped in the wind. Warships lit the sky with frenzied flashes of aether-light.

Boom. Boom. Boom.

At another cry from the bugle, a battery of mangonel arms came up with a thunk. Burning barrels and huge clay pots arced upwards, trailing smoke and tails of flame. A sound like a sigh filled the air. From the corner of his eye Devon saw Bataba back away.

'Grab hold of something,' he warned.

He didn't turn to see if the shaman obeyed. Suddenly

pitch and phosphor exploded ahead of them and bleached the forward windows. The bridge shuddered.

Devon felt the engines skip a beat. He eased the throttle then pushed forward hard. Bataba shot him a stern glance. Devon returned it warily. The Tooth juddered and lurched, then resumed its steady, rumbling progress. But something was wrong: the engine sound was coarser now, stuttering.

Teams of engineers were using hoists to reload the scorpions and mangonels, ratcheting the range adjusters, igniting heavy drums with dripping torches. A thousand silhouetted figures crowded the ridge before the city, black against the burning horizon. Behind the marching infantry, strings of bowmen dipped arrows into trenches of flaming pitch, raised them high and loosed them. Countless yellow arcs cut through the sky and fell, whining, before exploding against the Tooth's hull.

The engines stuttered again, seemed to pause, then lurched back to something less than full power.

'What's wrong?' Bataba demanded.

'The engine is overheating.'

'Can you fix it?'

'No time.'

Crackle. The scorpions discharged their spines once more, and moments later the heavy shafts pummelled the huge machine. *Crack, crack, crack.* Devon flinched at the successive impacts. Panicked shouting came from the corridors behind, then screams of agony. The Heshette had found and touched the poisoned, serrated spines.

'I told you to keep them away from those things,' Devon growled.

'They've breached through to the inner walls. The corridors are blocked!'

'Then cover them before you try to remove them!'
Sssssss.

A second volley of flaming arrows swept up, arced, and
fell like a shower of stars. Then the archers withdrew
and broke aside to the east and west. Hundreds more
infantry poured forward from behind. They were pushing
siege-towers. To the sides, heavy cavalry raced to join the
advance cavalry. A barrage of crossbow bolts lanced up
from both units. Devon could hear the infantry now, the
crunch of armoured boots, the rumble of massive siege-
tower wheels.

'We're now inside ballistic range,' he cried. 'The troops
will engage.'

Boom, boom, boom. The drums quickened.

'Archers on the roof!' Bataba shouted. 'Prepare to repel
boarders.'

The Tooth jolted, dipped forward, groaned, and
slowed.

'Trenches,' Devon said. He slammed the throttle back
to full. Engines screamed. Bolts and arrows smashed to
fragments against the window grille. The Tooth levelled,
tilted back, then slewed sideways. Curtains of sand sprayed
over the advancing infantry.

But the machine began to climb, Deepgate's war drums
thumping like its own heartbeat.

A tide of shields and spears broke around them. Grapples flew up from all sides. The Tooth struggled free of
the trench. Devon blinked sweat from his eyes and
knocked back a lever with his stump. The cutting arms
lowered with a furious hiss. 'Mow them down you said.'

'For Ayen!' the shaman cried.

Devon grinned, and activated the cutters.

The engines hacked once, twice, and died.

The Tooth jerked to a halt.

A sudden silence filled the bridge, as though every man in the Tooth and the army outside had paused. Devon turned to Bataba, his face bloodless. 'The propeller shaft,' he said. 'Get your men down there to fix it or we're dead.'

'How soon can it be repaired?'

'Not soon enough.' Devon rose from his seat. 'Fetch the priest.'

Below them, Deepgate's army charged.

Carnival backed away from the abomination. Her hand moved to the rope scar on her neck as though pulled there by some dark memory. 'Will I kill it?' she breathed.

'Someone already has,' Rachel said. 'A long, long time ago.' She found it hard to believe the thing was even standing.

Most of the angel was still there, but it leaned at an awkward angle, resting its weight on one leg. The other leg was withered and stunted, more bone than flesh. Three fingers remained on one hand, one finger on the other. Strips of intestine hung from its abdomen where leathery patches of skin – or perhaps just leather – had burst. Its yellow eyes were lidless and appeared to bulge, giving the creature an almost comical expression. It sucked air through a gap where its nose should have been. There was not a single feather on its wings, just tattered gooseflesh.

It was the most pitiful, wretched thing Rachel had ever seen, and yet she had a strong sense that Carnival was afraid of it.

Will I kill it? It was almost as if Carnival had asked for *approval*, but when did she ever need to ask anything of anyone?

'I'd be doing it a favour.' Carnival's voice trembled.

'No,' Rachel said.

The dead angel watched Carnival for some moments and it did not move. Then suddenly it bobbed its head back and forward, held out a closed fist, and said, 'Shing.'

Carnival flinched.

'Shing!'

'We don't understand,' Rachel said.

Mr Nettle had retreated a few steps back and was watching the dead angel warily. Evidently he had decided this wasn't Abigail.

'Shing!' The dead angel pushed its clenched hand again at Carnival.

'It's trying to give you something,' Rachel said.

'Shing!'

Carnival extended her hand and the angel dropped something into it.

'What is it?' Rachel stretched over to see.

Carnival held up the object: an ugly bone ring, somewhat chewed.

The dead angel lifted its chin. 'Shing,' it repeated, then shaped its mouth into something that might have been a grin, before it turned away and folded itself back through the door.

'Do you still want to kill it?' Rachel asked.

Carnival had paled. For a moment, she looked lost, confused. And then her expression darkened and, to Rachel's horror, the hunger was back in her eyes. 'Why the hell not?' Carnival said, and stooped to follow the other angel through the doorway.

Rachel grabbed for her, but hesitated. She had noticed Carnival slip the ring onto her finger. 'Come on,' she hissed to Mr Nettle.

Beyond the door a sweating red-rock passageway sank before them, and then rose again a short distance ahead. The dead angel paused at the bottom, beckoned to them. 'Grog,' it said. 'Ussis.' Then it turned and loped away.

'Did it just say what I think it did?' Rachel frowned.

Carnival stared after the monstrosity, her expression dark, and made no response.

'I suggest we head the other way.'

The scarred angel's fists tightened suddenly. She flexed her broken shoulder: bones cracked, and her skewed wing straightened. She grunted, and took off after Shing.

Cursing, Rachel ran after her. Somewhere behind her, Mr Nettle's crutch creaked.

Cressets dripped grease into congealed mounds and milky puddles on the floor. Rachel skipped round those, but the chain between her and Carnival sloshed through them and was soon soaked and glistening. Rachel's hand kept returning to her empty scabbard as she ran. Time was running out.

The red passageway ended at a heavy door. Shing halted, bobbed its head again, and attempted another ghoulish smile before it yanked the door handle. The door moved inwards with a sucking sound. Cold air rushed out and past them, and they stepped through.

Walls of white water thundered down into darkness on either side, forming a tall, misty corridor without floor or ceiling. They appeared to be standing on a ledge high on the wall of a vast cavern. *Or the edge of another abyss?* An ancient chain bridge zigzagged between the waterfalls and vanished thirty yards ahead where a weak red light suffused the mist. At this end the iron spans of the bridge looked weak; in the distance they seemed as delicate as lace. Looking down, Rachel saw nothing but frothing water

If this is hell, what lies below?

'Grog,' Shing said, and bounded on without hesitation.

They moved cautiously. The bridge was treacherously slippery. Rotten beams squelched and broke underfoot, sending fragments tumbling into the dark. Chains steamed and dripped. Rachel's leathers were soon soaked. Ahead, the red light grew steadily brighter, and gradually the deluge of water eased: first to sheets; then trickles like silver ropes; then drips. The mists parted, and they found themselves standing before Ulcis's palace of chains.

Without any visible means of support, the iron palace smouldered like an angry red sun in the darkness; amid a great knot of walkways, stairwells, balconies and platforms all stitched with chains. Huge braziers burned within. There were no walls, but Ulcis's palace was nevertheless a prison. Cages had been woven into the structure or hung from chains and hooks at every level. These were crammed full of people.

The Hoarder of Souls was slumped on a massive throne in the centre of his palace, watching their approach.

'Grog,' Shing said.

'He means god.' Ulcis's voice boomed across the void. 'His vocal cords rotted centuries ago.' He sounded regretful. 'Along with its wings and mind. I patch them up, but when the flesh is full of maggots, what can you do? This one is undoubtedly the worst. It never had the hunger to sustain itself.'

Rachel, Carnival and Mr Nettle stepped off the bridge and ducked inside the confines of the palace chains. The god's throne sat on a dais in the centre of a broad platform, surrounded by the numerous suspended cages. A carpet of bones covered the floor around him. Rachel loosened the leather straps around the burner and poison-song bolts at her hip. Cages creaked overhead and cold, hungry eyes turned to follow their progress.

'They are agitated,' said Ulcis. 'They smell meat.'

'Grog,' Shing said.

Ulcis reached down, plucked a bone from the floor, and threw it at Shing. It missed, skittered off the platform, then slipped between the chains and into the darkness beyond.

Shing bounded after it, but stopped before the edge, its shoulders slumped. 'Grog?'

'One day its survival instincts will fail,' Ulcis hissed, 'and I'll be rid of it for good. The things below this palace would soon tear it to pieces.'

'More of your slaves?' Rachel asked.

'The gates of Iril lie below,' replied the god.

'And what, exactly, is Iril?'

Ulcis smiled. 'Wouldn't you like to know?'

'Grog?'

'Leave!'

The creature hesitated, then bowed awkwardly and lurched back across the bridge.

The god of chains eyed Mr Nettle's crossbow indignantly. 'I suppose this other one is human. Or aspires to be.' His voice sounded like crumbling rocks. 'They *will* keep coming down here, from some implacable need to stand before a god. Great balloons or flying machines with sails, fins and propellers – I've seen it all. A man in a chair tethered to hundreds of sparrows, trailing feathers.' He made a dismissive gesture. 'I had the chair repaired.'

'This is Mr Nettle,' Rachel said, 'and he didn't come to stand before anything. He's looking for his daughter.'

'Have you seen her?' Carnival said.

Ulcis's face creased with rage. 'Are you feeling hungry, daughter?' he said. 'That time of the month?' He leaned back, parting his lips in a wet grin. 'How many have you murdered by now? Or have you forgotten them all? Do you remember your last scar? No? But now at least you remember your first.'

'I'll remember the next,' she said.

Rachel clamped a hand on her shoulder. *The chain. Don't forget we're chained.* But Carnival didn't move. She was staring beyond Ulcis's throne. There was movement in the darkness. Through the chains, other angels appeared: a handful at first, and then scores of them. They were in various states of decay, though none looked as bad as Shing. Ragged wings the colour of dust. Scraps of armour – corroded steel or bone plates, strapped over grey muscular torsos; curved swords, spears, maces and recurved bows.

'My lieutenants,' Ulcis announced. 'They remember you, daughter. You were once so pretty.' His voice was loaded with snide implication. 'Flowers and ribbons in your hair, so pretty then. They *all* remember you.'

Ulcis's archons leered at Carnival with such derisive pleasure that Rachel felt a surge of despair, almost panic. She'd seen that look before, on soldiers' faces after Hollowhill had been cleared of Heshette warriors; after the soldiers had been left alone with the women. Rachel had beaten four men unconscious after she found out what they'd done there. She'd beaten them until their faces were pulp, before she'd been dragged away screaming by the Spine.

Rachel's hand tightened on Carnival's shoulder. She could feel the scarred angel's muscles tensing like steel, her fists clenched, her knuckles white. The rope scar at her neck pulsed with each rapid breath. *No!* Rachel wanted to scream at the god. *Don't force her to remember!*

Carnival spoke quietly. 'What did you do to me?'

The god of chains rose, an unfolding landscape of flesh, and unfurled his vast wings. Chains of shadow lashed out behind him. 'Shall I give you those memories back, daughter? When they'd finished with you there was no point in taking your soul. There was nothing left of it to take.'

But Rachel knew that was a lie. Ulcis had tried to destroy his daughter's soul, to crush the humanity he so reviled. Yet he hadn't succeeded. Carnival had buried that part of herself even deeper than the abyss. She possessed her father's hunger and rage, but she still kept her mother's soul.

Carnival slipped off the ring Shing had given her and let it fall to the ground. That small gesture wrung Rachel's heart.

'The syringe,' Ulcis commanded. 'Bring it here.'

One of the angels approached, a creature seven feet tall. Naked bone gleamed where battle-scars had opened up its face, and ribs poked through gaps in its armour. Rachel studied the sword at its hip and the bamboo tube lashed beside it, then she frowned. This bastard was carrying her weapons. It handed Ulcis the Poisoner's syringe, still in the grip of Devon's severed hand.

'You came here for this?' Ulcis said. The hand twitched, tightened its grip further. The god regarded it without apparent interest.

'It's mine,' Carnival hissed, crouching, and the scars on her face contracted.

Rachel heard a creak of bone and glanced back to see Mr Nettle shuffle forward on his crutch. He levelled his crossbow at the god, and stared hungrily at the syringe.

Shit, what's his interest in the angelwine? Then it struck her. *His daughter's soul. So this is about to get very messy.*

No one moved.

The angelwine glittered: a distillation of souls that would restore an angel. Rachel now understood why Carnival had fought so hard to find it. Would it finally cure her hunger? End her torment? Could it remove her scars? Not only the scars she wore on her flesh, but those she carried inside?

That stuff brought Devon back from the brink of death.

And suddenly she realized why Carnival could never be allowed to have it.

Ulcis prised the syringe free from the Poisoner's dead fingers and flung the severed hand at his daughter. 'You may keep this – a gift from me.'

Carnival did not move a muscle, as the severed hand dropped to the floor at her feet, then scuttled away like a fleshy crab. But her scars flared brighter; her eyes darkened to the colour of murder.

Steel rasped, as the dead angels around them unsheathed their swords.

Rachel heard a click.

Ulcis's head snapped back, the hunting crescent buried in his right eyebrow.

Mr Nettle dropped his crossbow and charged.

His improvised splint broke apart, but his momentum still carried him forward, and he slammed into the god with a force that would have brought down a house. The throne pitched backwards, and Ulcis crashed to the ground underneath the scrounger. The entire platform shuddered, tilted; cages lurched and groaned above them. A hundred chains clinked and shivered.

Ulcis roared in anger.

Mr Nettle butted his head into the god's face.

His archons rushed forward to attack.

Carnival pounced.

But Rachel was ready: she grabbed the chain secured to her own ankle, and yanked.

The tightened chain halted Carnival in mid-leap. Her leg jerked back and she hit the ground face-first, snarling.

With one hand, Mr Nettle was wrestling Ulcis for the syringe. With his other fist, he was pummelling the god's face to a bloody mess. The archon nearest drew back its sword to cut him down.

Rachel threw the burner.

It struck the angel square in the forehead and exploded. A ball of flame engulfed the creature. It screamed, stumbled backwards into the archons behind in a cloud of burning feathers.

Mr Nettle had rolled free; his robes were on fire, but he came up on his hands and knees with the syringe in one huge fist.

'Mine!' Carnival leapt to her feet, her face creased with rage and pain.

The scarred angel flew at the scrounger, lashed an elbow down on his skull. The blow connected with bone-crunching force.

Mr Nettle grunted, shook his head once, then surged upright in an eruption of rags and muscle. One arm thrown around her neck, the other across her shoulder, he struggled to push her away. Caught in his awkward embrace, she scrabbled for the syringe, reached it, fumbled.

The glass tube of angelwine fell to the ground, rolled clear in a wide circle. Rachel snatched it up, then ducked as steel sliced the air above her head. Ulcis's lieutenants had closed the gap, and the tall, battle-scarred archon had just taken a swipe at her. With her own sword. Bastard.

'Give it to me, bitch!' Carnival shrieked. She had now disentangled herself from the scrounger and stood a few paces beyond him. 'That belongs to me!'

Still on fire, Mr Nettle wheeled, ran straight at Rachel.

The assassin sidestepped the big man easily, extended a foot. He tumbled head-first into the archon who had attacked her. Both sprawled to the ground, armour and ribs crumpling under the scrounger's weight. Pinned, the archon grunted, and tried to swing its sword.

Her sword.

Rachel ripped it from the angel's grip, then snatched the bamboo tube from the sword belt. And then she was running towards Carnival. 'Follow me! The chain! We're still chained!'

But Carnival's face was nothing but a snarling mask, eyes black with insatiable hunger.

Shit, not now.

As Carnival came at her, Rachel veered sharply, barely managed to duck under the angel's outstretched arms. She punched her assailant twice, once in the neck, the second blow in the shoulder. Carnival collapsed, hissing and spitting like a wildcat.

Too bright for you in here?

'Get up!' Rachel cried. 'The chain.'

A sword thrust to her side. The assassin twisted away. The blade sliced empty air an inch from her belly. Another weapon stabbed at her face. She caught the flat of its blade with the back of her hand, smacked it up, and sank her own sword into the archon's armpit. A yank and her blade was free, then arcing down to intercept the first assailant's rising stroke. Steel clashed, rasped. She spun, kicking the archon full in the face. The blow should have broken its neck. But it *grinned*, and bore down on her again.

Shit!

Behind it, the rest were closing in.

Rachel grabbed a fistful of Carnival's hair, dragging her upright as she ran past. She glanced back to see Ulcis rise and rip the crossbow bolt free of his brow. Blood poured from the wound and from his broken nose, huge chains of indeterminate darkness swirling behind him. Mr Nettle was still wrestling with the battle-scarred archon. He delivered one rock-crushing blow into the creature's face, before it struck him savagely on one temple and managed to throw him off. The scrounger slumped to the floor, unconscious or dead.

Carnival wrenched herself away from Rachel, furious, seemingly mindless of the chain that bound them together or the archons at her back, mindless of anything now but ripping the assassin apart.

'The chain!'

'Give me the syringe!'

Rachel slipped through the chains surrounding the platform, and reached the bridge with the angelwine still in her grip. The prisoners in their cages were howling, rattling the bars. The whole palace shook, as Ulcis's voice thundered after her.

'Kill them.'

Suddenly Rachel was jerked to a halt.

Carnival had found a different path through the complexities of Ulcis's palace. The chain between them was snagged, looped round another chain supporting the palace. Neither angel nor assassin could move forward. Carnival clawed at her, but couldn't reach. Behind her, Ulcis's archons were gaining on them. The fat god himself had joined the pursuit. His palace trembled under his footsteps. Cages creaked and swung all around him.

'Back,' Rachel cried. 'We're caught!'

For the first time, Carnival seemed to notice her manacled ankle. Her eyes traced the links back to where they had become snagged. 'I've got you now, bitch.'

'They'll cut us both down.'

'Not before I rip your heart out. The syringe – give it to me.'

'Behind you!'

Carnival spun about just as a huge archon, its lower face a grinning skull, reached for her. Plates of bone armour shifted as Ulcis's lieutenant swung its mace at her head with sickening force. Carnival ducked, darted inside the dead angel's reach. The mace looped around a palace support chain. Her fist snapped out, and the archon catapulted back, a jagged gap where its teeth had been. The other archons were weaving through the chains to engage.

Cursing, Rachel darted back to help her.

They had now surrounded Carnival: spears jabbed in at her from all sides, swords flashing and sparking on a tangle of chains. Most of the archons were enormous, twice her weight, but Ulcis's daughter was faster than all of them. Her scars seethed blood-red. Her eyes glittered blacker than the abyss itself. Unarmed, she attacked with fists and feet and teeth, and the fury of a thousand Scar Nights.

And she was driving them back.

Unable to find space to deploy their weapons among the chains, Ulcis's archons were retreating.

Rachel snaked through to join her, and thereby freed the snagged chain. 'Now move,' she cried, sliding her sword back into the scabbard on her back.

Panting like an animal, Carnival paused for a heartbeat and glanced around in apparent confusion, before she noticed Rachel and tore after her, yelling, 'Mine! Mine!'

Rachel raced past the thundering waterfalls without further hindrance, and slammed into the opposite entrance. The door burst inwards and she fell through. Carnival was at her heels, still spitting, snarling.

'They're after us, you rabid bitch.' Rachel scrambled away. 'Forget the syringe and move!'

They pounded up a rock-lined passageway. Dark tunnels slipped by on either side.

Which way?

Rachel didn't have time to stop and think. Carnival was close, and behind her sounded the crashing armour of Ulcis's lieutenants. She ploughed on, trusting to blind luck, gripping the syringe like some stolen gem.

Rachel now knew what she had to do with it.

Suddenly she was back in the chamber where they'd encountered Shing, cauldrons bubbling all around her, the butcher's block before her. She was going too fast to stop, so she leapt over it. Her shin struck the edge of the block with a crack of pain, and she fell.

'Mine!' Carnival lunged at her.

Rachel drove her heel into Carnival's neck, knocking the angel backwards into the first of Ulcis's lieutenants to burst into the room.

'Get up!' Rachel yelled, and she heaved at the chain, dragging Carnival along on her back. The angel's wings thrashed. A spear lashed out, struck the floor where her head had been a moment before.

Then they were up and running again.

Into darkness.

Rachel's lantern still hung from her belt alongside the poisonsong and the bamboo tube, but she couldn't light it without slowing down. Was there even any oil left in it? She had no way of seeing where she was going, but she charged ahead regardless, arms outstretched, feet slithering on wet rock.

Carnival's voice came from close behind. 'It's *dark*, Spine.'

Without pausing, the assassin closed her eyes tight and *focused*. Air currents unravelled, crystallized, full of subterranean sounds and smells: the distant chopping of knives, the roar of forges and hammering steel; the scent of cold water and denser odours of clay and minerals. She concentrated, sifted through them, searching for the one she wanted.

There!

Decay.

Rachel forced every scrap of strength from her exhausted muscles and ran faster. Her lungs burned. The odour she sought thickened, pulled her closer to her goal. She reached out her right hand, encountered iron bars, and swung herself into his cell.

'No!' Carnival screamed.

The chain around her ankle suddenly wrenched Rachel's foot out from under her. She thumped to the ground, all the wind knocked out of her. Then she began to claw her way forward, straining against the damned chain.

Sounds of battle behind: the clash of weapons. Ulcis's

archons had caught up with Carnival and Carnival didn't seem happy about it, from the sound of her reaction.

As the chain at Rachel's ankle slackened, she dragged herself further into the cell, searching the ground with fumbling hands.

Feathers.

Stone.

Metal?

Dill's chain mail felt cold and thin, his skin as slick as tallow beneath.

Catch me.

Rachel stabbed the syringe into his chest, pushed the plunger all the way down – and collapsed to the ground, exhausted.

'He's dead,' Carnival howled. 'He's dead, you stupid bitch. You can't save him!'

Torchlight flooded the chamber, as Ulcis's archons massed outside the cell.

'He's dead,' Carnival wailed. 'He's already dead!'

Carnival moved over and lifted Dill's wrist to her mouth. She bit deeply, and sucked, then threw his arm aside. 'Do you see what you've done,' she dropped to her knees, 'you stupid, selfish . . .' She couldn't find the words for her frustration.

Rachel was panting, her arms now hung heavy, empty. She turned at a commotion among the archons gathered outside the cell. They were retreating from the bars. Their master had arrived.

Blood streaked the god's battered face. His massive chest rose and fell from exertion. He said, 'You, my child, have seriously pissed me off.'

Rachel stared up at him, at the bulwarks of flesh, the breasts, the overlapping chins. His eyes glowed like burning coals. In one hand he gripped an enormous iron sword, scraped and serrated from long use. She felt like laughing.

There was a cough behind her. Rachel dragged her eyes away from the obscene god to Carnival, caught her startled expression, and turned to follow her stare.

Dill was sitting up.

31

ON THE BRINK

Devon slammed the cell door open. 'Get up,' he said.

Sypes flinched. The old priest had not moved since the Poisoner had last seen him. He was still lying naked and shivering among the fragments of his walking stick.

'Put this on.' Devon threw the Presbyter's cassock towards him.

Sypes still did not move.

Devon dragged him upright, and thrust the cassock into the old man's arms. 'Wear it. You must be recognizable.'

Without his stick, Sypes had to lean against the wall for support. His thin arms and legs trembled as he pulled the cassock over his shoulders, and let the hem tumble to his feet.

'There,' Devon said. 'Now you look almost human again.'

But that was a lie. There was nothing much human left in the old priest. He was all skin and sinew, mottled with purple and yellow bruises, more corpse than man. The cassock engulfed him, seemed to drag his stooped frame even closer to the ground. Grey eyelids drooped over misty eyes that did not lift to meet Devon's.

The Poisoner had to help him from the cell. He all but carried the old man along the crew quarters companionway and into the innards of the Tooth. Sypes shivered and coughed and his knees buckled constantly, despite Devon's assistance. The priest weighed almost nothing.

By the time they reached the corridor leading to the outer hatches, Sypes had started to drift in and out of consciousness. Devon had to shake him whenever he sensed him fade. 'Just a few more steps, old man. We're nearly there.' The Presbyter mumbled incoherently and batted his hands about as though dismissing invisible servants.

Heshette bowmen packed the hot, cramped corridor. They were loosing off arrows through rents in the hull left by the barrage of scorpion spines, whose serrated shafts had been knocked away and dragged aside to leave room. Piles of them now lay against the inside wall, their poisoned barbs covered in rugs and heavy blankets. Outside, war drums boomed a constant dirge over the clash of steel and the shouts and screams of the attacking army.

'Over here' – Devon dragged Sypes the last few feet – 'by this hatch.'

The hatch door had been ripped away and pitch-smoke wafted through the gaping hole. Two bowmen crouched there, sheltered one at each side, alternately firing arrows along the length of the hull. Outside, burning wood keened and snapped and whistled. Arrows and bolts whizzed and whined and tore screams from their targets. Great wooden wheels grumbled, boots clumped, and hoofs thundered. Over it all, the war drums endlessly beat out the pace of battle. Bataba waited over to one side, half his tattooed features lit up by flames.

'Most of the ladders have been repelled,' the shaman explained. 'But the siege-towers are moving into place and we have no more pitch. We cannot hold them back any longer, so this is your last chance, Poisoner.'

Devon peered outside, then jerked his head back as an arrow smashed to splinters against the wall behind him. Two more followed it in quick succession. He frowned, then grabbed Sypes's cassock and pulled him over, exposing him to view at the open hatch. Firelight washed over the priest's face for an instant, before Devon yanked him aside. Another arrow shot through the gap, and whistled past the old man's ear. Sypes did not appear to notice it. Instead he muttered something about stonemasons.

'There's always one,' Devon muttered. He waited a moment, and then thrust Sypes back to the opening, like a marionette. This time there were no arrows.

A chorus of shouts outside: 'Hold your fire. Hold your fire.'

Bataba echoed the command to his own bowmen. The sounds of battle died. The drums stopped beating.

Devon edged behind the priest and peered over his shoulder.

Fully half of the Tooth's hull was already on fire. Glinting armour and flames seemed to stretch to the horizon. Visored helms looked up at him from the crush of shields. Corpses, peppered with arrows, littered the battlefield. Pockets of flame sent up boiling columns of tar-smoke. Four intact siege-towers loomed black against the bloody sky. Two others were closer, but ablaze; embers raced skywards through their charred skeletons like tiny fleeing souls.

Trumpets sounded and, beyond the main mass of

infantry, scattered units of cavalry regrouped. Three riders broke from the nearest unit and urged their horses forward. Ranks of soldiers parted to let them through.

Devon muttered to Bataba, 'Tell your men to keep their bowstrings slack. Shoot these men and it's all over. We need time.'

The three riders threaded through the army. Devon recognized the insignia emblazoned across the breastplate of the nearest. This was Gullan, sergeant of the cityguard regulars – a tall, broad-shouldered man astride a fierce courser that snapped at foot-soldiers who got too close. The other two, Devon presumed, represented reservist infantry and cavalry divisions. The soldier to Gullan's left wore dented plate and a peaked helm with winged cheek-guards. He carried a shortsword and had a wooden buckler strapped to his left arm. The man to his right wore a chain hauberk over boiled leathers, and rested a light crossbow on his saddle-horn. Gullan sat easily on his courser between them, ignoring the horse's ill temper, his eyes fixed on Devon.

Devon shouted down, 'I have a proposition for Clay.'

Shouts and jeers went up from the nearest foot-soldiers. Gullan raised a hand and the noise died. 'I'll hear it,' he said.

'I'll speak with Clay,' Devon said, 'not his boot boy.'

'I have Captain Clay's authority to parley.'

'Is your leader afraid to approach me himself?'

A score of crossbows lifted at this remark. In response, Devon pushed the Presbyter forward, so that the old man leaned precariously over the edge.

'Hold.' Gullan held his hand out, palm down. Most of the weapons lowered. 'I will escort you to him, Poisoner.'

'Perhaps. Withdraw this army, and I will consider it.'

This caused indignation among the closer ranks of infantry. Swords rattled on shields. Gullan said, 'Say what you need to say, Devon.'

'This is not a matter of need. This is a matter of mutual benefit. Why else have I halted this machine on the brink of Deepgate?'

'The Tooth of God is finished,' Gullan said. 'Its only purpose now will be to serve as your tomb.'

'Shall I start the engines again before we speak further? How many more of your men should I crush before you hear me on equal terms?'

The reservist sergeant with the peaked helm spoke urgently to Gullan. There was a heated exchange between them, and then the regular said, 'Release the Presbyter and we'll talk.'

Devon felt a faint rumble through the floor. He edged Sypes forward an inch. It was a hundred-foot drop to the ground below. The Presbyter made no move to save himself. He remained as slack as a puppet in Devon's grip.

'You wish me to release him?' Devon asked. Then he whispered to Sypes, 'What do you think? Should I release you?'

Another rumble sounded within the Tooth, louder this time.

Sypes frowned down at the army, apparently confused.

'Wake up, old man.' Devon shook him. 'Better for us all if you appear lucid.'

The Presbyter's face tightened. He gazed over the upturned faces of the men beneath him, and blinked. And then he twisted, grabbed Devon's shirt with both hands and pulled hard.

Devon shot out his free arm to grab the lintel above his head, but his stump could grip nothing, and he fell forward, still holding on to Sypes with his good hand. The world swirled under him.

But instead of dropping into the mass of soldiers way below, he thumped against the hull just under the hatch, and swung back out. The Presbyter's cassock had snagged on something. They were both now hanging underneath the hatch. Devon wrapped his damaged arm around the priest's neck, and struggled to get a better grip with the other. Sypes gasped and choked.

Bataba and the two bowmen were pulling on the priest's cassock, trying to heave both men back inside the Tooth. Devon twisted, collided against the hull again and rebounded. Flashes of steel and fire and sky wheeled all around him. The cassock tightened around Sypes's neck till the old man's eyes bulged. His face was turning red but his fists still gripped Devon's shirt.

And then all at once they were being hoisted up, as the Heshette dragged them back inside the Tooth. Sypes lay wheezing on the floor. As Devon rose unsteadily, three crossbow bolts thudded into his chest and knocked him back down with the force of a hammer blow. A fourth caught him in the neck even as he fell. He felt his jawbone shatter. The steel tip jarred into his palate and blood flooded his mouth.

Devon rolled aside as a further shower of bolts and arrows shattered against the wall behind him.

The bowmen in the corridor returned fire.

'Gahh,' Devon croaked, lying on his back on top of the Presbyter. He could feel the wooden shaft lodged in his neck, its end pressing against his chest where the other bolts protruded. Air burbled in his lungs. Grimacing, he ripped the bolt from his throat and threw it away. Agony blossomed in his jaw. 'Gahh . . .' One by one he yanked out the others.

'Da . . . ness take you.' Devon spat blood and hauled himself upright. 'Damn you, Sypes. Tha . . . was sore.'

Presbyter Sypes lay motionless at his feet. None of the missiles had struck him.

'You had better be dead,' Devon growled. 'Tha . . . was unfeasibly—'

The corridor shook as, deep within the Tooth, engines grumbled to life. A roar went up from the bowmen in the corridor, answered by a savage bellow from the troops outside. Bugles and trumpets shrilled renewed orders. War drums began to pound.

'We're moving!' Bataba shouted.

Devon could feel it: the Tooth had begun to crawl forward once more. Its tracks were already crushing a wide path through Deepgate's army. A savage grin split his bloodied face. He felt the elixir answer his wounded body's demands, felt it curl around his lungs and heart – repairing, strengthening – and for a moment he even thought he heard the keening of thirteen souls. He grabbed Sypes by the loose skin of his neck and yanked him to his feet. 'Do you hear it, old man? Do you feel it in those brittle bones of yours? The end now. Everything you've done has led to this.'

Sypes's head lolled drunkenly.

'These deaths are *your doing*, Sypes.'

'Please,' Sypes gasped, 'Alexander . . .'

Devon smashed the priest's head against the hull, once, twice, thrice, until fragments of bone and brain covered the bulkhead. Then he pitched him out of the hatch.

'That damn repair had better hold,' he roared.

Bataba stared at him in shock.

'What?' Devon snapped. 'We're moving, aren't we?'

'It's alive, is it? Good, now we can kill it again.' The god of chains was still fuming. Occasionally he pinched his nostrils and examined the blood on his fingers with a mixture of horror and disbelief.

Rachel couldn't tear her eyes away from Dill as he tried to rise, but flopped back to the floor, where he sat trembling and rubbing his arms. His face was chalk-white on one side, black on the other where the blood had pooled. *And started to decompose.* The stench from him turned her stomach.

Dill reached to pick up his sword and frowned at it, opening and closing his mouth as though struggling to remember the name of the object. A black, swollen tongue slid between his lips. 'Word,' he said. 'Min.'

'Dill?'

No response.

'Dill!'

When he looked at her, Rachel saw that his eyes were colourless, not the sharp white of fear but a misty gelid hue. 'Dill, what do you remember?'

Dill wrapped his arms around himself and his gaze dropped to the empty syringe protruding from his chest. He plucked it out and let it clatter to the floor. Then he stretched out his wings . . . and winced.

Carnival and Ulcis were watching him intently: she with a look of lost hope; he with mounting ire. Swords unsheathed, two of the god's lieutenants blocked the exit from the cell.

Dill was healing fast. As Rachel watched, the bruises on his face paled and his missing feathers grew back with astonishing speed. His eyes seemed clearer than just moments before. He placed a finger inside his mouth and pulled back his lower lip to reveal several missing teeth. The finger came away bloody. 'Cold,' he whispered.

Ulcis sniffed contemptuously, and turned to leave. 'Lock the cell door,' he said. 'Let the freak devour her—'

With a clatter of iron, Carnival suddenly cast a loop of chain around his neck and yanked. The links snapped rigid and jerked the god off his feet. He crashed to his back on the flagstones.

She was at his neck in an instant, twisting the chain tighter. Ulcis gasped, and both archons at the door moved to attack her. But the god held his hand up, and they paused, uncertain.

'I want you to remember this pain,' Carnival hissed.

The god's face contorted with rage. He tried to say something, but Carnival drew the chain even tighter, and all that escaped his throat was a snarl.

'Send them away.' She loosened her grip and let Ulcis suck in a breath. His face bright purple, he tried to reach round for her, his mighty wings thumping for leverage against the floor.

'What do you—?' he began.

'Shut up!' Carnival twisted her fist again. She leaned closer, her teeth an inch from his neck. 'Get rid of those bastards or your head comes off. Then we'll see if you can grow a new one.'

Ulcis slumped, holding up his hands. 'Wait,' he gasped. 'Rebecca—'

The links bit deeper into his flesh. 'My name is Carnival!'

Blood bubbled from the corners of Ulcis's mouth, as veins ridged his neck and his eyes swelled.

The archons edged closer. Rachel slashed the air in front of them with her sword.

'Last chance,' Carnival warned. 'Do you want to see another aeon? Another day?'

Dill had finally found his feet. The bruises on his face had almost disappeared, and his eyes had changed colour. He regarded Carnival for a moment with a pale gold gaze, then turned to Rachel, a slight frown creasing his brow.

'Domestic,' she explained.

Ulcis waved a panicked hand at the archons. They backed off.

'Into the cell opposite,' Carnival growled.

The chain stretched just far enough to allow Rachel to pick up Mr Nettle's keys and lock the door.

'Now go,' Ulcis wheezed. 'Leave me.'

Carnival grinned. 'I won't abandon you like this, Father.' She grabbed his wrist and forced it, struggling, to her mouth. 'Tonight is Scar Night – or had you forgotten?'

The angel bit deeply.

The Poisoner shouldered several bowmen aside, then headed up stairs, past runners, warriors and wounded, through the cacophony of booming drums and clashing metal, rumbling engines and screams.

When he reached the bridge, he was in no better mood. He glowered at the Heshette councillors assembled, batted their questions aside with his stump, then slumped heavily into his control seat to peer out of the cracked and blackened windows.

Dawn turned the scene outside into an inferno. A

handful of churchships hung in the smoke, like angry red welts in a poisonous sky. Deepgate troops broke in waves against the now static cutters, falling over each other to scramble away from the advancing Tooth. Knots of Spine among them kept loosing off bolts in a concentrated assault on the bridge windows. Scores of men disappeared beneath the great machine. Some managed to jump up to the cutting arms and hang there. Many others tried and failed.

'Mow them down, you said,' Devon snarled.

Bataba did not answer. The shaman had withdrawn to the far edge of the bridge, his face pinched and ashen.

Devon slammed a lever forwards and the sharpened cogs began to turn. Most of the men on the cutting arms dropped quickly into the scoop below or were crushed beneath the Tooth's revolving tracks. A few held on longer, but as the cogs quickened they too were thrown back against the hull or down into the panicked mass of soldiers desperate to escape. The Tooth drove mercilessly over them all.

He banked the great machine to the left to intercept an abandoned siege-tower. The whirring cutters connected and ripped the structure into a cloud of splinters. Men leapt clear or died; a bloody mist fell over the jostling infantry. Devon resumed his southerly course, steering the machine up the ridge surrounding the abyss. Iron groynes broke under the Tooth's tracks with hollow booms, and all at once Deepgate appeared before them.

The city looked as Devon had seen it on countless mornings before: the dusty shambles of wood and tin of the League; the curved shadow thrown by the eastern scarp; the pool of smog over the Scythe, pierced by chimneystacks, cranes and mooring spines; clumped tenements furrowed by endless winding lanes. And above it all, wreathed in mist, rose the temple. Gaslights still glimmered weakly among the chains. Had anyone bothered to evacuate the city? Devon doubted it. Deepgate had always been a place to die.

The cutters were a churning blur beneath him. Cogs hummed and ticked and sent nervous vibrations through the bridge. Devon eased the Tooth to a halt, just yards from the edge, his eyes fixed on the city before him. He clicked a short lever back.

Bataba edged closer.

'This is what you want?' Devon asked.

'For Ayen,' the shaman whispered.

The cutting arms extended. Devon eased back another handle. Spinning blades lowered and ripped through a clutch of peripheral timber shanties. The houses exploded into shards of wood and tin. A soft ripping sound, and then the cutters bit into a foundation chain with a metallic shriek. Sparks geysered, cascading over the rooftops of the League two hundred yards away.

The foundation chain parted with a colossal crack. It collapsed and sagged among skewed streets and walkways, and then the League of Rope gave way like so much dry wood. Lesser chains snapped under the additional strain, cables broke and whipped free, and the great chain itself ripped a path through the city. Flames bloomed along both sides of the rent as gas lines tore open. Half a thousand buildings toppled, then slipped into the abyss. At the heart of Deepgate, the temple shook and tilted.

'Man or god.' Devon manoeuvred the Tooth around the rim towards the next foundation chain. 'Whatever Ulcis may be, this ought to get his attention.'

★

They left Dill's cell and for some time followed a sequence of gloomy passages before emerging at the mountain of bones below the abyss. The hunger had left Carnival's eyes; in its place shone something Rachel had never witnessed in the angel before. *Not peace, but perhaps . . . something akin to calm.* Carnival was drenched in blood, but she bore no fresh wounds. Her father's death had not, it seemed, grieved her.

Of the scrounger there was no sign. Rachel hoped the big man was still alive, that somehow he had escaped the Palace of Chains.

Dill stood to one side, quietly regarding the city of Deep. The forges were now silent. Ulcis's army had stopped making weapons and now seemed utterly confused, wandering listlessly through Deep's sculpted hollows and passages. Thousands of tapers winked in the gloom, threw long shadows over the slopes of bones.

Dill turned as Rachel approached, but his expression didn't change.

She held up her lantern. 'Are you strong enough to fly?' Physically, he seemed fine, but there was a faraway look in his eyes. One hand rested lightly on the sword at his hip.

'Where am I?' he asked.

'Do you remember *anything*?'

'Something.' He studied the chain linking Rachel and Carnival. It lay in a blood-soaked coil between them. 'Why are you two chained together?'

'Tradition.' Rachel shrugged. 'Do you remember my name?'

No answer.

'Rachel,' she said. 'And this is Carnival.' But if he recognized them, it didn't show.

Carnival was staring straight up, her head tilted to one side.

A whine, a rush of air and, thirty yards away, something huge fell from the darkness above and hit the mountain of bones with a colossal *crump*. Bones flew everywhere.

Rachel jumped, grabbing Dill's sleeve, and scanned the darkness overhead. Her sword was now in her hand, although she didn't remember drawing it. Strips of tin roofing floated down like enormous leaves. 'Was that a house?' she gasped.

Carnival nodded. 'More are on their way down.' She wiped blood from her mouth. 'A lot more.'

32

DEEPGATE FALLS

Dill lifted Rachel upwards from the mountain of bones while all around them a city fell from the sky.

Stones and beams and mortar rained down. Entire houses dropped past, shedding slates from their roofs, before punching massive craters in the brittle slopes below. Spans of chain and cable tumbled like deadly gossamer. Arched bridges and chain bridges and fluttering walkways smashed to fragments amidst jagged sections of cobbled street.

Most of this debris was ablaze. Tangles of timber and rope trailed smoke and embers. Showers of sparks and burning coals fizzed and whined, burst and scattered off the abyss walls.

They struggled skywards through the onslaught. Rachel clung tightly to Dill's shoulders, while Carnival shadowed them, as far as the chain between them would allow.

Dill watched it all with awe. Memories kept flashing in his head when familiar objects fell past, disconnected images that he couldn't weave together into anything that made sense. He recalled stone corridors, worn steps, dusty stained glass; twilight lengthening over a vast desert of rose-coloured sand.

Had he seen this city before, from another viewpoint? Spread out in a great bowl below him, pale avenues and walled gardens, clumps of rooftops and chimneys? He was standing somewhere high, crisp morning air on his face. In his bones he recalled the sonorous clang of a bell. *The Church of Ulcis?*

The chain at Rachel's ankle snapped taut when Carnival jerked aside as an old cistern dropped past them, emptiness booming inside it. It brushed her wing dangerously close. She hissed, 'The whole city is coming down.'

'Careful,' Rachel said. 'I don't need a feather trinket hanging from my ankle.'

Carnival grunted.

The falling debris grew thicker. A stone tower roared by, lights blazing in its windows as if the occupants were still busy within. Gas lamps and girders shot past like spears. A rusted bridge, dragging chains, tumbled into the depths, spinning end over end like a huge discarded toy. Pillars, arches and chunks of wall, some with windows or chimneystacks intact. A horse, still harnessed to a merchant's cart, whinnied and kicked the air as it plummeted.

Against this onslaught, they beat harder up towards the light, through clouds of dust and rainbow-laced curtains of water. Grit peppered Dill's head and shoulders, brought tears to his eyes. While Rachel buried her face in his shoulder, he kept his gaze fixed above, alert for anything that might strike them.

The smaller objects were almost impossible to avoid. Shards of glass, falling in glittering showers, tore their clothes and their skin. Broken tiles and fragments of wood pummelled them. Dill spun and twisted, dropped back and weaved through this deluge, endlessly trying to avoid the worst of it. Carnival followed their progress, the chain dancing between herself and the assassin.

Deepgate? Dill's memories surfaced with the name. The foundation chains; the League; the Warrens. He saw himself on a high balcony ringing a turret, remembered his cell beneath the belfry. *A chipped tile floor. Sunlight glimmering through a glass angel.*

His home? He was going home.

'This dust.' Rachel coughed into his shoulder. 'I can't see anything through it until it's almost upon us. Is there anything left of the city above?'

Dill squinted through the dust clouds. Chains hung like torn webs from at least a quarter of the city, leaving a gap through which he could discern blue sky. Flames flickered around the damaged edges and, even as he watched, another mass of buildings sagged towards them and broke free.

He shouted back to Carnival, 'Head there, over there! Less dangerous. The districts there have already come down.' Then he whispered into Rachel's ear, 'Some of the foundation chains have gone. From the edge to the hub, everything around them has been lost.'

'The temple?'

'I can see it.' Right there in the centre, a burning halo surrounded the Church of Ulcis.

'We would have heard it drop,' Carnival growled. 'That many wailing priests.'

Gradually the city grew nearer. Fresh showers of water occasionally drenched them, momentarily clearing the dust and smoke until it felt like they were flying through thunderheads. The air seemed to crackle and course with violent energy. Hairs rose on Dill's arms and on the back of his neck.

A roar and, a hundred yards away, an entire street ripped past, its houses ablaze, disintegrating into plumes of rubble. An old stonewood tree tumbled after it, its gnarled branches reaching out amid flailing chains. Carnival watched its descent. In the fleeting firelight, Dill saw a look of grim detachment on her face.

'We have to move faster,' she said. 'Ulcis's archons are free.'

'How many?' Rachel whispered.

'Fifty or more,' Dill said, after gazing into the depths. 'They're gaining fast.' He beat his wings with all of his strength. Carnival groaned in protest and lashed after them in pursuit.

Rachel drew the bamboo tube from her belt and popped open its lid. A musty odour emerged from inside; accompanied by a strange scratching sound. She closed it again quickly. 'Tell me when they get near,' she shouted. 'I can't see well enough.'

Now there were people visible among the debris: ragged men, women and children, tumbling head over foot, garments rippling. Screams and cries filled the abyss. One woman clutched an infant in her arms; its wail tapered away to nothing.

Beneath them the archons had drawn their swords. They circled as they rose, sweeping like great grey hawks through the falling debris.

'How close now?' Rachel asked.

'Close enough,' Dill replied.

'Take this, then.' She handed the tube to Dill. 'Open it and throw it in the face of the first one that gets near us.' Then, gripping Dill's waist between her legs, she leaned outwards and pulled her sword free.

Dill examined the tube. 'What's in here?'

'Hookfleas.'

A battle cry went up from the archons, as the closest moved to attack.

'Above!' Carnival shouted suddenly.

Dill glanced up just in time. He dived aside to avoid an iron spike as large as a temple spire.

'The Scythe!' Rachel cried. 'The shipyards are coming down.'

Massive iron skeletons thundered past. Mooring spines, gantries and cranes, huge winches and pulleys and rusted hooks, nets of blackened cable and chain. An iron funnel, belching smoke, thumped against the roof of a warehouse with a mighty boom that shook the abyss from side to side.

'We can't—' Rachel broke off and cried out in pain, as the chain confining her ankle tightened and her leg was jerked down savagely. Carnival had been forced to dive out of the path of a spitting furnace. They lost considerable height and suddenly were among their pursuers.

An archon with a cadaverous grin reached out and grabbed Dill by the ankle; sank its nails deep into his flesh. Rachel's sword drove down, aimed for the attacker's elbow. But the winged creature avoided her blow easily. It slipped away, leering, brought a scimitar up to strike.

Dill emptied the bamboo tube directly in its face.

Hookfleas burst from the tube with a chittering sound. The archon howled, dropped its sword, and began clawing at its face. The fleas had already burrowed into its flesh, were bubbling under its grey skin. Blood-smeared bone gleamed through rips opening in its cheeks and forehead.

'They'll burrow on into the brain and nest there,' Rachel shouted. 'It won't die for a while, if it can still remember how to fly.'

A second archon threw itself at Carnival's back, sword aiming for a point between her shoulder blades. The scarred angel spun, lifted a strand of the chain to parry. Steel struck iron. Sparks flew.

Rachel cried a warning.

Carnival recoiled as a brick wall plummeted between herself and her opponent. When windows rushed by, she lashed out half a dozen lightning blows through them, smashing glass each time. Then the wall was gone, leaving the archon hovering dazed and toothless. Carnival kicked the creature in the face and it tumbled away, snarling.

But the others were still closing, more than forty of them now. Huge wings pounding, they weaved through the onslaught of falling debris. The closest dived at Rachel and Dill, who drew his own sword. Did he even know how to use it? It felt so awkward in his hand. He threw the empty tube at the archon, but missed. The creature grinned triumphantly, then disappeared as a cargo hook slammed into it from above. Feathers skirled down after it.

'This is too much,' Rachel shouted to Carnival. 'Stay close to us. The chain . . . If something hits it . . .'

Dill swerved again, as the corner of a blazing building whoomphed by. Smoke engulfed them, and suddenly they were spinning, tumbling blind through turbulent, choking air.

'That was a warehouse!' Rachel yelled. Which meant the heavy industrial buildings that had once bordered the Scythe were falling now: factories and warehouses, foundries and mills, burning, booming, breaking apart. Monstrous chains thundered into the depths, slicing through clouds of seething smoke and dust. A knotted cluster of workers' shanties struck a crane and burst into planks and coils of rope.

A scarred archon in rusted half-plate armour engaged Carnival briefly, its spear flickering like a snake's tongue. Carnival was grinning back through her own scars. She fought with an arm span of chain, first snapping it taut to deflect the blows, then whipping it into her opponent's face. Three blows to counter every thrust her attacker made, soon reducing his face to shreds. She grabbed at the spear and kicked the archon in the shoulder, spinning it round. Carnival flipped the spear point over, drove it deep between the archon's wings.

An arrow hissed past Dill's ear. 'Archers!' he warned, pointing wildly in the direction the arrow had appeared from.

Carnival flung herself away in that direction.

'Wait,' Rachel cried – but Carnival was too lost in the frenzy of battle to remember the chain. Before Dill could react, Rachel was pulled free from his grip. Suddenly he was weightless. Alone.

Carnival shrieked as Rachel's weight yanked her from her course, and dragged her a dozen fathoms down before she adapted to the strain and clawed back some height.

Ulcis's lieutenants attacked as one.

Those level with Dill, a dozen or more, dived at Carnival herself. A score more beat up from below to where Rachel swayed like a pendulum. Swords, spears, cutlasses and sabres closed in like fangs.

'Spine,' Carnival yelled, 'make yourself useful.' She grabbed the chain at her ankle, then shifted her weight back, her wings thrashing at the air. Then she began to circle slowly, swinging Rachel beneath her.

Rachel looped her free leg around the chain, thrust out her sword.

Carnival increased her speed, circling over the assassin, then she dropped lower and leaned back into her wings. The muscles on her neck corded as she strained against the weight of the chain.

'Faster!' Rachel cried from below.

Wings lashing, quickening her rotations, Carnival pulled even harder on the chain. Rachel gained speed, drew level, and began to spin around her like a living mace.

From fathoms above, Dill watched them breathlessly.

The assassin's sword carved a bright circle through the surrounding darkness, once, twice, thrice around Carnival before it found the first of Ulcis's archons. As Rachel's blade ripped through it, the grey-skinned creature did not have time to scream. A cloud of blood and feathers followed the divided halves of its corpse into the abyss.

Teeth set grimly, Carnival was now using Rachel's momentum to increase their speed. Round and round the assassin spun, faster and faster, until the links taut between them sang and her sword seemed like a ring of steel.

Rachel clove another angel from shoulder to stomach, severed the wing of a third. Above, below, around, she whirled, her blade trailing arcs of blood. And all the while she was *parrying*, deflecting blows with astonishing speed. Steel clashed and sparked and flickered around her.

But it wasn't enough. Her opponents were faster. They swooped around the assassin, searching for a way past the whirring chain and blade. A hulking dust-coloured angel threw its spear, managed to catch Rachel's shoulder. As she cried out, Carnival bit hard against the spin, and swung Rachel over her head and back down with brutal force. The assassin smashed into the same archon, impaling it on her sword, and then she was torn free again.

Dill watched rapt. At the end of the chain, Rachel was spinning so fast he couldn't see her clearly. How could she still remain conscious? Blood flew in circles from her blade. Sparks and embers spiralled in a raging vortex behind her. Ulcis's angels were everywhere, thirty or forty of them, swerving, veering, circling. Parrying her blows, wounding her, they were going to tear her to pieces.

And, all around, the city fell. Great smouldering beams and crosses of iron. Chains, buttresses, turrets and scaffolding. Catwalks and stairwells, gutters and gables. Houses that spewed smoke, roared, and split apart among fizzing torrents of glass, cobbles and tiles.

The darkness deepened. And Dill glanced up.

A pendulum house the size of a warship filled the sky, three storeys of chain-wrapped stone and buckled iron plate. It would hit them full on.

He screamed, 'Carnival!'

She saw it, too.

Carnival heaved Rachel around one more time, and then folded her wings flat against her back. The assassin's momentum threw her beyond the circling archons, jerked Carnival after her. She only just made it as, inches behind, the pendulum house smashed into Ulcis's archons – and they were gone.

The city of Deepgate listed above him, torn open from edge to axis. Buildings swung below the temple from a score of foundation chains, still wrapped in tangles of lesser chains and cables. Fires raged across half the sky and motes of soot and embers fell like burning snow, but the sun was still visible through the dust-shrouded rent.

Ulcis's angels were nowhere to be seen – one way or another, they had returned to the depths.

Carnival was waiting for him, with Rachel in her arms. The assassin's body was covered in wounds, glistening red through countless gashes defacing her dusty leathers. Her head rested on the scarred angel's shoulder and her sword arm hung slack, the blade still dripping blood. She showed no sign of movement.

But as Dill's approaching wings blew dust around her face, she looked up wearily and smiled.

'How do you feel?' he asked.

'Dizzy,' she whispered.

He returned her smile. Then he glanced at Carnival. Dust enveloped her face and arms, covering her scars. She looked exhausted, but her eyes seemed a shade lighter than he remembered, and he was struck by the strange thought that she was pretty. He opened his mouth to speak.

'Save it,' the other angel said.

They flew on up – through the broken city and into sunlight.

As if a floodgate in Dill's mind had been opened, the memories of his previous life rushed back. He remembered clinging to a weathervane, turning with the wind under a darkening sky. He remembered circling his cell, carefully planting candles. Had he been so afraid of the dark?

He couldn't now think why.

He recalled priests in black robes shuffling through dim spaces; a vaulted corridor where the bones of his predecessors looked down from tall pillars; and Presbyter Sypes, muttering and grumbling, but unfailingly kind; also Bore-lock's whip; Adjunct Crumb's perfume.

Where were they all now?

Everything he knew was being destroyed. Deepgate was in ruins. One quarter of the city had fallen. Chains, cables and ropes hung from the edges where structures had been ripped away. Whole streets dangled over the yawning abyss. Just then, there was a mighty rumble and part of Lilley crumbled and fell. Fire engulfed the districts sur-rounding it, blackened chains interknitting with smoke. The temple itself tilted ominously, like a thin, cloaked figure bending to peer into a hole at its feet.

On the eastern perimeter of the abyss stood a vast machine the likes of which Dill had never seen. It was ablaze, funnels disgorging angry smoke from the summit of its yellow and black streaked hull. At its base long jointed arms held whirring cogs against one foundation chain, spraying sparks across the city. Deepgate's armies were pouring around this behemoth, inching siege-towers and ladders closer. Warships harried it from above with waterfalls of burning pitch and showers of bolts.

'Devon,' Rachel said.

Carnival studied the devastation. 'The bastard cut down my tree.'

Clouds of smoke rose over Deepgate and lifted the three of them up among the fleet of churchships. Mission-aries stood on the decks, gaping down, but their airships made no move to engage the Tooth. They seemed to buzz through the smoke without purpose.

Rachel's gaze moved between the churchships and the streets below. 'Those cowards could at least help them evacuate. They're doing *nothing*.'

Refugees were leaving Deepgate in droves. Crowds

packed the streets in creeping, shuffling lines. Many carried their possessions with them, or drove donkeys laden
with furniture, crates and barrels. Thousands had already
descended upon the army encampment, where a frantic
lieutenant was shouting orders, ushering the refugees
through the lines to where the camp encroached upon the
desert. But thousands more were moving in the opposite
direction, converging on the temple at the centre of the
stricken city. Streams of people tried to filter past each
other, till streets were either congested or completely
blocked and fights were breaking out everywhere.

Four heavy-set workers, en route to the temple, were
cutting their way through a family trying to escape the
other way. The wife was screaming over the fallen body of
her husband. More casualties choked the lane behind,
where a horse bucked and kicked among the jostling
crowd.

'Someone should tell them what's down there in the
pit,' Rachel said. 'They wouldn't then be so keen to get to
the temple.'

Carnival grunted. 'They'd only hate you for it.'

They flew over the clogged lanes of the Warrens and
high above the League of Rope, where fires raged far
beyond the edges of the rent. When they reached the
mountain-sized machine itself, they paused.

Battle raged below. Sappers were attacking the tracks
of the machine with rams and lances, dragging beams
from broken siege-towers nearer. Meanwhile soldiers
advanced, shields upheld, striving to reach ladders planted
against the hull. Dozens of men fell under arrow fire.
Grapples flew up, but most failed to find purchase on the
smooth surface and clattered away.

Dill and his two companions descended. From the roof of the machine, a stairwell brought them down to a hatch.

Inside, resistance was heavy, yet the scarred angel and the assassin dispatched the men they encountered with appalling efficiency. Both the chain that united them and the sword glistened freshly with blood by the time they reached the bridge.

Devon was hunched over a skeletal contraption, shifting levers, his attention fully on events outside. A bearded man with a heavily tattooed face stood to one side. When he saw them, his single eye widened in surprise and he murmured a warning to the Poisoner.

'Please come in,' Devon said, without turning. 'I'll be with you in a moment.' He pushed and pulled a few more levers before he turned to face them.

Outside, the grinding of metal ceased, the cutters lifting into view before the bridge windows.

'This is Bataba.' Devon indicated the bearded man. 'Heshette shaman and leader of those you slaughtered on the way in.' He eyed the fresh blood on Rachel's sword. 'I tried to warn him when we saw you approach. Providing you with an escort would have been less messy.' He gave a little shrug. 'Now he is angry, of course, and no doubt blames me.'

He made a dismissive gesture. 'On the day Deepgate falls, an angel, a leech, and an assassin rise from the pit.' He looked from one to the other, before his gaze finally settled on the chain between Carnival and Rachel. 'Scar Night must have been interesting.'

'Why are you doing this?' Rachel lowered the point of her sword to the floor. With her other hand she slipped the hood off the poisonsong bolt at her hip.

Devon snorted. 'It's what they want. Look.' He punched his stump at the window. 'The faithful are converging on the temple. The faster I cut, the more eager they become.'

'Half the city is trying to escape.'

'And if they do escape, I won't pursue them. I'm not unreasonable.'

'Ulcis is dead,' Rachel said. 'His archons are dead. There's nothing left down there.'

Devon raised an eyebrow. 'You found some evidence of that?' He seemed unconvinced. 'A tomb?'

'I drank him,' Carnival said.

Devon frowned, cupped his chin in his hand. His eyes flicked from Carnival to the floor and back. Then he looked up, amused. 'You drank him?' There was now an edge of uncertainty in his voice. 'You drank a god?'

'I could manage another,' she said.

Dill sensed blood in the air, the pressure of violence, like water building behind a dam ready to burst. And in response he felt something building inside himself, a force pushing back. Hadn't there been enough blood spilled? Too many lives already lost? He'd had enough. 'No,' he said firmly. 'No more killing.' He faced Carnival. 'Let him go. Let them all leave.'

'I think it's beyond that now,' Devon said, not unkindly.

'Enough!' Bataba snarled. He grabbed Devon's shoulder, swung him round. 'The city – finish it.'

Rachel said, 'There's nothing underneath Deepgate but bones, shaman.'

'Bones!' Devon laughed. 'What am I supposed to do with bones?' But his gaze then fixed on the freshly healed wounds on Dill's chest. 'The angelwine,' he said, 'you found it?'

'Dill died,' Rachel explained. 'It revived him.'

'Died?'

'I'm afraid I left your hand behind.'

Dill was stunned. *He had died?* His memories were now crystallizing. He remembered the fight on the mountain of bones, the pain in his chest before he blacked out. And then he remembered waking in the dark cell. Was there anything between?

Something . . .

A void, darkness. But he had a sense that this darkness cloaked other memories, lurking there just out of reach. 'How long was I dead?' he asked.

'Days,' Rachel said. 'Maybe a week. I don't know.'

'What do you remember?' Devon asked.

'Darkness.'

'That's it?'

Dill tried to shake the fog from his head. There *was* something else. A dream of shadows moving. Had there been a glimmer of light? Voices?

Devon frowned. 'That is not good enough.'

Behind him, Bataba suddenly leaned across the skeletal controls, reached for a lever. 'None of you,' he shouted, 'have any faith!'

The Poisoner wheeled. 'What? No—' He reached for the shaman's sleeve to stop him, but his stump was unable to find purchase. Bataba clicked the lever forward.

Engines roared.

Devon and the shaman were now struggling, fighting over the controls. The Tooth lurched, tipped forward, and suddenly they were over the precipice and falling.

33

POISONSONG

There was a moment of confusion, when Rachel found herself flat against the bridge windows, then pitched back fiercely as the chain at her ankle snapped taut. She struck the rear wall and air burst from her lungs.

A juddering groan from outside. The Tooth rocked, slipped, and settled upside down. The huge machine had been snared, barely, in Deepgate's remaining web of chains. Through cracked windows in the wall opposite Rachel saw the mighty links of a foundation chain among the tangle, and pitch darkness below it. One of the links had been half-sheared by the machine's cutters.

The partly sheared link was opening, stretching.

Carnival and Dill had been thrown into opposite corners of the bridge, and were now picking themselves up, dazed. The Heshette shaman lay unmoving between them. Devon was hanging from the control bank fixed to what had now become the ceiling.

Rachel heard the snap of cables and chains, and the Tooth lurched, slipped a fathom. The foundation chain groaned, the sheared link opening further. Rubble showered past the windows.

Devon swung above her, cursing, as she dragged herself

to her feet and staggered over to the windows, calling out to Carnival, 'Help me break the glass.'

Carnival and Dill joined her, while Rachel smashed her sword hilt against the scorched pane. When it didn't break, she tried again harder, putting every ounce of her strength into the blow. Nothing happened. 'What the hell is this made from?' she cried.

'Let me.' Carnival took the sword and struck the window a vicious blow with it. A fresh crack appeared among the others, but still the pane did not give.

'This isn't working,' Rachel said. 'Try the corridors. We need to find another way out.'

Just then the Tooth shuddered once more. Lesser chains broke, cables whined. A grinding, screeching of metal, and they sank another fathom.

'No time,' Carnival said. 'We're about to go down.' The muscles on her arms bunched as she drove the steel hilt into the pane, again, again, again. A crack widened. Carnival snarled, pummelled the pane furiously, faster than Rachel could see. Then she broke away, panting.

'It's giving,' the assassin said.

'Not fast enough.'

'Let me try.' Dill had moved in to crouch beside Carnival, his blunt sword in his hands.

'Back off, idiot,' Carnival growled.

But Dill ignored her this time. In both hands he raised the heavy weapon, and brought it down, point first, into the pane. The bridge rang with the din as the window exploded outwards.

Carnival stood and gaped at him.

'Out!' Rachel grabbed Dill's torn chain mail, and piled him through the window. 'Now you,' she said to Carnival. 'Go, before—'

The sound of snapping chains cut her off. The Tooth fell so abruptly that Rachel was thrown upwards. Her elbow cracked against something hard; her knee collided with her chin. The room spun, and she was bounced off a wall, or the ceiling, or the floor – she didn't know which. Then something wrenched hard at the chain holding her ankle. Still hanging on to the window, Carnival was dragging the chain towards her. Wind screamed around her through the broken pane.

For an absurd moment Rachel felt like shouting, *Get out of here. Just leave me.* But of course Carnival couldn't leave without her. They were still chained together. Carnival was intent on saving herself.

The Poisoner's hand grabbed Rachel's hair, yanked her back. 'You can stay with me a while, Spine.'

Devon had his stump wedged into the skeletal control panel. His cold eyes narrowed on Rachel. She reached for her sword, but it was gone, the bamboo tube gone too. And then she remembered the poisonsong at her hip. She tore the bolt free from its straps.

Devon sneered. 'You think that's going to make a difference?'

Rachel jabbed the bolt behind her, missed him. The bridge pitched and tumbled, knocking her against the controls, but Devon held on firmly.

'Let go of me, you—'

Carnival heaved on the chain till both Rachel and Devon were pulled free. For a heartbeat Rachel was weightless, then she thudded against the gaping window, beside Carnival. Devon slammed into her back. She felt a spear of pain in her side, heard Devon gasp.

One end of the bolt was embedded in her side, driven deep between two ribs; the other end had punched through Devon's jacket just below his heart. They were both bleeding, and five inches of blood-soaked shaft separated them.

No! Where is the tip? The Craw plague? Which end?

Devon's face creased. Flecks of spittle flew from his lips. He hooked a punch at her, all of his weight behind it, but his stump swished by an inch from her nose.

'Damn it!' he roared.

Then Carnival was dragging her through the window, out into open air.

Dill dived after the huge machine, wings closed tight, the tip of his sword piercing the air before him. Cutting wheels, dusty tracks and the scorched expanse of the Tooth's hull all tumbled below him. This thing was as large as the temple, spinning end over end as it fell. He veered to avoid one huge funnel, then dived again.

He momentarily glimpsed the bridge windows.

'Dill!'

Carnival swooped above him, and called down, 'I have her.'

His wings snapped out, and he slowed, allowing the great machine to fall away into darkness.

The scarred angel held the Spine assassin's limp body tightly in her arms.

'Rachel?' Dill gasped, staring at the blood dripping from a wound in her side. She didn't move or open her eyes, and he couldn't tell if she was still breathing.

'Rachel!'

'The reservist encampment,' Carnival said. 'We'll find a doctor there.'

'But you're still chained to her. The army will kill you.'

Carnival grunted, then took off skywards, her wings thumping like war drums.

Dill followed. As armies went, he supposed, it wasn't so big.

The Tooth juddered and shook and spun as it plummeted, but the Poisoner knew he would survive the fall. It might hurt, break every bone in his body, but he would heal eventually. He was more than a man now, broken bones meant nothing to him. For the angelwine boiled inside him. He could hear the souls clearly now, furious and raging, and every one of them had his own voice. They were a part of him. He realized they always had been.

He would find a way back to the surface, even if it took a hundred years. If he had to climb the entire abyss wall with rope and grapple, so be it.

And then he'd finish what he started. If Ulcis was dead, then the rest of the faithful would join him in oblivion. He'd hunt down Rachel Hael and make her suffer for her crimes. And Carnival: he'd lock that leech in a cell and watch her own hunger tear her to pieces. This fall was nothing more than an inconvenience. He had brought down the city. He had beaten them.

So he clung to the shattered window and waited. The Tooth toppled end over end, struck the abyss wall with a jolt that smashed the rest of the bridge windows. Devon still hung on. Air ripped and whistled through the broken panes, buffeted him and tore tears from his eyes. Still he hung on.

Soon now, surely. The abyss couldn't go on for ever.

He felt light-headed, nauseous, blood leaking from the wound in his chest. He squeezed the flesh there together, and watched it begin to knit, the skin healing. He grinned: mortal wounds were nothing more than scratches. Any amount of suffering could be endured, for a time. Devon knew this, it had been his life's work. Work he might expand upon now that he had so much time ahead of him. There was so much, in this life, still to learn.

An odd, shivering sensation crept up through his chest. The nerves there had begun to feel frayed.

A second wound suddenly opened, an inch below the first. A trickle of new blood emerged.

Strange. Devon clamped his hand over the wound, felt it start to heal again. *That's better. A temporary aberration, nothing more.* The bolt had clearly been poisoned. Which sort of poison? He racked his brains. It didn't matter. The new wound was healing. All his wounds would heal in the same way. He gritted his teeth against an impact that could only be moments away.

A terrible itching sensation swept through his torso, his arms, as though his entire upper body was swarming with lice. Five more wounds opened: three on his chest, two on his upper arm. He felt the skin break, felt fluids soak into his shirt. The poison was spreading. Or was it a disease? Devon moistened his lips, sweat beaded his forehead. He shook his head in confusion. These new lesions were already healing too.

The Tooth plunged deeper into the abyss, booming loudly whenever it struck the side wall. Devon clung on, sheathed in sweat, and itching all over.

Dozens of wounds were opening now. On his chest, his back, his arms and legs, and his face. They would heal soon, he knew. His wounds would always heal.

*

Mr Nettle joined the other dead at the bottom of the abyss. His newly-mended crutch sank among bones and rubble as he struggled up the slope. Chunks of debris still fell in places, but there appeared to be a lull, so perhaps the worst had passed. Deepgate glowed far above him, full of promise.

Abigail's soul had been stolen from him – for now. In a way, he was pleased it had found a temporary home in an angel. The daft girl liked angels. But he would find that soul again after he'd found her body. He'd have his daughter back. He was a scrounger. He could find anything.

The bonecrawlers ignored him. They were too busy sifting through the recently fallen treasures, pulling out sheets of tin, broken furniture, chains and timbers from the mounds of bones and ash. Some were shouting or fighting over their finds. Others merely sobbed, or lifted their faces to Deepgate and prayed. Ulcis was dead, but many had found a new god in his wake. The city, after all, had given them everything.

High overhead, a great shadow filled the circle of sky. Something stirred in the air, a faint tremor that reverberated through the abyss. The bonecrawlers felt it too. All were staring up now. The shadow grew larger until it blotted out the light from above. The scavengers watched in awe, lifting their arms in homage while the darkness grew deeper.

Returning his attention to his search, Mr Nettle hobbled on up the slope, his leg twitching with pain, his crutch slipping and sinking. He still had Abigail to find, somewhere. Somewhere, she was here. And she was near. He knew it. He could feel it in his bones.

EPILOGUE

They walked beneath the stars and under a cold thin moon, following the wide trail the Tooth had made in its progress from Blackthrone.

'I'm sorry,' Dill said.

Rachel huffed, 'Stop apologizing,' her breath misting as she spoke. 'I'm the one who should be sorry, for God's sake. I was supposed to protect you but I let you die.'

Darkness still shrouded that period of time for him, but Dill sensed the memories were still there. They would come back to him in time. 'Only briefly,' he said.

Starlight threw the shadow of his wings over the dunes. The Deadsands rolled on to the horizon, shining faintly like old, buckled silver.

'Do you think the Poisoner survived the fall?' he asked.

'Probably.'

'And the Craw plague?'

Rachel placed a hand on her bandaged ribs. 'That was an old bolt. I don't even know if the disease it carried was still potent.'

'But if it was?'

'Then he'll be pissed with me.' She winced, clutched her side.

'Are you feeling all right?'

'Bloody doctor, every stitch he put in is crooked.'

'Carnival,' Dill explained, and looked up to see her soaring high above, just a silhouette against the crush of stars. 'She was standing only a chain's length away from you in the doctor's tent. No wonder his hands wouldn't stop shaking.'

'Scar Night will come again,' Rachel said.

Dill made no reply. He wrapped one wing more tightly around her to keep her warm. 'Where will we go?' he asked.

She shrugged. 'The river towns? Across the sea?'

'What if it's endless? What if I get tired? I can't swim.'

'I'll teach you.'

'What if I can't learn?'

She sighed. 'Hold your head up, Dill. You always stoop too much.'

They walked for a while in silence.

'Dill?'

'Yes.'

'You were away for so long.' She hesitated. 'When you were dead, I mean.' Her eyes searched his. 'Can you remember anything at all?'

He thought about it, and halted mid-step. Suddenly he remembered everything.

'What is it? What did you see?'

'Iril . . .' he began.

Also by Alan Campbell

IRON ANGEL
Volume Two of 'The Deepgate Codex'

Visit **www.panmacmillan.com** to read more about all our books and to buy them. You will also find features, author interviews and news of any author events, and you can sign up for e-newsletters so that you're always first to hear about our new releases.

www.panmacmillan.com

GIFT SELECTOR
YOUR ACCOUNT
WISH LIST
WAITING LIST

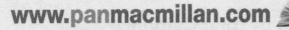

HOME | ABOUT US | IMPRINTS | TRADE/MEDIA | CONTACT US | ADVANCED SEARCH | SEARCH | GO

BOOK CATEGORIES | WHAT'S NEW | AUTHORS/ILLUSTRATORS | BESTSELLERS | READING GROUPS

Coming Soon...

Reading Groups

Competitions
Feeling Lucky?

Extracts
Sneak Previews

Interviews

Events
Meet Our Stars

Reviews
What The Critics Say

News & Awards

Editor's Choice
What We're Reading